# RESURGENCE

K.A. Emmons

www.kaemmons.com

ISBN: 978-1-7321935-6-7

# PROLOGUE

## *April 2197*

Seated on my bunk, I tipped my head back against the wall. I could hear the dripping of rain on the tin roof, but I was listening for something beyond that. A distant roll of thunder thudded through the cement walls of the barracks. Normally I wouldn't have startled, but tonight I was on edge.

The boy in the bunk above me snored softly; the rest slept peacefully. There were twelve bunks in that room, occupied by young men and women no older than twenty. I was the only one awake, the only one listening.

The clomp of boots on the pavement outside caught my attention. I held my breath.

A long silence was followed by the distant creaking of a heavy iron door. I shoved back the sheets. My rifle leaned against the end of my bunk, just like everyone else's. I grabbed it as I rose, tucking my pillow under the wool blanket. I melted back against the wall and into the shadows as the footsteps began to echo in the hall. At first, they were distant; then they came closer.

My muscles tightened as the door burst open and a shaft of light cut across the floor. The assertive footfalls entered the room and abruptly halted. I already knew who it was before he even spoke.

"Corporal Moran." His thick Irish accent filled the room.

I said nothing. My fingers tightened around the cold, black barrel.

He cleared his throat and spoke louder, repeating my name and rank.

Several soldiers stirred in their bunks, but no one woke.

My commander stepped farther in as I shrank back into the shadows. Walking briskly to my bunk, he bent down to snatch the wool blanket off what he was expecting to be me. He cursed under his breath when he realized I was gone.

He turned his attention immediately to the top bunk across from mine, grabbing hold of the sleeping soldier by the arm and shaking her roughly.

"On your feet!"

An inaudible murmur was the only response to his order.

"I said on your feet *now!*"

He all but dragged her down.

"What—sir? What's going on?"

"Moran," he barked into her face. "Where is she?"

"Over there, sleeping—"

"She's not sleeping. She's not in her bunk." He cut her off. "She's gone. Where is she?"

"I don't know, sir."

"You must know—you have to know. You're the only one she ever talks to."

Kess shook her head adamantly. "No, sir," she replied. "Sorry, sir."

He cursed loudly, then spun on his heels and marched for the door. He halted on the threshold, and I saw his shadow on the floor as he stabbed a finger in my comrade's direction.

"You see her, you hear her—you report to me. You understand?"

Kess hesitated, her eyes catching on my hiding place. She looked away just as quickly.

"Sir, yes, sir!"

She saluted respectfully and the door slammed in her face.

I squeezed my eyes shut, breathing again. Kess reached me in two quick strides. She clamped her hand over my mouth and shoved me back against the wall.

"Don't you dare say thank you, Lara. Don't you *dare.*" She hissed the words into my face. "Tell me what the hell you're doing, or I will go tell Donovan *exactly* what he wants to hear."

I peeled her fingers away. "Kess, tonight's the night."

"What are you saying?"

"I have to get out of here—I can't do this anymore, Kess. I *can't*."

"Do you want to get yourself shot?" She nailed me back against the wall again. "It's your night, Lara—you're on deck!"

"Kess, stop it. I know—"

"They'll *skin you* if you don't go." She dropped her voice. "There's been several sightings on the flats just this week—*this week*, Lara."

I swallowed. "You don't understand, Kess."

"What don't I understand?" she demanded. "Enlighten me!"

"I can't kill another one—I can't—I—"

"Lara, if you don't kill them"—her words severed my sentence—"they'll kill you. And I'm not talking about the recusants; I'm talking about the RGM—I'm talking about our bosses," she continued, her voice a harsh whisper in my ear. "The only reason you've survived this long is because we need you—"

"I don't care," I interrupted, pushing her away. "I didn't sign up for this! I didn't sign up to go crawl through the cold mud to kill rebels!"

"Did any of us sign up to be snipers, Lara?" She shook her head. "I suggest you get your act together and get out there. Don't run on your night. It's too dangerous. Everyone is on alert for you. Donovan's looking for you as we speak, for God's sake. Don't be a moron."

I wanted to object—everything inside me was screaming; I felt sick. But before I could say a word, she clapped her hands on my shoulders and shoved me forward. "Don't say a word. Get out there and go find him—now."

The hinges creaked as the door opened again; finally, I saw Kess's face in the sliver of light: deep brown skin, dark eyes, and a buzz cut. Her tone was steel, but her eyes were filled with concern.

"You'd better make up a good excuse."

Without replying, I took a few steps towards the threshold and then stopped. Turning around, I backtracked to my bunk. Hurriedly, I reached into my pillowcase and pulled out the familiar slip of paper. A tiny yellowed square, softened with age.

Kess sighed. "Why do you always take that thing with you?"

"You know why." I pulled on my jacket and boots. "It's the last I have of him."

Slinging my rifle over my shoulder, I buttoned my jacket and slid the folded paper into my breast pocket.

"I'll see you tomorrow, Kess," I said, stepping out into the hallway. "Hopefully…"

Kess didn't respond. She looked at me for a long moment before closing the door.

A migraine was already beginning to pound at my temple. I pushed my shoulders back and cracked my neck as I made my way down the hall and out of the barracks. Outside, the courtyard was spattered with rain and fluorescent light. My supervisor was in my face in a heartbeat, shouting at top volume.

"Where were you?"

"The jakes, sir."

"You're a liar, Moran." He shoved me backwards just as an unmanned Byrd aircraft began to lower silently onto the pavement. "I'll beat it out of you in the morning, you hear me?"

"Yes, sir."

"I'm sorry, I didn't catch that!"

"Yes, sir!" I yelled into his face, anger bleeding dangerously into my voice.

"Right now there's a job to be done," he continued. "You know what to do."

I gave a shallow nod, swallowing back the sick feeling in my stomach.

As the slender, almost translucent aircraft touched ground, its pressurized double doors hissed open. I climbed into the tight, body-sized space. The Byrd's tight interior was reminiscent of the small vintage helicopters the Irish Air Corps used to use.

"We're dropping you on the outskirts of Section New Dublin," Donovan told me as he leaned up against the side of the Byrd. "The exact coordinates have already been entered into ANI's system."

The Automated Navigation Intelligence system: my pilot and worst enemy.

I strapped on my helmet. "Will I ever be able to see exact coordinates for myself, sir?"

He shook his head. "This is a confidential mission, Corporal. Not a vacation."

I gritted my teeth and a moment later the doors zipped shut. My stomach lightened as the Byrd lifted into the air. A lifelike voice crackled in my headset.

"Good evening, Moron. Welcome aboard."

"*Moran*," I corrected the droid. "It's *Moran*. When are they ever going to fix this stupid thing—"

"Exterior temperature is 5 degrees Celsius. Interior temperature is eighteen degrees Celsius. Currently flying at an altitude of two hundred and forty-three meters. Currently traveling at four hundred and fifty knots. You will arrive at your drop point in approximately five minutes."

"Okay. Thank you, ANI."

"Your current body temperature is thirty-seven degrees Celsius. Heart rate eighty-seven beats per minute. Perspiration level: moderate."

I sighed. "Okay, ANI."

"Hunger level: moderate. Urine level: moderate."

"ANI, how do I shut you off?"

The moments ticked past. I blocked out the sound of ANI's rigid voice as I began going over my mental checklist.

*Just don't think. Just shut your mind off.*

"Dropping altitude," ANI announced a moment later. "Corporal Moron, prepare for drop-off."

I strapped on my landing pack, a tiny black engine that would ensure I didn't go splat on the rocky ground below.

"Engaging trapdoor."

A moment later the floor bottomed out from underneath me. I dropped silently out of the aircraft and hurtled down through the cold night air. The gentle hum of the Byrd gave way to the moderate wind as it whistled through my helmet.

I counted under my breath and pressed the button at the top of the landing pack just before hitting the ground. A blast of warm air punted me upwards again before gently fizzling out and lowering me to my feet.

I dropped to my belly and rolled into the shadow of a demolished wall, whipping my rifle into a ready position. I clicked off the safety, lifting up into a crouch. The rain pelted down in large icy drops.

"Drop-off affirmed," I whispered breathlessly into my built-in mic. "Activate night vision."

I slid my shield down over my helmet. The stripped, rocky landscape around me lit up as bright and vivid as daylight. The ruins of the city scattered before me in the distance. I could see the faint lights from the smaller cities that lay on the outskirts of the rubble.

"Okay… let's find these guys."

I was scared, but I knew Donovan would be listening to my every word. My every inhale and exhale. He would be checking the charts and monitoring my heart rate, my body temperature, my perspiration levels. I knew that everything Donovan could see, the rest of the Reformed Global Militia could see: my breathing patterns, my whispered curses, every time I had to pee—it was all being recorded, monitored.

I didn't want to find those guys, and I most certainly didn't want to kill them. I wanted to make a run for it. I wanted to get out of there.

*Don't run, Lara… Not on your night…*

Kess's words rang in my ears as I sat poised in the rain, scanning the rugged landscape around me. I'd already detected the faint glow of a flashlight in the distance, a glimmer that had quickly disappeared behind a small dilapidated shack.

I cursed in my head, leaning back against the rock. I was hoping that Donovan had been wrong, that they weren't actually out here tonight.

Noiselessly, I shimmied one hand out of my tight gloves and slid two fingers into my breast pocket. I took out the small square of paper and looked down at it through my shield. My fingers trembled as I held it in my grasp.

I'd been the one to find the note. I remembered the day like it was only a week ago. I remembered the agonizing worry in my mother's eyes as the landlady had handed her an extra set of keys to my brother's apartment. I remembered the way her voice had cracked as she called his name, her heels clicking on the linoleum floors. I remembered the light in the curtains, shining through the vines that draped the walls. The baskets of plants and flowers that seemed to hang everywhere. I remembered how she had taken the note from my small hand and collapsed, weeping, as she read it.

I'd been the one to fold it and keep it, even after everyone else had stopped reading it. After everyone had given up even the smallest hope of ever seeing him again. I'd taken the note from my mother's dresser and kept it under my pillow. I'd read it each night before I fell asleep, and I still read it now, every night, even though my brother had never been found and my parents and sisters had long since passed away. I still read it because it was all that I had to comfort me, one hundred and eighty years later.

I checked over the wall; I could see the light flickering gradually closer.

I looked back down at the brittle paper in my hands, then slowly, gently unfolded it. I read it silently before quickly tucking it back in my pocket. Then I squinted, raising my weapon once more. Easing the target into my sights, I held my breath. The light wavered in the sheet of rain, coming gradually closer.

*I'm sorry…* I whispered in my mind. *I'm so sorry.*

My finger slid over the trigger, twitching. I narrowed my eyes.

I could hear my heart pounding in the back of my skull.

I pulled the trigger. A crack rippled through the air.

The light went out.

*To my family:*
*I love you.*
*Don't stop searching.*
*Don't ever stop searching.*
*– Ronan*

# CHAPTER ONE
### *Icarus*


The sky seemed listless as it spun around me, a deep blue void. My perception lagged as I reached up and adjusted my headset. I tapped a button on the small screen in front of me, and the Kármán line swept up over me as I rolled. The Griffon slung forward, slipping into the folds of the thermosphere. I could just make out the hazy bow of the Earth's curvature. I dropped a few hundred feet.

In the distance I could see another aircraft just like mine. We mimicked each other in our motions. We flirted with a little less gravity; then we plummeted. Down, down, down, through the spectrum of the stratosphere, free-falling through the empty blue until the clouds finally yawned open to reveal the sparkling ocean. Haze hung in the air like rust suspended in the troposphere.

My fingers wrapped around the throttle and a clacking filled the cockpit as I dragged it back. The nose tipped downward as we pushed over into a steep dive.

"Descending," a female voice chimed in my headset.

ANI sounded so real sometimes. It was a little unsettling.

"No shit, Sherlock," I muttered, squinting as the coastline came roaring into view.

"Welcome to the Sands," she continued, in spite of my insults.

"Been here just a couple of times, but thanks." I pulled up just over the beach, sending sand billowing up like clouds underneath the aircraft.

"This section is currently graded level Fanta," ANI informed me. "External temperature: forty degrees Celsius."

"Didn't need to know."

"Internal temperature—"

With a touch of a button, I switched the channel on my headset. A favorite playlist burst to life.

I tapped a button on the back of my headset, activating the microphone, just as another metallic Griffon made its descent ahead. "How's it going up there, Aer?"

There was a split-second pause. Then a crackle.

"All right—until you started riding my tail."

A halfhearted grin twitched at the corners of my mouth. "You seen anything yet?" I asked.

"Negative," Areos replied. "Just a whole lot of sand."

He was right; it surrounded us like the color blue had only moments ago—sizzling hot sand. Blazing fragments of what used to be the suburbs of a pumping city—Los Angeles. Now known as Section C, short for Chaos. Because that was exactly what it was.

While we had been locked away in the Dimension, a hundred and eighty years had passed on Earth. I remembered living on the outskirts of this city like it was yesterday: going to school, sharing that tiny house with my quirky roommates and a driveway with the nutty old guy next door, the man who would become my teacher—and so much more.

And then there was Hawk.

I shook myself out of my thoughts, turning the music up. I sucked in a breath like I hadn't had one in a while, gripping the control wheel with a little more fierceness.

"It's a thousand frickin' degrees out," I muttered into the microphone. "Do they really think someone's wasting their time out he—"

I didn't finish. A bullet slashed through my left wing. I cursed, rolling immediately to the right.

"I guess so," I muttered.

"What's up?"

"I'm hit."

"Sh—"

I tapped a few buttons on the screen in front of me and jolted the throttle forward. The Griffon reared violently, then made a rapid climb to a higher altitude. I scanned the ground below, squinting through my shield.

"Icarus, to your right!"

Another blast cut through the hum of the Griffon's engines, but this time I dodged the bullet. Rocketing farther up, I kept a steady gaze on the sands.

"Come out, come out, wherever you are…"

A tiny black smudge blurred into the shelter of the scattered debris below.

I let go of a few rounds and watched as the bullets hammered into the ground around where the guy was obviously hiding.

*I missed on purpose, you idiot. Get out of here.*

This area of Section C was considered off-limits to the public. It was property of the RGM, and the RGM didn't like sharing—I had learned that the hard way.

"There's two," Areos announced.

"Do they both have weapons?"

"Just one, it looks like…"

I peered down, studying them for myself as I thrust the Griffon closer.

The two guys looked around my age. One wielded a semiautomatic. The other flipped me off.

I wasn't going to kill them if I didn't have to.

I shot a few more rounds. The two guys dropped to the ground, making lame attempts to shield themselves from the blasts.

I tilted my head, checking on the hole in my wing. My gaze shot back to the screen in front of me. I tapped to a thermal view of the ground below, watching as the two figures scurried like red ants across my radar. Areos fired a few shots, missing intentionally, I could tell.

Then, bang. Another hole blew through my wing.

I sucked in a surprised breath. Areos cussed in my headset.

"You okay, man?"

I shook my head even though he couldn't see. "I'm going to have to—"

The guy with the semiautomatic below blitzed me with another round for the fun of it—and this time an unhealthy sizzling noise followed the loud clatter of impacting bullets.

*Shit, shit, shit.*

"Okay, guys, I'm ticked now," I muttered through gritted teeth, upping the volume on my headset.

Warnings blared across the screens in front of me. My eyes scanned the smaller screen centered in my dash, cluing me in on how much ammo I had left to throw at them. A couple of rounds remained.

The guy below me hastily reloaded. I dropped out of the sky, leveling out over them, though I could tell from the sound of the Griffon's engines that I didn't have much longer.

I peppered the sand with bullets. The guy dropped the gun.

*Leave it... Don't pick it back up...*

But recusants were tricky beasts—and they never complied with my internal dialog. Not that I could really blame them—I was, after all, the "bad guy."

"Icarus, you're smoking!"

"Why, thank you," I joked sullenly.

"Can you please be serious?"

"I know, okay?" I barked into the mic, losing it. "I get it—I'm going to have to bail in a sec."

"No, no, no, don't—don't bail, not here," Areos shouted back. "We're like twenty miles from the base—"

"I won't make it that far."

I cursed our commander under my breath. Hatch had explained this as a "relaxing checkup on the sands." Relaxing, my *foot*. Sure, it had been graded level Fanta, the second of the three degrees on the ranking system for missions. Each level was named after a vintage soda and ranged from Sprite to Coke, Coke being an almost suicidal mission and Sprite being a basic sweep-up. Fanta was like Sprite with a little kick—but this was more than a little kick.

Sweat trickled down my neck as I throttled the aircraft forward, swerving out of the recusants' firing range. Unfortunately, that left me only several hundred yards away—smack in the middle of a debris field.

Areos cursed. "Icarus, pull up!"

"I can't!"

"*Pull up!*"

I knew it wasn't a good idea to bail. In fact, it was a very *bad* idea. My parachute would open up like a great big practice target, and the charred remains of the buildings below would not make for a soft landing—if I even made it that far. But then there was option B: staying in my Griffon and crashing like a kamikaze. That idea somehow didn't appeal to me.

I checked to make sure my chute was secure, then punched the foreboding red button at the base of my dash. The crystal-clear dome encapsulating me in the aircraft sucked back, exposing me to the arid, screaming wind. Instantly, I was unbuckled and ejected from the cockpit.

One minute the Earth was under me; the next it was over my head. The desert spun around me as the gusts of wind tossed me like a rag doll. I gripped the strap of my landing pack with one hand, searching for the button I'd only ever had to use in training. Meanwhile the ground was getting closer—fast.

My muscles locked out, my fingers shaking uncontrollably as they traced the strap.

*Where the hell is it?*

Finally, my index finger brushed the telltale shape of the button. Pressing it, I whipped back as the white parachute streamed out behind me. The dizzying motion around me abruptly steadied. I blinked into focus, swallowing back a wave of nausea.

Several hundred yards ahead and below, my Griffon pounded into the sand and exploded. A dirty orange blaze mushroomed up from the wreckage. Areos's Griffon circled the scene like a vulture; the growl of its engine ripped through the air.

Breathing heavily, I began to assess my surroundings. Between the wind and the force with which I'd been ejected, I'd drifted considerably, putting myself directly within the recusants' firing range.

*Beautiful.*

Areos made a sharp U-turn, streaking past overhead to swoop down over the pair of rebels below. They fired a few rounds but missed every time.

"Don't get shot, you idiot," I panted into the mic. "Seriously, I'm not worth it."

"Just shut up and get to the ground, all right?"

I didn't argue.

While Areos tempted the guy below to empty his magazine, I made a slow and painfully evident descent to the sands. I landed hard on a pile of sharp debris.

Grunting, I struggled to cut myself out of my parachute as it stifled me like a shroud. I crawled painstakingly over the debris, dodging jagged glass, fragments of what used to be windows. Shots cracked the hot air.

I stumbled to the ground, reaching into my flight jacket for my pistol. I kept my shield lowered over my eyes, locking out the torrents of sand.

"Touchdown affirmed," I huffed into my mic, making my way cautiously around the rubble scattered in my path. "Are they still—"

I stopped, mid-sentence, as I rounded a massive chunk of skyscraper. There they were, not ten yards away. I hissed curses.

"Icarus?" My radio crackled. "You all r—? Oh, shit…"

He didn't have to finish that question. They'd spotted me.

*Oh, shit* was right.

I threw myself behind a layer of rubble just as the familiar rhythm of bullets punching through metal exploded around me. I sank into a crouch, folding my head to my knees. When a pause inserted itself, I shimmied out from my cover just far enough to center the guy with the gun in my sights.

Areos swooped down over the two recusants again just as the first guy let go of another round. I fired fast, then fell back behind the ruins.

Even over the wind and the screaming engine of the Griffon, I could hear the beat of angry footsteps. I took a fortifying breath and forced myself to step out from behind my cover again, leading with the barrel of my pistol.

"Icarus!" Areos shouted in my ear. "What the hell are you—"

I shut off the headset. The music died along with his voice.

In front of me stood the guy who had just shot me out of the sky. He was dressed in ragged black civilian clothes, his face was coated in grit, and his eyes were alive with rage.

"Stop!" Spit flew out of his mouth as he yelled; he lowered his face to the sights of the weapon as he jerked it towards me. "Don't move or, so help me God, I will blow your head off!"

I shook my head, finger tense on the trigger. "I don't believe that."

"I mean it!" he shouted, taking a step closer.

"Okay, okay—okay!" I yelled back. "Just—just listen to me for a second!"

He spat a disgusted laugh. "Why the hell would I listen to a word you have to say, you dirty rotten—"

"Traitor?" I finished for him, shaking my head. "No, no, that's where you're wrong! I don't want this any more than you do."

In my peripheral vision I could see Areos dropping altitude. I knew I had about five seconds before he neutralized the screaming rebel in front of me. I had five seconds to convince him to put down his gun.

"Oh, you don't, do you?" He laughed mirthlessly. "Yet you're shooting the few—the *few*—who are willing to take a stand for freedom? Look at yourself! You're *one of them*—you're just one of their robots! You bought the story." He edged closer. "And now you think you're going to take away what little voice we have left?"

"I don't want to hurt you!" I yelled over the noise around us. "You don't know me—you don't know anything about me! I don't *want* to hurt you!"

For a moment he said nothing. His head lifted slightly as he stared, his expression darkening.

I swallowed, my heart accelerating as I held the gun tense in my grip. Slowly he took one hand off his weapon and lifted two fingers to the back of his neck, pushing aside his thick curly hair. I could see the beginnings of the small scar at the base of his head.

"Wrong again," he corrected me bluntly, his eyes drilling into mine. "You already have."

He pulled the trigger.

My head whipped backwards as I dropped to the ground, a bullet buried in my flesh. The last thing I saw was the flash of blood as Areos let go of everything he had. Then the world muffled and fell silent.

# CHAPTER TWO

*Fin*

**One year earlier. New Cornwall, UK. Night.**

Our third and final day was the most difficult. The sun had drifted below the horizon, plunging what had once been known as Cornwall, England, into thick darkness. We worked fast—hidden away in a dimly lit storage facility tucked behind a government building. Delta rifled through a long, shallow box of acrylic cards labeled "MIA – presumed dead." Areos stood behind her, peering skeptically over her shoulder. I kept watch at the door. I'd disabled the alarm system, but I was still acutely aware that we could be walked in on at any moment.

"Bingo…" Delta muttered under her breath, selecting several cards out of the stack.

I shot the two of them a concerned glance. "Isn't this risky? What if they find out these are identities stolen off the dead and the missing?"

Areos took the cards as Delta handed them up to him. "Not if we change the names to our own and do a little reprogramming." He began sifting through the stack. "How many of us are there at this point, anyway?"

"A couple of hundred," Delta replied before I could, shooting me a glance as she rose, shoving more identification cards into his hands. "You'd better work fast."

There was a small metal table tucked away at the back of the room. Areos threw himself down into the chair and tapped the slender screen that protruded from the middle of the table, waking up a blue glow.

"How do you plan to bypass the security system?" Delta questioned, positioning herself behind him. "You don't know the password—"

"I have my ways," he replied bluntly, shooing her away with his free hand. "This wouldn't be the first system I've hacked."

I checked back over my shoulder, peering through the window inlaid in the door, down the dimly lit cement hallway.

Areos just had to forge the IDs and we would be out of there. That was what I kept repeating to myself as I stood there, trying to steady my thoughts.

It had been almost a year since Icarus had miraculously returned to the Dimension, only to find it in shambles. We no longer lived by the code—we lived by a form of martial law. Of course the code was respected, but efficiency and order always came first—whatever whipped us into shape the fastest. And if that meant relentless training, little sleep, and a steady flow of harsh punishments, then so be it. At least, that was the ruling of the council, which now consisted of Mitsue, Delta, Azalea, and a few other students.

I almost didn't care anymore. I kept the letter from Sensei with me at all times, and I read it over whenever I began to despair. I read it to remind myself who I was and that everything would be made right in the end, somehow, whether the council accepted it or not. You can't stop a wave from breaking.

But even so, everything seemed empty without Hawk.

I squeezed my eyes shut, trying not to think about it—about her. Trying not to hear her voice echoing in the background. Trying not to relive that moment for the hundredth time, the moment I had rounded the corner and stepped into the hall to find Icarus standing there with tears in his eyes and Hawk's markings on his arms.

"Boom. We're in." Areos's voice pulled me out of my thoughts. His fingers tapped relentlessly against the screen. "How are we looking, Fin? Still clear?"

I swallowed, nodding. "Just be quick about it."

Areos finished with the ID cards and powered off the device. I held open the door for both of them and we filed out. Miraculously we escaped without detection. We crunched across the brushy fields, Delta in the lead. It was the middle of the night and we were in Cornwall, her territory.

"I've always wanted to visit England." Areos messed a hand through his blond hair. "But under the circumstances, I'd say three days is more than enough for me."

Delta grunted. "We barely scratched the surface of the true England."

Areos huffed, pausing only to glance down the hillside in the direction of the city, an agglomeration of vibrant lights and shimmering skyscrapers.

"It's a bit… built up."

"It wasn't always," Delta replied as we continued walking.

I kept quiet and listened.

The truth was, I wasn't sure why I'd even been asked to go with Delta and Areos in the first place. The two of them did most of the grunt work. I mostly watched and waited—and made sure no one got killed in the process.

"So everyone has a chip of some kind—a 'Fragment,'" Areos mused aloud as we trekked. "A connection to an expansive database of information with international contributors. Imagine what that implies for education—schools become obsolete. Everyone has access to the exact same information. That honestly doesn't sound too bad to me."

"It sounds dangerous," Delta snapped, turning to give him a sharp look. "If it was such a great asset, then why have so many countries fallen? Why are the forests vanishing, and—and the ocean, the smog…" She shook her head. "Things are different now, and not for the better…"

"Besides that, we've already seen a little of what the other side effects are," I added finally. "We've gained knowledge at the cost of reasoning, feeling, empathy—freedom. That's been taken away."

We reached the abandoned shed tucked away in the rubble of what looked like a tiny hamlet. It wasn't much to look at, but it acted as our portal between Earth and the Dimension. We crowded inside.

"But still, everyone has a Fragment except us." Areos rubbed his chin. "They all have scars as verification—the scars at the bases of their heads… I didn't see one person without it."

"It's definitely from the insertion procedure." Delta closed the door behind us. "It leaves a mark."

"Yeah. A mark we don't have," Areos countered, fumbling with the backpack slung over his shoulder. "Which means we'll be forging more than just ID cards."

"Look, we can't just run into this blind," Delta replied sternly. "This whole thing is… it's a lot worse than we imagined."

"We fake the scars, problem solved," Areos continued, as if Delta had never spoken a word. "We blend right in."

"It's not that easy."

"Psssh, why? Because you like to make everything so much more complicated than it has to be?"

Delta fell silent for a moment. I felt the atmosphere gradually shift around us.

"I recommend you both let me do the talking." Delta's tone suggested this was an order.

I reached out and opened the door of what was now the cavern. Light shredded in.

"We each have perspectives," I interjected softly. "Our own way of interpreting what we've witnessed over the past few days. Doubtless, the council will be eager to hear each of our accounts."

In the light her features ignited: red hair, narrowed green eyes. "It was my homeland. I daresay I know it best."

Areos grunted, brushing past both of us. "So? It's our *planet*. You don't seriously think Earth belongs to just you, do you, Delta?"

In response, she pursed her lips and stomped after him. I was left alone in the cavern for a moment; then I stepped out into the hallway and closed the door gently behind me.

Gaia met us on the training platform and ushered us into one of the safe rooms. I walked beside her.

"How did it go?" she asked quietly, giving me a sidelong glance. "What is Earth like?"

"Changed," I replied, "but not hopeless."

Delta grunted but made no remark until we had arrived at the appropriate safe room, where the council was gathered. We filed in and everyone took seats at the long table. Gaia gave me a gentle pat on the shoulder as she walked past us to join them. The three of us remained standing.

"… You have been sent back, back to Earth—you are the specially selected pioneers. The explorers." Mitsue's long monologue trudged on. "You have been sent back to Earth to assess what has happened to it, to give us a foothold of information to rely upon, and to help us chart an appropriate course of action with which to proceed."

Delta sighed. "Okay, great. Can we talk now?"

Mitsue slowly closed his mouth, glowering. "Very well."

Delta and Areos both began speaking at once, but Delta raised a hand for silence.

"The degradation of Earth is obvious—it has changed greatly, and the decay of Earth's natural resources is beyond what we could possibly have imagined," she began. "In an attempt to avoid a worldwide environmental and economic collapse, a band of the most influential nations have come together—the Unified Nations Collective, or UNC. From what we've discovered, this collective maintains a vast database of carefully censored information, which is available to every single person through a system known as Fragmenting: the installation at birth of a tiny but mind-altering chip inserted into the brain's cerebellum. The Frags connect every single person to the database, preventing them from 'thinking' outside it."

"Has the whereabouts of this database been confirmed?" Mitsue asked.

Areos shook his head. "We've only begun to scratch the surface of where it could possibly be kept and maintained."

"But because of the database and the Fragmenting practice, 'Information is free,' though not in fact," Delta continued. "As a result, the Reformed Global Militia protects and upholds this system, ensuring that Earth remains pure and purged of what they refer to as recusants—humans with defective Frags. The militia is somewhat reminiscent of Earth's old militaries, but it is different in that it has abandoned ethics; the vast majority of its soldiers are abducted as children and forced to train."

Mitsue's eyebrows twitched. "So future Earth is protected by child soldiers?"

I gave a slow nod. "Essentially."

Delta shot me a hard look.

"Anyway, the point is, in order to return to Earth, we'll all need protection—IDs, which we have obtained, and scars to prove we've been Fragmented—or else we're dead," she continued. "But in all honesty, we're not ready—we have only just begun to understand what we're up against! Yes, Earth remains… Yes, there is much we can do…" She shook her head. "But not yet. They are giants, and we are microscopic."

"I see…" Mitsue stroked his chin. "And… the rest of you?"

The question was almost a reluctant one, but I stepped forward anyway.

"What Delta says is true," I confessed. "Yes, things have changed vastly, and for the worse, though no one seems to recognize it. But we have the advantage, having been shut away in the Dimension—we have the ability to see things that they cannot, because gradual changes often go unnoticed. A frog will skip off the surface of hot water, but yet in water heating slowly, it will boil to its death." I looked up and down the table at the council. "That is what Earth is like. To those who live there, nothing seems amiss. To us, what lies on the other side of the cavern is hell itself."

I paused for a moment, steadying myself. Hawk's eyes were there every time I closed my own, reassuring me.

"But every trial Earth has to offer can only fuel us." I squared my shoulders and continued. "Yes, Earth is suffering and fading, but it is still good, and Sensei has raised us as his own children—his own sons and daughters—for such a time as this." My heart felt like lead in my chest, but in spite of it I smiled. "This is everything we've ever dreamed of. All that remains is for us to reach out and take what is already ours."

There was a moment of silence. Then Delta stepped forward to meet me.

"You think so highly of yourself, you would put others at risk, Fin?" Her words were hot with anger, and her eyes darted back and forth between my own. "You would send us out there to die? Is that really what you want?" She whipped around to face the council. "My god, we would have been better off just staying on Earth to get captured and killed!"

Areos spoke up. "No, Delta, Fin's right. It's not like it's going to just be the three of us—it will be all of us. I mean, isn't this what we've spent all this time and effort training for?"

The table in front of us was silent. Mitsue stared at what seemed like nothing. Azalea scribbled notes.

"Need I remind you, Mitsue, that I was the chosen member to lead this assessment mission?" Delta barked. "My word surely outweighs—"

Gaia cut her off. "Each of your accounts hold value. We must judge the situation without bias."

Delta's jaw tightened. She turned her attention to Mitsue.

"You're the leader, Mitsue," she stated, steely. "Who will you choose to believe? Me?" Delta paused only to shoot me a glance. "Or someone who worships a blasphemer…" She trailed off, and for a moment I could see the gears turning behind her eyes. It took but an instant to know exactly what she was implying.

I'd been walking on eggshells with Delta ever since I'd made the mistake of letting her read Sensei's letter to me, hoping, praying that her heart would soften and her hatred for Hawk would fade.

"But more than a blasphemer," she went on now, the softness of her voice hardly masking the razor sharpness hidden beneath. "A mortal girl who lived a mortal life, scarred by the sins of the world, indeed—"

A weight plummeted into my stomach. "Delta, no."

"—a rape victim whom Sensei had to swoop in and save from certain death," she finished, her voice louder now. She was staring directly into my eyes, an amused smile twitching on her lips. "Our foretold Sunrise, indeed."

A deathly silence fell over the room. I felt Areos's hand on my shoulder. Eventually someone must have said something, but all I heard was a shrill ringing in my ears.

———————

**Present day**

I took out my pocketknife, flipping the blade open. I stood before the skeleton of what must have been the most glorious oak in the forest. Its branches extended beyond themselves—reaching, it seemed, for something it had died trying to find. I felt like this tree as I carved yet another notch into its soft wood. Another notch to accompany the three hundred and ninety-nine others. This was its four hundredth scar.

Tiny flecks of wood trickled down the trunk as I carved, the blade cold against my fingertips. It was spring, but nothing bloomed. The wind only howled through the barren remains of the forest and swept over the rolling mountains. The evergreens seemed to be the only remaining survivors.

I put a little more pressure on the handle, digging in a bit deeper. Each notch represented one day. One day spent in the forest. Each night, I slept on the dry, rust-colored ground, the moss having long since faded from green to dead brown. Each morning the sun cut through the smog, and each day I walked. Where to didn't matter. Some days I descended to the valley where the ruins of the town lay; some days I climbed the mountain. The air was still clear at the top, the atmosphere untainted by the air pollution that seemed to ooze from New Dublin like pus from a wound. From the mountaintop, every-thing seemed far away; trees looked like smudges, and the rubble below disguised itself as boulders. I liked to imagine that's what it was.

Satisfied with my work, I closed the knife and stepped back. My breath painted the air.

Four hundred notches. Four hundred days.

I settled deeper into my jacket and continued past the oak. My camp was not far from the tree where I kept tally of the passing days. It was tucked between boulders from a rockslide and sheltered by fallen trees. Here I built a fire to warm myself. Here I slept. Here I made tea sometimes, just because it reminded me of Mom.

I closed my eyes, focusing on the crunch of dead leaves beneath my bare feet and not on the hollow ache in my chest that ran only deeper when I thought of her, or my father. Or my sisters. Or—

I stopped in my tracks as a sound like flapping wings interrupted the stillness. My gaze lifted immediately to the treetops; the world around me dimmed to blurry slow motion. I tuned out my other senses, listening hard. The towering evergreens stood unmoving, cracking the washed-away sky. I held my breath, turning around, scanning the forest. Then a fluttering—a blur of dark color.

My heart quickened as I took a breath, stepping forward, a name more familiar than my own already taking shape on my lips. Then, in a burst, a murder of crows sprang from the trees and tumbled into the air, chortling, seeming to mock me as they took flight.

I froze for a moment, not moving. I stood there and watched them fly away. Then I let go of a breath, a small puff of steam in the cold Irish air.

Crows. Just crows.

I pinched my eyes shut. Thinking—trying not to.

I felt detached from my body as I turned back around, placing one foot mechanically in front of the other. I rebuilt the fire and watched the flames until the gray sky died away to purple and then black.

*Where is she? Where is she...?*

I sighed, tipping my head back. Shivering, but not from the cold.

The army of tree corpses stood still around me. The wind came and went like the tide, but nothing else stirred. I knew these woods by now—I knew them after four hundred days, and I remembered them from when I was a boy, back when I would go for walks with Dad. I remembered the rippling vines and the birds, and the owls at night. The foxes and the hedgehogs, the crickets and the toads. I remembered a forest that was alive; I remembered my dad, the sound of his voice. Everything I had loved was gone.

Staring up into the opaque black sky, I searched for tiny familiar pinpricks of light. Stars I could no longer find in the veil of smog. Stars no one had seen for over a hundred years.

The sound of footsteps crunching through leaves snapped my gaze back down to the black woods. I stared into the darkness, alert now as my eyes narrowed. The steady footfalls continued, nearing, until at last, a faint huffing could be heard.

"Fin?" The word burst out, breathless. "You out here?"

My shoulders fell slightly, and for a moment I didn't reply.

More huffing and more footsteps. "Come on, man…"

I pulled in a slow breath, still hesitant. He'd been here only yesterday—I couldn't imagine what he wanted this time. I wasn't going to say anything, but then I heard him trip and fall. He hissed a made-up curse word.

"Fin, seriously."

I sighed, giving up. "I'm over here."

A moment later, my student stumbled out of the forest and into the small clearing. I could see his now neon-red hair even in the low light. The front of him was plastered with dirt and pine needles.

"Why didn't you answer?" he questioned, exasperated. "Didn't you hear me out there, calling you?"

"I think everyone within a ten-mile radius heard."

Deflated, he sat down across from me. He stuck out his hands, warming them over the flames, while he squinted at me like I was a stranger.

"Well?"

I gave him a firm look. "Haven't we been over this?"

"You want to be alone." Runner rolled his eyes. "But that's stupid."

"Is it, now?" I picked up a stick to shift the logs. "How do you figure that?"

"Because it's cold and wet and miserable out here," he blurted, for what must have been the hundredth time now. "There's no food—"

"Plenty of mushrooms are still growing," I interrupted. "Besides, I don't need food."

"What about friends?"

"I don't need them, either, and it's not like they need my help," I replied. "Look where that got Areos and Icarus." I jabbed at the embers. "I was supposed to protect him."

"You did everything you could have to keep Icarus from being captured that night, Fin." Runner looked at me earnestly. "The RGM has captured quite a few of us, not just them. It's just… the way Earth is, now."

"But I knew something was up—I should never have let him take off with Mitsue."

"Fin, Icarus is his own person. He *chose* to do what he did that night, and there's nothing you or anyone could have done to change his mind," Runner said. "It's not the end of the world—maybe it will even end up working out to our advantage."

"An international militia that raises assassins to protect the Unified Nations Collective and take out the rebels who disagree with their methods." I pressed my lips together, shaking my head. "I'm sorry, but I'm having a hard time understanding how that's going to work out for the best."

"I'm pretty sure Icarus hasn't killed anyone personally."

"That's not even my point." I threw down the stick. "He's the Sunset, Runner, and I promised Hawk I would…"

My throat tightened on the last words.

"You promised Hawk that you would look out for him," he finished for me quietly. "I know. And… and you tried. And you will."

A long silence amplified the crackling of the fire.

Runner drew a deeper breath. "I know that you miss her, Fin."

I swallowed, something in my chest tightening.

"But being a hermit out here by yourself forever…" He shook his head, looking at me. "It's not going to bring her back."

"I'm not being a hermit," I replied flatly. "I'm searching for her. And I'm not going to stop until I find her."

"She vanished in *another dimension*, Fin," he said, puzzled. "What makes you think you'll find her here—in *Ireland,* of all places? What makes you think she's even back on *Earth?*"

"I just know." I stared into the flames. "I know her. I can feel her."

"But why here?"

My mind immediately flashed back to the day we had gone to Howth with my sisters. The cliffside, the wind, the rushing sea.

*Bullets, bullets, bullets in my chest.*

"Because we return to the familiar." My voice was quiet as I looked up from the flames. "The senses may say she's no longer with us—that it would be impossible for her to return. But the words of the prophecy dictate otherwise—and above all else, my trust lies there. I'm useful here…" I paused. "Besides, I couldn't follow Mitsue or the other splinter groups into Japan or what's left of some of the other nations we've returned to."

"Why not?"

"Because they don't need me," I replied. "And honestly, I don't have the heart for it."

Runner stared at me for a long moment. Then, finally, he gestured to the forest around us. "Doesn't it bother you, of all people, that the forest is dead, Fin?"

My eyes shifted up to the pines. "Not a day goes by that I don't long to bring it back to life."

"Then why don't you?" he asked. "That's why we're here, isn't it? To make things better—to fix this fu—" He stopped himself. "*Messed up* situation."

"Because I can't, Runner. I've tried. I…" My words fell flat. I shook my head. "I've tried to heal the trees, to make new ones grow, but nothing happens. I'm not sure I have the power anymore."

"Sure you do."

I sighed. "Runner—"

"Fin, look," he interrupted before I could get any further than that. "You can't let this beat you. Hawk wouldn't have wanted you to—"

Abruptly, I put up a hand, rising to my feet. "Don't—don't mention her name. Not in the past tense." I turned and walked to the edge of the clearing, though I couldn't escape the intensity of his gaze. "I know you all have forgotten her already. I know no one believes she's out here but me…" I swallowed the lump in my throat, staring into the emptiness. "But I will never accept that she's gone—not when something inside me won't stop screaming that she isn't… she isn't gone. She's…"

My words cracked in half.

"Then don't," Runner replied quietly. "Don't stop searching for her, Fin. But don't… don't give up on *us,* either."

After a moment I heard him climb to his feet.

"Don't you *want* to fix the world, Fin?" he asked. "This is supposed to be our culmination! Do you think it's right that everyone has a Fragment with 'all the information they will ever need' inserted at birth? Do you think that's how humanity is meant to be living?" He sighed. "Maybe that's why we can't see the stars anymore. Maybe that's why the cities have been destroyed. Maybe that's why the birds are almost gone, why the ocean is fading away. Maybe–" He stopped, his voice wavering as he sucked in a breath. "Maybe that's why the trees are dead."

I pressed my eyelids closed, turning around slowly.

"Of course I want to fix it, Runner." I opened my eyes and looked at him.

He studied me sternly for a moment before solemnly nodding.

Shrugging off the knapsack he had been carrying, he shoved it towards me as he walked past. "Then eat," he said firmly. "And come to the gathering tonight."

I frowned. "Runner, I never go to the—"

"I know. That's why I'm asking you to come."

At length, I sighed and took the bag from him. "Fine, I'll be there."

Runner cracked a little side smile. "Good."

He gave me a few vigorous slaps on the back before walking off into the dark woods.

"Are you going to be able to find your way back to the portal down in the debris field?" I called after him.

"I think I've been here enough times to know my way back, Fin," he shouted back.

"All right then."

I turned and walked back to the fire. I heard huffing from the woods, then a soft thud as he tripped and fell. He shouted a made-up curse word.

# CHAPTER THREE

## *Icarus*

I sucked in a sharp breath as a needle pricked my flesh, releasing a generous dose of painkiller into my bloodstream. A warm hand came to rest on my back.

"Not too much," I said, wincing. "I have a mandatory appointment with my commander, and I need a level head."

"What you need is *rest*, Lieutenant," a stern female voice replied.

Charlie was probably a couple of years younger than me. She had big blue eyes, a bleach-blond buzz cut, and a tattoo of a rose stamped on the side of her neck.

"Screw rest," I said. "What's a little bullet to the shoulder?"

She rolled her eyes, though her lips twitched with a smirk. "You're such a dork sometimes."

I closed my eyes and attempted to focus on something other than the pain shooting up and down my spine.

"It takes my mind off the nine-to-five," I told her, gritting my teeth.

Charlie snorted. "You mean being the best pilot on base?"

"I mean the fact that I have to do their dirty work," I clarified.

"From what I hear, you've never even taken one of them out yourself."

"It depends on what qualifies as 'taking one out,'" I muttered. "I've shot a few because I've had to protect myself—in the shoulder, the leg, some other relatively insignificant place."

Charlie nodded as she retracted the needle. "Well, it looks like this is payback, then." She gestured toward my shoulder.

I exhaled a mirthless laugh. "Yeah, really."

I felt the scrutiny of her gaze for a moment, and then she tapped my arm.

"Where'd you get the ink?" she asked nonchalantly. "In-house?"

My throat tightening, I shook my head. "Before I came here."

I glanced down at the black bands wrapping my biceps and the circular marking that wound around my finger like a wedding band. The markings Hawk had borne her entire life.

"Interesting," she replied simply as she came around to the front of the examination table, seeming to sense that it wasn't something I wanted to discuss. "Can I ask you something, Lieutenant?"

I nodded.

"Why don't you kill them?" She glanced over at me. "The recusants. You're lucky you didn't die out there. Why didn't you just neutralize that guy when you had the chance?"

I looked at her for a moment. "Because it's not that simple. We have such nice, clean words to describe what we do. 'Neutralize'—it sounds so sterile. So detached…" I paused for a fatigued breath. "They're just like us. They're kids."

"They're killers."

My jaw firmed as I held her gaze. "And what are we?"

Charlie's eyes narrowed. As she spun back around to the tray of needles, I could see the faint scar on the back of her head.

"Charlie, you worked in the newborn ward," I began. "You helped with the implants. You of all people should be able to understand why they resent us. Why they're fighting us."

Her back stiffened. When she turned to look over her shoulder, her expression was steel.

"You want some pills to take with you, Lieutenant?"

I didn't reply at first. My eyes probed hers for a long moment—searching for something I couldn't find. Finally, I shook my head.

"No, thanks," I replied, my voice ragged. "Just tape me up and let me out of here."

---

Hatch had a habit of throwing things at pilots who didn't do their jobs. I was no exception; it didn't matter that my arm was in a sling.

"You want to tell me what the hell was going through your head?" She leaned back in her chair, boots up on the desk. Her green eyes shimmered hatefully. "Or should I get the real story from Areos?"

I shook my head. "He—he wasn't involved."

She quirked one red eyebrow. "That's not what it looked like."

I lowered my gaze to the floor.

Hatch's office doubled as a deranged sort of lab. The walls were white and mostly empty save one hanging photograph of a child soldier, a young teenage boy with deep-set eyes and dark hair. No one had any idea who he was; it was a little disturbing. Each wall was lined with tables covered in glass beakers and strange pieces of equipment. A black lab coat hung from a hook by the door along with a sophisticated set of goggles. What she worked on in there, none of us knew, but rumor had it our commander's alter ego was that of a mad scientist.

"Icarus, do you want me to play back the recording?" Hatch's question pulled me out of my thoughts.

"There's no need; I remember what I said with vivid clarity, ma'am."

Hatch's lips pressed into a thin, aggressive line. "Lieutenant, you are dancing perilously close to the edge of the precipice."

I opened my mouth to speak, then closed it, deciding it would be disrespectful to tell her that I was okay with that; I had some experience in falling off the edges of precipices.

"Lieutenant."

"Yes, ma'am?"

"Why didn't you shoot?"

"Because I didn't need to, ma'am."

Her expression didn't falter. Her eyes were hard, crowned by a deep scar that slashed through her right eyebrow and cut across her temple.

"Lieutenant, do you understand the meaning behind these missions—the reason why you do what you do?"

I swallowed an uneasy feeling, saying nothing.

After a moment she attempted a sympathetic smile. It didn't go over well.

"Let me ask you this, Lieutenant," she said finally. "When you're out there patrolling, what do you see?"

Sensing that she was going to continue, I made no response.

"Do you see flourishing towns and cities? Do you see a thriving, harmonious society?" She pushed away from her desk, swiveling to the window behind her to rip open the shade. "Or do you see a desolate snapshot of the human race hanging by a thread?"

Light shafted in. Beyond the window were rows of parked Trawlers—the sand-colored tactical vehicles we used for ground patrols. Past that was a wall trimmed with barbed wire, and beyond that, the wide-open desert. In the courtyard teenage trainees scurried into position, all dressed uniformly in black, and all with buzz cuts.

"I see a wound, ma'am," I answered. "A wound in need of mending."

My commander let go of the shade, which abruptly snapped shut. She swung back around to face me.

"Then do your job, and do not question our methods!" she shouted, slamming both hands down on the desk. "Don't tempt fate, Lieutenant—she has a habit of eating men like you alive, men who need to understand the system and why we do the things we do." Her eyes bored into mine. "Orders are not meant to be understood. They're meant to be followed."

I pulled in a deep breath.

"So I should have shot that guy?" I asked, ignoring the pain throbbing through my arm. "A couple of stupid kids with bad aim—"

"Not that bad, apparently." She flicked her gaze pointedly to my arm.

"He was two feet away when he got me."

Hatch shook her head, disgusted. "He should never have been that close."

"I thought I could talk him into dropping it."

My commander let out a laugh. "You thought so, huh?"

I nodded and Hatch sank into the metal swivel chair.

"Listen to me, Icarus," she said, reverting to my first name and dropping her voice. "I like you as a person. I respect you as a pilot—as one of our best. But if you make one more misstep—"

"You'll drag me out and have me shot."

Hatch's eyes hardened and she sprang to her feet, sending the swivel chair clattering away behind her.

"I'll rip those wings off your collar and ship you to the other side of the planet to scrub latrines for the rest of your life. Do you hear me?" she roared, reaching threateningly for another empty glass beaker. "Which, by the way, is what you'll be doing for the rest of the week—I don't care if your arm falls off!"

"Yes, ma'am!"

She stabbed a finger in my direction. "Neither of you are to leave this base for any reason."

My heart sank a little. "Yes, ma'am."

"Get out of my sight."

I didn't need to be told twice. I saluted respectfully and got out of there. I heard the sound of smashing glass as soon as the door had closed behind me.

Areos was waiting for me outside in the hallway, looking sheepish. His face was streaked with dirt and sand; you could hardly guess he was blond underneath the grit.

"How's the arm?"

I shrugged my good shoulder. "It's still attached to my body."

Areos clapped a hand on the back of my neck, giving me a sympathetic pat. I hated when he did that; it made me feel like his little brother.

"I hate those guys." He sighed, frustrated.

I shook my head as we made our way down the cement hallway. "Don't hate—that's what they do, and look where it gets them." I winced. "Hatred takes even truth and makes it·meaningless."

Areos sighed. "You sound more like Sensei every day."

A cold feeling settled in my stomach as I stared straight ahead.

"Yeah, well…" My words dropped off. "I miss him."

Areos fell silent until we emerged outside.

"Do you ever wonder where he is?" he questioned, drawing a deeper breath. "Do you ever wonder why the hell he left us to deal with this wreck on our own—with zero guidance?"

I squinted, gazing out over the bustling courtyard. The hum of generators lagged in the air. Trawlers churned up clouds of dust as they rolled past.

"If you think Sensei has left us without guidance, then I guess you haven't been listening, Areos," I replied, crossing my arms. "We're far from on our own."

"That's not what it looks like."

My gaze remained fixed on the desert ahead. "Then close your eyes."

"I can't. They hurt. I got pretty banged around up there—I think I lost a contact," he complained, rubbing his right eye.

I gave him a serious look. "Just be ready for tonight."

My comrade quirked an eyebrow. "Tonight? Is it already time for another…?"

I nodded.

He fumbled with the tactical watch strapped to his wrist. "It's… almost fifteen hundred."

"They'll be gathering by twenty-one hundred."

"Icarus, you got the same warning I did," he came back firmly. "We can't leave the base—that was an *order,* not a suggestion."

I tossed him a look. "Areos, name one instance in which I did exactly as I was told."

His jaw clenched irritably. "Icarus."

I stepped away from the door. "I've got a lot of latrines to scrub before we transport out."

"Icarus."

"Relax." I began to walk away. "Just relax. We'll figure something out."

"No—no, you always say that, but I'm not going to go along with your stupidity just because you keep telling me to relax!"

I turned to face Areos while walking backwards.

"Fine," I said. "Stay here. I'll go."

"You'll get your head chopped off."

I reached up and patted my freshly buzzed scalp. "Kind of feels like that already happened. That barber is a butcher—I swear he drew blood."

He studied my face like someone searching for sanity. "You just don't get it, do you? The RGM doesn't play games, Icarus—and it certainly won't play yours! You're screwing with fire."

"Would *not* be the first time."

His eyes narrowed into a glare.

"What's more important to you, Areos—this?" I gestured around. "What you see—or what you *know* is real?"

His expression softened slightly.

"Relax, Lieutenant," I repeated with a sigh. "I got us into this hell, didn't I?"

Areos looked down. "We both know it wasn't your fault—you can't blame yourself."

I gave him a mirthless salute before turning back around. "Too late."

# CHAPTER FOUR

## *Fin*

### Present day

I followed Runner's footsteps down the steep incline, avoiding my usual path to the portal at the base of the mountain. I'd done this so many times, the repetition was almost deadly. I had no idea what time it was, or how long it had been since Runner had left. I'd sat by the fire for what had felt like a long time. Now the purple traces of dawn began to awaken my sense of sight, though I knew the forest well enough by now to wander it blind.

My footsteps crunched across the thick carpeting of seeds and needles. The trees were stressed and yellow, even some of the pines now.

In the silence, my mind wandered back to the day Icarus had returned to the Dimension. The Sunset to his own people… who didn't believe a word he said.

*"You're a liar, Icarus."* Mitsue's heated words still rang in my ears. *"You are a liar and a blasphemer."*

Icarus had walked onto the training platform during sessions, and everything had stopped dead. I'd been the only one expecting his return.

An emergency gathering had been called. Mitsue had looked him square in the face from his seat of judgment at the council table and listed all the reasons why Icarus wasn't the Sunset—wasn't the one our prophecy had foretold. He had treated him exactly as he had treated Hawk. Everyone else had mixed views—the platform was chaos, but it didn't matter. In the end, the council and only the council had a say.

Icarus had stared straight ahead, saying nothing. His eyes were bloodshot and his face was as white as snow.

I had been too numb to think straight—to defend his case the way I should have. I'd tried to step forward, fumbling over my words, my voice cracking as I objected, but the council had shut me down.

"How can we trust your word?" Mitsue had seemed eager to make an example of me in front of the council. "How can we trust a thing you say, Fin? Your attachment to Hawk, your bias… It strips you of your credibility."

In the end, the council decided that even if Icarus, by some miracle, had made it out alive, even if Hawk had "paid the price for Icarus's redemption," they were *not* our patriarchs. They could not be trusted.

So what I had told Runner was true: I never went to the gatherings. Not since Icarus had returned to the Dimension without Hawk—and been scorned, shunned and treated like a pointless and unsolvable mystery. I never went because I never had anything to report. I never went because I didn't want to hear what other sliders reported. Not because I was afraid, but because I knew I had to preserve my faith—and our gatherings, though well intentioned, seemed to do nothing more than amplify the darkness around us, the darkness we had been bracing ourselves for, sealed away in our "utopia."

Since Icarus's return—which had shocked, yet not moved our new leader—Mitsue and the council had dictated the reemergence and our progress on Earth. Portals had been established all over the world, in America, Europe, Africa, Asia and Australia. We had all, in essence, returned to our natural worlds and lived amongst our own like soldiers in disguise, using our unique portals to transport back into the Dimension and report to the council. The Dimension had evolved from our home base to a place of reconvention.

*I should have been the one they captured that night. At least I would have been keeping my promise to Hawk. At least Icarus would be safe.*

I told myself this over and over again, though I knew full well he would never be safe. Not with Mitsue in power—Mitsue, who would like nothing more than for this blasphemous "self-proclaimed" Sunset to vanish from the face of the Earth.

*Maybe Runner was right: maybe Icarus was actually better off trapped in the chains of the Reformed Global Militia. So long as they never found out who he really was…*

I picked up my pace, weaving my way through the gray patches of brush until the tree line peeled away and the land leveled out before me. I pulled the collar of my jacket up over my nose, still somehow unused to the stench that hung in the air like a rusty veil. Ahead lay what had once been a village on the outskirts of Dublin.

The buildings, though crumbling from age, still stood mostly intact. Dying vines struggled to grow along the walls and decaying fences, and mold bloomed on the thatching. I walked silently to the church; its paint had long since peeled, and the bell had rotted away and crashed through the roof to the sanctuary, but its stark steeple still pointed skyward with seemingly iron resolve.

I pushed open the wrought-iron gate, which groaned quietly on its hinges. The dead vines still clung to the expertly crafted scrollwork. The garden lay around me, empty beds like freshly covered graves over which nothing grew. A spade stood against the weathered fence, whitened by age and the elements.

I closed my eyes, taking a trembling breath.

Since being back in Ireland, I'd done nothing but live in hiding. I focused all my time and energy on the one thing I knew I could still change: Hawk. I had to find her. I hadn't gone to the house where I'd grown up, I hadn't attempted to find my family's graves, but against my will, my portal had manifested in the church where my father, for many years, had tended the garden, trimmed back the rosebushes, tilled the ground, and planted bulbs in the autumn.

I focused on my feet as I quickly crossed the garden and slipped into the church through the back entrance. When I swung the old door open, a few rats scurried back into their hiding places. The daylight vanished as I shut it again.

My breathing seemed loud in the sudden, tomblike stillness. Everything smelled of decaying fabric and stagnant water. Slowly my eyes adjusted, and I began to make out my surroundings in the small amount of light filtering through the stained-glass windows coated thickly in grime and cracked in more places than they weren't.

Rows of empty pews waited in silence for a sermon that would never come. Rainwater dripped from cracks in the roof, and spiders' webs wrapped the chandeliers in such abundance they looked like suspended wasps' nests at first glance.

I steadied myself and walked down the aisle, all the way to where the pulpit had once stood. Above me was a hole in the ceiling, tunneling straight up into the steeple, and below, bashed into the rotted floor, was a gaping hole opening directly into the crawl space below the church.

Bracing both hands on the floor, I descended into the hole, careful not to drop myself directly on top of the bell embedded into the ground below. Immediately I felt the brush of cobwebs against my face, clinging to my beard. An assembly of roaches scuttled away.

Coughing, I swatted away the plume of dust.

I lowered myself to the ground, taking a seat on the rim of the massive bell. I swallowed, bowing my head, closing my eyes. Slowly, I began to tune out the muffled sounds around me; my mind quieted, beginning to visualize.

The sparkle of geodes. Damp, cold stone walls. Beyond that—a hallway. Mahogany wood, tall windows, light spilling in as it washed the ravine. The music of the wind, the dancing of the trees. The scent of incense. I breathed in, and somehow my lungs found that scent. The temperature around me suddenly plummeted.

When I finally opened my eyes, I didn't even need to look around me to know where I was.

Rising to my feet, I reached out for the familiar brass handle and turned it. With a slight push, the door creaked open. Light tumbled in through the windows to burn my eyes. I squinted, raising a hand to shield them, as I began to make out the shapes of the trees and craggy rocks beyond it: the side of the ravine.

The springlike breeze swept the length of the hallway, carrying with it the strong scent of pine and rain and morning, if it was possible that morning had a scent.

I blinked furiously, softly closing the door behind me now as I stepped forward. I stopped in front of the window, staring out.

The sky above was cloudless, tainted by the sun's rust-gold rays. It would be sunset soon. I could hear snatches of voices on the wind as my peers congregated on the gathering platform below. The clicking of tumblers caught my attention as someone opened the cavern door behind me. I turned just in time to see Mala step out into the hallway.

"Fin!" She looked surprised for an instant, then pleased. "I wasn't expecting to see you here."

"I wasn't expecting to be here."

"Hardly recognized you under that beard," she commented, brushing herself off. "And that long hair."

I pushed on a tired smile. "Been a while since I cut it." I cleared my throat. "I've been—"

"I know—wandering in desolation without food or water," she cut in, closing the door. "So Runner tells me. He's a bit relentless in attempting to be your supportive younger brother."

"I know he means well, but…" I sighed as we started down the hallway. "It's nothing he can fix."

Mala turned and cast me a look. "That's what I thought when you tried to help me, you know. Back when I still… clung to the few shreds of reality I could remember in my heart." She shook her head slowly. "I wasn't a big fan of your help—or you in general, to be honest."

A ghost of a grin passed over my lips as she elbowed me playfully in the ribs.

"But now," she went on. "Now, I would thank you for it. If it wasn't for you, I would still believe that I had to dig up the past and figure out who I really was." She looked over at me. "But who I am isn't in the past. It's here— this place… all of you… The power inside me. That's who I truly am. The rest is detail."

I listened, saying nothing for a moment.

"Maybe it's like that with you and Runner," she said at length.

"I don't know, Mala. He brought me a knapsack full of jerky."

She burst out laughing. "Good. Someone has to check on you."

"It's really not necessary—"

"—he says, as his appearance falls to ruin."

"That's what you call growing a beard?"

Mala swatted the question away. "Beards are for unattractive men to hide behind."

"What about Areos and Icarus?" I shifted the discussion. "Have they transported in lately?"

"They come when they can," she said. "Which isn't very often. The RGM keeps their pilots under lock and key—or at least that's what Delta says."

I swallowed. "Yeah? She's a pilot now?"

"A medic."

"She has enough experience in that area," I mused as we crossed the platform. "It must feel strange, being from Earth's future to begin with, yet now from the past, like every single one of us."

Mala reached up to scratch her forehead. "Yeah. Super easy to get your head around, right?"

———————————

When we arrived on the gathering platform, it was already crowded. Almost everyone was dressed respectfully in dark colors, causing those in black RGM uniforms to barely stand out.

My eyes scanned the platform as we pushed our way through the crowd. The council had already begun to take seats at the long table front and center. A fire was kindled in the middle of the platform, though its flames were almost translucent in the sun's harsh rays. I was scoping the uniforms for

Icarus when my eyes caught on a smudge of bright red. Runner stuck out like a sore thumb, but he waved as soon as he saw me.

Fighting his way through the crowd, he joined Mala and me.

"Glad you could make it," he said, seeming to address me, though he shot Mala a smile. "I saved a couple of seats for you guys."

"Where's Icarus?" I asked. "Areos? Are either of them coming?"

Runner shrugged, frowning. "I'm not sure, but they might still show up—who knows."

Mala's expression faded. Our minds both backtracked to that night on the sands. The night we had lost them.

*The night our "leader" made sure we lost them.*

My eyes shifted up just as Mitsue pulled back his chair and took his seat at the center of the table. Gazing over the crowd, his eyes clapped on mine for a split second, a coldness inside them. I looked away just as quickly.

### One year earlier. The Sands, Section C. Night.

I held my breath in the darkness, counting silently.

One, two…

In an instant, the transportation was over. We stood in what felt like a muffled tomb. Only moments ago we had been surrounded by the four walls of the cavern, but now what encompassed us felt strangely like—

"Sand?" The voice was Mala's. I couldn't see her in the darkness. "The walls have turned to sand…? Where the heck are we?"

Areos took a deep breath. "The transport must be complete… everyone good?"

Everyone was fine, and aside from myself, that included Icarus, Areos, Mala, and Mitsue. The council had decided to transport in splinter groups, and of all the transports Mitsue could have joined, he'd joined ours to LA. I knew our new "leader" had only chosen to accompany us because of Icarus. I was already on my guard.

We were all hesitant about our reemergence—everyone, that is, except Mitsue and the majority of his appointed council. According to him, we had spent more than enough time in training and it was time to move on. That was that. Now here we were, trapped, in a hole in the ground in the middle of no one knew where.

Icarus paced the small enclosure, assessing the situation.

"What if we run out of air?" Mala asked, sounding a little unnerved. "Is that possible?"

"Not if we start digging," Icarus said. "We're not that deep underground—listen."

Everyone was silent for a moment. A distant, almost inaudible rumble vibrated in the walls, causing small amounts of sand to trickle to the floor.

"There's something up there." Icarus was already beginning to scoop away at the wall with his hands. "Come on, we're not that far down—"

"No, stop." Mitsue clicked on a flashlight. We were under strict orders not to use our powers outside the Dimension. "We can't just blindly tear this thing apart."

In the beam of light I could now see Icarus standing in front of the wall at the opposite side of the hollow space. He turned slowly and looked at Mitsue, his long hair falling into his eyes. He hadn't cut it since he'd been back.

"It won't collapse," Icarus insisted.

Mitsue grunted. "How do you know that?"

"Can't you tell from the way your voice echoes?"

Mitsue opened his mouth for a quick reply that didn't come fast enough. Icarus gestured toward the ceiling, igniting an orb and shining it upwards.

"It's not sand, it's—"

"Metal?" Areos finished for him, stepping into the center of the space, craning his neck. "We're trapped under a… a building?"

Icarus walked back to the wall to keep digging, tossing the orb to Areos.

I studied the ceiling, saying nothing. Mala gaped up at the monstrosity above us, her face twisting into a terrified expression. "It looks like… doesn't it look like…"

"A massive frickin' piece of a skyscraper?" Areos offered, shifting the beam of light back and forth. "Yeah. Yeah, it does."

Mitsue stepped forward, folding his arms. "All the more reason why we shouldn't be shifting the sand."

"What would you have us do, Coach?" Icarus mumbled without looking up. "Stay here and suffocate?"

Mitsue's jaw set and he took a step closer, but not before I inserted myself between the two.

"Look, Mitsue, I think Icarus is right," I said. "That thing is huge—it's not going to shift if we tunnel out of here carefully. We have to get above-ground somehow."

I could see the gears turning frantically behind his narrowed eyes, but he gave no answer. He let us dig.

When we finally broke the surface, not five feet up, Areos clapped a hand on my shoulder. Keeping his voice low, he said, "Nice work."

I only nodded an acknowledgment. I hadn't done anything worthy of thanks. In fact, I could be blamed for the very fact that we had to put up with Mitsue's dictations. Hadn't Areos been the one who had tried so hard to convince me to take the leadership position? I wanted to tell him not to thank me for something I had only helped make worse.

*What would Hawk think of me now?*

I shoved the thought to the back of my mind as we each shimmied our way up through the sandy tunnel and onto solid ground. Mitsue flicked on the flashlight immediately.

"Shut that off!" Icarus hissed. "Someone might see!"

After a slight delay, the light went out. Mitsue tensed beside me.

"We can't see," he announced. "We have to be able to see."

"We have no idea where we are," Icarus shot back. "Staying alive is a little more important than seeing right now."

I could practically hear Mitsue's blood coming to a boil. I concentrated on helping Mala out of the tunnel. She sucked in a sharp breath as she climbed up, scoping our surroundings.

"What is all of this around us?" she asked, only loud enough for me to hear. "All these dark shapes…"

I squinted into the night, attempting to track her gaze. It took a moment for my vision to adjust; then I saw precisely what she was talking about.

We were standing smack in the middle of a debris field, surrounded by the ruins of what had once been towering buildings. Even in the darkness I could make out the faint shapes of windows. Turning back around, I scanned the desert around us. The rubble stretched on for miles.

"I thought we were supposed to be transporting into LA," she whispered.

I nodded slowly, still studying the darker shapes against the black. "I'm pretty sure we have, Mala."

"Guys, look," Icarus said. "I think… I'm pretty sure those are buildings in the distance." He carefully mounted a pile of debris, precariously climbing his way to a better vantage point. "I can see lights."

"There's no way of knowing what we're getting ourselves into with such little visibility," Mitsue muttered. "We can't just walk into this blind."

No sooner had he spoken than the same echoing rumble we had detected belowground broke the silence again. A beam of greenish yellow light swept through the air.

"Icarus, get down!" Mitsue hissed, falling back behind the rubble. "Someone's—"

I took cover in the mouth of the tunnel with Mala, scanning our surroundings until I pinpointed the source of the noise. Not a hundred yards away, what looked like a highly evolved version of an SUV sped past, churning up sand in its taillights. A large searchlight rotated on the roof, nearly nicking the top of my head as I ducked out of its range.

Mala let out a little gasp. "What was that?"

"Not sure," I said. "A vehicle of some kind—some sort of patrol, maybe."

Slowly the graveling of wheels on sand faded into the distance.

"We're going to get caught if we stay out in the open like this." Icarus jumped down onto the sand, breathing with a little more effort. "We can't just stay out here—I have no idea where we are, or what's going on, but that was *definitely* some kind of patrol."

"What do you suggest?" I asked, squinting to make out his dark shape in front of me.

"We exercise caution and get closer," Icarus replied. "We're sitting ducks out here—it's too dangerous."

"We could just go back belowground," Areos interjected. "We'd be safe until the sun comes up."

I was about to agree with Areos when a new voice cropped up—one that had, until now, remained calculatingly silent.

"I agree with Icarus," Mitsue said, keeping his voice low. "There's no reason for us to just sit out here, completely exposed."

"We wouldn't be if—"

Mitsue cut Areos off before he could finish. "If you three want to stay behind, that's your choice." He got to his feet, brushing himself off. "But for once, Icarus actually has the right idea. We didn't come back to cower in a hole like a bunch of scared kids."

"No one is suggesting that," I countered. "It's dangerous—we don't even know where we are."

"I'm fully aware of the fact, Fin. Thank you. If you're so concerned, why don't you stay here with Mala and Areos? Icarus and I will go."

A warning flag shot up in the back of my brain as Icarus stepped up, getting right in Mitsue's face. "I don't need you to come with me."

"I'll go," I volunteered, quickly climbing to my feet. "Let me go instead, Icarus."

"No, Fin." Mitsue didn't turn his head to look at me. "You stay here. Icarus has this—don't you, Icarus?"

Icarus said nothing, not moving.

*Don't fall for it...*

Finally, Icarus pushed past him. "Of course I do." He shot Mitsue a look over his shoulder. "Just keep that flashlight off."

A sinking feeling settled in my stomach.

"Icarus, no." Areos scrambled out from his temporary hiding place. "This is a bad idea. What if they're hostile?"

"We won't find out unless we get closer," Icarus replied firmly. "Look, stay here if you want, okay? Mitsue and I are going to get closer to see if we can at least start to figure out where we are and what we're dealing with." He paused, glancing around. "And how in the world this can possibly be LA…"

Together he and Mitsue rounded the pile of debris and evaporated into the blackness. I felt Mala's hand on my shoulder as she came up behind me.

"We can't just let them go," she hissed into my ear. "We have to stay together!"

"She's right," Areos said, coming up alongside us. "We can't just let them go off and die."

"That's not necessarily what will happen," I countered.

Areos grunted. "It's not necessarily what won't happen, either."

I sucked in a breath, thinking fast. I edged around the scattered debris; Icarus and Mitsue were already a few hundred yards off.

Finally, I gave in. "All right. Just… just stay close, okay? I don't want to lose you guys out here."

Areos gave a quick nod, motioning for Mala and me to follow. Everything was a dark, muddied blur as we ran. I could feel the sand shifting beneath me with each footfall; the wind began to pick up, howling through the destroyed remains around us.

"Dead ahead," Areos panted as we fell back behind the skeleton of an old vehicle. The lights from the buildings were probably half a mile away, and in the strange milky glow I could make out the two familiar figures. "They're almost there."

"Let's catch up."

We moved as fast and efficiently as we could. I stopped only when I heard Mala suck in a sharp breath, falling to her knees.

I turned around, extending a hand. "You okay?"

She pinned her lower lip between her teeth. "I caught my leg on something sharp—I couldn't see."

Bending down, I slipped an arm around her torso, quickly helping her back to her feet.

"Can you stand?" I asked as I searched for Areos.

"Yeah, I… I think so…" Mala replied, then tensed suddenly. "I think I might be bleeding…"

"Here, just…" I squinted, still scanning the sand. "Just lean on me, okay?"

Mala locked an arm around me, and we hastily made our way to the next viable hiding place, which came in the form of a shattered building. The wind blasted us with sand that hit our skin like a thousand tiny pinpricks as we attempted to shield ourselves.

"Where's Areos?" Mala had to yell the question to be heard, even though she was right beside me. "I can hardly see!"

"I don't know!" I struggled to peer past the rubble, still searching for some sign of the now three missing members of our group. "I told him to stay with us!"

"He must not have noticed we stopped."

I squinted, trying desperately to see. I could only make out dim auras of light in the distance, lights from the buildings ahead. Then one set of lights peeled away from the rest and began to move closer. For a moment I was confused; then a sick feeling punched into my gut like a fist.

*The patrol.*

I leaned closer to Mala. "That patrol vehicle circled back—I have to go find Areos and Icarus!" I shouted. "Stay here—do not move!"

"No, don't leave me here!" she protested. "What if they find me?"

"They won't if you stay low. I can't just leave them out there—we need them! I promise I'll come back for you."

I left her before she could say another word, charting a mental map as I sprinted in the direction of the lights.

"Areos! Areos, can you hear me?" I yelled as I tried to shield my face from the pounding sand. *"Areos!"*

Finally, there was a faint yell in response to my shouts, but it wasn't Areos.

Ghostly green lights flashed on the top of the vehicle as it skidded to a stop, splashing up sand and silhouetting a familiar shape against the blinding headlights.

I stopped in my tracks, my eyes burning as they widened. "Icarus!"

For a moment he stood there, paralyzed. Then he turned and ran. But not in my direction. Instead, he dodged around the patrol vehicle and towards the buildings—causing them to swing a sharp U-turn and launch into a hot pursuit away from the rest of us.

*Where is Mitsue?*

"Icarus, no! Stop!" Finally I spotted Areos, sprinting up ahead. He ran out in front of the patrol vehicle, arms raised high. Like a beast of prey, the vehicle abandoned Icarus and slammed to a stop.

I cursed through my clenched teeth: Areos had been spotted. They had him. There was nothing more I could do. He'd sacrificed himself to buy me some time—enough to hopefully catch up to Icarus before the patrol did.

I fell back behind a debris mound, sucking in sand with every breath. Stifling a cough, I checked on the position of the patrol vehicle. It hadn't moved. The doors were open now and three guys had gotten out.

Gulping back all inhibitions, I lowered my head and raced across the desert, dodging the range of the powerful spotlights. In the distance I could hear the wail of sirens, voices crackling over a speaker, barking orders for Areos to get down.

I ducked into the shadow of another destroyed building to catch my breath and finally caught sight of Icarus in the distance.

"Icarus…" I panted, scarcely able to detect the sound of my own voice. "Icarus! Icarus, st—"

A hand clamped over my mouth before I could finish, dragging me backwards. I writhed in the vise grip, throwing blind punches as the shadows sucked me back.

Above the wind and the pounding of my heart in my skull, I heard the roar of the patrol vehicle's engine. Throwing myself backward, I slammed my attacker into the sand beneath the weight of my own body, forcing them to release me. I scrambled to my feet. When I turned around, I found a gasping, sputtering Mitsue.

"Fin, stop!" he choked. "Stay where you are. You'll get us all killed!"

For a moment I just stood there, my mouth hanging open as I stared at him.

"You… you left him out there?" It was hardly a question. I stepped closer, standing over him. "You left Icarus out there?"

"I told him to stay here!" He scrambled to his feet, frantically clawing the hair out of his face. "I told him to wait until the patrol was out of earshot."

Still shaking from the adrenaline, I turned back around. The patrol vehicle was lost in a cloud of sand as it barreled past us—heading straight for Icarus.

"Fin, don't go after him," Mitsue barked through clenched teeth. "That's an order."

Heat boiled over in my center. I flung back around, fist first, and nailed Mitsue in the jaw. The force threw him to the ground. Pain sizzled in my knuckles as I turned and took off running, my focus zeroing in on Icarus.

For a moment everything felt strangely slow-motion, blurry. I skidded to a stop behind another piece of debris. The vehicle had already come to a grinding halt, green lights flashing and sirens blaring.

"One more step and we'll shoot!" a voice crackled over a loudspeaker as the front passenger door swung open. Then the driver's side door. Then the rear passenger doors.

Icarus stumbled to a halt, a series of red dots flickering between his shoulder blades. He slowly turned around with his hands in the air. One of the guards grabbed him by the arms to zip-tie his hands together. The other positioned himself behind Icarus for the escort to the vehicle, slamming him in the back of the head with the butt of his rifle. Icarus dropped to the ground.

I fell back behind the debris, a sick feeling tangling in my stomach.

*Look after him for me, Fin…* Hawk's voice echoed in my thoughts. *Look after Icarus.*

# CHAPTER FIVE

## *Icarus*

"Look at me." The ghost of Mitsue's voice haunted my thoughts. I lifted my head. I didn't want to—not because I was afraid to face him, but because I knew that if I lifted my chin, the tears would spill down my cheeks.

"Icarus, be honest with me..." His voice was muffled. "Do you truly expect us to believe in this place at the bottom of the ravine—these 'worlds' you've told us about? Do you expect us to actually believe that my student Raiden was down there with you, shape-shifting from form to form, waiting for *you*?"

I could still see him shaking his head. I could still feel the eyes of the council burning into me.

"Do you expect us to believe that Hawk, a convicted blasphemer, descended into the ravine to save you?"

*Hawk.* Her name seemed to echo. I looked down at my arms, tears obscuring my view of the markings. I raised a hand—the one that bore the ring—holding it up, shaking, for the council to see.

"Do you still not believe?" My voice trembled as I yelled. "Do you still... still not believe?"

*Do you still not believe...*

*Still...*

My words faded and twisted, drowning out, until at last my eyes flickered open.

I pulled in a deep breath as I struggled back up into consciousness, slamming my hand down on the alarm beside my bunk, a tiny screen that carefully timed our few precious resting hours. For a moment I lay there, breathing heavily.

Rusty strokes of sunlight slashed through the one small basement window. Sweat trickled down my neck.

For a moment, in that limbo between sleep and being awake, I could almost forget where I was. But the sounds of footsteps, the hum of engines, and the deafening whir of high-speed propellers quickly pulled me back to reality.

I squeezed my eyes shut, running a hand back over my stubbly head.

*Welcome back to Section C, Lieutenant. Or should I say, welcome back to Hell.*

It's amazing what scrubbing latrines for hours can do to a body. Pain seared through my shoulder as I closed my eyes again, swallowing away a dry feeling in my throat. My skull throbbed with a headache.

I rolled over onto my side. The screen was lit up dim blue.

*1900.*

I had a couple of hours to figure out how to transport to the gathering and back again before anyone noticed. We had already missed so many—we couldn't miss another. In order for that to happen I needed to be on my feet and thinking fast, but somehow, lying there, sweating, wounded, and aching all over, I couldn't seem to find the motivation.

I just wanted to go back to sleep.

I pressed my swollen eyelids shut with the heels of both my hands.

I was supposed to be out there, trying to understand how Earth had slowly slipped further and further from the light, how we had wound up swallowing all of this like it was normal. I was supposed to be the Sunset… I was supposed to be working with the anomalies—my family. The people I had grown to love in a strange way I couldn't quite put into words. I was supposed to be leading, somehow. *Leading.* Such a big, messy, complicated word. I had no idea what it meant.

*"Do you ever wonder where he is?"* Areos's words wove through my thoughts. *"Do you ever wonder why he left us?"*

*Where is he? Why did he leave us? Why did he leave me? I don't know what to do. I have no idea…*

I shook my head, forcing the nagging voice to be silent.

"I know you're with me…" I mumbled a whisper, pressing myself up to sit. "I know you haven't left me. I'm sorry I have such stupid thoughts." My legs swung over the edge. "Stupid, stupid thoughts…"

*Do you ever wonder why he left us to deal with this wreck? With zero guidance?*

I got to my feet. The room full of bunks was empty. I'd been privileged a few hours of downtime solely because of my injuries. I took advantage of my solitude.

"Shut up, shut up, shut up." I repositioned my arm in its sling, "You don't know anything—you're nothing like me. You're an unbeliever. I refuse to listen."

I struggled into a pair of pants and walked to the shower house. Stopping at a sink, I bent down to turn on the tap and splash a generous amount of cold water over my face. Large drops rolled down my neck and spattered my chest.

Blearily, I stared at my eyes in the mirror, bloodshot and puffy beneath a stubble-covered head. Blood spattered my bandages, and the color had drained out of my skin.

*And you think you were made to lead these people, Icarus? You? Really?*

"Didn't I just tell you to shut up?"

*Look at yourself. Seriously—you're talking to yourself in a bathroom mirror. You're living in denial of your own logic.*

"Logic and truth aren't always the same thing. Logic isn't always right." I shook my head, water dripping off my face. "No, sometimes logic is a liar—sometimes it's just a boundary: man-made and there just to keep everyone from going farther than anyone's gone before."

*Or are you just saying that to comfort yourself, Icarus? Are you just using that as a crutch to deal with the fact that you may just be alone—stuck in the desert, cleaning latrines for a militia that could have you executed and replaced in a heartbeat?*

My wet hands gripped the sides of the sink as I yelled at my reflection. "No, it's not a crutch! It's not denial—it's not illogical because Sensei told me he would never leave me! Sensei told me I was ready for this! And if Sensei told me I'm ready, nothing else matters—I don't care what things look like! I don't care how bad things get, or how many times I get shot, or if anyone even believes that I am who I say I am!" My face burned as I shouted. "None of it matters! I don't care how bad it gets. I believe in… I believe…"

My voice ran ragged, breaking apart as hot tears stung my eyes.

"I believe."

———————

I found Areos in the mess hall, poking at something unidentifiable with a fork and scribbling on a notepad with his free hand.

"Hey." I threw myself down on the bench opposite. "Finished with your punishment tasks already?"

His response was delayed, but he cracked a slight grin. "They went a little easier on me than you."

I grunted a laugh. "Isn't that usually the case?"

"I follow orders."

"While I disobey them."

"Which, I'm presuming, is why you're here." He lowered his voice, looking up. "Am I wrong?"

I scanned the mess hall in my peripheral vision, then leaned closer. "Listen, man—we have got to get off this base," I hissed. "We have to get to the portal. It's the reason we're here in the first place."

"The reason I'm here is because I tried to save your ass, Icarus."

"I know, I know." I let out a frustrated sigh. "But I mean why we're back on Earth to begin with. We didn't return to an apocalypse; we returned to something far more intricate than that, something we're *meant* to figure out."

"Yeah?" He still hadn't looked up. He took a bite of whatever was on his plate. "And how do you expect to do that, Icarus?"

I stared at him hard. "Not on my own, for starters."

Finally he looked up. He chewed, swallowed; then, rolling his eyes, he ripped the page he'd been working on out of his notebook and slid it across the table to me.

I quirked an eyebrow. "What's this?"

Areos stabbed at his food begrudgingly. "The plan—which you *will* follow or else I'm out."

I scanned the page, which was covered in notations.

"We can't just stroll off base and go AWOL, Icarus. It's not going to happen. We'll get caught, and we'll be drawn and quartered." He reached over to tap a place towards the bottom of the page. "There are a few patrols going out tonight—Trawlers will be going in and out, as per usual. That will be the best time to try to get past the gates."

My curiosity was piqued. "Are you suggesting we steal a Trawler?"

"We're pilots. We don't have clearance to operate Trawlers." He folded his hands. "Their engines don't start with the turn of a key. Each vehicle has a respective set of drivers and a sort of Breathalyzer installed in the dash. The unique chemical structure of each driver's breath has been coded into each Trawler's electronic system. Meaning, the assigned driver, or *drivers*, needs to breathe into the Breathalyzer in their *assigned* vehicle in order to start the engine."

He paused, squinting, as he weighed the facts. "Far more sophisticated than a thumbprint reader, and much harder to forge. So, no, not stealing one exactly…" He searched for the right word. "More like… hijacking."

Despite everything, I couldn't help but grin just a little. The word sounded interesting coming from Areos.

"Hijacking?" I leaned forward on my elbows. "Tell me more."

He ripped the paper out of my hands. "Don't get too excited yet—this is where you come in."

"Just tell me what to do, Lieutenant."

"Find a driver we can kidnap."

I blinked, studying him for a moment.

"Okay, funny," I hissed across the table, glancing around again. "Now seriously, what is the plan?"

Areos looked at me, unamused. "Seriously, that *is* the plan, Icarus. The only feasible way to get off this base is to take a Trawler—and we can only take a Trawler if we have a driver. And right now we don't have one."

"So you actually expect me to go kidnap someone?"

He flashed the paper. "Hey, I came up with the plan."

"You never asked me what part of the bargain I wanted."

"Because you're not great with planning. No offense." He folded the paper and stuffed it into his pocket. "Kidnapping seemed more in your ballpark."

I heaved a frustrated sigh, running my hands back through my hair.

"Don't make a big deal out of it." He cracked open the can of soda next to his plate. "Don't overthink it. You know this stuff..." He took a swig. "Medics will be going in and out most of the evening, Icarus."

I looked up. "What the heck are you talking about?"

He flicked back the metal tab with his middle finger and thumb. It broke and flew off the table. "The perfect candidate."

---

*We're going to get ourselves killed... We're going to get ourselves killed...*

"Shut up, shut up, shut up," I muttered under my breath as I walked down the long cement hallway. "This is perfect. Everything is..."

I stopped abruptly as a door swung open and my commander stepped out into the corridor. She grimaced almost immediately, giving me a quick once-over. Her bright red hair was a sharp contrast against her jet-black uniform. She gave a nod and I saluted.

"How's the arm, Lieutenant?"

"Sore as all get-out, ma'am," I told her, because I knew it was what she wanted to hear.

"Good." A smile twitched at the corners of her cracked lips. "I hope we've learned our lesson, Lieutenant."

"Yes, ma'am."

"What was that, Lieutenant?"

"Ma'am, *yes, ma'am!*" I shouted.

Her eyebrows pinched, she nodded again. She gave me a firm slap on my bad shoulder as she passed me. A bolt of pain surged through my arm. I bit the insides of my cheeks.

"As you were."

*Ow, ow, owwwww…*

When she had rounded the corner and vanished, I picked up my pace, the heels of my boots echoing in the emptiness. Silence descended as I came to a stop in front of the infirmary. I froze, my hand on the knob.

*Icarus, do you want to get off this base or don't you?*

I was about to force myself to do the deed when suddenly the matter was taken out of my hands. The door swung open in front of me.

Charlie's blond eyebrows rose as she halted on the threshold, jacket in hand, black tank top tucked into her pants.

"Lieutenant." She eyed me suspiciously. "You change your mind about the pain medication?"

Suddenly, everything I'd planned on saying went out the window.

"Uh, no, I…" I shrugged, racking my brain. "I just, uh… I—"

An expression of uneasy concern passed over her face. "You just what?"

*Come on, come on, come on!*

"I just, like—I think I—" I coughed, finally jerking my head towards my shoulder. "I think the stitches…"

"You want me to check them?"

I nodded, sweat beginning to trickle down my spine.

Charlie huffed an irritated sigh, shooting the wall clock a quick glance before gesturing me into the office. "I'm beginning to think you just like me taking your shirt off," she muttered, closing the door behind us and snapping on the light. "What did you do this time?"

"I don't know. It just hurts."

She pushed me back onto the examination table. "Okay, well, let's have a quick look."

I had about five seconds to figure out what I was going to do.

Charlie set her jacket down and walked over to the sink. I heard the water turn on as she began washing her hands.

"There's a few patrols out. I've got to get going," she explained quickly.

*Bingo.* She was going.

"So you're going out to the sands?" I asked, trying my best to sound only vaguely curious.

"Yeah. Why?"

I didn't answer. She dried her hands on a towel, rounding the front of the examination table and coming to a stop right in front of me. Her sharp blue eyes, narrowed to slits, drilled into mine.

"Why?" She pressed the question. "You want to come?"

Her tone was so serious that, for a moment, I was afraid to answer. Then I nodded.

"Uh, yeah," I replied finally, my anxious, cracking voice sounding a little pubescent. "Yeah, actually."

Charlie said nothing at first. Then she laughed, right in my face. "Sorry, Lieutenant. Last I heard, you boys were grounded for disobeying orders."

*News spreads quickly.*

She yanked my shirt off and pushed my head to the side like it was a piece of meat.

"They look fine to me, crybaby," she muttered, poking at them a little. "Now, I've got to get going, if you don't mind."

"But what about, uh…" Things were going downhill fast. I'd lost my suave in my old age. "What about the pain?" I asked pathetically.

Charlie slid on her coat and started zipping up. "There's an old saying my grandmother used to love," she said, already starting for the door. She paused only to throw a glance over her shoulder. "Suck it up, buttercup."

I opened my mouth to speak, but the door slammed in my face before I could get a word out.

Biting back curses, I pulled my shirt over my head and scrambled into the hallway. I trailed her outside and found Areos just beyond the door, as planned.

"Well?"

I gave a brisk nod. "She's heading out right now."

"Now?"

"I suspect she'll have to report to her supervisor first, though." I dropped my voice, squinting across the courtyard. "We should have just enough time if we move quickly."

It was dusk now, but the lights hadn't come on yet, offering us less visibility to work with as Areos gestured for me to follow him through the row of Trawlers, keeping ourselves as low as possible.

"How do you know which Trawler is hers?" I asked when we had finally ducked into the long line of tactical vehicles.

"Oh, you of little faith," he hissed, his voice a whisper. "You're the beauty, I'm the brains, remember?"

I rolled my eyes. "Thanks."

He pressed a finger to his lips for silence. I halted immediately. Over the hum of the engines around us, I could hear voices—one in particular—shouting orders. Shouts in reply.

"They're going to be over here any second," I urged him. "It's now or never!"

Areos didn't reply at first. He remained where he was, listening. After a moment, he nodded slowly, then reached up for the handle of the door to the backseat and gently clicked it open. He looked back at me.

"Now," he said.

I threw myself into the backseat without hesitation. Areos crawled in after me.

"We were standing right next to it the whole time?" I growled, trying to keep my voice down. "Why didn't you say something?"

"Because I was trying to listen!" He sank back behind the driver's seat. "Not the easiest task with you around."

I was about to respond when the rhythm of a loud clomping march came into earshot.

"Crap—what if she isn't by herself?" I muttered, suddenly terrified.

"She will be." Areos gestured for me to shut up. "She always is."

The driver's door swung open, moaning on its hinges. Areos shot me a warning look, sliding a finger across his throat. I wasn't sure if that meant "Don't say a word," or "We're going to die." Either way, I was barely breathing.

Charlie jumped up into the driver's seat. From where I lay, I could see little of what she was doing, but I heard her flip a few switches on the dash. Then, muttering, she puffed into the Breathalyzer. With a vibration like a drum roll, the engine roared to life.

I looked over at Areos, but his eyes were closed. He was thinking.

Charlie turned the radio on. Something that sounded like Mozart filled the speakers.

With a jerk, the Trawler lurched forward. At first, we moved steadily; then after a couple of minutes, Charlie let her foot down on the gas. The trajectory slammed me down on my bad arm, sending fresh spurts of pain firing through my shoulder. Thankfully there was enough equipment clattering around to disguise the soft thump as I hit the floor. There were no windows in the backseat—we were encapsulated by bulletproof steel—but I was guessing we were beyond the gates.

Charlie leaned back in the driver's seat and hummed aggressively along to the classical music. I could hear the gravel of sand and debris beneath the massive tires, and soon I detected the scent to go along with it; the foul smell that was always there, hanging in the atmosphere.

*What is the plan? What is the plan?*

I kept looking over at Areos, but his eyes were still squeezed shut. Reaching out with my foot, I delivered a solid kick to his shin. His eyes flared open and he shook his head.

*We're going to miss it—our drop-off point. She's going to drive right past it, and we'll be screwed.*

Craning my neck ever so slightly, I could see beyond the windshield to the terrain that lay ahead. Looming like a crouching giant was the familiar crumpled top of a skyscraper—one with a helicopter pad on top. I saw it from the air every day and would recognize it anywhere. A sinking feeling twisted in my core.

*Hawk.*

Charlie swung a tight turn to avoid the debris—just as Areos's hand slid down to his side for his pistol. I felt my eyes widen.

In a split second the gun went from the holster at his hip to the back of Charlie's head. A dull click cut through the commotion as he phased the weapon into firing mode.

"Stop the Trawler, now!"

I stared at him, dumbfounded.

Blurting a surprised string of curses, Charlie careened to a stop, sending up a spray of sand as the vehicle pitched to the side.

"What the hell are you guys doing?" Charlie shouted, flipping around to look at us. "*Icarus?* What is going on here? How did you guys—?"

"It doesn't matter," Areos cut in, both hands still positioned firmly on the pistol. "Just… just do what you're told and I won't shoot. Give me your gun."

Charlie's eyes narrowed, her face growing red. "You guys aren't allowed to leave base."

"Well, it looks like we found a loophole." Areos spoke steadily, though he was breathing hard. "Now give me your gun."

"Or what?" She shot him a condescending look. "You'll shoot me? Go ahead—*I dare you.*"

Areos swallowed. I got to my feet and opened the door.

"Icarus, what are you—"

My comrade's question was cut short as I leapt out, slammed the door behind me, and walked around to the driver's side. I opened the door for Charlie, who instinctively reached for her pistol. I grabbed her by the wrist before she got there.

"Let go of me, you son of a—"

"I will let go only if you promise me something!" I yelled over her, staring directly into her eyes. "You have to promise me."

"What? Promise you what?"

"Promise me you won't drive back to base and report us."

Charlie stared at me. "Are you out of your mind, Icarus? Of course I'm going to report you—*both* of you!" She twisted around to drill Areos with her fiery eyes.

I bit back a frustrated sigh. "Areos, put the gun down."

He didn't move.

"I *said* put the gun down, *now!*"

"Not until she gets out," he stated, keeping a level aim on Charlie. "Not until she's out of the vehicle."

My jaw set, I reached up to help Charlie down to the sand, but she shoved my hand away, jumping down herself. I slammed the door shut and Areos opened the back door at the same time. I fixed him with a cold stare and, begrudgingly, he phased his gun off and returned it to his holster.

Charlie turned and looked at me, her face still burning with anger.

"You do realize that with the tap of a button I can call for backup and report your acts of treason."

"I realize."

She folded her arms over her chest. "Then you'd better start explaining, Lieutenant."

In my peripheral vision I could see Areos shaking his head.

"It's not something I can really tell you," I said as she took a step closer. "It's something I… would have to show you."

"Show me?"

Areos shook his head more fiercely now. "Icarus, don't you dare say another word—"

My eyes flicked up to meet his, and in that instant, Charlie decided to go for her gun.

It all happened so fast—her hand, a blur, a silenced crack. Then Areos's eyes went wide.

Everything crashed to a mute. A sick feeling gripped my stomach. I felt frozen as Areos attempted to open his mouth to speak, then doubled over, crumpling to the ground. I turned as Charlie's index finger closed around the trigger for round two.

Lunging forward, I nailed her to the ground just as another deadly bullet launched down the barrel of the pistol. It shot the sky.

She let out a roar of rage. Twisting her arm into a lock, I wrenched the gun from her fingers and saddled it to my hip. I scrambled to my feet and dropped to the ground beside Areos, who was curled over his knees now, head pressed to the sand, hand clamped over his abdomen.

"Areos!" I put an arm around him, but he only curled in tighter around himself, a strained scream ripping away from him. "Areos, let me see it!"

"No!" he insisted, though barely able to form the words. "No—d-don't, Icarus—"

I rolled him onto his side, feverishly untucking his shirt to examine the wound. Blood drizzled over his belly, oozing from a hole the size of a dime.

Areos's fingers tightened around fistfuls of sand as he bit back another scream.

My heart sank. I pressed the heel of my palm over the wound and turned to look at Charlie, stabbing a finger in her direction as she got to her feet.

"If you call for help, I will make you wish you'd never been born!" I yelled hoarsely. "Get over here and help me! That's an order!"

Charlie froze for a second, staring at me through narrowed eyes. Then she sprinted to my side.

"He threatened me with a gun," she said lamely, then knelt down beside me. "I had no—"

"Just tell me if the bullet went through!"

Charlie slid one hand underneath Areos's back. "It didn't go through. It must be lodged in his intestines."

*I don't know what to do, I don't know what to do, I don't know what to do...*

"You're the medic!" I exploded. "Do something!"

"There's nothing I can do! He's bleeding too quickly!"

Breathing hard, I pinched my eyes shut for a split second, trying to think straight.

*Yes, you do know what to do... Yes, you do...*

I turned and looked at her. "Then get out of my way."

Charlie gaped at me, wide-eyed and seeming to have forgotten about trying to escape; then she snapped out of it and moved aside. I took a deep breath and closed my eyes, placing a hand firmly over the bullet wound. Areos writhed immediately, groaning through clenched teeth.

"No," he growled, "No, Icarus—we've sworn not to use our powers…"

Yes. I remembered. I remembered Mitsue's speech—I remembered all of it.

I couldn't have cared less.

"Shhh," I hushed him firmly. "Don't talk. And don't you dare think."

I knew by now that thoughts were the worst enemy; they were the black wolves, and the very last thing I needed. I felt Charlie's confused eyes on me, the hot breath of the wind across the desert, but I turned my mind away from everything around me. I thought of nothing. Instead, I felt.

*Who are you indeed, Icarus? Who are you that the Earth groans in long anticipation of your awakening?*

After all this time, Sensei's question still echoed: *Who am I?* Was I still truly unaware, or was I just too afraid to admit I knew the answer? Afraid because I knew that, once acknowledged, it couldn't be ignored? Afraid because I knew it would change everything?

A tingling sensation filled my fingertips, and a swirling motion substituted for my sense of balance. Gold flecks flickered behind my closed eyelids. In a surge, energy rippled the length of my arm and poured into my hand, pulsing from my fingers to penetrate Areos's skin. I felt him tense underneath my hand, but I didn't move. In my mind I saw something like fire, something I was holding back. Taking a steady breath, I let go. I felt the sting of metal in the palm of my hand.

Dizziness flooding over me, I opened my eyes. Areos lay motionless beneath me, but breathing. Slowly I pulled my trembling hand away, curling it into a fist as I did. The blood had vanished from Areos's torso, giving way to clean flesh. The bullet hole had disappeared.

Areos lay there for a second longer before struggling up into a sitting position, staring down at himself.

"Holy shit…" He gasped for air.

Catching my breath, I turned and looked over at Charlie. Her face had gone pale, and her eyes were twice as wide. Her mouth slowly opened, but I stopped her. Taking one of her hands, I placed the bullet in her palm.

"Pretty sure that's yours," I panted, looking her square in the eyes.

She gaped down at the bullet before she looked back up to me. "Icarus…" She stumbled over my name as she shook her head in disbelief. "What did you… How the…?"

I put up a hand to silence her. "Questions later," I said. "Right now, we have to move—we're already late."

"Late?" Charlie gripped the bullet. "Late for what? What are you talking about?"

"You'll see."

I heard Areos groan slightly as he got cautiously to his feet. "Oh, no—no, no, no, no, she's not coming with us."

I began to walk toward the smashed skyscraper ahead, not stopping. "She has to now, unfortunately. She knows."

"She wouldn't if you had stuck to the plan like you were supposed to!"

I spun around. "If I had stuck to the plan, you would be dead right now, Areos!"

Charlie's gaze swapped between us. Then she stamped a foot, returning to her normal self. "I demand to know what's going on."

"You demand?" Areos almost choked. "You demand, huh? You don't have the right to demand anything—you just shot me!"

"You threatened to shoot *me*!"

"But I didn't, did I?"

"Enough," I cut in before Charlie could counter. "The damage is done." I pointed a steady finger at Charlie. "No talking. Follow."

I grabbed Areos by the shoulders and pushed him forward in front of me, acting as a buffer between him and Charlie. I needed to concentrate on getting us all into the Dimension in one piece.

------

It was dark as we circled around the crumbling rubble to the mouth of the tunnel, covered only by a broken car door. I kicked it aside, stirring up a dusting of sand. I turned and gestured to Charlie.

"Get in."

"No. Why?"

I offered no explanation. I grabbed her by the arms and took her with me, plunging into the darkness. I heard a thud as Areos jumped down after us, pulling the door back over the opening.

"What the hell is wrong with you guys?" Charlie roared, kicking me away.

I didn't answer. I focused on steadying my breathing, leaning back against the sandy wall. "Areos?"

"Right here," he said.

"Can you handle the transport?" I muttered, closing my eyes. "I'm a little light-headed."

"Icarus, we're gonna get executed if we bring her in."

"Bring me in where?"

"Areos, there is nothing we can do now."

He kicked the wall, swearing.

"Areos…"

"Fine! Fine. Whatever. I'll—I'll do it." Then he muttered something under his breath about how he hated his life.

My eyelids flickered shut. "Thanks, man."

A long silence. Slowly everything grew cool, then cold. The soft sand gave way to rock walls trickling with condensation. The dull echoes of voices thudded in the small space with the sound of the wind. I took a deep breath, letting my head drop back against the wall.

Home. It used to feel so good. Now it was empty—echoing with everything it had once been.

I heard Areos feeling around for the door handle.

"It's freezing…" Charlie observed uneasily. "What happened?"

Everything illuminated as Areos pushed the door open. The first thing I saw was Charlie staggering back against the wall. "W-w-what's going on? Where are—"

"No questions." I reinforced my earlier statement, getting to my feet. "Keep your hat on and low over your eyes."

"And don't speak to anyone," Areos added angrily. "Unless you want me to turn you in for attempted murder."

"*What?*"

"Look, Areos, just—" I put a hand on his shoulder before he could take a step towards her. "Just forget about it—"

"Forget about it? She tried to—"

"I know," I said. "But we have bigger fish to fry right now."

Stepping out of the cavern and into the hallway, I gestured for my comrades to follow. The later we were, the more obvious our arrival would be. I was hoping to remain as inconspicuous as possible.

That was hard with Charlie.

"Where are we?" she asked, gaping at the view beyond the window. "Did you guys drug me?"

I gently tugged her away from the window, forcing her to walk in front of me.

"No," I whispered. "We didn't drug you."

"Then what the—"

"If you keep silent, I promise I'll explain later," I whispered as we emerged onto the empty training platform.

The sun was about to set; the gathering would be coming into session any minute. We made our way down the path carved into the side of the ravine, following it into the swaths of mist that were starting to rise. The gathering platform was full—the meeting was already in session.

*Shoot.*

Areos slowed to a stop, shaking his head. "They've already started. There's no way we'll get up there without drawing attention to ourselves." He turned to look at me, his eyes pleading. "We have to leave her here."

"Here?" I asked.

"Or lock her in a safe room."

Charlie grunted, sounding disgusted. "I'm not being locked away anywhere—I don't know who you guys really are, or where I am, but—"

"They'll find her if we just leave her here," I objected.

"They'll definitely notice her when we go waltzing up the platform steps!"

I pinched the bridge of my nose, thinking hard.

"There's a ton of brush—she can just hide here and wait." He lowered his voice, blocking my way. "We'll leave a little early. We'll be the first ones heading back up—we'll grab her and go!"

I shot him a dubious glance. "Like she's going to just sit here."

"Do I get some say in this?" Charlie piped up, joining our huddle. "Because I think—"

"No. You don't," Areos interjected sternly. "We are *not* taking you into the meeting. You have to stay here and hide until we come back for you. Believe me, you don't want to get caught. They do *not* treat intruders kindly here."

Already I was beginning to wish we had never attempted this. It was getting too messy—and the chances of us getting out of this clean were looking slimmer and slimmer.

I was about to object, an unsettling feeling sinking in my gut, but Areos was already shoving me down the path.

"Stay out of sight and don't make a sound," he ordered Charlie over his shoulder. "We won't be long."

Charlie looked ready to retort, but after a moment she did as she was told and disappeared into the brush.

"That was well handled." Sarcasm dripped from my voice as I turned to look at him.

He grunted. "She tried to kill me—I'm not taking her anywhere."

I didn't argue.

Silencing our steps within the murmur of the crowd, we mounted the platform as quickly as possible and ducked into the audience. We took seats at the back, and I immediately started scanning the assembly. Runner's bright red hair stuck out like a warning flag.

He noticed me after a moment and a smile spread across his face. He gave a low wave. Mala was seated beside him, and beside her, Fin, though it took me a few seconds to recognize him. His hair had grown out to his shoulders and he had a beard now. He didn't look up.

Looking away, I swallowed a pang of guilt and forced myself to tune in to Azalea's authoritative voice as she spoke from the center of the platform.

"For a year we have been back—for a year," she announced, stating the obvious, pacing. "And within that time we have learned little. Some of us have been living undercover as civilians, while others of us have, unfortunately, been inducted into the RGM, the Reformed Global Militia—this brutal military force that was established to protect and uphold the Unified Nations Collective. Its ranks are composed largely of young adults—taken from their families as children and raised to be warriors."

She stopped in front of the table, hands on her hips. Her eyes were knife sharp and her hair was pulled back into a tight bun.

"The ecology of Earth is changing—the forests, the ocean, the very air we breathe: the massive development of industry has overrun the Earth's ability to renew itself," she continued. "Technology is developing faster than people can come up with methods of sustaining it. The global change in weather patterns has created massive storms and unstable habitation, which has forced millions to evacuate from the countryside to the cities that still remain, surviving metropolises that lie beneath shrouds of smog."

Gaia pushed back her chair to stand. Her long dreadlocks hung over her shoulders, and her expression became determined.

"Ethiopia, my country, like many others, is in the grip of famine. With the soil depleted and the water so acidic, crops struggle to grow. Industry is practically nonexistent." She paused, her voice cracking. "Children are born with deformities from lack of nourishment, and often die before the age of two. The statistics are staggering—more people than ever are perishing from lack of food and safe water. Because of Earth's pollution and depletion, simple resources are no longer available."

"And the government-monitored Fragment makes it impossible for citizens to question what's happening to the Earth," Azalea added.

"Government-monitored?" A voice that sounded like Fin's spoke up. "You mean *controlled*."

"You could say that." Mitsue stroked his chin thoughtfully. "It's true that this age is far different from any other—the time of the internet, social media, and rigorous free speech has faded. But the fact that the information is within their governance isn't the scary part. As Azalea said, once 'logged on'—once the Fragment is inserted—there's no 'logging off.'"

"What's that supposed to mean?" said another voice.

"It means that the Fragment, inserted into the cerebellum, alters the entire brain—not only its higher functions like interpreting touch, vision and hearing, but also one's emotions and ability to reason and learn. The Fragment overrides these." He folded his hands on the table. "So, yes, while it is unnerving that the government is controlling information, they are in fact controlling something much greater…" Mitsue tapered off, his gaze crossing with mine as he scanned the audience. "They're controlling *you*."

A hush fell over the gathering of students.

"They control your ability to think. To reason. To understand that you are connected to a machine—that you *are* a machine," he went on, his voice low. "You can't decide whether it's right or wrong, good or evil, because the Fragment has programed you with indifference. To determine whether the Fragment is good or not has been taken out of your power."

"What if someone tries to remove the Frag?" Mala asked. "Like, surgically."

"The host would be terminated instantaneously," he replied gravely.

Azalea was pacing again. "There is a minority—those who were Fragmented with faulty hardware—who are becoming aware of the fact that something is amiss; that their freedom to think has been compromised," she explained. "The RGM is doing its level best to wipe out these 'defects,' these *recusants*, as they call them." She grunted, gesturing in my and Areos's general direction. "Some of our own are even lending a hand to help the RGM terminate—"

"Because we're *forced* to!" someone shouted.

"Which is why we have yet to close our doors to you," Mitsue said firmly.

"However, if we find that your position within the militia compromises our security in any way, you will be barred from entering the Dimension."

A cluster of opposing shouts immediately erupted, but Mitsue continued.

"But beyond this minority with defective Fragments, there is no one left on Earth with a completely unaltered mind—everyone has been touched." He looked around at the assembly. "Everyone except for the anomalies of Earth—who, for the past one hundred and eighty years, have been held just out of Earth's reach… waiting for this moment: our long-awaited culmination."

*Waiting for this moment.* He'd said this the last time we were here. Undoubtedly, he said it every time.

"So what do we do?" Azalea asked, not expecting to be answered. "We have discussed this over and over and over again—haven't we?"

No one said anything.

Azalea stared out at the gathering for a long moment, seeming to will a dramatic build.

"We live among them. We learn all that we can. We watch. We wait." Her jaw clenched, each word growing louder. "And we cut the disease off at the root—we destroy the database."

The majority applauded. The minority grumbled. A few remained silent.

I was one of the few.

Areos laughed, a short, sharp, irritated sound, as he leaned closer to me. "Good luck with that, children."

I pressed the heel of my hand to my forehead and sighed. Azalea had quieted the audience and was taking questions. I could feel a migraine coming on.

"We should go," I muttered. "There's no point in staying."

Areos nodded.

We were just rising to slip away when a pained shout cut through the air, silencing the audience.

"May I have everyone's attention, please?" Sharp, angry words.

I swallowed, my body going stiff as I turned around.

Delta mounted the steps to the platform, dragging a certain RGM medic with her, hoisting her arm high in the air when they got to the top of the steps. Charlie struggled to escape her grasp, red-faced and panting.

"We've had a security breach!" Delta announced loudly. "We have a stowaway."

A deafening roar arose from the crowd, then fell away; suddenly all eyes turned to Areos and me—the only ones standing.

Delta turned and looked at me. Her eyes narrowed and she gestured towards Charlie, twisting her arm with a little more force.

"Forgetting someone?"

# CHAPTER SIX

## *Lara*

Rain rolled down the plastic tent windows in large drops. I watched them, not touching the food on the tray in front of me. The mess hall was almost empty. Kess sat across the table, scribbling in a notebook and occasionally sipping soup from a Styrofoam cup.

"Think they'll make you go out again?" she asked, not looking up.

I said nothing for a long moment. Then I gave a shallow nod, shivering.

"I didn't get all of them," I murmured. "Only two."

"And that's not good enough for them." Kess's tone was mocking. "Are you all right? You look sick."

"I'm not sick."

"You're shivering."

I coughed into my elbow. "So?"

"They should send someone else—someone like me," she continued brashly. "I'm not as good a shot as you, but then none of us are."

My eyes refocused on the window. "Consider yourselves lucky."

"I don't. I consider myself incapable of being able to help my best friend, and that's frustrating, even if she does irritate me to no end at times—and get me into unnecessary amounts of trouble."

"Unintentionally."

"Psssh."

I rolled my chin into my hand. "I'd probably be dead already if you hadn't stopped me the other night."

"Probably."

I gave her a faint smile. "Thanks."

"You know how I feel about sentimentality." Kess scribbled fiercely. "You feel too much. Everything is always so… emotional with you."

I frowned. "Is that really such a bad thing?"

She glanced up, her large brown eyes serious. "For an RGM member? Yes."

I reached for the bottle of water on my tray and cracked it open.

"You need to stop acting like you're doing something wrong, Lara—you're not," she continued firmly. "There's nothing you can do—except what you're told. And yeah, sometimes it sucks, and sometimes somebody's gotta die. And sometimes you have to be the one to make that happen."

"They're kids, Kess." I stressed the words, lowering my voice. "*Kids.* Like us."

"They're nothing like us—they have no idea what they're talking about or what they're dealing with."

"And do we?" I whispered. "Do we have even the faintest idea?"

Kess's eyes narrowed as she scrutinized me. Then she bent back over her notebook. "I don't understand what you mean."

A long silence passed as I looked at her. I could see the faint scar at the base of her head.

"I know you don't, Kess," I said at last, rising from the table. "I know you don't."

I wove my way through the rows of long metal tables and stepped out into the rain. Zipping my jacket up to my chin, I trudged forward through the mud. It was getting late and the sky was fading from gray to a dark, angry blue.

I shivered, pushing myself forward across the courtyard illuminated by the stacks of burning brush. I dodged Trawlers decked out in grassy camouflage, avoiding groups of soldiers lining up for orders. Shouted commands cracked the air around me, peaking even above the low rumble of the engines and generators. Everyone was spattered with mud, their black caps pulled down to their eyes.

I felt self-conscious in my burgundy beret, a symbol of my rank as a sniper.

Several young new recruits stopped to salute me. I returned the gesture respectfully. As soon as I passed them, I picked up my pace, and once I was out of the courtyard, I ran.

The entire base was encircled by a barbed-wire fence penning in the courtyard and the cluster of dirty cement buildings that funneled out to line the dirt road leading off base. Rust bloomed over metal surfaces, and mud spattered everything within reach of the road. Water seeped into my already drenched boots as I splashed through puddles. Finally, slowing to a stop at a familiar cement building, I stamped off my boots and let myself in.

My commander looked up from the stack of paperwork on his desk. He lifted a finger for silence. Catching my breath, I closed the door quietly while he nodded and touched the tiny speaker tucked into his left ear.

He was a tall thirtysomething, with chestnut-brown hair, deep-set brown eyes, and downturned lips.

"Yes, sir… yes. Yes, I understand, sir…" Donovan eyed me suspiciously as he spoke.

I closed my eyes, struggling to steady my breath as shivers gripped my spine.

"Yes, that makes perfect sense, and I—" He stopped, sighing. "Yes, I will, sir. Thank you."

I pulled my collar up over my mouth and attempted to silence my coughs. After a brief delay, Donovan tapped the speaker again and looked up at me.

"Corporal." He gave a single nod. "What brings you here?"

I reached up to take off my beret, exposing what little hair the RGM had allowed me to keep. I took a deep breath. "Tonight, sir."

"Tonight? What about it?"

"The mission, sir."

Donovan straightened in his chair. "Yes, Corporal?"

My gaze drifted to the floor.

*I don't want to go, I don't want to go, I don't want to go…*

"If I… i-if I…" My words broke off as I coughed. "If I finish them tonight, could I… I mean, may I…" I swallowed, a hot feeling filling my head. I squeezed my eyes shut.

"Corporal?"

When I opened my eyes again, there were Donovan's own inquiring ones. One dark eyebrow arched.

"May I get a few days' leave?" I asked quietly.

Donovan's expression changed. "A few days' leave?"

"Yes, sir."

"Haven't we been over this before, Corporal?"

"Yes, sir."

"Haven't I already told you, many times, that this would be impossible?"

My reply caught in my throat, and I coughed violently into my elbow. "Yes, sir."

He squinted. "Corporal, are you unwell?"

I shook my head. "No, sir. I am well, sir."

"You don't look it."

I cleared my throat, gripping my beret in my hands and forcing myself to stand a little straighter. "I am *fine*. Sir."

He looked at me closely and then gave a slow nod. "So we will not talk of leave again?"

"No, sir," I said softly.

"I'm sorry, Corporal?"

I sucked in a breath. "No, sir!" I shouted, only to be thrown into a coughing fit.

Donovan pushed back his chair to rise. I lifted a hand to stop him as he rounded the desk.

"I'm fine—"

"You are not fine." He clamped a large hand over my forehead. "You're hot."

"I was out in the rain all night, that's all." I sighed, fighting to keep my voice level. "I'm just tired."

"You're an RGM sniper, Lara." He spoke firmly, looking me square in the face. "You're never tired."

I said nothing. After a moment, he stepped back, clearing his throat as he realized his mistake.

"Corporal," he corrected himself.

I bowed my head respectfully.

Donovan walked to the one window at the back of the room. He joined his hands loosely behind his back. "Do you know why we send you out there?"

I didn't answer. I knew he would.

"We send you out there because there are things—people—that threaten progress," he continued. "There are those who think that they can overthrow something that took decades to build—a unified militia, which rose from the dust to bring back order. Not peace… Order, Corporal. Order is different from peace. Peace is a choice… Peace is not something that can be forced. Peace is like the tide, coming and going. Here, gone. But order is a different beast, Corporal…"

He paused as a Trawler roared past the window, spattering it with mud. Then he turned to look at me over his shoulder. "Order is made of stone. Order, like medicine, can be administered. With or without one's consent."

Still I said nothing. Donovan watched me closely.

"We send you out there with a spring-loaded needle, Corporal," he went on after a moment. "We send you out there to administer that shot." He looked back to the window. "Luckily for you, that seems to be what you do best."

I swallowed. Donovan was silent for a few moments. He reached up and wiped the dust off one of the windowpanes.

"I've trained many soldiers—snipers. It's all I've ever known. I've trained everyone in this unit—I've taught them everything, exploiting their Fragments, *forcing* them to reach into the database in ways that very few of us ever do—that's where they get their power. I've taught them to take the lives that are no longer serving us without question. But you…" He turned around, giving me a long hard look. "I haven't trained you, Corporal. Not really. I showed you the basics. The rest came naturally."

I remained silent as he began to pace, hands still folded behind his back.

"You're as good a shot as I am. I'm not too proud to admit that. That's why you are where you are; that's why you outrank every other sniper on the base; that's why we send you out there," he went on. "I just wonder sometimes… where it all comes from." He paused in the middle of the room. "How you've learned to maximize the capacity of the database far beyond everyone else."

A tightness gripped my throat. "I just follow orders as best I can, sir."

My commander nodded after a pause. "Yes. Yes, of course."

I covered a cough and slid my beret back over my head. "I'm sorry to have bothered you, sir."

His eyebrows furrowed as he watched me form a shaky salute. After a brief delay, he returned the gesture.

I turned for the door, grasping the handle.

"Corporal."

I halted. "Yes, sir?"

"The recusants haven't been spotted since you last went out," he said. "I… I could be persuaded to give you a few days of leave."

I stared at him, grasping for words.

"This is a *rarity*. But you are sick—I don't care *what* you say." He sat back down, tucking the chair underneath him. "And I can't have you out of order—not now."

Something inside me lightened. "Really, sir?"

"Yes, really," he grumbled. "Now get out of my sight before I change my mind, Corporal."

I smiled, opening the door now. "Yes, sir," I said, then paused. "Thank you, sir."

# CHAPTER SEVEN

*Icarus*

"I try to be patient with you. I really do. I try, and I try—and I give you another chance and then another and—" Mitsue interrupted his own speech, slamming a hand down on the chabudai table in front of him. "And every time, Icarus, every *single* time..." Fury flashed in his eyes. "You disappoint me. In fact, you *disgust* me."

The gathering had ended prematurely. Dawn crept in through the glass wall at the far end of the room. I was alone with Mitsue in a locked safe room. I sat at the chabudai across from him, not saying a word in response.

"I've come to notice a pattern with you, Icarus, a cycle," he continued, stroking his chin. "Sensei pulled you from the mess you'd made of your life, and made you one of us, yet you seem determined to tear us down."

"That's the furthest thing from the truth." I looked him in the eyes. "You and I both know that. You were there. That first day, when I woke up in the dorms—you were the first person from here that I met, besides..." I couldn't bring myself to say her name. I swallowed and forced myself to reset. "You weren't so eager to get rid of me then."

"That was before you brought Mala into the Dimension—and Raiden after her."

"I didn't actually bring Raiden here."

"Indirectly, yes, you did."

I leaned back, still looking at him. "Why do you despise me, Mitsue?" I asked. "What did I ever do to you?"

He grinned mirthlessly, turning to look out the window. "I don't answer to you, Icarus—you may think I should, since you are, after all, the acclaimed 'Sunset' who is to come and save us." His voice dripped mockery. "But I know better. I know exactly what you are—a blasphemer and a con artist who has yet again jeopardized our safety."

"I brought in *one* person."

He whipped back around, slamming his hand on the table again. "One person is all it takes!"

For a moment, I did nothing. Then I forced a slow nod. "I'm sorry." I pushed the words out. "I shouldn't have brought her here. But I had no choice."

"We always have a choice, Icarus."

My jaw set. "You have no idea what the situation was."

"Really?" One of his jet-black eyebrows sprang up. "Enlighten me, then."

My gaze remained locked with his for a long moment before I slowly shook my head. "No," I said finally. "Decide what to do with me based on the evidence you have. I have nothing else to say."

Mitsue looked surprised. "Nothing?" he asked finally, sounding deflated. "Icarus with nothing to say?"

Finished with the conversation, I stood.

Mitsue jumped up immediately and seized my wrist. "Did I give you permission to leave?"

His face was only a few inches from mine. I could feel the edges of his angry words.

"Let go, Mitsue," I said quietly. "Let go before it kills you."

A silence hung between us as his expression slowly hardened. He began to speak just as the door burst open.

Gaia stopped in the doorway, a look of urgency on her face.

"What is it?" Mitsue barked, quickly releasing me. "What do you want?"

"The student body—the council. We're anxious to send them back," she said briskly. "There's no sense in detaining them longer and making it even harder for them to provide a reasonable explanation for why they were gone for so long."

"They will be sent back when I am through with them."

Her lips pressed into a thin line. "Unless you want chaos on your hands again, I suggest you speed up the process."

Gaia waited by the door, arms crossed, as a heated mixture of voices drifted in from the hall. Mitsue's hand curled slowly into a fist, and finally he stepped back, his dark eyes drilling into mine.

"You are to transport out and never transport back in—do you hear me?" He tipped his head back slightly, squaring his shoulders. "All three of you."

"Mitsue," Gaia blurted, "you can't just call the shots without the approval of the—"

"Of the council?" he grunted, cutting her off. "Oh, believe me, you would have been the only one to object."

He grabbed me by the shoulders and roughly escorted me to the door, pushing me out into the crowded hallway.

"Even so, it's not right!" Gaia yelled after us.

"Even so, I don't care," Mitsue muttered.

Everyone was clustered together on the training platform, whispering, talking, staring as I walked by. Even after all this time, after everything that had happened, I still wasn't hardened to the scrutiny and suspicion. My face burned as I was handed off to Azalea, who stood waiting in the hallway that led to the cavern.

"Keep him here while I speak with the other two," Mitsue ordered, giving me a harsh look as he turned to backtrack across the platform. "Don't let him out of your sight."

When he had vanished into the crowd, I let out the breath I hadn't realized I'd been holding.

*We are in so deep.*

The sudden touch of a hand on my arm yanked me out of my thoughts. Jerking around, I found Fin standing beside me.

"What happened?" He motioned toward my wounded shoulder.

"Oh, it's nothing—a scrape." I brushed it off. "Still can't heal myself, as pathetic as that is. But it's nowhere near as much damage as I've created tonight. I… I'm sorry."

Fin stared straight ahead, saying nothing for a moment. "Don't apologize to me, Icarus. Not when I know who you are."

"Who I am doesn't seem to make much of a difference." My voice shook as I leaned back against the wall.

"Truth never does make a difference, Icarus. Not unless it's believed."

I caught sight of Mitsue across the platform as he dragged Charlie towards the safe rooms. She wasn't making it easy for him.

"I should never have brought her here," I said, almost under my breath. "I should never have tried to transport in tonight. How can I ever expect them to trust me when I screw up every time they turn their backs?"

"Their faith is none of your concern, Icarus." Fin folded his arms over his chest. "You don't need to prove anything to anyone—you need no one's belief in you but your own."

"I try to believe," I replied. "Not for my sake, but for…"

Her name caught in my throat. I pressed my eyelids closed, but it was no escape from the memory of her eyes, her face, and her voice. It was all there, as vivid as if she were standing before me.

*The forest. The flowers in her hair.*

*"Icarus…"*

I sucked in a breath, an ache pounding in my chest as I folded my arms over my torso.

"Have you found any sign of…" My voice cracked. I cleared my throat as I turned to look him in the face.

Fin's expression grew distant. "No," he said. "Not yet."

Everything seemed to fade from my senses.

"It's been over a year…" he continued. "A year, and every last day spent searching… I haven't found a trace of Hawk. But I've gained nothing but hope. I've been taught what you must now learn, Icarus." He paused. "That it doesn't matter what other people believe. At the end of the day, it's what you believe about yourself that matters."

"You're a stronger man than I, Fin."

He smiled a little. "We're alike in many ways, Icarus."

I tipped my head back against the wall again, a tight feeling stinging in my throat.

"No, Fin, you look for the lost, while I just feel lost myself." I sighed. "I keep telling myself that this is my purpose—to be their Sunset. Their leader…" I cringed at the word, the same sharp feeling resurfacing in my chest. "But all I want is to be out there, looking for her like you are. Everything seems so meaningless without her… I've taken bullets; I've bled… but somehow no enemy has ever felt as real to me as myself," I told him numbly. "Somehow that stupid, stupid voice inside my head is worse than any bullet I've ever taken."

"You have no idea how loud your own thoughts sound in the woods." Fin sighed. "After four hundred days of solitude."

I buried my face in the palm of my hand, letting out a sigh. "What I would give to be able to come with you…"

"You're doing everything she asked, Icarus," Fin replied steadily. "She asked you to take care of her people… to lead them into—"

"Chaos?"

The murmur of the crowd escalated once again as the safe room door opened and Mitsue stepped out. Everyone crowded around Charlie, barraging her with furious questions as he ushered her across the platform. A guard joined them, dragging Areos.

"Hawk believes in you, Icarus." Fin stepped closer to speak clearly into my ear over the noise. "If all else fails you, at least remember that."

Before I could reply, Mitsue came to a halt before me, and Fin slipped away into the crowd.

"Let go of me!" Charlie finally succeeded in yanking her arm from Mitsue's grasp. "What the hell is your problem?" She turned and gaped at me with fury in her eyes.

"Icarus, Areos." Mitsue cleared his throat loudly, turning to look at the two of us. "I hardly need to explain the danger you've put us in by bringing in an outsider."

"We didn't intend to bring her here," Areos explained through gritted teeth. "Our situation was dire."

"And that's why you have been trained here," Mitsue replied tersely. "So that you know how to handle such situations. But then I forget that you yourself were only recently an outsider."

Areos opened his mouth to speak, but I cut in before he could say a word. "So we're banned now?"

Mitsue jerked his head in assent. "In effect, yes."

"I see," I replied flatly. "Then I guess we should be going—we've already been gone too long." I pushed on a fake smile. "So I appreciate the release."

Mitsue's expression wavered uncertainly. Then he stepped closer. "You may mock me all you like, Icarus." He lowered his tone. "And you may believe whatever you like about your identity—I'm sure it will give you some comfort as you languish in the desert, putting bullets in the heads of rebels—innocent people who hate the RGM's agenda as much as we do."

I gritted my teeth, stepping up to him. I left only inches between our faces. "You have *no idea* what it's like out there, Mitsue." My tone was steel. "Don't talk about things you don't understand."

"I understand perfectly, Icarus—I understand that you are on the very brink of making the same mistakes Hawk made…" His lips twitched. "And you know how I dealt with her."

The words that had been tingling at the back of my throat faded with the pulse of my heart. Fresh blood surged into my arms, and my fingers curled to fists. Everything around me slowed.

*Don't, Icarus. Don't.*

I took a deep breath, trying to steady myself, but I couldn't hold it back any longer. My fist launched into Mitsue's face.

Staggering, he fell back into the wall opposite, and I dove after him—as a pair of firm hands grabbed hold of me from behind.

"Icarus, stop!" Areos yanked me backwards. "It's not going to make a difference!"

Azalea rushed to Mitsue's side to help him up, but he shoved her away. His lip was split and bleeding; a chunk of hair had come loose from his braid to hang in his face. He clambered to his feet, struggling to breathe, as he stared at me.

"You are worthless, Icarus!" He stabbed a trembling finger in my direction. "*Worthless!*"

Areos tightened his grip on my arms, twisting them behind my back.

"It seems only right that you bear her markings," Mitsue hissed, still keeping his distance. "You're both the same—liars."

I heard the sound of hinges as the door to the cavern opened behind us. Areos hauled me towards it, though I resisted every step of the way.

"If you ever dare to come back to the Dimension, Icarus, I swear," Mitsue yelled after me as I was dragged backwards into the darkness, "I will have you executed—I'll kill you myself if I have to!"

Charlie stepped in and slammed the door shut behind her. Only then did Areos release his grip on me. I jerked away at the same time, breathing hard. Heat radiated off my face, and the knuckles on my right hand pulsated as the commotion around us faded away.

"Who the hell *was* that guy?" Charlie's angry question echoed in the empty space.

I took a slow breath and searched for an answer, but none came—there was nothing left inside me to say. The words crumbled along with my insides. I slowly turned to the wall and slammed my fists against the cold stone just as it gave way to sand, pounding it over and over until my knuckles were raw.

"Icarus." Areos's voice was firm. "*Stop it.* Just stop it."

I shook my head, pressing my forehead to the wall.

*Hawk…*

"W-what just happened?" Charlie stuttered. "The-the walls are sand again! What the literal—"

"We're back on Earth," Areos answered, brushing off the question. "The transport is over. We have to get out of here." Then, under his breath, he muttered, "God knows how long we've been gone…"

"Back on Earth? *Back on Earth?*" Charlie repeated. "What the—what does that mean?"

"Just help me find the tunnel opening, okay?" His voice grew more distant. I heard the muffled sounds of his footsteps. "We have to get back aboveground."

The sand stung in my bloody knuckles. I gritted my teeth and peeled myself away, forcefully ignoring the voice in my head. The one I had told Fin about. The one I had shouted at earlier. The one that now repeated Mitsue's words loud and clear: *worthless, worthless, worthless, worthless...*

Light suddenly poured down on us. Areos, bracing himself in the tunnel, became a silhouette.

"Are you guys coming or do you want to stay down there?" he called.

Charlie snorted. "I'm not letting you out of my sight until I get some answers."

"You attempted to kill me," he replied bitterly. "Expect nothing but an eternal silencing from yours truly if you dare breathe a word about anything you saw."

Areos was the first to climb out, then Charlie. I was last.

Squinting, I lifted a hand to shield my eyes from the sun. Even with the smog, I could see it was high in the sky.

Charlie squinted at our surroundings. "It was dark when we found the tunnel... How can it possibly be noon?"

Areos shot me a level stare. His lips formed a silent curse.

"That was yesterday," I replied numbly, wiping my bloody hands on my shirt. "And yesterday's gone."

Charlie looked back at me, her forehead creased in confusion.

"And the day after that, probably..." I murmured, taking a couple of steps forward. "Come on."

Areos fell into step behind me. "I knew we should never have done this. We got stuck there a lot longer than we expected—it's been days here," he ranted, furious. "And we have literally no excuse to cover us. You do realize that, right?"

"I do realize that you are getting on my nerves, Aer." I glowered over my shoulder at him as we rounded the massive decaying building. "Stop talking."

"Seriously, Icarus, you don't understand—"

I put up a hand, slamming to a halt. "Seriously, stop talking," I said, silencing him.

"What is it?"

I shook my head once, straining to listen. Attempting to mute everything except the sound I could have sworn I had detected.

Charlie came up alongside us. "What's wrong?"

"*Shhh!*"

I stepped slowly forward to the edge of the building. Then out into the open.

A dull click, as clear and distinct as the pounding of my heart, caught my attention as the muzzle of a pistol slid up to press into the side of my neck.

I froze, my eyelids sinking shut. I didn't need to look to know who it was. I had already seen the jagged scar in my peripheral vision. In the hazy distance, parked Trawlers surrounded Charlie's abandoned one like it was a crime scene.

I heard Areos curse quietly behind me.

"Lieutenant." Hatch said my name steadily through gritted teeth. Her eyes barely shifted as she noticed Charlie and Areos behind me. Her lips thinning, she kept pressure on the gun. "You just can't seem to grasp the concept that orders are meant to be followed, can you?"

———

"You don't understand. I'm—I didn't do anything! It's their fault—I was taken hostage; my Trawler was *hijacked!*"

Hatch motioned for one of the guards to tighten the bands that bound Charlie's arms. Areos and I wore matching sets. Hatch paced the dim hallway slowly. We stood at the loading bay, waiting for the black door to rise.

"If you were hijacked, you most certainly would have reported it."

"No, no, no, no, you don't understand. They pulled a gun on me. There was nothing I could do—I couldn't call for backup."

"You three should be grateful we're not putting you to death—which would have been my first choice," Hatch grunted. "But where you're going, they have a way of getting what they want out of troublemakers like you."

I attempted to move my wrists into a more comfortable position in the bands, but the cool metal only dug in deeper.

"Where are you sending us?" I asked.

Hatch paused mid-stride and turned on her heel, giving me a toothy grin. "That's for me to know and you to find out, Lieutenant," she replied. "You can ponder that on the flight—along with the consequences of your seditious actions."

"Seditious?" Charlie spat back. "My actions were the complete opposite! I was just trying to—"

"—help the wounded, but you were kidnapped. Right." Hatch pursed her lips, nodding vigorously. "Whatever your excuse, the evidence is stacked against you, I'm afraid."

I sighed, swallowing back the pain shooting through my shoulder. "She's telling the truth, ma'am. It was my fault."

My commander's eyes flickered to me. She folded her hands behind her back. "I'm more disappointed in you than anyone, Icarus," she replied, ignoring my last statement completely. "You show true skill—talent, even. But talent unrestrained and unrefined can be a very dangerous thing. And I cannot—I *will not* put the RGM at risk for your sake." Her stern expression turned to one of ice. "It will be hardest for you where you're going."

"How do you mean, ma'am?"

"I mean that you struggle with taking orders." She stepped closer. "You struggle with your conscience—that siren that wails silent to all but you. For you it is everything…" She placed a hand on my good arm, on the black band that wrapped it. "Learn to silence it, Icarus—or one day it may silence you."

I looked at my commander for a long moment. Then the pressurized door slid up into the ceiling. A black, unmarked cube truck stood open in front of us.

Finally, Hatch stepped away from me, gesturing to the guards. "Clear the mess."

"No—no, please!" Charlie begged as the guards grabbed hold of us, dragging us forward. "Please—I swear, I had nothing to do with this! Please!"

We were pushed down into the back of the truck. Without hands to balance, I stumbled and collapsed onto my bad shoulder. Areos and Charlie landed beside me.

"Safe travels," Hatch called after us.

"No, wait!" Charlie's voice cracked as she yelled hoarsely. "You don't understand!"

I struggled up into a seated position just in time to watch the door roll shut, swallowing Hatch, the guards, the light. The air inside the truck was cold, the surface beneath us steely. I heard Areos struggling to get to his feet, but as the truck lurched into motion, he dropped to the floor again.

I squirmed back against the wall, trying not to focus on the pain still tearing up and down my arms. I sucked in a breath, resting my head against the vibrating side of the truck.

Charlie was breathing frantically beside me. "Where do you think they're taking us?"

I shook my head slowly, closing my eyes. "I guess we'll find out, won't we?"

# CHAPTER EIGHT

## *Lara*

I'd been dropped off by an outgoing patrol in the countryside—in the middle of what seemed like nowhere. It was RGM property, acres and acres of abandoned farmland and meadows reclaimed by the Earth's wild fingers—although *abandoned* wasn't really the right word. After all, no one had left of their own choice.

Wrapped in my jacket and shivering to keep warm, I trekked across the Irish countryside: faded fields dotted with boulders and sprinkled with bullet casings. The green grass was gone, replaced by straw stubble. The trees were just shells of trees; the tall, scraggly skeletons surrounded me as I entered the forest, if it could even be called a forest anymore. Dried moss crunched beneath my feet. It seemed too cold to be spring.

I coughed into the collar of my jacket, then peeled off my beret and paused, glancing down at it in the dull gray light, my fingertips white against the burgundy.

*Don't stop searching. Don't ever stop searching.*

I crumpled the beret and shoved it into my pocket.

The trees began to look familiar; the needles grew golden under my feet. I scanned the trunks, searching for notches I'd carved carefully at eye level.

I took a sharp turn at the first slender mark I found, carved discreetly into the rust-colored bark. The second mark I found on a pine, the third, the fourth; the fifth was on a stump. I picked up my pace, winding through the deadwood. My fingertips brushed the soft, rain-soaked bark as I steadied myself.

The ghosts of voices swelled in my consciousness.

*"Why do we hurt the trees, Ronan? Why do we scar their faces?"*

*"We're not hurting them, Lara—look… see how I don't press the blade too deep? See how it draws no sap?"*

I swallowed, my fingertips trembling as they traced the markings I'd etched so many years ago.

*"We scar the trees so that we can find our way home, Lara…"*

I pushed myself forward, my feet seeming more and more like lead weights with each step. In a broken whisper, I began to sing, attempting to drown out the voices in my head as they grew louder.

A right turn, a left, a long straightaway through a yawning row of black pines. My boots pounded against the soft ground.

Finally, I halted and glanced around, a somewhat paranoid habit of mine to ensure I was alone.

I ducked into a thick patch of brush, trying my best to move quickly without breaking any of the dry branches or dead hanging vines. I left as much evidence as a ghost would. I picked my way around thorny bushes, barely noticing their sting as they brushed against my legs. Finally, I broke through to a small clearing. In the center stood a weather-beaten cottage, a simple, boxlike structure with two faded glass windows frosted in mildew, a slate roof licked with brown moss, and a door bound in the clutch of dead vines. A dead tree grew up directly through the center of the structure to burst through the roof and skyward.

Clutching my collar, I proceeded across the patch of dead grass and up the two front steps, pausing on the tiny covered porch. The old wood moaned beneath my weight. Shaking, I brushed aside a cluster of leaves, feeling around for the familiar smooth handle. Glancing over my shoulder, I checked my surroundings one last time before I brushed aside the dead vines and gave the door a firm push. It shrieked quietly on its hinges, grinding slowly open. I stepped inside.

I felt for the matchbox, then lit a candle on the small table beside the door. It was always the first thing I did—or used to. It had been so long. I tore the coverings off the windows; milky white light pierced the glass to fill the room, igniting microscopic particles of dust. I shook my head, gazing around.

A table and a bed were the only furnishings, and each was coated in a thick layer of dust. Dead foliage hung from the ceiling, and the walls were lined with shriveled grapevines. A great, thick oak grew silently in the middle of the room, stretching up and through the roof. Shelves dotted with pots of what had once been flowers stood along one wall, brown and covered in dust.

I walked across the room and lifted one of the flowerpots, examining the caked soil. I took one of the brown petals in my fingertips, kissing it.

"I have missed you, my friends."

I set the pot back down. Taking a deep breath, I pressed my fingertips deep into the hard soil and began to slowly exhale, dipping each finger up and down as if playing an invisible piano. I resumed my song, singing under my breath as the dried flowers began to gradually twitch, as if moved by a fierce wind only it could feel. I watched as shades of green trickled steadily into the leaves, moving up the stems and into the petals, which began to blush shades of pink, yellow, orange. Their smooth, velvety textures returned in a wild flourish, drizzling the flower heads like a honey glaze, seeming to spill down and stain the soil a damp, earthy green.

I leaned in, gasping for air as if I'd been holding my breath the whole time. I inhaled the sweet smell of poppy and my lips turned in a smile. I set the pot down and reached for the next one, inserting my fingers into the soil. The deadheads swirled, morphing back to life at my touch.

I snatched a scrap of cloth from one of the shelves and got to work on the table, wiping away the dust and tucking my face into my shirt to avoid a coughing fit. I then turned my attention to the window, swiping away the grime until I could once again see beyond it. I placed the candle on the table. I gathered armloads of the succulents and spread them across the table's surface, brushing my fingertips over the walls on each trip across the room. The vines seemed to twitch from each encounter with my skin, trembling as green rinsed over them like the dribbling of a fresh spring rain. I swirled my index fingers like a conductor and watched as tiny green grapes grew out from among the leaves, ripening to a deep purple.

I took another breath as I paused at the head of the table, closing my eyes. I blew out as if a birthday cake stood before me, and not a small army of dead plants. Crackling fingers of green sprang up before me as my breath rolled across their leaves and the plants came back to life, sending puffs of what looked like fog up into the air; small, barely audible, childlike sighs seemed to amplify the effect.

As plump leaves began to push from their branches, I turned on my heels, satisfied, and walked a few paces to kneel down beside my bed, pulling a shallow cardboard box out from beneath it. I opened the lid and ran my fingers lightly over the dresses Mom had made for me so long ago. I bent my head closer. They smelled strongly of dust, but I didn't care. I breathed them in anyway. My favorite was a dress that looked like an oversized T-shirt. It was soft and gray, and it reminded me of the days I'd spent with my sisters.

I untied my boots and slid out of my starched uniform, folding it carefully and placing it on the floor beside the bed. I stuck my arms into the sleeve holes and pulled the soft fabric over my head. I pulled back the blanket and dropped into the bed, then lay still for a moment. I folded my hands behind my head, linking them over my scruffy excuse for hair, and gazed up at the ceiling. Dried brown blossoms hung lifeless and dust-coated.

I squinted up at them, tilting my head slightly to one side; then I reached out with one hand, twirling my finger. The flowers trembled only the slightest bit, not easily convinced. They never were. I guided the vines with my finger, back and forth in a sweeping, hypnotizing motion, coaxing them closer. Fresh green life crept slowly into the leaves, and gradually the rust-colored blossoms began to assume their usual white radiance. I let my eyes close, still swaying my fingers from one side to the other, rippling them rhythmically back and forth until at last I felt something soft nuzzle against my fingertips.

I cracked a smile before even opening my eyes, knowing full well what it was. Flecks like snow fluttered down to brush against my face. White wisteria vine wove between my fingertips and down my arm, squeezing me gently before releasing me from its grip. I breathed in the residue of its scent off the palm of my hand.

Green moss bloomed up the tree trunk in the center of the room now, and plumes of white draped from the ceiling like curtains of shimmering pearls. The massive bloom above me swayed in the dull flicker of the candle-light. It was almost dark now.

With one hand, I reached down without looking and retrieved the famil-iar square of paper from my jacket pocket. I didn't open it or read it. I just held it tightly in my hand, snuggling beneath the blankets now. My eyelids closed for just a moment.

**One hundred and sixty-six years earlier. Dublin, Ireland.**

College was the last place on Earth I'd wanted to go. No school could teach me what I needed to know, or answer the questions that plagued me in the dark hours. No human could. But I knew I had to leave somehow, and I couldn't bring myself to run away. I loved my parents too much to devastate them like that.

I'd lived the first eighteen years of my life with bare feet, grass-stained knees and buttercups in my hair. I spent my days outside the city, running the cliffsides and exploring the forests with Ronan, Brigid, and Anna. Even after Ronan disappeared, we still returned to the forest and the cliffs, until Brigid went away to school and Anna eventually married. After that, I still went, believing, deep down, that Ronan had left a clue in his letter—that, if I kept searching, I would find him somehow. But that year, everything changed.

It started with the flowers—the flowers I had picked in a field only to look down and find that roots had sprung from their stems to wrap around my arm. Fresh moss exploded with my every footfall, leaving a winding path of green footprints to chase me through the woods. Seedlings sprouted every time my hand brushed the Earth. I wasn't afraid—I was terrified.

I had no idea why this was happening, or how to control these strange abilities. I couldn't tell my family; I didn't know how. So I kissed my parents goodbye, holding back the tears as I kept my feet firmly on the pavement. I boarded the train headed for college and sat by the window, watching for hours as the landscape whipped by in blurs of green and lighter green. Dread seemed to sink in with the rain as it pounded down, turning gradually to sleet.

A sudden feeling of sickness came over me. Anxious, I rose and made my way to the next train car. I wasn't sure what was amiss at first. I had never been on a train before, so I figured it was just an effect of the motion, but then I began to realize that something was off. I had no explanation for the feeling, I just… *knew*. My pulse quickened and sweat sheathed the back of my neck. Some passengers slept, while others were served coffee or silently read books. The train rocked rhythmically.

I continued to the next train car, which was empty. I took a few steady breaths, attempting to calm myself—wondering what on earth was wrong with me.

*Jump.*

I couldn't tell if it was an audible voice or merely a thought—but it was strong. Stronger than reason, and blaring like a siren in my soul.

*Jump. Now.*

The train jolted back and forth, falling out of normal rhythm. I stumbled and fell against one of the seats. I scrambled to the emergency exit window, hesitating only a moment, my fingers pressed against the cold glass. A fierce vibration rattled through my hand. My heart pounding, I flipped the red levers and the glass dropped out, shattering onto the tracks. I dove after it without hesitation.

I slammed into the ground. The Earth felt like iron, and the rain pelted me like bullets. Everything spun over my head, the grass flipped up to where the sky should be as I rolled and rolled and rolled—and then stopped. Then a sound like the crack of lightning pierced the air—only ten thousand times louder.

I scrambled up into a seated position, clutching handfuls of dirt as though the ground would pull itself out from under me.

The train collided with a massive fallen tree that lay across the tracks. It buckled and rolled from the rails, slamming to its side and tearing into the tree line on the opposite side of the tracks. A ringing sound hissed in my ears until the sky suddenly flashed red. Flames bellowed from the engine, and a tumbling plume of crimson ripped down the length of the cars, spreading to the pines. Shrapnel launched into the air, spattering the landscape like bullets from a machine gun. I flattened myself against the wet grass, pain tearing through my body as I braced myself.

Suddenly I felt two hands clamp firmly down on my shoulders and pull. In shock, I didn't struggle against it, though something in the back of my mind screamed warnings through the fog. My eyelids lulled shut, then opened. Pine trees swam above me; icy raindrops pelted my face. I felt strong arms beneath me, carrying me. The rhythm of footsteps pulsed through my body.

Slowly my vision cleared. I saw the face of a stranger bent over me as he set me gently to the ground. I scrambled backward, digging my heels into the ground.

"Stop—w-w-who are you? Where are you taking me?" I shouted, though my voice sounded muffled. "Where did you—how did you—"

An old man stood before me, wrapped in a heavy overcoat. His face was wrinkled with sun and age, his eyes were a dancing green, his head was crowned with rusty salt-and-pepper hair, and his jaw was swathed in a thick beard. He stepped back, lifting his hands as he knelt down on the soaked ground.

"I saw you fall."

"I-I-I d-don't understand—who are you? Where did you come from?" I reached up to touch the back of my head. I tasted blood as it drizzled from my nose. "Who are you?"

He knelt before me and looked me straight in the eyes. "The voice that told you to jump."

I gaped, then squirmed farther back, thudding against a tree trunk. I shook my head fiercely. "No—no, no, no, no, that—that is not... that is..."

"Did you not hear a voice?" he asked.

I stared at him for a moment, breathless and unable to answer.

"Is there not another question you wish to ask, Lara? A question far more important to you than who I am—or how I know your name?" Gently he reached forward and placed one large leather-soft hand on my forehead. "We have but a moment, dear one—ask it quickly."

A warm, liquid substance seemed to pass from the palm of his hand and melt into my skin. A numbness stretched over me, and all of a sudden, I could no longer hear the roar of the fire on the other side of the tracks. Parting my lips for a trembling breath, I looked up into his deep-set eyes.

"W-w… who am I?"

"One who heeds the voice within." He took his hand away.

"I don't know what that means, sir."

"I am not *sir*," he replied, getting to his feet. "I am your teacher. And you have a greater mission than I."

I stared up at him, unable to move. I slowly lifted my fingers to my nostrils. My skin was dry, the taste of blood gone.

He extended a hand to help me up. Dazed, I took it.

"You must run, Lara, and let no one know you survived—tell no one where you are, who you are, or what you are capable of," he told me quietly. "You seek identity—and someone you have lost. You will find what you seek, but you must first find them in here." He laid a hand over his heart, looking earnestly into my eyes. "That is the only way you will find them out there."

I blinked through the rain. "How did you know? That—that I lost…"

"Do not ask me now, Lara—you must go. Go, and run as far away as you can. Never stay too long in one place. Keep moving," he continued, an urgency in his voice. "You were not made for this world, Lara."

"How do you mean?"

"You possess unique abilities—abilities you must learn to harness. As an anomaly, your face will not wither, and your body will not age," he answered. "You must never let them find you, or know who you are."

I took a shaky breath, looking down at myself and then back up at the mysterious man before me.

"Now go," he said, stepping aside and gesturing toward the deeper part of the forest. I took a step backward, then another, my eyes remaining fixed. The sky glowed orange behind him.

"Run!" he bellowed, his voice echoing. "Run, Lara!"

I obeyed. Turning, I streaked through the trees. But in a moment, the urge was too great: I had to look back. Halting in the cold rain, I looked over my shoulder. But no one was there, only the lonely trees swaying against a grieving sky.

The man was gone.

# CHAPTER NINE

## *Fin*

I stood at the tree and carved notch four hundred and one. The sky had cleared to a strong shade of blue, dulled just slightly by the smog. The ground was covered in dew, and the air reeked of decay. Wood curdled and fell away from the pressure of the blade. I heard the sound of footsteps in the distance, but I didn't stop my work.

"Hey." A familiar voice ventured closer. "You left the meeting early."

"As I said, I have a pretty low tolerance for the gatherings these days." I pulled back the blade to blow away the sawdust. "Besides, I could tell Mitsue was eager to see the back of me."

Runner grunted. "Who the hell—er, *heck*, cares what Mitsue wants? The guy's on a power trip—he's been on one ever since you refused the position."

"Don't remind me." I pocketed the blade. "It haunts me even in my sleep."

"If you could go back and do it all—"

"No."

I turned to find Runner staring, holding two plastic cups. "But you didn't even let me finish the question."

"Because I knew what you were going to say."

"What was I going to say?" He extended one of the cups.

I raised an eyebrow. "What is it?"

"Cocoa," he said. "They still make it, you know—I stopped in one of the outer cities before I came here."

"I'm not drinking anything from those cesspits." I brushed it away, walking past him. "And you were going to ask me if I would take the position after all if I could go back and do it all over again. I wouldn't—I still know that I can't, that it's not what Sensei would want, and I cannot and will not go against what I know in my heart to be true." I glanced at him over my shoulder. "You know?"

Runner's shoulders slumped forward as he slowly began to follow me. "Whatever. I'll drink both."

We walked in silence for a moment.

"You missed the big fight."

"What fight?"

"Icarus decked Mitsue after you left," he said, sounding suddenly animated. "You should have seen it."

"Why?"

"Because it was hugely entertaining."

I heaved a sigh. "No, I mean why did Icarus hit him—what instigated it?"

Runner hesitated. "Mitsue made a few choice comments about Hawk..."

For a moment I didn't reply. We walked in silence.

"Well," I said finally, keeping my focus firmly on the course ahead of me, "I hope he hit him good and hard."

"Good enough to get banned, apparently."

I stopped short and turned to look at Runner. He stood several yards back, gulping the contents of one of the cups.

"What?" The question came out in a sharp tone of disbelief. "What do you mean, banned? Icarus was—?"

"Excommunicated, basically," he clarified, wiping his mouth with the back of his hand. "But not just him. Areos and that chick they work with—Charlie, I think her name is." He shrugged. "But yeah. They're not allowed back in the Dimension. Not that it makes a huge difference; they weren't even coming to, like, any of the meetings anyway."

"It makes an enormous difference," I corrected him. "Icarus is the back-bone of our movement while Hawk is gone—he embodies both the Sunrise and the Sunset. Hawk granted him that—we need him."

Runner squinted at me. "You say that like her disappearance is tempo-rary…"

My jaw set as I resumed my steady pace.

"No, no, no, Fin—Fin, don't get me wrong." His footsteps quickened. "I know you believe it *is* temporary—but I still don't understand… what makes you so sure that she's out here? I mean, Icarus lost her in another *dimension*, Fin—a completely different world."

"I know."

"So what makes you think she's here?"

I pulled in a steady breath, still staring straight ahead. "Because I trans-ported here for a reason, Runner. I didn't dictate with my mind where my portal would open up. I let my heart do that, and it brought me here." I threw a hand in the direction of the trees. "I *refuse* to believe that's for nothing."

"But according to the notches on the tree, you've been doing this for, what? Four hundred days?"

"Four hundred and one."

"Don't you think it's time to give it a little rest? We need you, Fin—the Dimension needs you. Especially now that Icarus and Areos are gone."

"They need me no more than they need you or any one of us, Runner," I said firmly. "They don't want me—don't you see that? They don't want me or Icarus or Hawk—or even Sensei!" I halted and turned to face him on the incline. "Why do you think he left, Runner? Why do you think he's not here? Because he abandoned us? Because he doesn't believe in us anymore?"

My voice echoed in the empty woods. Runner stared at me as I slowly shook my head.

"He left because he believes in us." My voice was quiet now, my breath lingering in the air. "He left us because he believes we can do this—the things he always told us we could do. But what have we done with our freedom but make fools of ourselves—bogging everyone down with rules we can barely keep ourselves?"

"You probably keep them better than all of us put together, Fin."

I shook my head. "No. No, Runner, I'm not as good as all that."

"How so?"

I turned away, continuing up the base of the mountain. "I love her."

"Right—but isn't that like a rule? Everyone is supposed to love every-one."

"No, I mean…" I sighed, shaking my head. "It doesn't matter."

"Oh… *oh*, you mean—"

"Just forget I said anything."

"Stuff like that cannot be unsaid, dude."

I pressed the heels of my hands to my eyelids.

"Like, you're in love with her? Dude—did you ever—"

"Yes." I severed his question with the answer. "Yes, I told her once. A long time ago. It's not something I want to discuss."

"Why?"

"Because I have no right to," came my ragged reply. "I—she… Look, Hawk and Icarus are the Sunrise and the Sunset, the *patriarchs*, the ones the prophecy foretold. They belong together. I think the only reason Icarus and I have gotten through this is our common belief in Hawk. He's just as devastated as I am without her. Do you actually think I would come between them? I promised her I would help him—"

"And you have, Fin."

"I *wouldn't be* if I allowed myself to be carried away by what I feel for her." I hoisted myself up over a large boulder in the path. "I would be doing the exact opposite."

"But what about you?"

"What *about* me?"

"Are you going to be okay?" he asked. "If—I mean, *when* you find her, and she goes back to Icarus—are you going to be okay with that?"

A strange feeling instantly tightened in my joints. I slowed to a halt and glanced back at Runner. His eyebrows quirked as he gave me a knowing look.

"Of course," I replied firmly. "Runner, what I care about is *finding* her. That is *all*."

Runner and I parted ways, and I hiked onward in silence.

The air was devoid of the usual birdsongs I remembered from my boyhood, when my sisters and I roamed the woods like the wild foxes did. We had lived a good half hour from here, but since returning to Earth, I hadn't gone back to see if the house was still there, or if it had been destroyed long ago. Seeing the church and the garden in ruins was already more than I could bear. To see the woods where Brigid, Anna, Lara and I had played—built our "clubhouse," fought with swords made of dead branches, and made up new "noble" names for each other—I wasn't sure what it would do to me. But thinking about it, and my sisters and my parents, made me wonder whether I had lied to Runner when I'd explained why I was looking for Hawk—why I had to find her.

I'd made it all sound so honorable. But was it? Was I really so relentless in my search merely because of loyalty to my own—to Icarus, to my pledge to Hawk? Or was it just that I couldn't accept that I had lost her, too?

My thoughts tormented me as I walked in the quiet, staring up at the withering pines. I ached to heal them. My fingertips brushed the tall, dead grasses, but they remained exactly as they were.

"Why can't I heal you? Why, why, why…?"

I clenched my jaw, breathing deeply as I closed my eyes.

"Sensei, why did you choose me?" I asked, my voice no more than a rough whisper. "I cannot heal… I feel no power. In this shadow of death I feel nothing but darkness. Why did you choose a doubter like me?"

My throat was tight as I opened my eyes again. The sky was blue and rust, flickering before my eyes like a light before it goes out. The trees groaned listlessly in the wind. I sank to my knees, burying my face in my hands, bowing over my knees until my forehead made contact with the earth. For a moment I remained there. Tears stung my eyes and the wind grew stronger around me.

"Why do I doubt?" I whispered. "Why am I so afraid…"

A tear squeezed past my eyelid and rolled down my cheek. With one shaking hand and then the other, I reached out and pressed my palms to the moist ground, sinking my fingertips into the dead moss. Breathing heavily, I didn't lift my face from the earth. Instead, I whispered to it. Again and again and again, until my voice rose like the mountain before me.

"Wake up… wake up… *wake up!*"

Despite my shouting, my pleading, my relentless hoping, the forest still hung dead around me. I was no longer sure who I was calling to: the forest or myself.

# CHAPTER TEN

## *Icarus*

We were in the truck for a half hour. I counted. We were then transferred to a high-speed Griffon for what felt like an eternity. We made a few stops. Unlike the darkness we'd been confined to in the back of the truck, one flat green light on the ceiling illuminated the interior, and two metal benches lined the Griffon's cool steel sides. That was all.

Charlie sat across from me. Areos was curled up on the floor as far away from us as he could get, his eyes shut and his mouth hanging open. Biting my lip, I squirmed in the bands clamped around my wrists.

"How's the shoulder?" Charlie asked.

I shot her a look. "What do you think?"

"Wishing you had been the one to kill the little lice-bag who shot you yet?"

I shook my head, holding back a breath as I shimmied farther back against the wall. "No, I'm wishing I could heal myself."

Charlie stared at me. "So you can heal him, but you can't heal yourself? That makes no sense."

"Welcome to my life." My voice was flat. "You would think I'd be able to, after training for so long in the Dimension…"

"The Dimension." She tested the word, narrowing her gaze. "What the hell are you talking about, Icarus?"

"The place we took you to. The Dimension."

"Okay… Which is…?"

"An actual extra dimension in space."

"Okay, funny. Seriously, though."

"Seriously." I winced, still painfully attempting to roll my wrists in the bands.

Charlie snorted. "You expect me to actually believe that? You're psycho."

"How is that any harder for you to believe than that I could levitate a bullet out of Areos's body and reseal the wound?" I asked. "I can heal, I can channel energy, I can also kill if I want to… but I learned how to control those powers, in the Dimension."

"No. No, I think I was drugged."

My head thudded back against the cold side of the Griffon. "Whatever. Don't believe me."

"But if I don't believe you, it literally makes no sense that Areos is alive."

"With no thanks to you," I reminded her. "Is it really so easy for you to just shoot someone?"

Charlie said nothing for a moment, but I felt her eyes on me. "I've learned to be hard. I was very young when they took me," she explained. "Mom tried to stop them and they killed her."

My eyes scanned her face as the gravity of her words sank in.

"That's when my training began. They said I was best suited for the medical field." She grunted, shaking her head. "I wanted to be a soldier. I wanted to learn to kill—it's kill or be killed."

I took a slow breath, unsure of what to say for a moment.

"Charlie, I… I—"

"Shut up, Icarus, please," she spat, shaking her head. "I don't want your sympathy."

The hum of the engines filled the air for a moment.

"I wasn't going to give you any," I replied, my voice quiet. "I was going to say that I know how you feel."

The expression on Charlie's face didn't change, but before she could say anything, we slammed into whitewater turbulence. Areos startled awake, and I braced myself against the wall as best I could.

"What's happening?" he grumbled.

"More turbulence," Charlie replied briskly, clearing her throat as she seemed to brush off our conversation. "We've been on this thing forever—you think we'd land soon…"

I glanced around the Griffon's dim interior for a moment, willing my eyes to see through the walls. "We're starting to descend. I can feel it."

"I wonder what country we're landing in," Areos muttered, rolling over onto his side. "Who wants to take a guess?"

No one was in the mood.

Wherever we were, it was dark when we finally landed.

"Can I ask where we are, sir?" I questioned the armed guard as he dragged me by my bad arm. "Where have we landed?"

He jerked me forward, only tightening his grasp. "Ask nothing." I thought I detected a British accent.

The guards ushered us into a truck, and after a short ride we were transferred into the curved car of a Bullet—a much faster version of a train. One tiny window dotted each side. It took a while, but eventually the Bullet lurched forward. I braced myself against the wall, my head resting on the window.

Charlie heaved a sigh behind me, seated against the wall opposite. "If it weren't for you guys, I'd be stuffing my face with food and heading out to the sands to pick up bodies right now."

"Wow. You're really missing out," Areos muttered, seated as far away from her as possible.

I closed my eyes, listening: metal over metal as the train shot along the track. The bulletproof glass hummed.

"Why didn't they kill us?" I muttered, unsure if I'd spoken aloud. "There was no reason for them not to…"

"Hatch said why," Areos responded finally. "We're too skilled to die."

I shook my head. "No… She said that where we're going, they have a way of getting what they want out of us."

"Meaning what?" Charlie mused. "Imprisonment? Torture?"

"So much to look forward to, either way," Areos grumbled.

My jaw tightened. "If you plan on just sitting here and doing absolutely nothing, then yeah."

"What do you expect us to do?" Areos sounded dubious. "We're tied up and locked in a Bullet going hundreds of miles an hour. That doesn't give us much elbow room."

"But we still have our minds intact." I drew a steady breath. "We have plenty to work with."

"What are you talking about?"

I barely heard Areos's question. I stared out the window into the blackness, the gears in my mind turning as I began focusing on my wrists and the way the metal bands felt around them—then imagining how they normally felt, with nothing to restrain them. I glanced down at the black bands wrapping my arms, Hawk's words coming back to me in full force.

*It's not something I can talk you through. It's something that will require you to believe in yourself… If you don't trust yourself, then forget it… Internalize it, Icarus… Internalize the feeling…*

I took a silent breath, my gaze flicking back and forth across the glass. I thought of bashing a hole through the window—wielding a massive orb of energy to do so. I would need my hands to do that. My hands freed. In my mind's eye, I began to visualize myself channeling—energy pulsating between my hands—stepping back, taking careful aim.

A familiar warmth began to rush the length of my arms, trickling into my fingertips. My hands instantly heated. The clang of metal against metal rattled in the air as the bands blew off my wrists in one swift motion and impacted against the wall opposite. Charlie cursed, throwing herself out of the way. I swallowed back a feeling of dizziness and slowly turned around.

In the car's dim illumination, the bands glowed hot red on the floor at Charlie's feet.

She stared up at me, eyes wide. "Holy *shit…*"

I flexed my wrists, bringing my hands up in front of me. I returned her look with a serious glance. "Believe me yet?"

"I…" Charlie swallowed. "I'm starting to."

I backed away a few paces, pressing my palms together until the beginnings of an invisible orb of energy separated them. I rocked the energy back and forth between my palms for a moment, molding the orb until it was humming recklessly between my two hands, strong enough to jerk my arms slightly as I held it.

Areos watched me closely. "Icarus, are you sure we should do this? I'm sure they have security cameras in here. What if we get caught?"

"Don't worry. I already took care of those."

A puzzled expression crossed Areos's face and then vanished. "Icarus—"

"Areos, our only other option is to stay trapped in this Bullet car and see where it takes us—and for all we know, that could be to our graves." I passed the orb from hand to hand. "Do you trust Hatch—I mean, really?"

"She's a sadist."

"Exactly—"

"But—"

"We have to run *now*, Areos." I cut him off, turning my focus back to the wall across from me again. "We *have* to *try*. This may be the only chance we get."

For a long moment he said nothing. Neither did Charlie, surprisingly. Then finally Areos gave a single nod.

I rolled my shoulders back, listening to the rattle of the tracks. I didn't throw the orb; I simply let go. It passed through my fingertips like a rush of fire, and twice as hot. I stumbled backward, failing to catch myself as a deafening sound like an explosion rippled around us. A hissing filled my ears.

Charlie scrambled to her feet, retreating to the end of the car with Areos. A hole as big as the back end of a Trawler had been punched into the side of the car. Faint traces of dawn spilled in with the red-hot glow from the tracks whirring past below us. The landscape, though barely visible, was just a sweeping blur. The Bullet was moving way too fast to make out any of it.

Scrambling to my feet, I ran to free Areos and then Charlie from the bands that restrained them. The color drained from Charlie's face as I began to channel the bands from her wrists. She leaned toward me.

"Icarus," she whispered, so quietly I wouldn't have heard over the rush of the wind if she hadn't been so close. "How are you real?"

With a rush of energy, her bands clanged to the floor. Breathing heavily, I shifted my gaze back to her eyes.

"It's nothing I can explain," I replied, my voice equally quiet as I took her by the hand. "It's just something you have to believe in—long enough for us to get off this thing."

We ran to the edge of the car, then halted, clutching the sides of the jagged opening to avoid getting sucked out into oblivion. But then again, that *was* where we were bound anyway.

Areos turned and looked at me, his eyes wide but still doubtful. "Icarus, you cannot be serious."

*He's right. You're insane—you know it deep down. You're all going to die.*

I shook my head fiercely. "Shut up…"

"What?" Areos snapped.

"I wasn't talking to you, Aer." My jaw set. "Ready?"

Charlie gave my hand a squeeze, her fingers still wrapped around mine. "Ready."

Staring into the darkness, I tried to make out the shapes of the trees and whatever else was out there. Everything was a rush. There was no way to know what we were jumping into headfirst.

I took a deep breath. "Go!"

Suddenly, there was a feeling like a wave crashing down on us, tossing and turning and spinning us into oblivion. It reminded me of waking up underwater—in the rapids below the ravine. Except now there was no water to soften the blow that came when I hit the ground.

The last thing I heard was Charlie shouting my name, and the roar of the Bullet as it screamed past and vanished into the night.

# CHAPTER ELEVEN

## *Lara*

Kess had been my best friend, my *only* friend, since I'd been inducted into the RGM. She was my age, sort of. I still *looked* seventeen, and she *was* seventeen, so I counted that as close enough.

Kess, like most of the other recruits, had been taken from her parents and trained by the RGM. Everything she knew she had learned from the RGM. She spoke the way they had taught us to speak; she walked the way they had trained us to walk—shoulders back, eyes straight ahead and slightly down. She had a scar on the back of her head like we all did, me included. Except my scar hadn't been inflicted on me. I'd made my own scar, and no one had been the wiser. Kess, like everyone else, had a Fragment—a tiny chip that had been inserted the day she was born. Because of this, she could kill mindlessly, carry out orders efficiently, and be braver than what I considered humanly possible.

I'd asked Kess once if she missed her parents, and she had said no. Because that was what they all said—that was what I had said when someone had asked me the same question once, except I was lying. I missed my parents, because I didn't have a Fragment inserted in my cerebellum. Some days this felt like a blessing, and on others it felt like a curse.

But the greatest wonder of all was the fact that no one had found me out yet—no one had discovered that I didn't have a Fragment. But now, in the clutches of the RGM, it was just a matter of time until someone noticed something was different about me. I couldn't kill a rebel without a second, third, fourth thought. I couldn't kill without throwing up afterward. I couldn't carry out orders without question. All I'd ever wanted to do was bring everything to life—my fingertips were filled with it. I'd been running from it—the life bursting out from behind me like a trail behind a star. I'd left home to escape the life that seemed to constantly chase me—and now… now I was forced to silence that urge, laying it aside for a weapon to kill and destroy.

Sometimes I wished I *had* a Fragment, something to take away the feelings and the pain—the guilt, the fear, the nausea. Something that would make me a machine, silence my thoughts. Something that would make me stop wishing I could rewind time just to see them once more. Something that killed me inside just like I was forced to kill the recusants—the misfits with defective Fragments. The freaks of society, the misaligned gears in the machine.

Unlike these rebellious kids, I didn't have a *broken* Frag, though; I had *none*. I was the greatest recusant—I was the last one in existence.

And so I lay in bed in the cottage in the woods, staring up at the wisteria hanging above me with tears streaming down my face. I asked the same question I had been asking for *so* long now.

"Why did you choose me…? Why…? I'm not strong enough—I try to be… I just hide it until I can get away and empty out everything I've been holding back… Why did I have to be different?" My voice came out in a fragment of a whisper. "Why does this have to hurt so much?"

I was one flickering star in the bleak vacuum of space, helpless and drifting. I knew what light was, yet I told no one.

It only hurt because the hope inside me kept rising and crashing like waves against my conscience with each breath I took. I *wished* I'd given up on the world—because to give up is to lose hope, and when hope is lost there is nothing left: nothing can touch you, nothing can hurt you, you can sink no deeper. But for every trigger my finger pulled, flowers bloomed from the Earth with the very same touch. Even in this death, this hell… I couldn't stop seeing the hope everyone else had lost so long ago. The ultimate form of intelligence—a Fragment connecting you to everything you could ever wish to know, all the knowledge the nations together possessed, yet it left out hope. It forgot peace. It skipped faith. It missed love altogether. How heavy a price we had paid to know everything, for without these things we knew nothing at all.

I hoped. For that was all I knew how to do, despite everything. I'd *come* from before it; I had existed longer. I knew of things that no one left on Earth knew about; I knew about love and faith and the wild, rushing feeling of the ocean wind whispering in my ear—what my father had told me was the voice of God. And because I knew all of these as intimately as friends, I somehow couldn't see darkness even when I was looking it straight in the face. No, out of its depthless eyes I glimpsed nothing but a promise that I, being the last of the light, would outlast the darkness and restore everything that had been lost.

I only wished I could restore *everyone* I had lost too.

I pushed back the quilt and rose from bed. I could tell the fever had left; I was no longer shivering as I walked to the window. I didn't bother wiping the tears from my face; the sky wept too. Droplets of rain spattered the faded old windowpane.

I had these few days. That was all. Then I would have to go back. I would have to go back out into the muddy fields and hunt down the recusants before they succeeded with another retaliation. I would have to center them in my crosshairs and pull the trigger on yet another fifteen-, sixteen-, seventeen-year-old with a defective Fragment.

How did we know they were defective? We knew because they questioned the system. No mind altered by a Fragment would cause someone to question our ways—it wasn't within the Fragment's programming.

I pulled my jacket over my shoulders and stepped outside. The smell of creosote stung in my nostrils as I stepped off the porch and onto the soft ground. The acidic rain fell in large icy drops, pricking against my skin like the tips of needles. I waded through the tall grass in the clearing, scanning the tree line before tipping my face toward the sky. Dim, blue-gray clouds churned overhead. The rain soaked my buzzcut, raising chill-bumps across my scalp and down the back of my neck. I missed the rivers of hair I'd had before my induction.

I stood in the rain for a while, eventually sinking to my knees and sprawling out on my back. When I closed my eyes, I could practically hear my mother's voice chiding me, calling me back inside, just as she always used to when my siblings and I had done this: thrown ourselves down in the grass to soak in the summer rain. She had always said we would catch cold, but I had never been able to understand how something so beautiful could give me a cold. The icy sting of each drop, the cool breeze on my face—it made me feel alive.

I listened, but I heard nothing beyond the patter of the rain and the sigh of the wind. No rabbits rustling in the brush, no wrens warbling from the fading branches of the evergreens.

*If only I could heal the forest without exposing my hideaway...*

Lying there in the forest, so far from the base, it was easier to imagine that the world was still how it used to be. It was easier to feel as I had before the powers had changed me. It was easier for me to imagine what I had been like before the RGM had found me that day, wandering the fields like a lost child, like most of the other recruits. I had no identity, no parents, and no memory—or so I pretended. Donovan had been the one to find me that day, to lead me into his office and put me through a seemingly endless inquisition. I'd listened and hardly spoken a word. I didn't know why he ordered them to keep me—I didn't know what he saw in me—but it was because of him that I was still alive. Alive, and on leave, and lying in the rain, wishing I could turn back time.

Two more days. Then I would be back out there, rifle in hand and mud soaking into my boots. And I would have to pull the trigger.

---

"Lara." Kess slapped me on the back, her lips pressed into a narrow smile. "You're back."

I nodded, zipping my jacket up to my throat as we walked briskly towards the barracks. "I'm back."

"Can't believe Donovan gave you three days of leave, you lucky little lice-bag."

"I was a little surprised," I agreed. "But I was sick—I'm over it now; don't worry."

Kess grunted. "Like I care. We all catch each other's shit around here."

"Not as much as I'll catch from Donovan if I report in late." I tapped the tiny screen latched to my wrist. "I'm expected at twelve hundred."

"Better move yourself." She did a double take. "But change first—you're a mess. What did you do, go rolling in the mud?"

I smiled a little, inwardly. "I'll change, don't worry." I slid on my beret. "I'll talk to you at dinner."

She hesitated as we passed a group of kids lining up for formation, dozens of tiny pairs of boots splashing in the mud. They couldn't have been much older than nine or ten. I swallowed back a sick feeling, keeping my eyes steadied on the ground in front of me.

"If you're not out there, you mean," Kess answered once we were past them.

My muscles instantly tightened as I turned to look at her. "What?"

Kess took a measured breath. "They've been picking up some activity out there."

"And now I'm back. How convenient." I kicked a rock in my path. "Do the recusants just wait for me to be on duty to screw with us?"

"Maybe they like you."

I sighed, scanning the monotone horizon that lay beyond the barbed-wire fence. "Maybe so."

"You think that's what Donovan wants to see you about, getting you back out there?"

"No, I'm sure he just wants to welcome me back." Sarcasm dripped from my tone.

She rolled her eyes. "Are you gonna be okay with it?"

"Guess I'll have to be."

"Since when?"

"Since you told me I couldn't run," I replied flatly, marching forward through the drizzle. "Since the fresh country air knocked some sense into my head."

"Look, Lara." She fell into step beside me. "I'll put in a word with him—maybe I can get out there tonight instead."

"And I'll have to live with guilt for the rest of my life if something happens to you?" I shook my head. "No. Besides, he's never going to approve."

"But why you?" Her words were edged with irritation. "Why does it always have to be you? Why not someone else—why not me? I haven't been out there for weeks. They should give you a break."

"I had three days." My voice was ragged as the metal door ground open and we stepped down into the barracks. "That's more than I could have wished for."

"Your sudden compliance is scaring me."

I slowed to a halt in the dimly lit hallway, turning on the heels of my boots to face her. "Maybe I just know when I've been beat, Kess."

Her dark brown eyes scanned my face analytically for a moment; then her lips firmed. "If there was ever somebody who didn't know when they were beat, it's you." She paused abruptly, shooting the door a glance before stepping closer. "Do you think Donovan doesn't know that? Lara, he's trying to break you!"

My throat tightened. "I... I don't think so, Kess."

"Of course he is!"

"Why would he?"

"Because he's broken the rest of us!" Kess whispered. She was quiet for a moment, regarding me. "But he hasn't broken *you*, Lara... Not yet, anyway."

A heaviness lingered in Kess's eyes—something almost like concern, which the Fragment should have eradicated from her system long ago.

Without a word, I stepped around her and continued down the hallway. I felt the scorch of her gaze.

I washed and changed my uniform, avoiding my own eyes in the mirror. When I reemerged outside, it had stopped raining. Trawlers barreled past, heading beyond the wire. Smoke billowed up into the air at the far end of the base where massive piles of brush were burning. I dodged the muddy spray, walking quickly.

I'd been ordered to meet Donovan in his office. I couldn't ignore the sinking feeling in my stomach as my fingers crested the handle of the rusty metal door. Every muscle in my body was tense, my fingers already straightened in anticipation of a respectful salute, but as I stepped inside, I found my supervisor's office vacant.

Dimly lit by the glow emanating from the surface of the desk, which was itself a light source, the room around me was layered in thick stillness. The blinds were shut and the air was stagnant.

For a moment I just stood there, unsure whether to remain. I checked the screen on my wrist.

*1205 hours. Donovan's late.*

Straightening my shoulders, I stepped farther into the room. As Trawlers roared past, I felt the floorboards rumbling beneath me. I walked to the window, pulling one of the metal blades down just enough to peer out into the courtyard, looking for some sign of my commander. I saw only children in black uniforms, lining up for formation.

I snapped the blind shut again, turning slowly to scan the bare, dimly lit walls. I walked over to the desk.

Papers were scattered on the surface, illuminated in the soft light radiating up from below. Lists, carefully printed RGM paperwork, requests, task schedules. A photograph peeked out from between the pages: two people, a man and a woman with friendly smiles and the sea shimmering in the background. The image listed to the side, as if taken by a child. There was a thread-slender screen protruding up from the desk's center, displaying a login screen with blank fields. An open notebook sat shoved off to one side.

Cocking my head, I tried to make out the hastily scrawled word at the top of the page without moving anything. What the spidery letters spelled out was almost as familiar to me as my own name.

*Howth.*

Maybe it was just the memories that had me standing there, seemingly frozen in place. Howth, and the cliff walks, and the many, many memories I had there. Ronan—and what little I could remember of him.

Below that was a task list, and other notes written in Irish Gaelic. I couldn't remember enough of it from school to read more than bits and pieces. I was stuck on the single word at the top. The ink looked fresher than the rest of the items on the list, and there was no bullet point beside it, almost as if it wasn't even a part of the list. Almost as if it was something else entirely.

The clomping sound of boots startled me out of my thoughts. I quickly stepped around to the front of the desk again, heading for the door just as it swung open. Donovan's frame was silhouetted against the dull white light. He paused only a split second before stepping in and closing the door with a heavy hand. He scrutinized me without saying a word. I immediately saluted.

"Corporal." He gave a single nod, walking to his desk. "Sorry to have kept you waiting. At ease."

I relaxed.

"We have a new lead on the recusants," he began. "I just came from the head office."

"Sir?"

"We've picked up some activity in multiple locations—this place is turning into a bloody hotbed for these lice-bags," he went on, hastily clearing his desk. "We've got a few on the outskirts, the leftovers from the last mission."

A sick feeling twisted in my stomach as I recalled the night.

"But now we've picked up something else—something interesting." He shuffled a stack of papers to one side of the desk, snapping the notebook shut. "Wicklow Mountains, New Glendalough. One of our pilots tried to smoke them out—quite literally, if you catch my drift."

Chills raced the length of my spine as my mind reeled back, recalling the training we'd undergone using Death Vapor.

"Fortunately, it exposed their whereabouts, just as we had hoped," he finished.

I cleared my throat hesitantly. "But Glendalough, you say? In the Wicklow Mountains? How did we detect them that far out?"

Donovan gave me a stern look. "There are some things about the RGM that even you cannot know, Corporal Moran."

The knot in my stomach grew tighter. "And what exactly makes the targets so interesting, if I am allowed to ask?"

Donovan cracked a throwaway smile. "Because of the potential identities of the targets."

"I… I'm afraid I don't understand."

"The day you left, Corporal, a Bullet pulled into our northern station, a car that was supposedly carrying three delinquent RGM members from another base."

"Which base?"

"That I cannot disclose," he said. "But the Bullet arrived at the station with a hole ripped through the side of it." He looked at me for a moment, then set the stack down. "And the car was empty."

I swallowed, hard. "But… but how is that possible?"

My commander pulled his chair underneath him, taking a seat at his desk. He made no reply.

"So, you think they're the ones out there—the recusants?" I asked, puzzled, still turning the idea over in my mind. "RGM members?"

"That's for you to find out, isn't it, Corporal?" he replied, opening a drawer and setting the notebook inside. "A Byrd will be waiting for you in the courtyard in ten minutes."

I was already starting for the door, a queasy feeling churning in my stomach.

"Oh, and, Moran?"

I stopped. Turned.

Donovan looked at me for a long moment. "Bring them back alive."

"*Alive,* sir?"

He nodded, folding his hands.

"But, sir, I don't underst—"

"Orders are not supposed to be understood," he snapped. "They are to be followed, Lara…" He faltered, then cleared his throat. "*Corporal.*"

I stood there, staring hollowly at my commander. Then I saluted.

"Yes, sir."

# CHAPTER TWELVE

## *Icarus*

Everything was dark, cold and spinning around me. My senses felt shut off, all except my hearing, which filled my head with an echo like wind howling through a cave. Then, a whisper. A word I couldn't quite make out churned in my mind, repeating itself until finally I heard it as close as if it were being spoken into my ear.

*"Icarus…"*

I willed myself to speak, but somehow, I couldn't. I lay there, helpless, listening.

*"Can you do this for me, Icarus?"*

I knew the voice. I knew it as well as my own.

*"Don't let them down… They need us…"*

I tried again to speak, to say her name, to move my hand and reach out to touch her, but it all seemed impossible. My body was like dead weight.

*"They need both of us, Icarus…"*

*Both of us, both of us, both of us*—the words rang in my ears, ached in my mind. *If they need both of us, Hawk, then where are you? I lost you in another dimension—how can I find you on Earth? I carry your soul inside me—I know you're out there… but where?*

*"How do I bring you back, Hawk?"*

*"Don't let me down, Icarus…"*

*"Hawk…"*

I felt the warmth of her hand on my chest. My fingers felt like lead, but I slowly managed to grasp it.

*"Please don't leave me…"* My lips barely separated as I whispered. *"Please don't leave me, Hawk…"*

"Icarus."

I swallowed; the darkness began to lift to gray and then white. My eyes slowly blinked open, finding the world twisting in purple bokeh. A blur of a face hovered over me. I still clasped a hand.

"Icarus, can you see me?" A muffled voice. "I don't think he can see me—Areos—"

My eyelids sank shut.

"Icarus." A different voice. "Can you hear us? Come on, man…"

Suddenly the back of my head was throbbing—or maybe I had just become aware of it. I felt tears stinging in my eyes as I sucked in a breath and pressed myself up into a seated position, digging my fingertips into the soft ground.

"Whoa, whoa—take it easy, man, okay?" Areos pleaded. "You might have a concussion—or worse—"

"I don't have a concussion," I growled, opening my eyes with difficulty and squinting at him. "I don't… h-have…"

I felt the Earth slipping underneath me and then myself falling. An arm caught me, strong and solid.

"Areos, we've got to get him away from the tracks," Charlie instructed.

I felt myself lifted from the ground—two hands grasping my shoulders, two more around my ankles. The painful drumbeat carried on inside my head.

"They'll be looking for us. They'll know we've escaped as soon as the Bullet pulls into the station at god knows where," Areos continued.

"I know, I know—but we can't worry about that now, Areos. We have to get him somewhere safer. Somewhere I can take a look at him," Charlie shot back.

My mind struggled to piece together everything that had happened.

*The fall…*

Blowing off the bands, channeling the orb, blasting open the side of the Bullet, and jumping out—it all came surging back.

"Where are we?" I mumbled.

"Just stay still," Charlie ordered harshly.

I asked nothing else, and quite frankly, I was in too much pain to speak intelligently. After a few minutes, I felt myself being lowered to the ground again and heard Areos and Charlie panting for breath.

"Check him," Areos commanded breathlessly. "Not that there will be much you can do to help."

"Okay, look. Are you the trained RGM medic here?"

"No, but I'm also not the one who tried to kill someone only a few hours ago."

"You aimed the gun first."

I winced, tipping my head back against the earth as the ground seemed to spin around me.

"Stop fighting with me and just let me do my job, you son of a…" Charlie's voice trailed off to a growl.

Again I was dragged backwards, but this time a little more gently. I felt my head lower into Charlie's lap. Then she peeled open my eyelids.

"Owww," I groaned, fighting to close them again. "Stop…"

"Icarus, keep your eyes open for me, okay? Don't be a baby."

I struggled to do as she said, though what little light there was burned my eyes every time I opened them.

"How many fingers?"

I swallowed, then choked on my own spit.

"Shit, shit, shit—this is bad." Areos's voice came closer. "Icarus—"

"Just shut up! Give him some room to breathe," Charlie shot back.

I gasped for air, attempting to roll to my side, though Charlie's firm grasp prevented me from moving.

"Fingers—how many? Come on."

I blinked a few times.

"Three."

"Okay, good."

Areos groaned. "Wow, futuristic first aid is so advanced."

"Futuristic?"

"Ignore him…" I mumbled. "My head hurts."

"How bad? Do you feel sick?"

"No, just dizzy," I slurred. "I hit something… when I…"

"You smashed into a boulder, Icarus," Areos replied before I could finish. "For a few minutes there, you were out of it completely."

"Do you think you can sit up?" Charlie asked.

Areos grunted. "I thought you were enjoying having his head in your lap."

"One more word—one more, and I swear I'll—"

Taking a steady breath, I struggled my way up into a seated position. They both fell silent.

I rubbed my eyes with the back of one shaking hand.

"I'm fine. I…" I blinked a few times, my vision gradually coming in clearer. "I think I'm fine." I carefully touched the back of my skull. "Am I… am I bleeding?"

"No, but you definitely have a lump."

"What about my arm?" I passed her a sidelong look. "The stitches okay?"

"They look fine."

I focused on breathing, scanning our surroundings for the first time in the faint scattering of dawn light. Trees surrounded us, tall grasses, large craggy boulders, all washed in muted gray. The wind ebbed through the creaking branches and the sky churned restlessly with clouds.

"Areos is right," I said finally. "We need to get away from the tracks before they find us." I winced, fighting back the pain. "Wherever that Bullet is bound, whoever is expecting us—they're going to come looking for us when they find the car empty."

"And destroyed," Areos added, his tone swamped with pessimism. "I wouldn't be surprised if they're already looking for us."

"Think you can stand?" Charlie asked me, largely ignoring Areos.

I winced a little, but nodded.

Areos stooped down to wrap an arm around my torso, helping me to my feet. "Take it easy."

"I'm fine, I'm fine."

"Okay, guys—which way…?" Charlie squinted, scanning our surroundings. "It's gotta be like… zero five hundred hours…"

"No idea. Let's just move forward," Areos returned irritably.

But the lighter it got, the more our surroundings became apparent. I could see now that there weren't just a few trees—we were in the thick of a forest in god knows where. It rolled out like a carpet, surrounding us for miles in every direction. There was no sign of life, and by life I don't mean just that of humans.

Most of the trees were dead, and the rest were dying. A silence hung in the air. No chirping of birds, no rustle of small animals in the brush, no signs of insects. Without the wind, everything would have been perfectly static.

"Where… where do you think we… are?" I asked Areos, gulping back the pain as we trekked. "There's something strange about this place…"

Areos shot a glance up at the trees and shook his head. "Not sure… That tree looks like *Pinus sylvestris*, possibly."

"English?"

"A Scots pine. Which doesn't narrow it down hugely—but it has my suspicions leaning toward Europe." I could practically hear the gears in his head turning. "Maybe England. Ireland."

"Or Scotland or Wales," I added mirthlessly.

He grunted. "I'm just thinking out loud, okay?"

"What we need is to find some form of civilization," Charlie declared from up ahead. "Civilization brings road signs and landmarks. That will help us figure out where the hell we are a little faster than a tree."

Hours ticked past, gruelingly slow and uneventful. Finally we broke through the tree line to a wide-open field dotted with sizable slate-toned boulders and remnants of what looked like it had once been a tiny village. Ruins of buildings littered the landscape, along with jagged pieces of steel and metal sticking out of the ground like monuments to what had once been.

"Europe for sure," Areos mused, leading me over to one of the boulders to take a seat. "Look at the architecture—what's left of it anyway."

I sat down slowly, rubbing the back of my skull. A lump the size of a goose egg had formed.

Charlie was already picking her way through the rubble, investigating our new environment. Areos rushed to catch up, making his way over to what remained of a cottage: a couple of decaying walls covered in a thick layer of dry brown moss. Beyond the ruins there was a long stretch of valley, yellowed grass morphing gradually into foothills and then mountains. The view was vast, lonely, and void of life. I could relate.

I pressed two fingers to my eyelids, shoving back the voices whispering in the dark parts of my thoughts. Hawk's voice was one of them, part of the dream that had overlapped so effortlessly with reality. Darkness and the echoing of her last words. The touch of her hand.

My gaze followed Areos as he wove his way through the rubble. Charlie was even farther ahead now.

As I sat in silence watching them, a strange feeling filled my gut. For a moment I wrote it off as an effect of hitting my head, but then I happened to look down, and my mouth ran instantly dry.

Half hidden in the swatches of dead grass was a small metal sphere dulled by rust and weather but unmistakable in shape.

"Whoa—guys, stop!" I shouted.

Areos, about fifty yards off now, turned around and looked at me. "What's wrong?"

I made a few driving motions with my finger. "I just found a land mine!"

Even from here I could see my friend's face go white. "*Shit...*"

I took an even breath. "Think you can retrace your steps?"

Areos didn't move.

Charlie finally slowed to a stop. "What's going on?"

"Minefield—potentially," Areos relayed, not moving a step from the ruins where he was still planted. "Icarus just found one."

"Maybe that's the only one," Charlie offered optimistically.

"I don't want to find out," I replied. "Something obviously happened here. We'll have to find some way around it—and be more careful in future."

"If we don't get ourselves blown to smithereens trying to get out of here, you mean?" Areos shouted back, picking his way slowly through the tall grass. "Jeez, man, you could have said something a little sooner."

I carefully shifted myself away from the mine at my feet, scrutinizing the ground.

Areos slowly made progress. Charlie followed right behind him and then stopped abruptly. She stared at the ground, arms wrapped tightly around her torso.

"What's wrong?" I yelled to her just as Areos arrived by my side again.

"I found another one!"

Areos cursed, breathing heavily beside me. I bit my lip.

"Can you step around it—carefully?"

"What if there's another one just below the surface?"

Areos cupped his hands over his mouth. "That's a chance you'll have to take! Move!"

I slapped his arm, getting to my feet.

He shot me a look. "What?"

"You can't just tell her to move, Aer. What if there's a group of them right there?"

He looked at me for a second, then shrugged one shoulder. "What else is there to do—go out and get her?"

I gave a brisk nod, straightening up. "Good idea."

"I was joking."

"I'm not."

He stared at me in silence for a moment, his gaze shifting briefly to Charlie and then back to me.

"Icarus, are you frickin' crazy? You're hurt!"

"I'm *fine.*"

"You are *clearly not.*"

I sighed, squinting out over the field to where Charlie was still standing, petrified. Her face was red from the wind and her eyes were huge. I'd never seen her scared before—I mean, this was *Charlie.*

"What do you want to do, Areos?" I asked icily. "Leave her out there and hope she can find her way back without stepping into her own grave?"

"I did, didn't I?"

He was right. But something was different about where Charlie was standing, I just knew it. I could feel it, just as I had sensed the mine planted in the grass at my feet.

"Stay there. I'm coming out to you!" I yelled through my cupped hands. "Don't move."

As if guided by a sixth sense, I slowly made my way through the grass and around the scattered remains of the demolished houses. I didn't think about where the mines were; I just focused on getting to Charlie and trusted the instincts that seemed to guide my every step.

"Icarus." Charlie shook her head dubiously when I came to a stop in front of her. "Have I told you how insane I think you are?"

I scanned the ground for a moment, studying the mine I could see and letting my senses inform me of the others' locations. I reached out and took her by the hand. "You've hinted at it a few times."

---

Taking the long way around the minefield, we headed for the mountains. We hiked through the woods until our feet were sore, and made it to the foothills by nightfall.

We found some shelter beneath two large triangular rocks leaned up against each other and surrounded by a thin scattering of pines. I built a fire and Areos went deeper into the forest to gather more wood. Charlie sat with her back to one of the rocks, facing me from the other side of the flickering flame. Twilight settled over the landscape like freshly fallen snow.

I placed a hand on my bad shoulder, willing myself to focus on its healing as I leaned my aching head back against the stone. For a long time, we sat in silence. The crackling of the wood was the only sound to disturb the quiet woods around us.

"You're staring," I muttered finally, not even checking.

"So?" Charlie grunted.

"So…" I winced, pressing my fingers against the wound. "You're distracting me."

Charlie laughed. She stared into the fire between us.

"How, Icarus?" she asked the flames. "How did you do it?"

I rolled my shoulders back, trying to relax. "Get you out of the minefield?"

"Yeah, that—and melting your bands. And blowing a hole in the side of the Bullet car, and…" Charlie trailed off, shaking her head in disbelief. "'The Dimension'… That is what you called it, isn't it? That place…" She blew out a sigh, pressing her fingertips to her brow. "That impossible place—the whole thing is *impossible*."

My gaze shifted up to meet hers. "Says who?"

Charlie made no reply. Her eyes twinkled with flecks of orange and gold.

"Says you? Says most of the world?" I offered. "Well, let me tell you something: they've got it wrong. They've *all* got it wrong, and that's why Earth's like this. Because no one believes."

"In what?"

I thought for a moment before I finally replied, "In something so much realer than all of this—where nothing is impossible. Nothing."

"And… the Dimension is that place?" Charlie questioned.

"No." I slid my hand down to my chest. "That place is in here."

She tilted her head to the side, saying nothing for a moment.

"I don't understand," she said quietly. "What you do… who you are… It scares me in a way." She laughed a little. "Intrigues me… inspires me, even—though that word is so antique I could hardly tell you what it means. But I don't understand you or the things I've seen, Icarus."

A smile twitched at one corner of my mouth. "I didn't either when I was initiated. The first time I saw the Dimension, I thought I was going insane. I thought there was something seriously wrong with me…" I paused, thinking back. "But then I always knew that."

"I think everyone who meets you does. I mean, you're a weirdo." She laughed. "You're the dot on the chart that fricks with the rest of the data: you make no sense."

"Nothing makes sense. Nothing that's real, anyway." I poked at one of the burning branches with the toe of my boot. "It's the things that seem to make sense that are usually the lies."

She looked at me for a long moment. Then she shook her head. "Okay… So it's okay that I don't get it—or you."

"Totally okay."

Charlie rose, taking a few steps forward to gaze into the dark woods around us. The glow from the fire illuminated the scar at the base of her head. I looked away almost as soon as I noticed it, a bitter feeling mixing with the turbulence inside me.

She didn't understand because she *couldn't*. The Fragment didn't allow her any choice.

Finally, she broke the silence. "Icarus… can I… can I ask you something?"

I nodded as she turned around to step closer to the fire again. "Sure," I said.

Charlie hesitated; then her eyes flicked to mine. "Who is she?"

"What are you talking about?" My heart seemed to descend to my stomach.

"Hawk." She sat down across from me again. "You called her name when you were delirious."

"It's not… She's not… something I can really talk about." My voice frayed at the edges as I avoided her eyes. "You wouldn't understand—" I stopped, kicking myself inwardly. "I'm sorry." I drew in a sharp breath and then exhaled, still staring at the ground. "I know you know what it's like to lose someone…"

"What, my mother?" She half rolled her eyes. "I don't miss her. I've never missed anyone, really—I don't even know what that… what that feels like. Just tell me about you for once."

"Me?"

"Yes, you. Tell me about Hawk."

I tipped my head back against the triangular rock, unwilling to answer. Since the day I'd come back, since the day I'd been forced to tell the council everything, I hadn't spoken of Hawk. I didn't need to. She was in every thought that crossed my mind, every breath I took. Her markings wrapped my arms, and her soul dwelled inside me. She was the reason behind everything I did. I didn't need to talk about it.

But Charlie was waiting for a response. Charlie, who had been robbed of her ability to hope and dream and reason. Charlie, who had been ripped away from her parents—who had lost her mother and couldn't even miss her. She was sitting across from me, waiting for me to give a response.

"I met Hawk when I was at school," I began, leaving out where and how long ago. "She lived next door… It's complicated how we met, but she… she knew about my abilities. She had abilities too—she's the one who brought me to the Dimension, who became my teacher, who taught me how to control my powers." I pressed my lips together, staring up at the sky. "And I love her."

"What do you mean by love?" she asked.

"What does love mean to you?" I asked in return.

Charlie seemed to consider it for a moment. "I don't know. Sex?"

I shook my head. "Indescribably beyond that."

"Then I don't understand what you're talking about."

"Sure you do."

She shot me a puzzled look. "What?"

"You save people's lives. You drag wounded men and women off the front lines and do everything in your power to help save them." My voice rose as my explanation gained momentum. "What do you call that?"

Charlie stared at me. "Um. My job."

"Yeah, but *why* do you do it?"

She looked no less puzzled. "Because I would be executed if I didn't."

I suppressed a sigh. "Never mind."

———

"Are you guys hungry yet? Because I'm honestly starving," Charlie complained.

Areos and I exchanged a glance.

"We don't require food for survival," he replied over his shoulder. "That stuff is for wusses."

It was dawn, but the sun had yet to make it over the peak of the mountain rolling high before us. We trekked onward in its cold blue shadow. Icy droplets of dew licked the swatches of decaying moss and absorbed our weary footprints. I was sore, Charlie was hungry, and Areos was, unsurprisingly, muttering about how much he hated his life.

"Oh, right—*superhuman*." Charlie feigned a tone of awe. "Forgot."

Dead leaves crunched under my feet as I stepped over the withered roots of massive dead trees.

"I wish there were animals we could hunt," she grumbled behind us.

My fingers curled around a tree branch as I continued walking; the incline was growing steeper. "What happened to them all, anyway? Which species were the first to go?"

Charlie huffed. "I know about as much as you. I didn't pay attention in training—and that was a bit before my time, Icarus. Jeez…"

"You must remember some of it, though."

"The larger mammals were the first to go, they say—the ocean animals. And then the bees disappeared."

"Which explains all this." Areos gestured toward the dying forest around us. "They pollinate somewhere around ninety percent of all wild plants—not to mention crops. No wonder there are so many nations in famine."

"And all of the animals that ate those plants died off."

I gazed at our surroundings as we walked, a sinking feeling in my chest.

"Thankfully some species are still kicking. Plus, the RGM has been able to save some species," she continued, sounding like a commercial. "Farm animals, certain species of wild animals… I think maybe some aquatic species…"

"But those are experiments," Areos responded, pushing aside several branches. "Most of which are failing. Mass production through factory farming and artificial insemination methods, cloning, splicing—you would have thought things would have progressed far beyond that."

"It has. They've figured out how to manufacture simulated meat and plant varieties." She ducked out of the way as Areos let go of the branches. "Who needs the real thing when you can just formulate it yourself?"

I winced, trying to focus on something other than the pounding headache I had. "Earth, apparently."

Within an hour it was raining. With most of the leaves having fallen years ago, the droplets pounded down without obstruction, soaking us. The trace amounts of acid burned my skin.

"Icarus, you're shaking." Areos fell back beside me. "We should stop."

I shook my head. "We've come this far."

"But we don't even know where we are," he argued. "We have no idea where we're going—what do you expect us to do? Just march on into oblivion?"

I wrapped my good arm around my torso, trying not to think about how cold I was.

"W-w-we have to keep moving. They'll find us if we stop."

Areos gripped his scalp, letting out a frustrated growl as we came to a stop. "Icarus, who's going to find us all the way out here?"

"He's right," Charlie panted, leaning forward to rest her hands on her thighs. "We've been trekking through these frickin' woods forever. There's no way they'll—"

A twig snapped, cutting Charlie off.

My heart rate skyrocketing, I made a motion to turn around but never got that far. Areos's eyes widened as he focused on something behind me. I heard footsteps approaching.

"Stop!" a voice boomed. "Don't move a muscle."

# CHAPTER THIRTEEN

## *Fin*

"Fin…"

My eyes slowly opened to the sound of my name. Blurry outlines of pine trees swayed above me. My heavy eyelids wavered, then closed. The sensation of the hard ground beneath me sank into my awareness. The cool morning air. The persistent rhythm of raindrops dancing on my face.

At first, I couldn't think, trapped in the purgatory between being asleep and being awake. The voice was without substance to back it up, but then it repeated, and with it came an alarming sense of familiarity.

"Fin."

My eyes opened; the trees were reverently still now. Startled, I sat up, looking around me. A pile of ashes was all that remained of the fire I'd built. I hadn't returned to my usual camp; instead I'd spent the night close to the summit, sprawled beneath the creaking pines, searching for the stars I couldn't find. Listening for sounds that never came. Now, at last, I heard something.

I stood up, turning, searching my still surroundings.

"Fin…"

It was a voice, but at the same time it was like the wind. It spun through the trees, pushing my long hair out of my eyes. My gaze darted back and forth;

my heart beat a bit faster.

"Sensei?" My voice was a whisper. "Sensei, is that you? I can't see you."

The wind only rolled, with a sound like the laughter of a stream rushing past, invisible. My eyes sought tangible evidence.

"Oh, my son, stop searching for that which you already possess." Sensei's voice spoke from every direction. "Did I not tell you that you were like me? That you were born for such a time as this?"

My whole body trembled as I drew a breath. "Sensei, I don't know what to do. I don't even know what I am doing now, not really."

"Stop doubting yourself, Fin."

I lowered my gaze to the ground without speaking. Everything stilled around me.

Suddenly, I heard gentle footsteps behind me.

"Did I not make myself flesh, blood, and bone for your sake—so that you would finally see, feel, trust that I am with you?" Sensei's deep voice was so clear, so close I could almost feel his breath. "Did I not tell you that if you only believed, you would see the Earth burst open beneath your fingertips?"

The words pounded through me like sonar. The hairs on my arms rose.

"Why can't I heal the forest?" My voice faded in my throat, along with the question. "Why can't I find Hawk?"

"You seek answers in places they do not dwell."

"What answers do you not have, Sensei? You know everything—you know the very contents of my heart."

"All that I know, all that I am…" He spoke softly. "I've given it to you. You are no longer a child that you should seek answers from any external source. Do not doubt your own capacity."

His voice circled around now to emanate from directly in front of me. I felt his breath and the warmth of his presence.

"Put to death this ache inside me and I will never doubt again," I whispered. "I am filled with grief for what I have lost—grief so strong it will not let me go, and I can find no way to escape it. Grief that has tainted me, and in doing so, tainted her…"

"You feel you have betrayed Hawk?"

A sharp pang filled my chest. "I did betray Hawk. I forfeited a secret I should never have trusted anyone with. And now everyone..." My voice cracked, and I lowered my gaze to the ground again. "Everyone knows what happened to her."

"Fin, we are not what happens to us," he replied softly. "We are not our pasts, our presents, or even our futures—we stand outside them. We are only ever as much or as little as we believe we are. Hawk is no different. Hawk discovered this slowly... and has overcome it at last." A feeling of warmth manifested on my shoulder from a hand I couldn't see. "Now you must do the same."

"But, Sensei, how?"

"Allow yourself to answer that question." I saw breath in the air. "Keep asking—keep searching. If the question is eternal, if the search is everlasting, the answers will rise to meet both. Trust yourself to answer."

The hand began to melt away from my shoulder now; a gentle wind was once again stirring in the trees. I grabbed hold of it before it could vanish away—and felt my fingertips close around solid flesh. I stared into the places where I knew his eyes were staring back at mine.

"Tell me, Sensei, please..." My words were desperate, ragged, as I clutched his weathered hand. "Is she here? Am I looking in the right place, am I—am I right to feel that she is here, on Earth? That she is not lost, not gone, but..." I trailed off, losing breath. "But here?"

The stillness was upended by the wind, by the rustling of the dead leaves. The gentle, ebbing laughter.

"Oh, my son." Sensei's voice grew from a whisper to a roar. "Nothing is ever truly lost."

Then, like reemerging from water, I woke up. Bolting upright, I clutched the earth beneath me, breathing as if I never had before. The wind rustled through the tall pines and tousled the remnants of brush below. I pressed my face into my palms, trembling and attempting to steady my rapid inhalations.

I'd come to learn that dreams of Sensei were never just dreams.

I stood up, a wind rising at the same time to greet me, blowing back my hair. Chills ran the length of my arms. The rain showered down, every bit as icy as it had been in the "dream." The fire had turned to a pile of blackened ashes among the patches of dead grass and vines. I unzipped my jacket, shedding the extra layer to let the rain soak into my skin, tilting my face towards the sky.

*Nothing is ever truly lost… What does that mean? How is that possible?*

Tucking my jacket under my arm, I descended the slippery decline, heading back down the mountain once again. My hair and clothes were soaked by the time I was close to the base of the mountain. I was lost in thought, going over every question I had asked and every answer Sensei had given, so much so that I didn't hear the faint sound of voices until I was almost upon them.

I slid to a messy halt in the blanket of pine needles. Three figures stood in a cluster, far enough away that I couldn't make out any of the faces—only the fact that they were all clothed in black uniforms.

Up until now I'd been able to avoid detection by the RGM. After a year, I knew where the base was; I knew how their scanning systems worked, how far their patrols went, and had managed to avoid all of them—for good reason. In human terms, I was twenty-three years old, perfectly fit, and bore a scar at the base of my skull just like everyone else. I was prime material for induction into this military's ranks.

Icarus and I seemed to be the only ones who truly knew Hawk was still alive—and believed her to be who she said she was: our Sunrise. If I was inducted, that would be the end—there would be no one left to look for her.

There was no time to hide: I was already exposed. I could see no other way around it than meeting them head-on—and throwing together as strong a cover story as I could muster.

"Stop!" I shouted, forcing myself forward. "Don't move a muscle…"

I was already with the RGM, I decided: I was a spy. That was why I wasn't in uniform. I was British—I knew I could twist my accent enough to make it seem authentic—and I was—

"Fin?" one of the figures said as I came closer. "Is it really…?"

I stopped in my tracks, finally close enough to see their faces. My jaw slackened.

"Areos?" I could hardly believe it. "What on earth are you doing here?"

"I could ask you the same thing," he said, stepping forward to meet me, folding me into a firm hug and slapping me on the back. "You scared the living daylights out of us!"

As he stepped back, I noticed the young woman I'd seen at the gathering, and Icarus beside her. His face was pale, and he was a mess of dirt and blood; he held one arm against his side, bent awkwardly at the elbow. He made eye contact only briefly before glancing away.

Without hesitation, I walked up to him and put an arm around his shoulder.

"Come on," I said. "Where I usually camp isn't far from here. Let's get you out of the rain."

The young woman studied me with steely blue eyes, staying where she was for a moment. "Wait, wait, wait—weren't you at that meeting they kidnapped me into—the one in—in that… place?"

I gave a shallow nod as we started walking. "That's me."

"Speaking of which…" Areos spoke up from the lead, shooting me an anxious look. "Where exactly are we?"

I climbed over a massive craggy rock obstructing our course. I reached out a hand to help Icarus when I got to the top, but he shook his head and continued slowly by himself, keeping his eyes down.

"That would be Ireland," I replied, pulling my focus back to the question. "What's left of it, anyway."

———

"Oh my god—real food." Charlie snatched the knapsack Runner had given me, eyes round. "My quality of life just got exponentially less apocalyptic."

Areos and I exchanged a glance. He sat across from me on the other side of the fire I'd just finished building.

"She's always like this," he muttered. "I forgot how tedious it is, dealing with humans."

"You look pretty human to me. And I might also add that you're not that super to deal with either." Charlie ripped open a stick of jerky. "The both of you kind of suck."

"You were the one who tried to annihilate me," Areos shot back. "I don't think anyone's topped that yet."

I looked back and forth between the two of them, raising an eyebrow. "You tried to kill him?"

She chewed contemplatively, then shook her head. "It was self-defense—but he'll never let it rest."

"If it wasn't for Icarus, I would have died," Areos clarified firmly.

"Speaking of Icarus," I cut in before Charlie could make a comeback. "Where *is* he?"

He had slipped away while I was building the fire.

"He was just over…" Areos craned his neck, peering around the structural beams holding up the shelter. "Icarus?"

I lifted a hand before Areos shouted for him again. "It's okay. I'll go look for him—he probably just needed some space."

Getting up, I ducked out of the shelter and into the rain again. The forest spread silently around me, dripping in rusted shades of blue. I peered between the trees as I started walking, listening for footsteps.

I headed for the edge of the woods, following the trail Runner's numerous visits had carved through the overgrowth to the place where the forest flung open, revealing the ruins of the town, resting like dry bones in the palm of the valley; the peeling white steeple rose from the center like a ghost.

Near the edge was a scattering of rocks, like benches placed there specifically for taking in the visceral brokenness sprawling below. Icarus was seated stiffly on one of the larger boulders, staring out. I approached quietly and stopped beside him.

"Mind if I join you?" I asked.

He shook his head without looking at me. Dark circles marred his eye sockets, and his hollow gaze remained fixed on seemingly nothing. Above the deceptively realistic scar at the base of his cerebellum, a massive purple bruise flourished, swollen to the size of an egg.

"What happened to you?"

"I hit my head on a boulder when we bailed out of the Bullet," he said, sounding numb.

"Areos didn't heal you?"

"Areos can't heal. He was just beginning to master channeling when we reemerged."

I followed his gaze out to the ruins below.

"What are we expected to do about all of this anyway?" Icarus went on, his voice ragged. "The darkness is considered progress. No one sees it as anything otherwise—no one has the capacity to."

"The Fragments prevent them from seeing reality as it is." I sighed. "The council feels that the best course of action is to track down the database itself—if we can shut down the database, every Fragment fails and the system crumbles."

Icarus winced, moving his wounded shoulder experimentally. "Yeah? And how do they propose we go about doing that?"

"From what I've heard, they're lying low in several nations, scrambling to collect data—piece together clues, gather as much information as they can, and pool it at the gatherings, hoping a lead will surface…" I paused, my brow creasing. "They've made little progress, but they see no other alternative."

Icarus said nothing. He stared out over the ruins below.

"I think they believe this is something they can kill at the roots," I continued finally. "Something we can disable as if it's a machine."

He exhaled sharply, almost a laugh. "But it's not a machine, is it? It's people—*humans*. Charlie…" He turned and looked at me for the first time. "And thousands of others just like her, growing up detached from their own souls—unable to even truly know themselves. It all seems so complicated, but it's not. We *are* the darkness… and we don't even realize it."

I nodded slowly, my head heavy like the weight in my chest.

"Have you…?" The question faded as he asked it. "Has there been any sign of her?"

My eyes traced the faint outline of the church steeple far below, obscured by the rising swaths of smog. "No. Not yet."

The patter of rain filled the silence between us.

"Do you think she's here?" he asked quietly. "In Ireland? On Earth, even…"

"Yes," I replied without hesitation. "Yes, I know she is."

Icarus hesitated. "I lost her in another dimension, Fin…"

"It doesn't matter," I responded, refusing to even let myself consider it. "I feel her here—in everything. I know I'll find her."

My words were followed only by another long silence. Finally, Icarus sucked in a pained breath, lifting his face from his hands; his eyes squeezed shut and his Adam's apple moved as he swallowed.

"My god, Fin. This is all my fault." His voice was husky. "If I hadn't revealed who we were back then—if we'd been able to stay on Earth—things might never have come to this. But I destroyed our chances of that!"

"Icarus, you *cannot* know what would have happened."

He shook his head as though he were in pain, his fingers curling into shaking fists. "I *brought* her attacker into the Dimension—I let him win! I led her to the worlds beneath, Fin. Don't you get that?" His eyes opened wide now, brimming with tears as he turned to stare me in the face. "I'm the reason Hawk sacrificed herself." He beat his chest with his fist. "*I'm* the reason she's gone! She's gone because I—b-because I…" Icarus's head bowed and he crumpled to the ground on his knees. I immediately grabbed him by the arm, kneeling down to support him, but he shook out of my grasp.

"Don't!" he sobbed, pushing me away. "D-d-don't—don't touch me."

"Icarus, I want to help—"

He cut me off before I could finish, straightening up only to grab me hard by the shoulders.

"No! I don't *want* your help—I don't want you to help me. I want you to *hate* me, Fin!" he yelled, only inches from my face. "I killed her, Fin! *I killed her!* Why don't you hate me?" With dirt-streaked hands he gripped his face, smothering another agonized sob. "Why don't you hate me as I hate myself…"

I said nothing for a moment as I blinked back tears of my own. I took a deep breath and let a flood of warmth emanate down the length of my arms.

Firmly taking Icarus by the wrist again, I jerked him back up to his feet. I grabbed him by the back of the head and pulled him into my arms, pressing my palm, now pulsating with healing, directly against his wound.

For a moment he was disoriented. Then he started fighting me.

"No—no! Fin, don't heal me—I don't deserve it! Just let me go!" His voice tore out of his throat, wretched. "J-just let me die!"

I pressed my fingertips harder against his skin. With the other hand, I grabbed him by his wounded shoulder, channeling a stiff surge of invisible energy into his body. It pounded through me like sonar, enough to knock the two of us apart, sending us sprawling backwards onto the ground.

For a moment we both lay still. I breathed for what felt like the first time in a while, slowly pressing myself up from the ground, brushing away a streak of hot tears.

Then Icarus scrambled to his feet, gasping for breath. Shaking at the knees, he began to frantically check himself over. The bump on the back of his head had vanished, and his shoulder looked perfectly normal. He stood there staring as I got to my feet and brushed myself off. I looked him in the eyes.

"I don't hate you, Icarus," I began, my voice shaking. "I love you like a brother."

He lowered his gaze to the ground and I stepped closer.

"Look at me!" I yelled, my voice cracking. "Look at me…"

He obeyed, tears welling in his angry eyes.

"You are the Sunset, Icarus!" I shouted hoarsely. "We *need* you. *This world needs you*, and Hawk…" Her name winded me. "Yes, Icarus… She sacrificed herself for you. Not to make you something you never were before, not because you were worthless, but *because* you *are worth* her very life—"

I stopped, closing my eyes for a second, fighting back the lump in my throat.

"She gave up her soul for you," I went on quietly. "Because she knows *who you are* and she *believes in you*…"

Icarus stared at me, grief twisting his expression. I stepped closer and placed one hand firmly on his now healed shoulder. Tears rolled down his cheeks.

"Maybe it's time you started believing in yourself, Icarus."

# CHAPTER FOURTEEN

## *Icarus*

*What is wrong with me?* That was what I kept asking myself over and over again as I lay awake that night.

*Am I still so weak, while the voices inside my head are so strong? Am I still so much at their mercy?*

Fin had told me to believe in myself, and what I wanted to tell him was that sometimes I did. Sometimes I was the Sunset, and I would find Hawk, and the darkness wouldn't win. Other times, I *was* darkness itself. I was a contradiction wrapped in skin. Two forces of opposite natures, bound inseparably. Each day I chose which one to be.

My heart ached inside my chest, longing for Hawk, longing for things to be different. Longing…

*Oh, Sensei, did you lift me out of hell only to lead me into the wilderness to die?*

Through the hole in the roof of the shelter, my eyes searched for stars in the blackness. Though my eyelids became heavy, I forced myself to keep them open until I couldn't anymore.

———

When I opened them again, it was morning. I felt stiff as I peeled myself up off the hard ground, rubbing a hand over my face. Out of habit, I favored my left arm. Then I remembered that Fin had healed it the day before.

As I looked around, I realized I was alone. I stooped to duck out of the shelter—just as a strange, fluttering sound from overhead caught my attention. I stepped outside, straightening up, straining to see past the haze. I caught only a split-second blur in my peripheral vision, a chaos of white motion, the sound of feathers beating the air. *It sounds so much like...*

My pulse pounded as I took a few steps back, keeping my eyes on the treetops. I shielded my gaze with my hand, scouring the sky. I slowly spun, searching, blinking back the sunlight.

*Come on, come on...*

The sound came again. The soft beating of wings steadily grew louder, louder, until the tactile notes hardened to something far more rigid. The unmistakable scream of an engine.

My mouth ran dry as the treetops began to stir, the noise escalating from a gentle hum to a grumble—to an earsplitting roar as the Griffon ripped past, eclipsing the sun to give me a split-second glimpse of the aircraft's underside.

The ground rumbled beneath me as the sound pulsed through my body. I turned and ran, breathing hard as I dodged rocks and jumped over roots sticking up out of the ground.

"Fin!" I yelled, searching the forest for some sign of life. "Fin—where are you?"

"Over here!"

I raced through the trees, following the sound of Fin's voice as the roar of the engine whooshed past. I almost slammed into him.

"Fin." I panted, clapping a hand down on his shoulder, pointing frantically with the other hand. "That was a—"

He nodded rapidly. "Yes, I saw it."

Areos and Charlie, who had been only a few yards away, ran to meet us. Charlie squinted up at the sky.

"Do they normally fly this way? For, like, training or patrols or—"

"Never," Fin interrupted, taking a few steps forward. "I've been living out here for over a year. I know their routines, their patrol ground. It's a wasteland out here, and there hasn't been any recusant activity, to my knowledge. Even if there was, there's no way they'd be able to detect it." Fin turned to look at Areos. "Remember? You're the one who figured that out."

"Right—their detection scanners can only extend so far before losing the signal," he agreed. "There's no way this would be within their range, way up here in the mountains."

"Then why the hell is it out here?" Charlie's eyes were still glued to the sky.

"That's a great question," Fin replied.

"It may be for some other reason," Areos offered, sounding deep in thought. "It could be bound for another base or something…"

He trailed off as the unmistakable scream of the Griffon's engine returned. Ahead in the forest, I could already see the Griffon's shadow as it rippled through the trees, sending what looked like tiny particles fluttering to the ground. I knew exactly what the particles were before they had even hit the forest floor.

My voice was hoarse as I whirled around. "Split up!"

"W-why? What is it?" Charlie shouted, her hands over her ears while Fin and Areos bolted. "What's happening?"

I gave her a hard shove, scrambling up the incline myself. I glanced back over my shoulder: sure enough, clouds of rosy pink lifted from the sawdust as the strange substance fluttered to the dirt.

"Death Vapor," I said tersely. "We have to get away from here—we have to get away from each other! They found us…"

Sunlight streaked through the dead trees around us as we ran, Charlie still beside me. Fin and Areos had taken off in the opposite direction, and I could no longer locate them past the inflating clouds of pink.

Charlie and I were both sprinting, running parallel, ducking beneath low tree branches and jumping over rocks and withered roots. I was becoming all too aware of another oncoming roar overhead. I could feel an unnatural pulse tickling the ground beneath me.

"Charlie, we *have* to split up!" I yelled as we ran. "Just keep going straight—keep running!"

"What if we lose each other?" she yelled.

"I'll find you!" I shouted back urgently. "Just go! Now!"

After a split second of hesitation, she surged forward, and I turned left and sprinted uphill. The Griffon ripped past overhead, a flashing shadow, followed by the soft pattering of what could have been mistaken for raindrops.

I gave it everything I had, willing myself forward as fast as my legs could carry me. A quiet hiss emanated from behind me as the vapor began to roll through the forest. Sweat trickled down my forehead as I furiously tore through the brush, clawing my way farther and farther up the rocky incline.

*How did they find us?*

The clouds seemed only a few yards behind. I could already smell traces of what I had only ever heard described: a strong, bleach-like odor.

*No, no, no, no, no—you have to stay ahead of it... Stay ahead of it... You can do this...*

Every muscle in my body burned. I forced every ounce of energy I had into my legs, grappling my way up the mountain. At first, I was almost neck and neck with the deadly plumes billowing behind me; then I began to pull ahead.

I turned to look back just as something snagged my ankle. My legs crumpled beneath me and I impacted hard against the ground. An agonized shout escaped me as I struggled, panicking.

*Get back up, get back up, get back up...*

My vision was already growing hazy. I could barely see as the cloud rolled over me like an ocean wave. I held my breath. I fought to sit up, to free my ankle from what I could feel was a mangled root, though my efforts seemed only to entangle it further.

I pinched my burning eyes shut, beginning to feel light-headed from the lack of oxygen.

*Just pretend this is a pranayama. Don't breathe.*

A tingling sensation broke out over the surface of my skin, and my stomach churned. I peeled one eye open for a split second, only to find a swirling haze of pink. I kicked my legs furiously to escape. I was still holding my breath when I finally collapsed, yellow specks flickering across my closed eyelids.

*Don't breathe… don't breathe… don't…*

My thoughts were cutting in and out like a bad radio signal. My body felt ten times heavier against the cold, hard ground. My fingertips closed around fistfuls of soil.

"Icarus! Where are you?"

Everything was muffled; I felt like I was underwater, straining to hear something above the surface.

"Icarus! Icarus, *answer me!*"

Finally, my brain caught up.

"I'm here." I choked out the words.

"Icarus, don't move," the muffled voice stammered, hoarse coughs severing the words. "Keep—keep talk—"

"I'm—I'm h-h-here—" I tried my best to yell back, my hands cupped over my mouth. I leaned forward, gagging hard.

Then I felt a hand on my shoulder. At first it merely brushed me, but then it tapped me again, more firmly this time, as if to be sure. Then the fingers dug in.

"Icarus!"

I choked into my hands and squinted up, barely able to make out the faint outline of her frame as she seized me by both hands. "Charlie—?"

She responded only with ragged coughs and gasps—and a firm jerk that almost ripped my arms out of their sockets. My foot finally came loose. I struggled to my feet and we took off, running blind, our hands interlocked. My head was pounding, my watering eyes slits as I searched for a way out of the vapor. Pulsating yellow lights hammered at my vision.

"Icarus, this way!" Charlie shouted, giving my arm another firm tug.

I stumbled after her, the ground seeming to level out under our feet as we gained speed.

As suddenly as the cloud had come, it dissipated. A clear meadow swung open in front of us, blurry and wavering; we ran until we couldn't, then collapsed into the dead grass. Coughing violently, I pushed myself up long enough to make sure we were actually free of the clouds. Death Vapor could only reach so far before losing its highly concentrated potency.

We were up pretty high now; I could see from here where the thick fuchsia fog began and ended. It swallowed hundreds of yards of the dense woods below and wafted up past the treetops like a neon mushroom cloud. Faint wisps of pink reached past the edge of the trees like long fingers, scattering in the gentle breeze.

I covered my mouth with the crook of my arm, coughing hard. Charlie rolled to her side on the ground, choking.

I sized up our surroundings: sprawling mountain meadows and no sign of civilization. I squinted up at the cloudless sky: no sign of the Griffon.

I turned to look at Charlie. She lay motionless on the ground, gasping like a fish out of water, her cheeks as bright red as mine probably were. After a second, she peeled open one eyelid and stared up at me.

"What?"

I coughed. "You just saved my life."

She coughed. "So? Get the hell out of my face."

Charlie pushed away my hand when I offered it and pulled herself up to a seated position, rubbing her eyes with the crook of her arm.

I peered out over the meadow. "Weird."

"What?"

"The Death Vapor." I pointed. "Fin and Areos took the exact opposite direction, but it seems like the vapor only followed us."

"The pilot probably heard your big mouth."

"Very funny." I shielded my eyes with my hand. "It seems strange, though, doesn't it? I mean, how did they detect us up here in the mountains?"

"He was flying low. He probably saw us. We were all standing there together in a clearing." She coughed some more.

I shook my head, not disagreeing but dubious. "If he saw all of us, why didn't he attack Fin and Areos too? He could have easily circled back to them."

"So what are you saying?"

I studied the pink mushroom cloud. "Nothing," I answered. "Nothing yet."

I turned back to face her as she climbed to her feet.

"You okay?"

She nodded briskly. "Never better. You?"

"Oh, I'm great."

She rolled her eyes, walking past me to take up the lead.

"Come on," she called over her shoulder. "Let's go find the boys."

———————

Unable to circle back through the blooms of Death Vapor, we journeyed parallel to the forest, trekking in the general direction that Areos and Fin had run. By late afternoon we were in a completely different part of the forest. The mountains swelled and rolled, covered in wilted brush and dead flowers. Dirty streams flowed in the crooks between rolling peaks that must once have been the purest shades of green. Ashy gray clouds congested the sky.

"You think they made it out?" Charlie asked, coming to a stop on the ridge, looking down over the twin basins pooled below in the valley. "What if they got stuck in the…"

I slowed to a stop beside her. "No, they made it out. The vapor didn't even travel that far—you saw where it began and ended. The pilot was trailing *us*, not them, remember? We'd better keep moving."

"Isn't that kind of stupid, though? To just keep blindly moving forward?" she huffed. "What if we're not even moving forward. What if we're going backward? We don't even know where the hell we are. We could be heading straight for a base—straight into their range of detection."

"You think?"

Charlie's face was flushed and spattered with dirt. She walked past me. "I have no idea, but it's a possibility, don't you think?"

"Well, yeah, but there's really nothing we can do about it," I reasoned, thinking it over as we walked. "I mean, there's no way to know."

"Just keep your head on a swivel."

"My head's *always* on a swivel," I shot back.

"Like when you didn't see that root."

I glared at the back of her head, not countering.

Carefully finding secure ground with each footstep, we descended the rocky slope into the valley, where a narrow stream trickled down to one of the lakes. Large boulders studded the bending landscape, offering some cover as we proceeded.

It was good to have both arms in working order again, though I felt my ears tinge red at the very thought of my conversation with Fin. I called it "conversation"—I was still too much in denial to use the proper word: *breakdown*. Yet Fin hadn't thrown it in my face like I would have if I had been him: *Icarus, this is your fault—you're the reason my family is dead. You're the reason Hawk is gone. I hate you—you're pathetic.*

Yet somehow, Fin had forgiven me. Fin didn't hate me. Fin "loved me like a brother."

I couldn't help but feel that I didn't deserve that love or respect from him. I couldn't help but still feel, deep down, that he should have been in my shoes; he should have been the Sunset anomaly. He had everything I lacked; where I stumbled, he soared.

*Why, Sensei? Why did you choose me? Why me?*

They were old, tired questions. Ones I had turned over in my mind a thousand times.

We were making our way alongside the stream now, splashing through the shallows whenever the boulders prevented us from staying on dry ground.

"So why did you do it?" I asked, breaking the silence. "Why'd you risk your neck to pull me out of the Death Vapor?"

"It wasn't a big deal."

"It kind of was."

She huffed a frustrated sigh. "Fine. Whatever. When I made it out and realized you were still in there, I just…"

I fell into step beside her and saw that she wore a puzzled expression.

"I don't know," she concluded finally. "I guess I thought it would be unfortunate not to have your… interesting abilities at my disposal."

"When have they ever been at your disposal?" I snorted. "That's not the real reason."

"No?"

I shook my head. "No. I think you thought it was the right thing to do. I think you love me."

She turned up her nose. "Like I'd be physically attracted to the likes of you."

"I don't mean love like physical attraction," I clarified. "I mean love like you care about what happens to me—the same way I love you."

She halted in the middle of the stream and turned on her heels. Her large eyes connected with mine.

"What did you just say?" Her brow creased in confusion.

I looked at her for a moment, my gaze flicking back and forth between her eyes. "I said I love you."

Charlie opened her mouth to speak, but for once had nothing to say.

"If the situation had been reversed and you had been the one trapped in the vapor, don't you think I would have done the same thing you did?" The question came out sounding almost urgent. "Don't you think I would have run in there to get you?"

Her lips twisted into a frown. "Would you have?"

"Of course!" I said. "Of course I would have—I wouldn't let you die. I would do whatever it took to make sure you were okay, because I care about you. And when you care about someone, it means that you *love* them. It means you would sacrifice things, maybe even your own safety, maybe even your own…" I stumbled on the last word, a sinking feeling settling in my gut, "maybe even your own life for them."

She still looked lost at sea. But after a moment her lips yielded a little smile and she shook her head. "You're a strange one, Lieutenant." She turned and started walking again. "But your ideas are interesting."

I reached up to stroke my forehead, standing there in the middle of the stream, water trickling over my boots. There was a strange feeling taking flight inside me, something I couldn't name, but something that seemed to resound in the meaning of those words.

*Maybe even your own life…*

That was love. That was what Hawk had done for me—without hesitation. Without a second thought.

*"She sacrificed herself for you. Not to make you something you never were before, not because you were worthless, but because you are worth her very life…"*

An almost inaudible click jerked me out of my thoughts. An unmistakably familiar sound.

I froze, my mouth suddenly dry. Charlie was a few dozen yards ahead or so, sending water splashing up from the stream with her every step.

Without moving, my eyes scanned our surroundings, searching the tall grass for any sign of life. I didn't see anything—but I felt something. My heart started pounding.

"Charlie, get down!" I shouted, diving behind a rock.

A stiff, suppressed crack rattled the air—followed by a ragged scream as Charlie fell into the water.

# CHAPTER FIFTEEN

## *Fin*

"I can't believe they looked for us—all the way out here, Fin! That makes no sense, literally *no sense…*"

Logic and reality were apparently at war in Areos's mind, and he grappled with them loudly as we walked. It had been hours since we'd dispersed to flee the Death Vapor, and Areos had been the first and only member of our party I'd been able to track down.

"Maybe they figured out where exactly we jumped off and tracked us from there?" He scratched the stubble on his chin. "But even then, our course was entirely random. The chances that they actually tracked us are slim, and the chances that the pilot saw us from the air? Even slimmer."

I let my fingertips brush against the dried bark on the trees as we trekked along the edge of the woods. "Did they ever plant some kind of bug on you guys, or whatever the equivalent would be these days?"

"No, they didn't tag us with any kind of tracking device, to my knowledge."

"Well, if anyone can figure that out, I'm sure you can," I told him, scanning the silent forest around us. "But right now we have to find Icarus and Charlie."

"How about just Icarus?"

I cast him a brief, unamused look over my shoulder. "Learn to let things go, Areos."

"Why? Why should I let something of that scale go?" he spat, clearly ready to rehash the ordeal. "She—she literally shot me, Fin! Like… okay? I just let that go?"

"I left my whole family behind, Areos." I had intended my response to be stern, but instead my voice sounded numb. "I lost Hawk."

"Because of Icarus."

"Blaming someone else for the way things are—resenting them, hating them—what good will it do, Areos?" I shook my head. "Resentment is like drinking poison and waiting for the other person to die. It doesn't hurt them; it hurts you."

He kicked at a small rock, sending it skidding over the parched grass. "Yeah, well, maybe I don't care."

"I think that's anger talking."

He let out a frustrated sigh. "Look, I love you, man, but sometimes your optimism gets old."

"Optimism." I tried the word out, my gaze still up in the trees. "Is that what you call it?"

"Yeah—yeah, that's what I call it. That or delusional—take your pick."

I didn't say anything. After a moment he growled, "Look, Fin, I'm just sick and tired of all this, okay?"

"Of what?"

"Of this! Walking around the stupid woods like we're actually going to restore Earth. Look around you!" He swept an arm out in a wide gesture. "Look at this place—look at the world! It's dead, it's broken, it's *screwed*." He kicked another rock. "People are robots, the ecosystem is wasted, the economy is tanking, wars are raging—everything that could possibly have gone wrong has!"

I kept walking, making no response.

"I'm tired of all these stupid council meetings and having to listen to all these stupid kids—yes, *kids*, that's what we all are, last time I checked—talk like this is some kind of science project, like we're actually going to find this top-secret database of information, shut it down, and *ta-da!* Earth is restored!

Everything is sunshine and rainbows!" His face was red as he fell into stride beside me. "It's a bunch of crap. None of that is actually going to happen."

I nodded my agreement. "Not for you, anyway, if you keep talking like that."

"Fin, please." Areos turned to give me a pathetic look. "You're like the last somewhat sane friend I have. Do you seriously believe that's what's going to happen?"

"Sunshine and rainbows?" I quirked an eyebrow. "No."

"Okay. Thank you."

"Restoration of Earth?" I nodded. "With all my heart, yes. Do you really think this is how Sensei intended the world to be?"

"No clue," he said curtly. "I honestly don't know Sensei that well, and I can't say that I would place my trust in the values of a withering old man who disappears halfway through the game, who has no teeth, and mills around in pajamas. I can barely understand a word he says."

My eyes widened, and despite the seriousness of what my friend was saying, I had to suppress a laugh. "Are you serious? That's how Sensei appears to you?"

He rolled his eyes. "And he doesn't to you?"

"Far from it." A smile passed over my lips as I considered his words. "He's vibrant in every sense of the word. Weathered, yes, but the wrinkles are like etches in stone, carved over time and each like a monument to his experience. He's tall, his hair is long, his eyes are bright, deep, and ocean like—and he's Irish, of course." I laughed. "He's everything my soul was thirsty for."

Areos said nothing for a moment; then his expression soured. "Well, it must be pretty thirsty again now, seeing as he abandoned us all."

"Abandoned?" I shook my head. "He's simply left us alone in the throne room to see what we'll do with the crown."

He sighed. "It's so annoying when you talk in riddles, Fin."

I quickened my pace, ignoring his comment. "It's a choice, Areos. It's all a choice. Some stare at the crown, longing for it—wishing things could be the way they used to. Some pick it up, some even try it on—but precious few of us will ever wear it like it was tailor-made for us."

Areos only looked more puzzled, so I went on.

"Do you think we're here by accident? Do you think this is all a mistake, that—that Earth should have been 'fixed' long ago? Earth isn't a machine, Areos. It's a living, breathing being. It's people and plants and animals and…" I smiled as my fingertips brushed the bark. "It's trees… forests, woods, mountains, roaring oceans. We cannot fix Earth, Areos. One does not fix a broken heart or a bleeding wound." I turned and looked him square in the face. "One heals it."

Areos stopped at the edge of the forest, beside the same rock where Icarus had sat only the morning before. He looked out over the valley and heaved a sigh.

"I understand what you're saying, Fin. Really, I do," he began, his voice calmer. "And I admire it. But I cannot believe it… Not when Earth looks like this. Not when everything around us is falling to ruin. No." He shook his head. "I'm sorry, but no. We don't choose reality, Fin—we can only choose whether to accept it or not."

I stood there and looked at my friend for a moment, but before I could reply, a voice called out, "Yo! Guys!"

"What the…" Areos muttered irritably, giving a small begrudging wave to my neon-haired student, who was climbing the slope to meet us. "Runner… what a surprise."

Runner scampered to a stop, making a wild gesture with his arm. "You guys—did you see the sky over there?" he shouted at the top of his lungs. "I think a cotton candy machine exploded!"

Areos rolled his eyes. "Yeah. Death Vapor. We know. It almost killed us."

Runner resumed his climb.

"What brings you here this time?" I called to him.

"I came to get you, man," he yelled back. "You need to be back there— we need you."

My muscles tensed a little, a feeling of dread mixing in my stomach. "Why? What's going on?"

"They've called an emergency gathering, and Delta explicitly told me not to tell you." He grinned, wiping the sweat off his face. "So I thought I'd better let you know."

I started down the slope to meet him. "Did she mention what it was about?"

Runner shook his head. "Nah, not really. But I have a few guesses."

The gravel shifted beneath me and I slid several yards, digging in my heels to come to a stop in front of him. "What are your suspicions?"

He rubbed the back of his neck. "You know they've been searching for the anchor at the end of the chain—the motherboard holding this whole thing together."

I nodded. "The database, yes."

"Well." He straightened, taking a breath. "Rumor has it, they may have found it."

---

Areos was reluctant to transport back to the Dimension after Mitsue's threats, but I promised I would take responsibility for him. We transported from the portal in the floor of the church, but to my surprise, it was not into the Dimension.

"Where on Earth are we?" Areos asked, feeling cautiously around in the tiny dark space that now encompassed us. "This doesn't feel like the cavern."

"That's because it's not the cavern." Runner fumbled with what sounded like a doorknob; there was a creaking sound as a door opened slowly. "It's a utility closet…"

"A utility closet *where*?" Areos asked.

"Shhhh." Runner lifted a hand for quiet. "Last time I really freaked out the janitor—I didn't realize he was mopping the hallway."

My eyes began to adjust as light peeked in. Seeming satisfied after a moment, Runner waved us forward. The three of us emerged into a long white hallway lined with doors and framed modern art. The sounds of traffic and pounding bass filtered through the walls.

"This way," Runner directed, leading us down the hallway and fixing his hair simultaneously. "They're meeting up in Mitsue's suite."

My eyebrows quirked. "Mitsue's? You mean we're in—"

"Osaka." He stretched the word, leading us up a winding, ultramodern staircase. "This is where Mitsue's been holding meetings about the database research."

*Why am I not surprised?* I thought. Beyond the numerous windows we passed sprawled the city shimmering in shades of neon. The major cities of Japan were still thriving, though I couldn't help but wonder for how much longer.

Several floors up, Runner halted in front of a door, then pushed it open to reveal another hallway. This one was constructed entirely of sheer glass.

My insides went light as I stepped hesitantly out onto the sheer glass floor. Thousands of tiny lights twinkled below us, rippling veins of bright colors and motion, churning like lava in the darkness. A thick, glowing haze hung in the atmosphere, blurring the skyline.

Runner proceeded down the hallway, stopping at the end to knock firmly on one of the reflective glass doors. Treading carefully, I came up beside him. He rocked back and forth aimlessly on his heels, waiting for a response, but none came over the tumultuous murmur of voices from within. He tried again, this time banging with the side of his fist. The door finally rolled open.

Delta stood on the threshold, her eyes narrowing into a glare. She wore a black skin suit, and her hair was pulled back into a tight braid. Her dry lips pressed together angrily as she stared at us, sizing up the situation in a rapid glance.

"*Runner,*" she began irritably, but I cut her off, stepping forward.

"We would like to join the gathering."

Delta looked at me for a moment, uncertainty flickering through her eyes like a meteor. "I'm afraid that isn't possible."

"According to the dictates of the code—"

"Which we are currently *not* subject to," she sliced in curtly. "Look, Fin, it's for the best."

"Delta, *please.*"

"*No.* And you can beg and plead all you like, but—"

A new voice interrupted from within the room. "Delta, who is that?"

"*No one.*"

No sooner had she said this than a familiar face came up behind her.

"Oh… Fin." Mitsue's eyebrows lifted when he saw me; his hair hung down over his shoulders. "Do come in."

Delta's eyes widened and she whirled around to face Mitsue. "That's not a good idea."

Mitsue rolled his eyes. "Why not?"

"Because—b-because he's just—"

Mitsue lifted a finger for silence. "Delta, you mustn't allow your emotions to interfere with leadership." He rudely nudged her aside. "Come in. Join us."

I said nothing, my guard rising as I followed him into the room, Areos and Runner behind me. The room, like the hallway, was completely translucent. A long metal table ran the length of it. The council were seated on one side, and a handful of Mitsue's students occupied the other.

"I see you have your student Areos with you," Mitsue commented out of the side of his mouth. "That wasn't wise, to bring him here."

"You banned him from the Dimension, not every gathering—every student has a right to attend," I replied quietly but firmly. "And I doubt you want to make another scene in front of the rest of the council."

Mitsue didn't reply to this, but I saw his jaw tighten.

"You interrupted a discussion about the database, Fin," he began, gesturing for us to take a seat at the table. "Up until now we haven't had much new information, but Gaia has requested this meeting for the specific purpose of discussing a new lead that has apparently surfaced."

"Behind closed doors, I see," I commented, sitting down across from Gaia. She wore a long gray dress with a high collar, and her dreadlocks were woven into a bun; she looked tired. "Shouldn't such gatherings be held in the Dimension—and be open to the rest of the student body?"

"It's for everyone's good, Fin," Mitsue responded. "We wouldn't want anyone getting their hopes up."

"Is that wise?" I inquired. "Allowing emotions to interfere with leadership?"

He gave me a hard look. "Be *grateful* that I'm even allowing you to be involved."

Areos grumbled irritably under his breath as he sat down beside me.

Mitsue resumed his seat at the table and glanced down at his papers. "My students have just been filling us in on their progress, which has yielded some interesting results. The database is indeed a detached source to which all Fragments are connected."

One of the young men across from him nodded vigorously. "Think of it as what they used many years ago on Earth—a Wi-Fi network. This is a network of sorts, that you 'log in' to."

"Except in this case, there is no way to simply 'log out,'" Gaia added. "We know that when the Frags are inserted into the cerebellum at birth, they activate immediately, connecting its host to the database—a constantly updated, monitored, and censored information source. This activation is permanent. The only way to log out is to remove the Frag..." She looked around the table. "And Fragment removal terminates the host instantaneously."

"Which means it's unstoppable," someone said.

"No, not at all." The first student spoke up again. "It only means that the Fragments cannot be removed. If the database itself was terminated, the Fragments would simply stop working—thus disconnecting the hosts in the safest way possible."

"We don't *know* that it would be safe, necessarily," Gaia countered. "If Frags kill the hosts in the event of removal, what happens in the event of a disconnect?"

Delta stared out at the city, her arms crossed over her chest. Mitsue looked irritated as he flipped through his paperwork. No one had an answer.

"Billions of people... billions of tiny Fragments." Gaia held up a sliver of air between her finger and thumb. "A golden key to all the education you will ever need, and for free..." She glanced around at us. "Or is it free?"

"Speak plainly, Gaia," Mitsue muttered, still looking over his papers.

"Fine. I will. You placed me on this project, Mitsue. As an experienced slider, someone who has grown up within the Dimension, you said I was the one you wished to work with, to collaborate with on this project—"

"With my supervision."

She ignored his comment. "We've found the database."

Mitsue froze, his pen slipping from his fingers as he turned to stare at her. "I beg your pardon?"

Gaia glanced across the table at a pair of students. They nodded.

"And you didn't feel the need to mention this earlier?" Mitsue asked.

"I didn't wish to disrespect leadership by speaking out of turn," Gaia replied.

My gaze switched back and forth between her and Mitsue. Everyone else was silent. Delta still hadn't moved.

"Please." Mitsue pulled at the collar of his button-down shirt. "Tell us what you've discovered, by all means."

Gaia pushed back her chair and got up from the table. "It's not something I can tell you. It's something I have to show you."

Mitsue sighed through gritted teeth. "By all means—"

"Not here," Gaia interrupted. "Your elevator acts as a portal, correct?"

"Yes, yes. What of it?"

"Follow me," she replied simply.

Before Mitsue could object, several of the students jumped up from the table. Soon everyone had followed suit, leaving him with nothing to do but begrudgingly follow. I took up the back as we filed through Mitsue's luxurious, spotless apartment and crowded into the elevator. Surprisingly enough, the walls were opaque. The tiny space quickly filled with a hushed murmur as everyone began speaking at once.

Areos leaned into my shoulder. "You have any idea what she's talking about?"

I shook my head. "No... but I get a feeling you do."

He smiled mirthlessly, nodding. "Hold on to what little faith you have left, Fin," he whispered. "You may be about to lose it."

I swallowed; I had a sinking feeling in my gut despite my efforts to ignore his comment. The doors glided shut, and a moment later the ambient yellow lights flickered off, submerging us in darkness. A hush fell over our small group, though even in the silence I could still detect Mitsue's anxious breathing.

This gathering was not going according to his plan. I was sure the only reason he had allowed us to join was to subject me to some display of his dominance and power. He hadn't been expecting this surprise announcement.

In a moment, the pulsing sounds of the city around us rolled away. The air grew gradually warmer, and a soft, leafy breeze emanated from just beyond the doors, which slid open a moment later to—

"There's nothing there," someone said.

Gaia pushed her way to the front, the first to step out. "Don't worry. We're on solid ground. It's just dark—very, very dark." She channeled an orb of glowing purple energy, using it like a flashlight for us to see by. "And that's exactly why we're here."

"I don't get it," Runner said, stepping cautiously out after her. "Why does it need to be dark? Where are we?"

As we filed out, I turned around immediately to assess what the elevator had just transformed into. It was hard to tell exactly, with so little light, but the structure in front of me resembled a yurt, except this one was made of clay and straw. As my eyes drifted upwards, I felt the breath escape from my lungs.

Stretched out above us was a velvet blanket of stars. Hundreds of thousands of stars, the rim of the Milky Way galaxy, so bright the landscape around us was almost faintly illuminated in their soft white glow. I couldn't believe it.

Wonderstruck, I turned back around to face Gaia as she began speaking again.

"For many months now, we have been trying to track down the database—to figure out where it is, and how exactly it works, information we must know if we are to even attempt to shut it down." She clasped her hands together, extinguishing the light. "Those who are in research positions on Earth have done their level best to search for clues, and those of us who are RGM members have risked much to aid in tracking down highly classified information." She paused. "But recently, I realized we've been looking in all the wrong places. It was just a suspicion at first—and that's why I said nothing to the council. I didn't wish to raise false hopes."

Mitsue shifted uncomfortably, probably not even aware that he was standing beside me.

"It's documented, recorded evidence that in the year 2097, this system of Fragmenting began," she continued. "The process of controlling Earth's population by controlling their minds and censoring what information was available to them."

"We know this," Mitsue stated.

"Yes, yes, we do know this," she agreed. "But we weren't here that year. We weren't on Earth—none of us were. And it seems now that we've been so focused on shutting down the database—'fixing Earth'—we've been so busy shouting that we haven't listened. Not really."

Areos sighed, sounding irritated.

"What else happened that year? Does anyone know?" She waited a moment for a response, walking softly around the outer edge of the semicircle we had formed. "Something important happened. Something beyond just the christening of the Unified Nations Collective—something bigger. Something that took place in order for humanity to even be able to accept such a thing; the sugar to chase the medicine…"

Gaia gestured towards the brilliant sky above.

"And I've brought you here, to my natural world, Ethiopia, so that you may see it tonight." She stopped between Mitsue and me. "See that tiny speck? It looks like a star, but it's moving, and much closer, blinking slightly."

Everyone's neck was craned back as we all stared up into the night sky, searching for the object. My eyes having fully adjusted now, I spotted it almost immediately. A faint, satellite-like speck swiping through Ursa Major. Its course seemed almost listless in comparison to the many other satellites— or whatever they called them now. I didn't know.

"In 2097, nations came together in an initiative to launch a capsule into space, a supposed mission to send research drones to Saturn. But oddly enough, the drones were lost before the capsule even surpassed Earth's orbit.

The mission failed. But the capsule remained in orbit…" She paused, looking up. "The mission was called Eolas, a Gaelic word…"

My heart skipped a beat; my eyes widened. The tiny dot flickered onward through the blackness.

"For knowledge…" I finished, my voice fading in my throat. "The database…"

For a long moment no one spoke a word, not even Mitsue. We stood there silently in the darkness, staring up at the sky, up at that one tiny dot— so vastly beyond our reach.

"The research mission was a cover-up," Areos breathed, shaking his head. "It was *meant* to fail. It was just to win the people over, to create a foothold for the creation of the UNC—and a Reformed Global Militia to protect them. To protect 'progress' with a program that would change Earth… Fragments…"

Gaia sighed. "A program that didn't hit Earth like a fireball, but slowly boiled its inhabitants alive. Small changes no one would notice until… until they *couldn't notice* anymore."

Mitsue stiffened beside me. Before anyone could say another word, he spun on his heels and stormed back into the tiny hut from which we'd emerged. With one last glance at the sky, I turned and took off after him. Areos was right behind me.

"Get out of this transport," he seethed as soon as I had shut the door behind us. "Or I swear to god, I will throw you out myself!"

"Mitsue, what is *wrong* with you?" Areos blurted. "Are you so proud, so—so *full of yourself* that you're going to bury your head in the sand and ignore the facts? Because that's *exactly* what Gaia and her students just presented—facts!"

"Speculation, mere *speculation*," Mitsue corrected him, disgusted. "But then, of course, you're just a human fledgling—and a traitor at that! You wouldn't be able to understand these things."

"Mitsue, Areos is *right*," I cut in. "Gaia's information… It's solid stuff, it makes *sense!* It explains why we haven't found the database—it's not even on Earth!"

The elevator door slid open, revealing Mitsue's apartment once again. He strode out onto the glass floor, gripping his head in his hands, hissing curses under his breath.

"Mitsue, why are you fighting everyone?" My voice dropped as I slowly followed him. "Have you forgotten who it is you're at war with? Because it isn't us!" I stopped in the middle of the room, watching as he paced. "It's not even them… It's you."

That was the trigger that sparked the explosion. He whipped around, jabbing a finger in my direction. "Just *shut up*! Just *leave*, Fin—leave me *now*!" Spit flew out of his mouth as he yelled hoarsely. "Take this traitor." He pointed accusingly at Areos. "Go back to your train wreck of a country to keep looking for your dead girlfriend, and *leave me alone!*"

The words were sharp ones. For a moment I stood there, in the middle of the glass floor, absorbing their impact.

"Your hate and envy will kill you if you don't let it go, Mitsue." My voice was quiet when I finally spoke. "It's *destroying* you."

Mitsue turned to face me, the neon light reflecting in his furious eyes. "Then let it."

---

Twilight was settling in as we emerged from the church back in Ireland. The stark white steeple towered over us to crack the darkening sky. I stopped in the churchyard, resting my hands on what was left of the old wrought-iron fence.

"My father loved this place," I mused quietly, staring up at the hole where the bell used to be. "He didn't attend services; he just tended the gardens and the grounds. He always said he felt God more in the trees and the flowers." I felt a faint smile pass over my lips. "Maybe that's why my sisters and I loved the forest so much—we even built a hideout in the woods and pretended we lived there."

"You must miss them all." Areos stuffed his hands into the pockets of his uniform. "Your family."

I nodded silently. Words were too weak.

"I never really knew mine," he said finally. "I mean, I wasn't, like, an orphan. I had a family… They were just never really there. I was never high on their priority list, and they were never high on mine either. I know it must hurt like hell because it's different for you… but at least you had them when you had them. If that makes sense."

I thought about it, looking around at the crumbling village as I breathed in the night air.

"Yes, it does," I replied quietly. "It does make sense."

We both stood there a moment longer before Areos carefully pushed open the gate, the hinges groaning loudly in the silence.

"What a night." He exhaled the words, reaching up to rub the back of his neck. "The database isn't even on Earth… What are we going to do now?"

"Reevaluate, I suppose…"

Areos shot me a look. "You don't ever frickin' quit, do you, Fin?"

I shook my head as we started back through the ruins. "It's not in my nature to quit, Areos. It's not in my nature to give up on anything."

"But what if sometimes we should?" he asked, almost hesitant. "What if… what if we are meant to let go of certain things? You even said yourself that we have to let go."

"Of hate, yes," I agreed, keeping my eyes on the path ahead. "Of hope? No. No, that I'll keep holding onto."

Areos sighed and rubbed his eyes. He said nothing else until we had made it to the edge of the ruined village; then he stopped.

"Fin, I can't go back with you," he said. "I mean no disrespect, but I feel pointless wandering around out here. We walked for miles and miles, and we haven't seen a trace of Icarus or Charlie—I think it's more than probable that they may have been captured. Or worse."

"Areos, you're wanted by the RGM—they're probably still out there looking for you," I cautioned. "What if Icarus and Charlie *weren't* captured?"

"What if they were?" he countered. "You said the New Dublin base is close by—what if they're already there? What if they're dead?"

"Don't say that."

"One of us has to say it, Fin. It might as well be me." He gazed in the direction of the city, where a faint glow illuminated the sky. "Let me go find the base and see if Icarus is there. I'm an RGM pilot, remember? I actually know some things about how the system works. If anyone can find them, it may just be me. Now that we're out of the woods, I know I can find the base—I've known pilots who have been there before. I can find it."

I frowned slightly, considering the implications. "Let me go with you, then."

"No. Are you kidding? If they catch you, they'll induct you." He looked me gravely in the eyes. "You wouldn't be able to handle it, Fin—not what they would do to you, but what they would make *you* do."

"Fine," I said finally. "If you think you should go, then go, Areos. I trust your judgment."

"And I trust yours." He faltered, tilting his head to one side. "Well, most of the time."

I laughed slightly, then gave him a firm shove. "Away with ya. And don't get yourself shot, all right?"

"Wilco." He gave me a halfhearted smile; then his face turned serious once more. "I hope you find what you're looking for, Fin."

I bowed my head in a nod, my heart sinking a little as I considered the mission that still lay ahead of me. "Thank you, Areos."

------

The walk back into the forest was a quiet one after we parted ways, but not lonely. My mind was still reeling from the gathering and what we'd learned there, and in a way, I was grateful for the time alone to digest it. But after a while it became harder and harder to think about Earth and our mission and all the technical details that it entailed. All I could think about was Hawk.

My heart ached in my chest; my fingertips brushed the bark on the massive trees as I walked slowly. I couldn't return to camp with remnants of the vapor still hanging in the air, so I blazed a new route, my feet carrying me farther into the mountains.

"Wake up, wake up, wake up…" My voice was somewhere below a whisper as I spoke to the trees. "Wake up…"

Somehow, the air was sweet, like a memory of what it used to smell like: wild honeysuckle, rich dew, thick carpets of bright green moss, robust conifers and pines. It was all there, so awake and alive in my mind. I'd been able to heal Icarus; I *knew* I could heal the forest. I just needed to let it out through my fingertips…

I started to focus, coming to a stop in a clearing. I placed my hands on the towering giant before me: a pine tree skirted by a golden carpet of needles. I pressed my fingertips into the bark, I rested my forehead against the trunk, and I tried with all my might to focus.

But the ache in my chest was all I felt. A hollow, throbbing ache.

I let out the breath I hadn't realized I'd been holding, sliding down to the ground to kneel, my forehead still pressed against the dry, deteriorating bark.

"Hawk, I know you're here…" I whispered, my voice trembling, "I believe it more than anything… just… please just let me find you… Please help me…"

I repeated the words over and over again until my voice grew so quiet it faded altogether. The air was cool, my heart wild, and the forest silent around me.

Then a long, familiar, shrill cry filled the atmosphere.

# CHAPTER SIXTEEN

## *Lara*

"Wicklow Mountains? *Wicklow Mountains?* You have got to be joking with me."

I sat on the edge of my bunk, giving my rifle one last examination. Kess sat on the bunk across from me, a black turtleneck pulled up to her chin and her elbows resting on her knees.

"Orders are orders." I ran a rag over the barrel. "They're meant to be followed, not understood."

Kess rolled her large brown eyes. "Says who?"

"Says Donovan."

"And what the hell does he know?"

I grabbed a fistful of ammo, loading my magazine. "Donovan started out just like the rest of us, you know. It's not like he wanted this life either. Maybe he just wanted a normal life—a wife, children, a home."

"And is that what you want—a normal life?" She tipped back her head, a look of doubt in her eyes. "Is that what a normal life is like, Lara? Being a wife, being a mother? Having a home?"

I reached for more ammo. "It's different for everyone. But there's nothing wrong with being a wife or a mother. Wanting those things—it's okay to want those things."

"And do you want those things?"

My hands hesitated slightly. I thought about it.

I couldn't recall ever being asked such a question, and now I wasn't even sure how I would answer. What Kess didn't understand—couldn't understand—was that I hadn't grown up in the RGM like she had, and my life hadn't changed solely because of my induction. My life had always been different. I had always been different. Maybe it could all be traced back to the day Ronan had disappeared, but even that was a faded memory.

*What would a normal life have been like?*

"Lara?"

Kess's voice tugged me out of my thoughts. I blinked back into focus, continuing to load my weapon.

"I don't know," I replied quietly. "I don't know what I want."

---

"Good afternoon, Moron, welcome aboard," ANI greeted me.

I strapped in, rifle tucked at my side. "*Moran.* For the hundredth *thousandth* time."

"Exterior temperature is ten degrees Celsius. Interior temperature is 18 degrees Celsius. Currently flying at an altitude of two hundred and seventy-four meters. Currently traveling at five hundred and seventy five knots. You will arrive at your drop point in approximately three minutes."

I started running through my checklist, sliding on my helmet and making sure everything was in working order: the shield slid smoothly; the night vision worked—

"Command, do you copy?" I spoke into the mic.

A pause. A slight crackle followed by some white noise. "Copy, loud and clear."

I frowned. "Signal sounds weak. Don't be surprised if I lose you."

"Copy."

I continued through my tasks, trying to tune out of my thinking mind.

"Your current body temperature is thirty-seven degrees Celsius. Heart rate is one hundred and ten beats per minute. Perspiration level: high. Hunger level: not applicable. Urine level: moderate."

"Just *shut up*, ANI," I growled, struggling to squeeze my fingers up inside my helmet to mess with the mic. "Can you hear me now, sir?"

A long silence. Bleeps echoed in the small cabin around me, then a hissing sound as we began to descend. My insides grew light.

"Dropping altitude," ANI announced. "Corporal Moron, prepare for drop-off."

I tightened my chin strap and secured my landing pack, unbuckling now to sling my rifle over my shoulder. I closed my eyes and started to focus, willing myself to shut off my brain.

*Don't think; just act. Just act.*

Such a funny word, *act*; it could mean to execute a plan, to *do* something. But it could also mean to put on the mask and to pretend to be someone else, someone you *weren't*. I couldn't help but feel like I was doing both.

"Engaging trapdoor."

A loud hiss cut through the relative quiet, and an instant later the floor dissolved under my feet. I dropped silently through the air, the hum of the Byrd there one moment, gone a second later. I tapped the button at the top of the landing pack when I was fifty feet from the ground. A jet stream of air immediately billowed out to soften my landing at the edge of a lake.

I checked the screen on my wrist. *1300.*

"Drop-off affirmed," I said quietly into the mic, catching my breath.

The Byrd that had carried me here was already a mere speck on the horizon. I quickly turned, assessing my surroundings. I took a few silent steps, then dropped down behind a large boulder to think. I was already sweating bullets in my grassy-camouflaged skin suit; my sage green helmet felt like a lead weight.

*Okay... Game plan.*

I started tapping the screen, accessing the briefing Intel had sent me. I opened up the map and quickly found the red dot. Target. Then I scrolled until I located the green dot. Me.

They were a few miles away, but heading in this direction. There was a stream that ran through the mountain pass and trickled down into the static blue-gray basin. They appeared to be making their way towards it.

I swallowed back a queasy feeling, looking back up at my surroundings. Dead trees stood guard at the water's edge, bowing forward like tired old men to surrender their branches to decay in a watery grave. Yellow algae smudged the lake's surface, and the sticky ground began to swallow my boots every time I stopped for more than a moment.

I checked the map every five minutes, making sure I was still headed in the right direction. When I wasn't looking at the map, I made an effort to cleanse my mind of it all. I listened to the gentle breeze, the resistance it met among the tree branches, the water lapping quietly against the muddy shore. The distant sound of the mountains, a voice composed of the billowing wind in the grass. I listened like it all was music, letting my fingertips brush the bark on the trees as I walked.

"Oh, wake up, wake up, wake up…" I murmured under my breath, gazing up at their wilting boughs. "You're too beautiful to fade away like this…"

My mom had once told me that she had never known a girl to feel things as deeply as I did. I remember asking her if that was good or bad. *Both*, she'd answered. And now, I felt as though I finally knew what she meant. One who loves profoundly will grieve profoundly—and my world was in shambles.

*Never stop searching.*

What had my brother meant by that? What had been going through his head when he wrote that note? Where had he gone?

I tried to remember his face and his voice, but there was just a void where he should have been. I had been so young; everything was blurry and pastel at that age. Bright and rushing like a river; here and gone.

Pausing in a clearing, I checked the map. I was gaining altitude; I could feel it. The red dot was a little closer.

I continued up the incline, digging the toes of my boots into the rocky soil. I tried my microphone again, checking to see if my commander could hear me, but after a few minutes I had still received no response. Finally, I had to assume that they couldn't hear me. I was alone out here.

*Alone—without the supervision of the RGM. If ever there had been a time to try to run...*

I forced these thoughts to the back of my mind. I couldn't—it was too risky. There was no way to know if and when they would pick up my signal again. *No, I would apprehend the targets and bring them back to base alive, regardless of whether a Byrd picked us up or I had to walk them all the way back to Base New Dublin at gunpoint.*

I felt my brow crease as I considered Donovan's irregular order. Why did he want them alive? When did the RGM *ever* condone letting a recusant live? What did they plan to do with them once they had been apprehended?

I was puzzled, to say the very least. Still, I kept walking, checking the map as I went. I thought back to the night I had tried to run, the night that felt like so long ago. The night Kess had probably saved my life by persuading me to abandon the idea. I couldn't help but wonder what would have happened if I'd tried.

Finally, I reached the pass between the peaks. I walked along the edge of the rocky stream, climbing over sizable boulders just to avoid the splash my boots would create when they hit the water.

I heard voices—snatches of words on the edge of the wind. I dropped behind a boulder, flattening against it. I checked the map, watching for a moment as the blinking red dot moved gradually closer, millimeters away on the screen. I sucked in a breath, sliding my rifle into position and lowering myself to my belly in the overgrown grass.

Footsteps, footsteps, and then, finally the first one passed me. I lay motionless in the grass, my finger poised over the trigger, my mind racing. I sized her up instantaneously: a dirty RGM uniform, a buzzcut and a neck tattoo. She splashed through the stream, completely unaware of my presence.

Then another one walked past. Another RGM uniform, just as dirty, but this one was different. He looked around like he could see everything. His head was covered in dark stubble, and his jaw was rough and unshaven. He was tall, lean and muscular, with clear blue eyes. My finger went to the trigger.

He froze in place for a moment, seeming to have heard something. His counterpart continued, noticing nothing out of the ordinary. I waited a moment to see what he would do, my finger trembling on the trigger.

A few seconds ticked past, accentuated by my beating heart.

Then he exploded into action, diving behind the closest boulder and shouting to the girl to get down.

I pulled the trigger, aiming easily just past her thigh. The bullet made a small tear in the leg seam of her pants, but didn't touch her skin. She flailed, screamed, and dropped to her belly in the water as I leapt to my feet, gun poised.

I whipped my shield down over my eyes and activated day mode. Everything sharpened instantaneously. *X-ray.* I saw through the rock to where his body was hunched; I saw his heart pumping in his chest. *One hundred and twenty beats per minute.*

"Stay down!" I yelled through the mouthpiece in my helmet. My voice seethed out, distorted through the speaker. "Do not move…"

The female lifted her face from the water, gasping, and raised her hands. The young man surged out from behind the rock, inserting himself between the muzzle of my rifle and the young woman.

"Stop!" he shouted, breathless, his arms in the air. "Don't shoot."

I scanned his organs through the crosshairs, stopping when I got to the heart. "Are you an RGM member?"

I had no intention of shooting him, but I couldn't let on—not when it was two against one. I had to bully them a bit.

I watched his heart, his lungs, his rapid breathing. Numbers were popping up on my shield, memos about his blood type and other details I didn't care to know. I deactivated X-ray mode, looking him in the face now.

His skin was sheet white as he dropped his head in a single nod.

My thoughts raced. I gestured with my rifle. "Step aside."

"No!" he yelled back. "I won't!"

"You will, or I will move you myself—" I gritted my teeth, stepping forward, finger poised on the trigger. "I said *move!*"

His hands instantly snapped up defensively in front of him. Though he hadn't even come close to touching me, I suddenly felt something strike me—a force I couldn't see. The gun flew out of my hands and I fell backward to the ground.

Gasping for air and scrambling to my knees, I reached for the pistol packed at my hip. The young man hadn't changed position, except now his hands were closer together. I was expecting to see some kind of weapon, but instead I saw nothing. Thin air.

"Get down on your knees, now!" I shouted hoarsely.

He dropped to the grass obediently. The female was still in the stream, hands raised. The pistol shook in my grasp as I walked slowly backwards to retrieve my weapon, dead set on aiming it right back in his face.

My stomach dropped as I picked up my rifle. The trigger had completely melted into the guard.

"What the…?" I didn't finish.

I turned around and looked at him, flicking X-ray back on. His heart rate had skyrocketed, his eyes had dilated, and his adrenal glands were working double time. I looked up at his skeletal face.

"What did you just do?" The question came out uneven. "W-what just happened?"

The young man kneeling before me said nothing. I got to my feet, slung my busted weapon back over my shoulder, and walked over to him, stopping a few feet away.

"Who are you?"

He squinted up at me, as if trying to see my face past my shield.

"Explain what you just did." I held up the rifle by the straps, feeling somewhat at his mercy as I realized he could do the exact same thing to the pistol I still pointed at his forehead. "How did you just do that?"

"That I couldn't say."

"Couldn't, or will not?"

"Couldn't."

A strange feeling formed in the pit of my stomach. A sensation like the sick, restless feeling that had gripped me that day so long ago. The day I had left my family, the day I had boarded the train and left behind everything I had ever known. It was the same feeling I'd had when I heard the voice.

*Jump.*

He couldn't explain? He couldn't explain what he had just done? He couldn't explain knocking me off my feet and destroying my rifle—without even touching me? He couldn't explain the—the *power* that had just come out of his hands…

*Power…*

I stared at him. I couldn't think straight.

I sucked in a breath, reached up, and tugged my chin strap loose. My fingers trembled as I shoved my pistol back into the holster. I pulled off my helmet, sweat trickling down my forehead.

I looked down into his eyes. "What's your name?"

Surprised, he stared at me for a moment. "Icarus."

I studied his expression long and hard. "Well, Icarus, unless you and your friend want to be executed, I suggest you do *exactly* as I say."

----

"You both were on a Bullet headed for the north station," I said.

"We had no idea where it was going, but yes," Icarus replied.

"How'd you escape?"

Icarus faltered, a twig snapping beneath his foot. "Why haven't you killed us?"

"They want live specimens this time." I nudged him between the shoulder blades with the muzzle of the pistol, keeping up appearances. "I've been ordered not to kill you. Either of you."

"Are you taking us to the base, then?" the girl, Charlie, asked, giving me a suspicious once-over.

"Enough! I don't want another word unless I speak to you first!" I'd put my helmet back on, but the distorter was off now, letting my normal voice flow freely through my shield.

I'd locked bands around both of their wrists. They walked in front of me as we trekked through the woods, my mind grappling for a plan.

*What am I doing, what am I doing, what am I doing?*

The truth was, I wasn't sure what I was going to do, I just knew one thing for sure: there was something different about Icarus—something I'd never seen before—and I couldn't let the RGM find out. I was testing the waters, considering the idea that my radio wasn't working. They might have lost the signal, and this might have been the perfect time for me to vanish off the radar—taking both of the recusants I'd found with me.

I carefully led them farther and farther from the base, praying under my breath that the RGM wasn't watching.

Finally, I grabbed Icarus by the arms and shoved him back against a massive dead oak. He made no effort to resist. My breathing was ragged as I scrutinized him.

"If we get caught—if we go back—" I almost choked on my own voice, the various outcomes of this act of rebellion churning in my mind. "You can't breathe a word about…" I trailed off, still hardly able to believe what he had done.

Icarus's eyes searched mine; my hand was still locked in a vise grip around his wrist.

"You say that as if we're not going back…" he said quietly. "You say that as if…"

He didn't finish. He didn't need to.

I nodded.

"But I don't understand…" Icarus's brow creased. "You're helping us? Why?"

I might have answered that one. I might have told him that I had to—that this was my chance to finally, finally escape this hell. I might have told him that he wouldn't be able to survive where I was taking him, not with his… the way he was. I might have told him that I knew, because I was like him. I might have told him that being in possession of an uncanny ability was not unfamiliar to me. I might have told him he was the *only* other person I had *ever* met who was like *me*…

But before I could speak, my headset began to crackle and the familiar roaring whir of a Byrd began to slowly make its approach. My heart sank in my chest.

"Moran, do you copy?"

Icarus couldn't hear it; only I could. There was still this look in his eyes: part confusion, part hope. It was all about to be ripped away—*beaten* away— and he had no idea. That same feeling still tingled inside me. That same feeling that had said *jump*—that same feeling I'd had in the woods when the old man had spoken.

"Yes, sir." My voice wavered; tears stung my eyes. "I copy."

A crackle, a brief hesitation. "Have you apprehended the targets?"

Charlie had come to a stop beside us now, terror in her eyes. Icarus's were brave and probing. I couldn't speak until I had pulled my gaze away.

"Yes, sir."

"Move into the meadow. A Byrd should be landing momentarily."

I felt sick—like I was drowning. I swallowed hard, pushing Icarus back in front of me.

"Yes, sir."

I was out of my mind. There was no way we could escape. There was no way they wouldn't find us. And now Icarus knew that's what I'd intended— to run away. If he told the RGM, I would be executed for treason, all for two brief moments of an overpowering urge to run.

For a moment I'd felt almost as if Icarus was my answer. And now I was forced to hand him over to the wolves.

# CHAPTER SEVENTEEN

## *Fin*

I stood frozen in the middle of the forest clearing, every muscle in my body locked with tension and every thought having vanished from my mind. For a moment I wondered if my senses were playing tricks on me. I scanned the treetops, my heart in my mouth. A dense silence hung in the air.

I drew a long breath, closing my eyes to listen. No sooner had my eyelids closed than a set of claws grazed my back, followed by a burst of feathers streaking past overhead.

*Make that talons.*

My heart was pounding, swelling to ten times its natural size.

For over four hundred days and nights I had dreamed of this exact moment, visualized it so vividly I felt as if I had already lived it ten thousand times over. Now it was actually here, and suddenly I was frozen and light-headed and staring through tears as another shrill cry rattled the forest. An echoing shriek of a hawk, but not just any hawk.

*Her.*

She was somehow brighter than the darkness around her, spiraling up into the trees, flapping her wings, showering me in feathers as soft and white as a first snowfall.

"Hawk..." I breathed her name.

She tilted her head, looking down at me as she circled, then let out a long piercing cry. A smile burst across my lips.

"Hawk!"

She replied with another call, swooping down to run her talons through my hair. She tucked her wings and wove deftly through the trees. I wasted no time in sprinting after her, smiling still—laughing through the tears as they rolled down my cheeks.

The pounding of my bare feet against the ground and the whoosh of her wings filled the forest. I ran after her, losing track of everything but the pure white feathers. We raced through the trees and the brush and over knolls covered in dry grass. She bulleted over streams and I splashed through them; she soared over piles of boulders while I climbed each of them.

Finally, as we came to a clearing, I dropped into a breathless heap in a soft bed of golden pine needles. The blood pulsed through my head and I couldn't seem to drink in enough oxygen. I rolled onto my back and closed my eyes. When I opened them again, she was still there, unlike my dreams of her, in which she would always be gone.

Hawk hovered for a moment, then descended and landed lightly on my chest. She tilted her head to the side, giving a throaty trill as she examined me. I immediately lifted a hand to her soft downy chest, and she stepped up to perch. I sat up, looking deep into her small dark eyes as I furiously blinked away tears.

I gently stroked her head, running my fingers over her soft neck and wings.

"I knew I would find you," I whispered, a tear rolling down my cheek. "I knew I would…"

Hawk trilled again, quieter now. She hopped lightly from my hand to land on my shoulder, nuzzling her head against the curve of my neck. I could feel her heart pounding through her soft chest. I wanted to pinch myself to make sure it wasn't a dream, but I could barely move, barely breathe.

"Is this real?" I whispered, turning my face slightly to rest it against her soft feathers. "Or am I dreaming this? You…"

She made no sound; there was a slight hesitation. Then a twinge of pain as she nipped my earlobe with her sharp beak.

"Ow! Okay, okay! I get it—it's real." I lifted her on one hand again, bringing her in front of me so I could see her eyes. "*You're* real."

Hawk's eyes didn't leave mine. The withered forest hung silently around us, the sky already beginning to brighten incrementally with the brushstrokes of dawn. I felt as if I'd only just now awoken from four hundred days of sleep.

Slowly, I leaned closer to touch my forehead gently to her tiny one.

"I missed you *so much...*"

---

Though I couldn't recall having closed my eyes, I awoke from a deep sleep to patches of sun on my face and soft, downy feathers brushing against my skin.

A brilliant yellow sun sifted through the slouching pines. The ground had dried overnight, and the air was filled with a scent like straw and mulch. Hawk was still nestled beside me. I was sprawled on my back, my T-shirt soaked with dew. Everything felt so much less bleak that morning, but I believe I would have thought the same had I awoken in hell, as long as Hawk was by my side.

Never had I once doubted that I would find Hawk—I'd *known* that I would. I'd felt her presence all along, as if she were part of me. Yet somehow now that I had found her, it felt less real than when I had only imagined being with her again. It felt like a dream.

She stirred, but didn't open her tired eyes. I lay there next to her for a long moment before finally peeling myself up off the ground. I lifted a hand to shield my eyes as I scanned our new surroundings. We were much higher up in the mountains, far from the location of my camp. I knew there was no way we could go back, not now—not after the attack.

Why had the RGM been out this far? It seemed unlikely that the pilot had just happened to be passing by. Something didn't add up.

I'd been one of the few to scout out the conditions of Earth before our reentry. I knew a little of what made the RGM tick—how this militia worked and what sort of equipment they had at their fingertips. Their highly advanced radar could comb the landscape for miles, searching for unfamiliar or suspicious activity, but even with such advanced technology, their signal was still swallowed by the mountains. I *had* heard that, in some cases, the RGM would attach a tracker to a member's helmet before particular missions, but this was never a secret to the member themselves. Icarus, Areos, and Charlie didn't have them. There was no way they could have detected us way out here.

I rekindled the fire I'd built the night before and watched Hawk as she slept. Her wings were tucked close to her body and she was nestled into the thick blanket of golden pine needles.

After a little while she stirred, this time opening her sharp, dark eyes.

"Good morning," I greeted her softly as the flames took.

She responded only by closing her eyes again. I grinned.

"It's colder this far up. I usually return to the mountain's base to camp, but… well, it's a long story."

She murmured a trill.

"I know—we have nothing but time. But first we need to come up with a plan."

Hawk peeled open one eye inquiringly.

I half rolled my eyes. "You know very well what I'm talking about."

She didn't reply because she couldn't.

"This!" I gestured wildly at her, though still grinning helplessly. "You being an animal."

She gave an aggressive sort of chirp.

"*Raptor*. Sorry. But the point is, you're not human—not that you *were* a human, you were a slider, but you know what I mean. You need your alternate form back."

Hawk replied with a throaty trill.

"I know—I know you gave your soul to Icarus… But we'll find a way to work around that—there has to be a way."

She preened her long milk-white primary feathers. I poked at the fire thoughtfully.

"I've seen Icarus, Hawk. He was here just yesterday."

She hesitated, turning her head to look at me.

"He escaped the RGM—they sent him and Areos and Charlie to Ireland. But then yesterday, there was an attack. Apparently, we were spotted from the air, though I'm still unsure how. They attacked us with Death Vapor. Icarus felt we should all split up, so we did, but after it was all over, Areos was the only one I found again. We walked for hours looking for Icarus and Charlie, but we couldn't find them, and we couldn't venture back into the forest to search for them further because of the vapor."

Hawk listened intently, making no sound.

"They say the stuff takes about twenty-four hours to clear, so I plan to hike back down today and see if I can figure out what happened to them. It seems unlikely that Icarus would have…" I stopped, clearing my throat and refusing to allow myself to dwell on the implications. "I'm sure he's fine, wherever he is. Areos is inclined to believe that he and Charlie may have been captured, which, I'll have to admit, is a possibility."

Hawk gave me a look.

"Charlie? She's a medic from the base in Section C. That's where they came from. She's… a long story. She got tangled up in it all by accident, and now she knows too much."

Hawk looked away. I circled back to Icarus.

"He misses you, Hawk. When he came here, he was… broken. He feels responsible for what happened—with you."

She let out a long shrill call, flapping her wings a few times but remaining on the ground.

"I know, I know. I told him it was your choice—it wasn't his. But you know how he is."

Hawk made a sound like teasing laughter.

"'Look who's talking'?" I reiterated. "I could turn the tables, I think—Icarus's stubbornness is nothing compared to yours, Hawk. I've never met a more pigheaded, righteous—" *beautiful, loving, faithful* "—doggedly persistent individual in all my days," I finished, setting the stick aside now that the fire was roaring. "He's nothing compared to you. At least he listened."

Hawk shot me a look. I laughed a little.

"I know, you *do* listen…" I trailed off, gazing at her. "When I can find the words."

We talked for a long time—well, I did most of the talking. But she didn't need to speak for me to understand her. We were beyond needing words.

The forest soon warmed with the hazy sunlight. I put out the fire and began my long trek down the mountain. The ground was plastered with pink powder. Only a faint scent of the poison lingered in the air. Hawk soared overhead, a stark silhouette against the smoggy sky. I tried not to glance up every other second, but it was impossible not to.

Between my vantage point and Hawk's bird's-eye view, we made a thorough search of the woods, combing it for any sign of life. Eventually, close to what remained of my camp, we spotted someone. But it wasn't Icarus.

"Hey, Fin!"

I squinted at the distant figure, bleached by the sunlight, then detected bright red hair an instant later. I lifted one hand to wave as Hawk swooped down and sank her talons into a thick tree branch to perch fifty feet above.

"Runner," I greeted, meeting him halfway, "I'm glad you came."

"That's a first." He laughed. "Why?"

I grinned. "I found her."

His puzzled expression remained a moment longer, then melted into one of surprise.

"No way!"

I nodded, gesturing towards the tree Hawk was perched in. "Although I think it would be more accurate to say that she found me."

Runner gaped up at her, clutching a fistful of spiky red hair. "Wow. She looks… different."

"She doesn't have her slider shape at the moment."

He shook his head. "No, like, I just meant she looks paler. Like, before, she had that classical desert-hawk look—with like the brown and the speckles and…"

I nodded, biting back a smile as I looked up at Hawk myself. She leapt off the branch and took to the air, letting out a long, loud cry.

"Still sounds the same," Runner added wryly.

I took a few steps forward, gazing up into the sky after her, shielding my eyes with my hand.

"I need to help her, Runner," I told him quietly. "I don't know how I'm going to do that yet, but we need her back with us."

"Well, it looks like she's back, however the hell—*heck* that happened."

"I have no idea how she found her way back," I admitted. "She'll tell me in time, I'm sure. Even though she's returned to Earth, she still bears Icarus's punishment. She redeemed him with her soul; it belongs to him now. She can't shift; she can't do any of the things that she used to. She's trapped in hawk form."

"Huh." He was squinting up at the sky. "That sucks."

It was a gross understatement, but I nodded.

"So… now you have to figure out a way to make her a human again…" Runner's gaze remained on the sky a moment longer; then he turned to squint at me. "How're you gonna do that?"

How *was* I going to do that?

"I'm sure it will come to me," I resolved, refocusing. "Anyway, this can't be the reason you transported from Japan and came all this way—"

"Oh, I didn't transport from Japan," he interjected. "I left Ethiopia and went to Rome for a bit, actually."

"Rome?" I questioned, puzzled. "What's in Rome?"

"Good food still, thankfully," he replied. "Nice people, few RGM members to avoid."

I looked at him inquiringly. "Is that what you do with all the free time on your hands, Runner? Travel around and eat?"

He shrugged. "Why not? It's free."

"You don't need food."

"But I enjoy it, and there's nothing else to do," he said, defending his case. "Mitsue's in fits, and the rest of the council is in a tailspin. No one knows what to do next."

"I never agreed that obliterating the database was our mission to begin with," I said. "We don't even know what we're dealing with. We could kill everyone by destroying it—if it was even within our reach to destroy—we have *no* idea."

"How do you think things will get better, then?"

I kept myself in the shadow of Hawk's wings as we began to walk.

"It's not worth much—what I think," I replied after a while. "What I *think* can often be self-focused, misguided, or simply wrong. It isn't really about what we think as much as it is what we believe. If we believe, the right choices will become apparent to us; we will not need to muscle our way to the right conclusions. You know what I mean?"

"Sort of," he replied. "I never quite get all of it, though, when you speak in riddles like that."

"Metaphors?"

"Whatever. Confusing shit." He winced. "*Stuff.*"

Hawk dove down through the trees, twisting in midair before mounting the next updraft and taking to the sky's great expanse again.

"Have you told Icarus?" Runner asked hesitantly.

"We're still searching for him. That's why I hiked down here, actually—to look for him. Areos went to the base to see if Icarus and Charlie had been captured…" I frowned. "I'm not sure how he plans to figure that out without getting caught himself."

"And as an ex-RGM member, they'd probably lop his head off."

"Let's not assume the worst," I replied firmly. "Areos is smart. He'll find a way. Until I hear news from him, I have no reason to come to any bleak conclusions. When Icarus is found, I'll tell him about Hawk."

Something inside me twinged. I pushed the feeling away.

"Until then, we have work to do," I finished.

Runner stopped walking, turning to look at me as we came to a stop. "We?" he puzzled. "What do you mean, we?"

"I mean that I'm not the only one with a mission to fulfill," I explained. "You've been in the Dimension for some time. You've trained, you've trusted, and you've accomplished many things with that trust, Runner." I paused. "Can I ask you something?"

He bobbed his head in a nod.

"When you look at Sensei, what do you see?" I asked slowly. "He appears different to every one of us… How does he appear to you?"

"Sensei?" Runner said nothing for a long moment; then he grinned. "Sensei looks like *fire*."

I smiled, looking back up at Hawk again for a moment and then back down at my student. "Runner, you've grown much. I think it's time I stopped referring to you as merely a student—I think you're a good deal more than that now." I clapped a hand on his shoulder. "Go back to the Dimension and help the others train and prepare themselves. They are still training, right?"

"Yeah, under Mitsue's supervision."

I looked him squarely in the eyes. "Maybe it's time they followed a method other than his."

Runner looked interested. "You mean, like, defy him?"

"I guess you could put it that way," I agreed slowly. "And I have reason to believe Mala has already been helping quite a few of the younger students with their training. I'm sure she would welcome the help."

Suddenly he looked even more interested. "Mala? Really?" A grin twitched on his lips. "But what about you? I mean, I've gotten used to coming out here and trying to help you keep your spirits up."

I smiled. "Don't worry about that, Runner. My spirits are up," I promised, then turned serious. "One more thing."

"What's that?" he asked.

I shot a quick glance up at the sky. "Don't mention anything about Hawk to anyone, please."

"They're going to find out sooner or—"

"I know," I said. "Just… promise me. For now, say nothing."

He looked at me for a long moment.

"All right," he agreed. "I promise."

# CHAPTER EIGHTEEN

*Icarus*

"**B**ullet 501 pulled into our northern station, allegedly carrying three renegade RGM members—you were one of them. This particular car was found to be partially destroyed—torn open in an impossible way. What weapons did you have?" Commander Donovan's eyes were dark, like his hair, like his smoke, like his soul. He wore a decorated black uniform and stared me down like I was a dangerous animal. His eyes seemed older than the rest of him. I was guessing he was in his early thirties.

Smoke hung in the air between us, and the room was cool and dark. My hands were still bound behind my back. His were free: one rested on the surface of the table; the other brought a cigarette to his lips.

"What weapons did you have?" He repeated the question, exhaling a puff of smoke.

"I didn't have any weapons."

"That seems impossible, wouldn't you say?"

I stuck my tongue in my cheek, considering the situation from his point of view. "But things that seem impossible often aren't."

He took a long drag off his cigarette and exhaled slowly. "What do you take me for, Lieutenant?"

I said nothing.

"*How* did you do that kind of damage to the Bullet car?" he asked, his gravelly voice dropping to a mechanical tone. "*How* did you escape?"

"With my bare hands, sir," I replied truthfully.

"There were two other members with you."

"Yes, sir."

"Where's the third?"

"Depends on which one you consider the third."

Donovan's jaw tightened.

"I don't know, sir," I replied before he could strangle me. "We got separated when the vapor hit."

"And it was just the three of you out there in the woods?"

"Yes, sir."

There was no way I was betraying Fin's position. He was a friend, yes, but beyond that, he was searching for Hawk. No matter how much I wished I was in his shoes, I knew he was the only chance we had of finding her.

"And you were separated from your comrade? Areos, I believe."

"Yes, sir."

"Did he assist in your escape?" Donovan asked. "From the car—did he do any of the damage?"

I shook my head.

"Icarus, what do you think of New Dublin?" he asked, in an abrupt, fake-out kind of way. "Is it up to the standards you were accustomed to in Section C? Do you find it as welcoming?"

My brow creased. "Welcoming isn't exactly a word I would use to describe Section C, sir."

Donovan tapped his cigarette, sending ash fluttering to the cold cement floor. "Oh, but you will once you've acclimated to your new home, I think. You'll soon be pining for the luxuries of Section C."

I waited a few seconds. "Sir, why is it that the orders were for us to be brought in alive?"

"Who told you that?"

"I'm a fighter pilot, sir," I reminded him. "I was out there every day, with commands to squelch disobedience."

He chuckled under his breath. "Of course you were. We're the Reformed

Global Militia… We cannot incline our ears to any opposing voices. We must drown out all but ours—isn't that what Hatch always says?"

The words were sharp ones. Almost resentful.

"You know Hatch?" I asked.

Donovan's gaze hardened. He said nothing—then the back of his hand whipped across my face. Pain sizzled through my jaw; my head was thrown to the side.

"Speak only when you are spoken to." The order was gruff, but freakishly calm. I slowly turned back to face him, the side of my face burning. "Lieutenant, you and your comrades were sent here because you explicitly disobeyed orders—you on more than one occasion. You also kidnapped one of your comrades, apparently?"

"That wasn't our intention."

"You miss my point, Lieutenant." His voice was neutral, his eyes lethal. "You were already a delinquent, but now you've rebelled against the very organization that spawned you. Now you're a *recusant*."

"So why haven't you had me executed, then?" I asked, my voice ragged.

"Perhaps we have other plans for you and your little friend." He dug a pack of cigarettes out of his breast pocket. "Or perhaps, here, we simply relish prolonging one's suffering."

His expression grew thoughtful as he studied the blackness around us. "Lieutenant, have you ever been to the Olympic Games?"

I could tell by the way he said it that he wasn't actually talking about *the* Olympics. Something inside me was already sinking. "No, sir," I replied quietly.

A smile twitched at his lips. "Well, you're in for a treat."

---

At Base New Dublin, the "Olympic Games" were a method of punishment. It involved hours of grueling physical endurance: rolling a massive, two-hundred-pound tire back and forth for hours on end, push-ups, pull-ups, bear crawls—all in a sopping pit of thick, shin-deep mud. Once finished, you were required to wear your dirty uniform for the next three days and go without food.

No, scratch "punishment": it was a method of *torture,* and I wasn't even the one doing it. Charlie was.

That was how it worked. You screwed up, your buddy went to the Games—and you were tied up and forced to watch.

The pit was dug at the far end of the base, right next to the burn area. It was dark now, and a large spotlight shone down into it. I was literally tied to a chair and seated at the edge, looking down at my comrade, who was barely recognizable under the slathering of dark brown sludge as she dropped to the ground to start the push-ups. The mud sucked her in up to her elbows.

I kicked myself over and over again as I sat there, watching helplessly. *What was I thinking?* I was such an idiot! Groveling and begging for forgiveness had been what was needed in my interrogation, not trying to teach Donovan a lesson. I'd come off as a loose cannon—someone to be broken. And Donovan seemed to have an intrinsic knack for breaking people.

Boiling over with rage and remorse, I had tried at one point to serenade Charlie with a pitiful speech about how unbelievably sorry I was. She replied only by flipping me off.

I heard footsteps approaching; I didn't look up to check who it was.

"Donovan invited you to the Games?" said a tense female voice. "He must've taken a real shine to you."

"Did you come here just to rub it in?" I attempted to jerk around to look at her, but it was a useless effort. "Why did you try to help us? Or was that some messed-up psycho head game, like this is?" I gestured with my head in the direction of the mud pit below.

A hand clamped down over my mouth from behind. I felt her nails against my skin and her hot breath as she leaned in.

"I hope you know how to show proper gratitude to someone who tried to help you, Icarus," she whispered. "You do that by keeping your mouth shut and not breathing one single word about what I…"

I made no effort to nod.

"I tried to do something stupid. I failed. If you told Donovan about it, I swear to god I'll tell Donovan about *you*," she whispered, releasing her grip with a slight jerk. "That is, if he doesn't already know."

"I didn't tell Donovan anything about you." I stressed the words. "Nothing—his questions had nothing to do with you. It was about the Bullet and how I escaped. And what do you mean 'if he doesn't already know'?" I asked finally. "How could he know about me?"

A long pause, filled with the splash, splash, splash of mud as Charlie continued with her tasks, a foreboding sergeant standing over her, shouting orders.

"Donovan has a nose for these things," she said at last.

"And you would know because?" I craned my neck, trying to catch a glimpse of her.

"Because I know," she replied sternly. "You've been in the RGM for what—a year? Less? I've been here for *five*, Lieutenant. I've learned a good deal in that time, I promise you."

"You sound bitter about it."

She stepped around to the front of my chair. Placing her hand on the back of it, she leaned in. Large green eyes. Fair skin. A faint spattering of freckles. A blond buzz cut capped by a burgundy beret.

"Why do you think I wanted to save you out there?" she whispered, seeming to search for something in my face. "Because I thought you were a freak of nature? Because I didn't understand how you obliterated my rifle?"

She shook her head briskly, answering her own question.

"No. I tried to save you because I…" Her voice snagged in her throat. "I felt like I was meant to find you. I saved you because you're the first person I've ever… I've ever found who's like me," she whispered almost frantically. "And that's why I didn't tell Donovan what happened."

My eyes widened. "What do you mean you're like me? Who are you?"

"Moran!"

The young soldier in front of me snapped to attention.

"Donovan wants you in his office," the voice called. "Oh five hundred hours—first thing tomorrow morning."

She gave a curt nod, her face sheet white. My mind was churning as I stared at her, detecting something strangely familiar about her face.

"Moran..." I tested the name out carefully. "Is that your last name?"

Her gaze flicked to me suspiciously. She gave a tentative nod.

"What's your first name?" I asked.

She turned on her heel and began to walk away.

"None of your business."

---

"I hate you, Icarus. I hate you, I hate you, *I hate you*. You know what? Next time they interrogate *me*, I'm going to run *my* mouth and get *myself* a frickin' invitation to the Games to watch *you!*"

"I'm *sorry!*" I repeated for what felt like the hundredth time that night. "I didn't know that would happen—I would have gladly taken your place!"

Charlie snorted, throwing me an angry look. "Are you saying I'm incapable of doing it?"

I dragged a hand wearily over my face. "No, Charlie, *obviously not*. I'm just—I'm *sorry*."

She snorted again, pacing the small windowless cement room; dried mud caked her skin. I sat on the floor with my back to the wall.

"Whatever," she muttered, taking a large breath to say more, though she only repeated the word with more emphasis. "*Whatever*."

Neither of us said anything else for a while. I lost myself in thought.

"There's something going on with the sniper who captured us," I announced at length. "Moran."

"You mean the loser who tried to help us escape and then changed her mind three seconds later?"

I shot her a glance, my head back against the cold cement. "Let's face it, Charlie—we wouldn't have been able to anyway. And she knew it."

"Then why'd she even try to get away in the first place?"

"Because she saw."

"What? Your outburst?"

I tilted my head. "She saw I had power—that's why she tried to save us. Even when she realized she couldn't, she didn't tell them about me…"

Charlie halted in the middle of the room, mud oozing from her boots. "Why, though? Why wouldn't she tell them what you did?"

"Because for some reason she had mercy on us."

Charlie raised one blond eyebrow. "Mercy? What is it with you and these strange words that make no sense?"

I withheld a sigh. "It's a bit like love."

"Okay… so like me dragging you out of the woods?"

I shook my head. "More like… if I screwed something up royally, and you had the opportunity to get back at me but chose not to." I shot her a pointed look. "That's mercy."

She frowned, reaching up to wipe the mud out of her eyes. "I guess I don't like mercy."

But Moran did. An Irish RGM sniper—the best of the best, it seemed, judging by the amount of respect she received from her comrades, yet she'd decided not to report my actions.

*"You're the first person I've ever found who's like me."*

What did that mean?

Who *was* she?

# CHAPTER NINETEEN

## *Lara*

The Byrd had flown me and my two captives back to Base New Dublin. I'd sat mute, a sick feeling in my stomach. I'd kept staring at Icarus, both flabbergasted and amazed, but also horrified at the thought that I could lose him to the RGM. I didn't know what they were going to do to him. For all I knew, they were planning to test a new method of execution and needed guinea pigs.

I felt nauseated as I sat considering the potential outcomes, and even more so when I pondered all the things I should have done to help them escape. I shouldn't have been so selfish—I shouldn't have tried to run away myself. Maybe if I hadn't, they could have gotten away.

But the thought of freedom… Oh, it had been so tempting. How I had longed so desperately for it.

When we arrived back at the base, my prisoners were escorted away to a cell. Icarus was to be interrogated, which only left me with an even more intense feeling of dread as I sat on the edge of my bunk in the barracks, trying to stay calm, trying to think, with Ronan's note pressed between my fingertips.

Icarus would report me; I knew he would… This was it. This would destroy me. There was no way I would get away with disobeying orders on that scale. Yes, I'd abandoned the idea, but I'd tried my utmost to rebel, and in the eyes of the RGM, that was enough for a death sentence. But to my surprise, Icarus's interrogation came and went, and I was never summoned.

When I'd finally ventured outside, I found that the Games were in session, and Icarus was the spectator. I tried my level best to get the upper hand over him—threatening to tell Donovan everything I knew if he so much as breathed a word about what I had tried to do. But keeping it together was harder than I expected.

There was something so different about him. My guard had slipped, and I'd said too much: I'd told him *why* I had tried to save him.

I kicked myself a thousand times after that. I didn't know Icarus; I couldn't trust him, not yet—not with something this important. I had to protect myself.

That was what I told myself that night when I couldn't sleep. That was what I told myself as I rose the next morning, washed, and changed into a starched uniform. That was what I repeated to myself over and over again as I walked the muddy road to Donovan's office.

I found him standing at the window.

"Sir." I saluted.

He gestured for me to relax. I stood in front of his desk and waited for him to speak. I noticed that everything that had been on his desk the day before was now gone. Everything was tidy and spotless: no trace of the papers, notes and the photo that I'd seen before.

"I trust you slept well, Corporal," he began at length. "After your grueling hike yesterday."

"Yes, sir."

"Quite a ways up there, wasn't it?" He stared out over the street. "Your trek into the Wicklow Mountains."

There was a brief pause.

"Well?" he said abruptly. "Aren't you going to tell me about it?"

"Tell you about it, sir?"

"Yes, Moran. The details."

My stomach sank. *The details.*

"It went without a hitch, sir," I began as he turned from the window to face me. "I followed the map. I found the targets. I apprehended them."

"That easily?"

I cleared my throat softly. "There were two of them, sir. I don't know that I would say it was easy, but everything was done as efficiently as possible, I can assure you of that."

He walked over to the desk, but instead of taking a seat, he remained standing. He looked me straight in the eyes. "I can always count on you to carry out orders with the utmost efficiency, can't I?"

"Yes, sir."

He leaned forward slightly. "Did you experience any technical difficulties?"

I nodded. "Yes, sir. The signal for my headset was lost. I couldn't hear you or reach you until I had finally apprehended the targets."

"You couldn't hear me?"

"No, sir."

Donovan gave my face a slow once-over before his eyes locked with mine again. "What a pity," he began softly. "Because I could hear you loud and clear the whole time, Moran."

My mouth ran instantly dry as I stood there and stared at my commander, every muscle in my body tightening like a spring. A sickening surge of dread filled my belly.

"Yes, that's right," he affirmed with a nod. "I know. I heard it all, Corporal—the conversation. The idea."

I went cold, watching as a grin twitched on his mouth.

"You never lost the signal," he explained smoothly. "You simply believed exactly what I wanted you to believe."

My voice was frozen in my throat.

"Yes, Moran. I made you think that you had lost the signal—I made you think I couldn't hear you because, since the day you were inducted, since the day I began training you, I knew." He leaned forward. "I knew there was something more to you than met the eye. I knew you were different."

My heart dropped. Suddenly snapping out of it, I began shaking my head violently. "No—no, you are wrong. There is nothing different about me! I am ordinary!"

"Oh, but you are *not*, Moran." He almost laughed. "You are the furthest thing from."

"I swear to you, I am the same as every other soldier here."

"Not every soldier would run. Only the cowardly or the insane would attempt that, and I know you to be neither," he said, searching my face. "You tried to run because you wanted to save the recusants you found. You wanted to save them because you are *one of them*."

He put up a hand before I could say a word.

"I wanted to know what you would do when no one was watching you, Moran," he went on intently. "I wanted to see how you would handle the situation if you were out there entirely on your own. I wanted to find out."

"Sir, please, I swear—"

"What, Moran?" He cut me off with a question of his own. "That you're not a recusant? That I'm mistaken? I have proof! You cannot deny your own actions!"

"I am a soldier!" My voice came out in tatters. "I am an RGM sniper— I wish the militia no harm! I wish only to do my duty!"

"Your duty?" he reiterated. "Your *duty?* Are you serious? Helping escaped, renegade members of the RGM further succeed in running away? How on earth does that equate to doing your duty?"

It didn't. I was only digging myself in deeper. I sucked in a breath.

"You heard everything?" I asked quietly.

"I did: the moment you found them, the struggle that ensued, and then your decision to help them."

*The struggle.* That was what he had heard. I'd disposed of my busted weapon as soon as I'd arrived back on base, before anyone had seen. My commander had no idea exactly *what* the struggle had consisted of. For this, at least, I was grateful.

"And now you will have me executed," I concluded.

My statement was followed by an agonizingly long silence.

"Did I say that?" he asked.

Almost unable to believe what I had just heard, I looked up at him.

"Did I say I would have you executed?" he repeated, his face unreadable.

"I… I assumed."

"Lara," he said finally, his voice dropping as he reverted to my first name, "I knew long before I sent you out there. These events are an affirmation of my suspicions, not a revelation."

My mouth went dry. "But if you knew all this time…"

"Why did I not turn you in?" he asked when I trailed off. "Why did I not report you and have you executed like every other host with a defective Frag?" He tossed me a look, as though the answer to this question was already evident. "If you found a valuable tool, Lara, would you throw it away simply because you were told you must not touch it?"

I waited for him to go on, saying nothing.

He shook his head. "No. I wasn't going to lose something I'd spent my life looking for."

"You were looking for me, sir?" I asked in surprise. "I don't understand."

"You don't have to. You only have to accept that I will not report you–" his gaze was firm "—if you, in turn, do something for me."

My stomach was already in knots, and this did nothing to lessen the effect. I stared with dread into Donovan's eyes, feeling as though I were shrinking.

"The day may come that I will ask a favor of you," he explained quietly. "And when that day comes, you will obey me, at all costs."

I searched his eyes for some scrap of something I could trust. I nodded.

"These are changing times, Corporal." His voice was still quiet. "We live on shifting sand. We think we have accomplished, we think we have conquered… but in a tinder-dry forest, it takes but a spark…"

Something strange passed through his dark brown eyes, an expression like fear and hope married together, a fleeting something I could scarcely identify before it had dissipated and he once again straightened.

"You will speak of this to no one, Moran," he stated coldly. "No one— do you understand?"

I gulped, nodding. "Yes, sir."

"I cannot hear you."

"Yes, sir!"

"Good." He gave a single nod. "You may go."

I saluted, turned and started for the door. I hesitated. "Sir?"

He lifted an eyebrow and waited.

"The recusants who are being held prisoner…" I began, trailing off.

"Yes?"

I faltered. "What will be done with them?"

Donovan's eyes narrowed slightly. He hadn't moved. "Is it any concern of yours, Corporal?"

"No, sir."

"Quite right, Corporal."

I opened the door and stepped back outside into the cool, early-morning air. Generators hummed, young trainees scurried to and from the bath house and barracks, and the occasional shot sounded as the more experienced soldiers began target practice out on the nearby flats. Fog hung in the air, and the damp landscape sprawling before me was an ombre wash of browns and grays, scented with ash and gasoline.

My surroundings were grim, yet I could somehow see the beauty as I stood there at the edge of the base, trapped in a moment of stillness. For a moment there was no Donovan, there was no secret, there were no favors to be asked of me, and there was even no Icarus. In a few moments the base would burst to life and I would be forced to move on, to go about my daily routine and pretend that everything was normal when nothing was; nothing had been since the day Ronan had left us, and standing there, I couldn't help but feel that nothing ever would be.

I was about to take a step forward when a cold hand clamped down over my mouth from behind, jerking me backward.

I snapped into fight mode, delivering a sharp jab to my assailant's ribs with my elbow. A male voice grunted as I knocked the wind out of him, along with a few choice words, but he didn't release his grip.

"Stop moving!" he hissed. "I'm not going to hurt you!"

I drove the heel of my boot into his shin and wrenched away, but before I could put any distance between us, he grabbed me by the shoulders, slamming me back against the side of the building.

"Not a word—" The hand clamped over my mouth again; his grip was like iron. I stared into a set of wild hazel eyes. "Not a word and I swear I won't hurt you."

I finally focused: he was tall, slim, with a wiry build and a buzz cut. His cheeks were swathed in stubble. I recognized his RGM uniform immediately, though his jacket, which would have been badged with his respective rank, was missing.

I shoved him away, hard, but he instantly grabbed me by the shoulders once more.

"People who grab you from behind and drag you behind a building rarely wish you no harm," I growled icily. "Release me."

The young man shook his head. "I'll release you after you tell me what I need to know."

I quirked an eyebrow. "I don't have to tell you anything—"

"I'm an RGM member; surely you must see that!"

"I see an impostor!" I gave him another firm shove and it was finally enough to jolt him away. Before I could turn to escape, he stopped me in my tracks again—but this time it wasn't by force.

"I believe you have information about the two new prisoners here."

I halted, my heels sinking into the muddy ground. I turned around and looked at him, giving him another long once-over. "It depends on who's asking."

"I am an RGM fighter pilot from Section C," he stated.

"Section C," I repeated carefully, staring at him. "Isn't that where…"

"They're here, then?"

I stepped closer, folding my arms over my stiff black uniform. "Why do you want to know?"

"He's my friend."

"He?" I asked, coming to a stop in front of him. "I thought you just said there was more than one."

A brisk nod. "Yes, ma'am. But it's… it's Icarus I'm trying to find."

*Icarus.*

A telling look must have washed over my face.

"He is here, then. I knew it!" His jaw clenched as he looked me right in the eyes again. "Take me to him. Now."

My eyebrows twitched. "I don't have to do one thing you ask. You do realize that, don't you? With one scream I could have every gun on this base aimed at your skull, boy—is that what you want?"

He stared at me, not afraid, but seemingly puzzled. "I don't think you'd do that."

I grunted dubiously. "You have no idea who I am. What makes you think that I wouldn't?"

He gave this a nanosecond of consideration before giving his calm, collected reply. "Because you would have already."

I closed the gap between us, getting right in his face and narrowing my eyes. "How do you know Icarus?"

He scanned my face, an inquiring look on his own. "I told you: he's my friend. We both served in Section C." Then he spat the question back at me. "How do *you* know him?"

He was cocky and a renegade—I knew it by the look of him, the smell of him, the sound of him. I wasn't inclined to like him, so instead I decided to put him in his place.

"I know him because I'm the one who captured him," I said firmly, not looking away. "And I'll do the exact same to you in a minute."

"No, no, no, wait!" he hissed as I turned to leave. He clutched my wrist, though this time his fingers didn't close nearly as tightly. "I'm sorry. I just— it was you? You were the one who captured him?"

"Them," I corrected him coolly. "And yes. Is that so hard to believe?"

He didn't respond to the question and he didn't let go. "Please, tell me where they've taken him!"

I shook my head. "I can't do that. I don't even know who you are."

"A friend."

I frowned. "I'm afraid that's not good enough."

He opened his mouth to reply but was interrupted by a voice over a loudspeaker, calling all personnel to the courtyard for daily assignments. In just a moment, the base would burst to life. In a moment, everyone would be outside.

"You'd better get out of here, *now*." I dropped my voice. "You'll be discovered!"

A resolute expression had settled onto his face. "I'm not leaving without Icarus."

"Then you won't be leaving at all," I hissed back, "because they'll capture you too! Now go!" I insisted feverishly. "Get out however you came in, and hide in the woods!"

"But I must speak with you!"

I was already walking briskly away. I paused only to turn and glance at him over my shoulder. "Just go—I will find you."

"When?" he blurted. "And—and how?"

"I know the woods like I know myself," I told him firmly. "I will come to you tonight. Now go!"

There was a moment of hesitation as he stood there staring at me. I glanced back over my shoulder as I walked away, but he was already gone.

# CHAPTER TWENTY

## *Fin*

"My father used to say that the forest is essential. He never quite explained what he meant by that; he didn't have to. I grew to know what it meant the more I spent time in it."

Hawk was perched several branches above me. She peered down, her head tilted to the side, watching with intent eyes as I climbed the massive elm.

I reached up and took hold of the next thick, rough branch, testing its merit before giving it my full body weight. I squinted up through the sunlight at Hawk. She hopped up to a higher branch, staying just out of reach.

"What?" I inquired, giving her a look. "What's that face for?"

She flapped her wings.

"I have tried to heal the forest, Hawk," I replied. "My mind, my heart—they're just not working together. I don't know why."

I wiped the sweat off my forehead. My hair was tied back in a knot, and my beard was laced with sweat. Spring was turning slowly to summer, and the temperatures were beginning to reflect the transition.

"It feels like I'm trying to *make* something happen, not just allowing it to flow effortlessly," I confessed as I searched for my next foothold. "It's a strange feeling… It never used to be that way."

Hawk chirped a laugh, seeming to entice me farther up the tree.

"You can laugh about it—you, the Sunrise!" I countered, climbing higher. "I'm just your humble servant. A gardener who seems to have lost his green thumb."

She lifted herself to the next branch, stretching her strong ivory wings as she did. I couldn't help but pause a moment and watch her, smiling to myself. For a slider who could no longer shift or execute power in any form, she was still mightier than all of us put together. In her sharp eyes, I could still see the Sunrise.

As I looked at her, resting between two branches, my mind drifted back to the dream I'd had of Sensei. I was beginning to realize that I'd completed my mission to find Hawk, and now a new one had been granted me: I had to find a way to help restore her to her alternate form.

But how could I do that? How could I, when Icarus held her soul? Her soul was what made her the slider she was. When Sensei had brought her into the Dimension, she had become far beyond human. Now she had given that power to Icarus.

As I climbed the rest of the way up the tree, I couldn't help but wonder what that left me to work with. I brushed away the thought, reaching for the next branch and the next until at last there were no more. My toes gripped the bark as I balanced and stood, attaching my hands to two other branches.

The endless view of the Irish countryside opened before me. In the distance were humps like the backs of dragons: mountains frozen forever in shades of brown and gray; hills and valleys and lakes that used to be alive and bursting at the seams with birds and deer and foxes, and humming with bees that pollinated the blankets of flowers that covered the valleys and grew along the shores of the lakes.

I heaved a sigh, slowly turning my head to take it all in. Hawk was perched just above me, on the tip of the highest branch. The wind ruffled the feathers on her face as she peered at the world far below.

"I told Areos that we couldn't fix this," I said softly. "I told him we could only heal it. I believe in those words more than anything, yet what do I know about healing?" I turned to look up at her. "I don't even know where to start."

Before she could reply, a crack rang through the air, and the bough collapsed beneath me. The air was sucked out of my lungs as I felt myself slipping.

I dropped a few feet—then caught myself on a lower branch with both hands. The bark bit into my skin, and I caught my lip between my teeth as pain seared through my palms and rippled up my arms. Hawk shrieked and barreled down through the branches to find me, landing on the same branch.

"I'm all right," I panted, gazing around for another more secure branch. "I'm fine, I swear…"

I swung back and forth until I had built up enough momentum. Then I swung myself to land on a stout branch a bit lower. I straddled it and leaned back against the tree trunk to catch my breath again. Hawk gazed at me for a moment before fluttering down to join me.

Dry bits of leaves and bark showered down like dust. As I reached up to swat away the particles of debris, I noticed my hand was bleeding. Spreading my palm, I examined the cut.

"Just a little scrape," I said, wiping the blood on my jeans. "I'll heal it when we get—"

I stopped and stared at her, a sudden idea roaring in my thoughts, silencing all else.

Hawk tilted her head from side to side, staring at me. I glanced back down at my hand, at the pooling blood.

*What do I have left to work with, indeed…*

———————————

Lifeblood—such an expression. It seemed to encompass the very meaning of this wild ride we had all respectively found ourselves on since entering the Dimension and realizing who we were as sliders. Blood was reason; blood was identity. We all carried this blood within us, this thrust to find the why behind our existence; we were all in this race, and we would all arrive at the finish line… only to find that it was a starting line.

I couldn't help but feel, sitting there in that tree, looking from my hand to Hawk, that I had found my reason for being. I'd found my purpose.

I climbed back down the tree and built a fire, ignoring her questioning looks. We were high in the mountains of Wicklow now; there was no one and nothing for miles. We were alone and tucked into a small clearing between clusters of birch trees. The fire burned between us until I finally rose to join her on the other side, resolved in what I must do.

"Hawk, just because you left the Dimension does not mean you left my thoughts—you were in every single one of them…" I paused, my heart beating a little faster from letting myself say it. I took a steady breath.

"Before Icarus even returned, I pieced together what had happened to the fallen sliders, and realized who Raiden really was… that Edwin had been racing you through time, stealing the lives and powers of other sliders to keep himself immortal. I knew he was the one down there with you, and that you would have to defeat him in order for you or Icarus to make it out alive," I explained quietly, looking into her eyes. "I also knew that Icarus would never come back to the Dimension unless a sacrifice was made to bring him back. We created the code, we established the law, so we had to live by it. The only way so-called justice could be upheld was if…"

I swallowed back the rest as Hawk looked down at herself.

"Edwin stole the lives of other sliders," I started again. "He exploited the laws of entanglement by taking lives. Death can be the only result of such selfishness. But what if it was used to give life, Hawk?" I asked, my voice coming out softer now. "What if… what if we used it to give you back yours?"

Her eyes darted up to meet mine, suddenly wide and alert. She stepped back, shaking her head violently.

"Hear me out, Hawk, *please*—hear me out," I quickly continued. "We're all sliders—you, me, all of us—but buried beneath each slider is a human. Let me give you my human side, just as you gave Icarus your soul."

She looked startled, but I put up a hand before she could make a sound.

"I'll still be a slider, Hawk. I will still be just as I am now—in fact, it will force me to snap out of this stupor I've been stuck in since we lost you! It will force me to be the slider I am, to stop fearing it. And you…" My voice faded; my gaze softened. "It will give you back your human form. Not your powers, but your ability to go find Icarus and reclaim them."

Hawk took one more step back but then stopped. She wasn't shaking her head anymore.

"You weren't made to live like this, Hawk. Sensei doesn't intend for you to spend your days and nights out here in the wastelands—he expects more of you than that. Can't you see?" I searched her face. "He created you for so much more…"

My throat tightened, and I stopped.

"Hawk, I would do anything for you," I said softly. "I would give up my *whole* life for you, never mind just my human side until yours is restored. I'm only asking you to let me. For you, and for us…"

Hawk stared at me, not moving. Then at last she stepped closer.

Kneeling before her, I looked inquiringly into her eyes and she stared up into mine. Finally, she bowed her head in a consenting nod, and a faint smile passed over my lips.

I took my knife from my pocket, the one I'd used daily to carve the notches into the oak tree, marking the days I'd spent searching for her. Now I used it to make similar cuts on the palms of my hands. Blood rose to the surface of my skin. Lifeblood.

Hawk spread her wings, giving me permission to make the same careful cuts along her flesh. My hands trembled as I did so, a feeling of sacrilege tugging at my conscience as blood began to stain her pure white feathers.

When I finished, I drew a quivering breath. "Ready?"

Hawk nodded and kept her wings spread wide. I leaned closer and gently allowed my hands to make contact with them. Our wounds bled into each other, my blood spilling into hers and hers into mine.

A strange swirling, dizzying sensation came over me, at first like rain, and then like floodwater. The sounds around me seemed to ebb and fade away with the white noise that filled my ears. I felt my body less and less, until it seemed almost as though I didn't have one at all. Something scorched me from the inside like a flame, then turned to ice.

It felt like there was lightning in my veins, coursing through me. My body went weightless, and for a moment the earth seemed to slow… stop.

Then sound came roaring back into my senses, and I was no longer kneeling but standing. My eyes were closed, and the dizziness came in one last surge before it, too, faded. I leaned forward; my forehead made contact with skin. Feeling slowly returned, and with it, the realization that the wings I'd so gently taken in my grasp were no longer wings.

They were hands.

# CHAPTER TWENTY-ONE

*Icarus*

I was in a sterile white room, alone and reclined in a chair with various arms and intimidatingly scientific-looking apparatuses extending from it. There was a long slender needle stuck in my arm and another in my leg. My hair had been shaved down to the skin, and my skull was covered in tiny, sticky metal sensors that were transmitting whatever information they were gathering to some sort of probably equally scary-looking system located elsewhere. Everything was blindingly bright and stank of bleach; a sizzling hum akin to a dying streetlight substituted for silence.

I'd been startled awake at 0600 hours and dragged off my cot by an armed guard. Charlie had been similarly roused, except she had sworn loudly through the whole process and at one point tried to bite the guard's hand.

As soon as we were out of the cell, a cloth sack was slipped over my head. After a while, I was totally disoriented. Yard upon yard of echoing cement floor passed under my feet, and I could no longer hear Charlie. The sack was removed only when we had entered the smelly room with the sizzling lights.

A nurse with a pinched face, wearing gray, robe-like scrubs, had then replaced the guard.

"Sit," he said. Like I was a dog.

I hated it, but I did everything I was told to. They shaved my head, took my temperature and blood pressure, and checked my reflexes. Then the needles were inserted. I squeezed my eyes shut as they pierced my flesh.

"What are you doing to me?" I'd asked at one point.

The nurse had looked at me with cold, gray eyes and then continued with his work. After I was all hooked up, he told me to stay still and quiet, and that he would be back soon.

I didn't like the word *soon*. It was ambiguous and left lots of room for interpretation. The nurse apparently defined *soon* as a very, very long time.

I was tired. I wanted to close my eyes, but I was afraid to. I needed to stay alert. I needed to pay attention.

Eternity seemed to pass as I sat there and examined the ceiling, listening to my heart pound like fists against a locked door. I wondered what was going on, where they had taken Charlie, and what on earth they were planning to do with us.

Finally, the nurse returned. Wordlessly, he started picking off the leech-like sensors.

I cleared my throat after a minute or two of silence. "Verdict?"

"Perfect health."

I squinted at him through the bright lights. "Is this like a complimentary checkup? Does it come with my stay?"

This didn't amuse him. He finished with my head, removed the needles, and then tapped the screen on his wrist. "Patient number zero-seven is ready to exit."

There was a brief silence. Then a long dull tone sounded, and a door at the end of the room slid open with a *psshhh*. The guard strode back in, stern-faced and armed.

"We will see you again soon," said the nurse.

That word again: *soon*.

Before I could say another word, the sack was back over my head, and I was once again being forcefully towed down the hallway.

After a while I heard the heavy grinding of an iron door. The guard pulled the sack off my head and gave me a firm push. I stumbled into the room, and the door slammed shut behind me. It took a moment for my eyes to adjust in the dimly lit cell. A moment later I noticed Charlie seated on a bunk, her head shaved down to the skin to match mine.

She blinked sluggishly. "Icarus?"

I dropped onto a cot opposite hers. "They examined you too?"

"Yes! What the hell was that all about? They acted like it was just routine," Charlie said, puzzled. "But being a medic, I know that's not true."

She got up and started pacing, her heavy footsteps thudding on the cement.

"Maybe we'll find out more the next time they drag us back in there," I said.

"What do you mean?"

"The lice-bag who stuck me full of needles made it pretty clear that this wouldn't be my only trip to the infirmary."

Charlie's footsteps halted. "Really?"

I nodded.

"The nurse that worked on *me* said they wouldn't need to see me again," she informed me, confused.

"Are you sure?"

"That's what he said." Charlie frowned thoughtfully, looking at me. "They must have found something."

A twisting feeling tugged at my gut. "Or didn't find something…"

"What?"

I touched the back of my head lightly. "I don't have a Fragment."

"That's impossible, though. Everyone does."

I sighed. "Not me. I'm… I just don't have one."

Charlie shook her head. "I don't understand."

"That's right… You… *can't* understand that I *don't* have one because you *do*…" I took a deep breath. "The database won't allow you to know that there was a time when no one had Fragments. It won't let you even consider the idea that someone could not have one…"

Charlie's eyebrows knitted together in confusion. "I don't get it."

"Okay, then just—just don't think about that part of it, okay? They obviously saw that your Fragment was intact and that you're not a recusant. They won't bother you now. I'm surprised they even brought you back here."

I thought back to the night on the Bullet and our escape after I'd blown open the side of the car. I rewound to our grueling trek through the woods with my injuries, the minefield, and finally finding Fin. I retraced our steps to Fin's shelter, recalling that night and the following morning when the Griffon had spotted us and attempted to smother us in Death Vapor. I remembered my order to split up, though Charlie had stayed by my side, and how the Griffon had seemed to make a U-turn, gliding back over the forest just to follow Charlie and me…

It would have been impossible to see us from the air that day. I knew: I'd been up there. There was no way he had just spotted us. He'd already known we were there.

My gaze shifted to Charlie, to the tiny scar at the back of her head.

Charlie had to have been the one being tracked; she had a Fragment, and though I wasn't sure, I couldn't shake the feeling that there was some sort of tracking hardware wired into each Frag. How else would they be able to track down RGM members if they went missing? It would make sense, and it would explain how they had found Charlie and me: they had been tracking her.

All day, I considered the implications of my theory as I paced our cell.

If they were tracking missing members through their Frags, they wouldn't necessarily have realized that I didn't have one… They would probably have assumed I had a *defective* Frag, which, to them, would explain my behavioral tenancies. I mean, that *was* the reason Hatch had sent me here, wasn't it? For disobedience.

I had way too many questions and very few answers. I could only hope and pray that Areos and Fin were safe—and as far away from this place as possible. Charlie was asleep now, her head tipped back and her mouth hanging open. She didn't stir as the large iron door creaked steadily open.

Corporal Moran stepped in, unarmed. She checked over her shoulder before softly shutting the door behind her.

"Corporal," I said softly.

She quietly crossed the room and stopped in front of me. "I've been trying to come to you, but it has been impossible."

"I'm surprised to see you here."

The expression on her face was conflicted, unreadable. "You know I would have helped you escape if I could, Icarus."

"I don't know that for sure," I replied steadily. "I don't know you at all."

"I can understand your suspicion. But if you knew what I went through to be where I am today…" Her words faded as she pressed her eyes shut for a moment. "I know you don't trust me, Icarus—and you don't have to. But I am going to get you out of here. I *swear* it on all that I am. You have something we need, Icarus, whether anyone realizes it or not—*we need you.*"

"What are you talking about?" My eyes grew narrow as I stared at her.

"Icarus, you have capabilities that no one on Earth has."

"You don't know that."

"Yes, I do."

"Yeah?" My eyes shifted back up to hers. "And you would know this because you're like me, right?"

She nodded hesitantly.

"And what do you mean by that, exactly?"

She didn't answer. Instead, she scanned the room and walked over to a tiny weed growing out of a crack in the leaky cement. I watched, not sure what to expect.

Moran lifted a hand, palm spread, to hover just above the tiny seedling. For a moment nothing happened; then, slowly, the tiny sprout began to tremble. I sat there stunned as the plant swelled and cascaded down the wall. Abruptly she balled her hand into a fist, and it halted its progression, swaying back to stillness.

She turned back to give me a hard stare. "Do you believe me now, Icarus?"

My mouth opened, then closed. I swiftly crossed the cell and stopped beside her. My gaze shifted from the plant to her face.

"How did you do that?" I dropped my voice to a whisper. "Who are you?"

Her emerald eyes stared up into mine, sharp as knives, with a softness hidden beneath. There was something so hauntingly familiar about her, but I just couldn't put my finger on it.

"I've already told you," she replied quietly. "Someone like you."

"But how?" I whispered, almost more to myself than her. "How is that possible? There are no sliders left on Earth…"

"Sliders?"

"People like us," I replied. "I've only ever seen one person do what you just did to that plant—Fin."

"I know nothing of sliders and nothing of this 'Fin.'" She shot a wary glance towards the door. "But I must talk fast, Icarus. We don't have much time, and I must leave you before we are discovered—your friend is here."

"My friend?" I repeated.

"Areos."

My mouth ran dry. "Did they…?"

Moran shook her head, apparently perceiving my thoughts. "No. Fortunately, the stupid boy chose to grab *me* for his inquisition," she replied. "He demanded that I bring him to see you, but I told him that was impossible."

"You need to tell him to stay away."

"I told him to get off base and hide—that I would find him tonight if I can get assigned night patrol…"

"They want him back," I told her gravely. "Donovan told me so—no doubt to examine him too. You have to *make sure* he doesn't come back. Tell him I said—"

"Examine?" she cut in. "They were examining you?"

"They brought me to some sort of infirmary early this morning," I explained. "Charlie too, except it seems they want me back. I think it… I think they know I don't have a Frag."

Moran's eyes were as large as saucers. "What did this *infirmary* look like?"

"It was pretty empty, really, except for a weird-looking chair, where they hooked me up to a bunch of—"

"That's not the infirmary."

I looked at her, swallowing the rest of my sentence.

"What, then?" I asked.

The color had drained from Moran's face. "That's the experimentation lab."

# CHAPTER TWENTY-TWO

## *Hawk*

Everything was ablaze. I felt like I was melting away to nothing, and for a split second I was filled with terror. I felt disconnected from the only body and form I had left; I was spinning, completely disoriented. I wanted to scream, but I had no voice. Then, as quickly as it had begun, it was all over. The fire ebbed away like a receding wave, and I was breathing again. Everything was still a blur, still swirling, but after a moment the fog began to lift.

First came sound: the gentle crackling of a fire. The familiar swish of wind dancing in the treetops. My own lungs gasping for air, except now, there was the tone of my own voice in each inhale. The sensation of touch returned: hands in mine. Skin against skin. A warm forehead against my own. Gentle breath on my face.

I opened my eyes, blinking a few times as everything came back into focus. A set of familiar, sparkling green eyes met mine. Eyes I'd stared into for what seemed like eternity, yet somehow this felt like the first time I'd ever seen them. I drew a breath, my lips curving into a smile.

"Fin."

That was all I could manage. That one word, yet it felt as if the whole world were inside it.

I stepped back, breathing heavily, looking down at myself, down at my legs and arms and hands and feet. A white tunic covered my arms halfway, a soft leatherlike strap looped over my shoulder, joining to the belt that circled around my waist, and soft, fitted green pants ran to my knees.

My head was spinning as my hands flew up to cover my smile. I looked up again at Fin, at his long hair and beard; he smelled of the mountains after the rain. Tears welled in my eyes, and I laughed, almost a sob, as I repeated his name again, this time a joyous shout as I threw my arms around his neck and buried my face in his chest.

"*Fin!*"

He folded me in his arms and spun me around. "Hawk!"

He set me down, pulling away just enough to look at me. He cupped my face in his hands and looked at me, tears glimmering in his eyes.

"It's really you..." he whispered, stroking my cheek with his thumb. "You're human..."

I reached up for one of his hands, giving it a gentle squeeze. "Thanks to you."

A tear slipped down his cheek, but he smiled. "Look at you. I can hardly believe it..."

I studied myself again, every bit as dumbfounded. This time I noticed something I hadn't before: over my shoulder hung a long braid, as pure and white as my feathers had been. My fingers brushed it, and I looked up at Fin. "My hair is... white?"

"It... seems so." He stepped closer to examine it. "You gave your life to Icarus, Hawk—your soul. You may look—and feel—a bit different than you did before."

I was already noticing the differences as he spoke. Aside from my hair, my skin was pale and my nails were white and opaque.

"Fin." I looked up at him. "What color are my eyes?"

The question seemed to catch him slightly off guard. He opened his mouth as if to respond, but then didn't. His eyes seemed to trace every feature of my face before slowing and seeming to delve into my eyes. He exhaled quietly, saying nothing, and for a moment it felt like everything stopped.

"They're as they have always been," he replied softly. "But you are changed, Hawk."

"Human…" I sighed. "I haven't been a human in so long… Is it… is it wrong that it should feel so… good?"

A far-off look lingered in Fin's eyes as he stared into mine. Then, slowly, that same smile reclaimed its shape.

"I don't think it's wrong," he said, reaching up to brush a loose strand of hair out of my face. "I think it's perfect…" His voice faded, then collapsed to a whisper. "I think *you* are perfect…"

For a second my gaze shifted back and forth between his eyes. I wrapped my arms around his neck, resting my head against his shoulder.

"I missed you so much, Fin…" I whispered, tears blurring my vision. "Thank you…"

For a moment he said nothing. I could hear the pounding of his heart in his chest.

"For what, Hawk?"

I pulled back, looking up into his face, his deep, green eyes.

"For not giving up on me." My response was a cracked whisper. "For never giving up…"

He started to reply, then stopped abruptly as something else caught his attention.

Around his bare feet were bursts of bright green: fresh spring grass. He stumbled backwards slightly, startled, as the fresh new growth chased his footsteps, breaking out across the ground as he stepped backward a few paces.

My fingertips came to rest involuntarily against my lips as I stood there, staring wide-eyed as a mossy green path painted itself across the ground in the shapes of Fin's footprints.

Still walking backwards, staring at the ground, Fin caught his heel on a root. Tripping, he steadied himself against the trunk of the massive dead elm. With a sound like a great, slumbering groan, a warm auburn hue shot from Fin's fingertips, rippling up the trunk of the tree like a raging river, wrapping the trunk, spiraling farther and farther up, gaining speed and momentum until, with a great and roaring surge, the branches exploded into life. A green so pure it was nearly iridescent rippled its way through every branch until it had reached the very top, where it stopped, disseminating into a puff of what looked like breath.

I could practically see Fin's heart pounding through his T-shirt. He stared up at the treetop, gasping for air. Blinking, I followed the lush mossy path towards him. Finally, he looked down at me.

I smiled. "You've changed too, Fin."

He stepped closer to me again, the forest floor coming to life beneath his every footfall. "It's… it's back," he whispered, staring up at the tree. "I don't know about you," he said breathlessly, extending a hand, "but I'd say it was time we woke the forest up."

My eyes slowly traced their way up through the foliage, which glimmered in the sunlight. The massive branches above us were filled with life and leaves, reaching skyward like worshiping hands. I looked back at Fin, unable to keep my smile at bay. I grasped his hand.

Our footsteps quickened and, together, we ran through the forest, a river of life flowing behind us in rich ripples of deep green as plants pushed up through the ground. A sound like ten thousand children taking their first breaths filled the air around us, rising like an anthem from the groaning earth as it stretched and awakened beneath our pounding feet, as Fin's fingertips brushed against every single tree.

Like ice melting, the decaying world of browns and grays gave way to explosive emerald shades of *life*.

# CHAPTER TWENTY-THREE

## *Lara*

There was a puzzled look on Areos's face as he stood there, arms crossed, in the thick of the woods. The sun had set some time ago, and the forest was dark.

"How on earth did you know where to find me?" he asked, his voice dry and monotone. "I could have been anywhere."

I crossed my arms to mirror his stance. "I told you I know these woods. Didn't you believe me?"

"Have you given me a reason to believe you?" he asked. "For all I know, you could be lying about having captured Icarus. You could have told me to hide out here just so that you could come and shoot me later. See? You even have your rifle with you."

"I'm on patrol. Of course I have my rifle," I huffed. "Did you really think I'd risk my neck sneaking off base just to talk to you? I was able to get assigned to night patrol this evening."

"They patrol this part of the woods?"

"You bet," I lied. "You're lucky I found you first. Someone with a crueler disposition might have done much worse than merely finishing you with a bullet."

Even in the darkness I noticed his eyes widen. I grinned inwardly. "Anyway, we're here to talk business, aren't we?" I questioned.

"Yes. Yes, of course."

"Icarus."

"Yes—Icarus." He stepped forward. "I have to figure out a way to get him out of there."

"Yes, we do," I agreed. "And sooner rather than later."

"We?" he reiterated. "What do you mean, we? I need nothing more than information from you—Lieutenant?"

"Corporal."

"Corporal." He nodded. "Since you are obviously sympathetic to the cause—"

"Which is lucky for you," I interjected. "Since you could have grabbed someone who would have shot you on sight."

"Oh, but I wouldn't have grabbed just anyone."

"Really?"

"Yes, really." He rolled his eyes. "I scoped you out."

I raised an eyebrow. "Scoped me out, huh?"

He began a reply, then stopped. "Not—not like that."

"Right, right." I let out a wry laugh. "Not buying it."

He sighed, flustered. "Okay, Corporal, look. I need to break in there and get my friend out," he announced. "Your job is to help me figure out how, and when would be the optimal time to do so."

"My *job*?" I repeated, staring at him in the low light. "Who do you think you are?"

Like someone who had just realized that Earth didn't spin circles around them, his lips flapped uselessly for a moment before he cleared his throat. "You don't understand."

"No, I think you're the one who doesn't understand," I replied, my voice rising. "I don't care how much is at stake here, or what kind of superhero mission you want to turn this thing into—this base is not like the one you're used to, Areos. This isn't Section C! They will *gut* you here. They're already looking for you! Do you understand?"

"That's not possible. They don't even know if I'm still alive or not—they have no way of tracking us!"

"They tracked one of you somehow," I replied. "I could see the dot on the radar the entire time. I'm not exactly sure how they did it… but that's how I found them. The RGM tracks members all the time, but we usually know about it. This obviously wasn't the case here."

"Maybe there's some kind of tracking device in the Frag." Areos rubbed his jaw. "Something the RGM can activate to track MIA members. That would explain why they tracked Charlie and not us. It would explain why the pilot chased Icarus and Charlie with the Death Vapor, not Fin and me…"

My curiosity was piqued. "Who is this Fin? Icarus mentioned him too."

"A friend," Areos replied absentmindedly. "A colleague. I left him back in the mountains—I came to find Icarus. And I'm not leaving until I've gotten him out of here."

My jaw tightened. "Then you'd better be ready to cooperate."

Areos heaved a sigh. "But the thing is, I hate group projects…"

"I'm sure you'll accustom yourself to the idea," I deadpanned. "Unless you would rather share Icarus and Charlie's cell…"

He quickly shook his head. "I can deal with you."

"How flattering." I shot him a look. "We'll have to handle this very, very carefully—I have even more at stake than you do, Lieutenant."

He quirked an eyebrow. "Yeah? How's that?"

My mind reeled back to Donovan's office and our conversation. His words ricocheted in my skull.

*"I knew there was something more to you than met the eye. I knew you were different."*

I pushed the thoughts to the back of my mind, refocusing.

"Never mind," I replied sternly. "If you want to help me save Icarus, there's a lot we need to go over—"

"Help you? You're the one helping me."

I rolled my eyes. "Look, we don't have much time. They're running experiments on Icarus. They started early this morning and they're planning on continuing."

"Why?" Areos sounded as shocked as I had been when Icarus told me. "What are they planning on doing with him?" The color had drained out of his face.

"I don't know," I replied at length. "They usually just slaughter recusants—that's what I do practically every day. I do their dirty work. I take out the 'bad guys,'" I grunted. "Which merely equates to anyone who so much as breathes a word of disagreement with their methods. Which makes the situation even more unique…"

We were both silent for a moment.

"Areos, tell me about Icarus," I said finally, refocusing. "I need to know everything: about you, about him—and about what exactly 'sliders' are."

I could see the bright whites of Areos's eyes as they probed mine.

He stepped closer. "First, we need to find a better hiding place."

"I'll do better than that," I said. "Follow me."

---

"My brother, Ronan, and I built this place—my sisters too." I pushed aside the brush that encompassed the clearing. "It feels like ages ago. It *was* ages ago…"

I could hear Areos beating through the brush behind me, trying his best to keep up. "What do you mean?"

"It's a long story."

"We have a little time."

A wry laugh pushed past my lips. "Not nearly enough, trust me."

Weaving my way through the trees and tall grass, I led Areos into the clearing, in the middle of which stood the cottage, dark, silent, and looming like a remnant from another life. The moon had risen in the shape of an impregnated crescent, though its milky glow was tainted by the layer of smog in the atmosphere. It illuminated the cottage and the clearing, transforming the slick shingles and glazed windows into shimmering reflections.

Areos took only a few strides before standing still, gazing around him as if he had just stumbled into another realm. "Whoa."

I walked past him, my footsteps silent against the thick layer of dead grass. I took the steps all at once and shouldered open the creaky door. I glanced over my shoulder.

"Are you coming?" I asked brusquely. "Or are you spending the night outside?"

"Sorry." He mounted the steps. "I've just never seen anything like this before."

"Really? I would have guessed you've seen lots of abandoned and decaying places, Lieutenant." I stepped into the cottage.

He grunted, following me inside and shutting the door behind him. "Oh, believe me, I have."

I dug the matches out of the drawer and went about lighting the candles.

"You know that I don't have a Fragment," Areos began. "As hard as that would be for you to believe—I doubt your robotic mind will even be able to comprehend the idea. But suffice it to say, I oppose the way things currently are," he went on, in that same arrogant tone. "However, I, unlike some people, see that there's nothing to be done about it. It's too late—this is survival of the fittest, whether it's a recusant, an RGM soldier, or otherwise."

I blew out the match. "That's your hypothesis, huh?"

"It is."

I turned to look at him; the room was now illuminated by the candles. "Sounds a little dreary."

His arms were crossed and his lips were pressed into a tight, irritated shape. And though his eyes reflected the glittering yellow flames around us, they were hard and unyielding.

"It may sound dreary to you, Corporal, but to me," he said, "it sounds logical."

I studied his grave expression for a moment before cracking a small grin. "Logic is indeed precious."

"Are you laughing at me?"

"No, Lieutenant. I wouldn't laugh at you."

I sat down on the floor by my bed, setting the candle down a few feet in front of me. I gestured for him to come and sit, but he wouldn't until he had defended himself.

"I simply like to see things for what they are."

He crossed the small room and lowered himself to sit on the floor, folding his long legs awkwardly in front of him.

"I realize that you may see my worldview as being… pessimistic, Corporal," he went on. "But I have seen things that no one should have to. I have done things that… for a long time I had trouble dealing with. You have never been in my position, Corporal. You cannot know what it is like."

I swallowed, nodding. "You're right, Lieutenant. I have never been an RGM pilot."

I stopped there, and for a moment he seemed somewhat satisfied.

"But," I continued, "I have been an RGM sniper. So I think I know just a little of what it feels like to wade through waist-deep mud, in the rain or snow, to lie in wait for someone to come just close enough to feel the sting of a bullet. I know a little of what it feels like to kill, and to wish it could be you instead of them—to wish…" I trailed off, a lump forming in my throat instead of the words that should have been there. "I know a little of the darkness, Areos," I finished quietly.

He looked as if he had been struck, his expression of confidence having faded.

"I see it, I feel it, I smell its rotting stench around us." I shook my head slowly. "It's easy to despair—anyone can do that. It's hard to hope. It's hard to see the light when the sun's gone out of the world. But just because all we can see is darkness doesn't mean the sun's not there, does it? Anyone can look around at the world and point fingers and call names and make statements and write data. But I was taught that when you find yourself standing at a crossroads, the most rewarding path will always be the roughest and the rockiest. My training didn't teach me that; my parents did."

Areos studied me for a moment, his eyes filled with a strange presence I couldn't describe. Finally, he pulled in a breath, seeming to break out of his trance. "Who *are* you?"

I glanced down at the tiny screen on my wrist. "I have six hours before I have to report back, so listen carefully, because I won't have time to say anything twice."

He nodded, his eyes never having left my face. "I'm listening, Corporal."

I studied him for a moment, my eyes tracing the features of his face, before taking another steady breath.

"Please, call me Lara."

# CHAPTER TWENTY-FOUR

## *Icarus*

The lights flicked on in buzzing succession. "Both of you up—now!" The loud accented voice cracked through the first taste of sleep I'd had in what felt like ages. I peeled my eyelids open to find a blurry outline of Donovan towering over me, contrasted against the blaring white lights.

"Rise and shine." He lowered his voice to a monotone calm. "We have a special visitor."

I swallowed, then choked on my own spit. I bolted upright, coughing and rubbing my eyes. Charlie groaned, muttering inaudibly as she rolled up to a seated position on her cot.

"Who?" I croaked.

"Someone who enjoys the Olympic Games," Donovan replied flatly.

Charlie whimpered a curse word. "B-b-but I just got out of my muddy uniform!"

"Oh, don't worry. You won't be performing tonight," he replied dryly, his eyes still focused on me. "You get to watch your buddy here give it a shot this time."

In less than five minutes, I was outside in the cool, foggy air, being shoved down into the familiar muddy pit. I fell about ten feet and landed on my hands and knees. As if on cue, a massive spotlight burst to life, illuminating my mud-splattered face as I gasped for breath and turned to look up at the rim of the pit.

Donovan stood with his hands behind his back. Charlie was tied to a chair beside him, writhing against the ropes that wrapped her torso. The guard who had pushed me stood, statue-like, at the edge. I scrambled to my feet just as a familiar figure stepped into view: a woman of medium height, dressed all in black, with a swath of short red hair and a scar slashing down across her right eyebrow. She cracked a sadistic, toothy grin as she peered down at me, the toes of her thigh-high boots peeping over the edge of the pit.

"Icarus." She wiggled her fingers in a wave. "I hope we are in for some good, lively entertainment this evening."

My jaw slackened as I stared up at my commander, sinking deeper into the mud. Hatch chuckled, gesturing for Donovan to come join her. After a moment of reluctance, he walked over.

"Look at him, Don—look at him staring." She grinned, folding her arms over her thin, sunken chest. "So confused, so frightened—just like you were."

Before he could answer, she cupped her hands over her mouth to shout down to me. "Stop staring, Icarus. I'm afraid I am not fond of people who stare!" she yelled hoarsely. "I will have to shoot you the next time you stare— oh, doesn't that make this even more fun now?"

I swallowed, feeling suddenly sick to my stomach.

"Let's see five hundred push-ups!" she wailed. "With your face in the water!"

I threw myself down onto my hands and feet in the mud, lowering slowly from a plank position to my belly, making sure my face submerged fully into the stagnant water. Then I pushed myself back up. I did this ten times, then ten more, then ten more after that. Hatch perched herself on the edge of the pit now.

"Come, come!" she insisted raggedly, whipping a flask out of her coat pocket to take a swig. "Show us what you've got!"

*What is she doing here? Why is she here?*

All the possible reasons for her sudden appearance disturbed me even more than her presence did.

I did the push-ups until I reached five hundred. My face was dripping with mud and dirty water as I stumbled to my feet, only to fall to my face again. Hatch burst into laughter.

"Again, Icarus, again." She interrupted herself as she took another swig. "No—no, let's have some pull-ups now."

My fingers curled around fistfuls of mud, every bone in my body seeming to shake in its joint. I crawled to my knees and willed myself to my feet again. I walked over to the bar at the far end of the pit. It was too high for me to reach from a standing position.

"Five hundred, Icarus!"

I tuned out the sound of her voice, lunging up to grab the cold, slick bar with both hands. My abdominal muscles burned as I pulled myself up until my chin touched the bar and then slowly lowered down again. Wincing and panting for air, I repeated the action over and over and over again until I roared in pain with each rep, my muscles feeling as if they were shredding.

Hatch laughed, clapping. Donovan stood behind her, stone-faced.

Charlie shouted to me from her chair. "You've got it, Icarus! Don't give up!"

I tried to focus on her words instead of the pain, though it felt almost impossible. But after a while I became aware of a tiny voice from within me, which, as I went on, seemed to scream even louder than my comrade.

*You're the Sunset, Icarus. You're the Sunset—Hawk trained you for this! This is nothing. You've got this.*

I rewound and replayed those words, putting amplifiers on every syllable until they were all I could hear—until, at last, something inside me began to own them.

*I'm the Sunset… the chosen… I've got this. This is nothing.*

I finished the routine with a mandatory roll across the pit, coating myself thoroughly in mud before clambering to my feet and saluting my superior officers. Hatch was still seated on the edge, but the smile on her face had flattened to a hard frown. Her sharp eyes bore down on me in an enraged glower.

"Don, take these nice young people back to their cell," she said, feigning calm as she gestured for the guard to remove us. "No food or water for Icarus."

I crawled up the gradual slope and walked obediently beside the guard all the way back to our cell. I collapsed onto my cot, breathing for what felt like the first time. Charlie stood in the middle of the room, staring at me. She didn't speak until I finally turned my head sluggishly to look at her.

"What?" I panted raggedly.

"You," she replied simply. "They made you do five times more than what they made me do. How on earth did you get through it?"

"I don't know…" I panted. "I just believed I could do it."

"You believed it?"

"Yeah…" I squeezed my eyelids shut, focusing on my breath. "I just… I kept thinking about how I needed to get through it for her."

"Her?" Charlie asked quietly. "You mean Hawk?"

I nodded.

She straightened, sucking in a long breath simply to blow it all back out again in disbelief. "How can thinking of someone or something—how can merely believing something get you through all that?"

I thought about Charlie's question for a moment, thinking back to the day Areos and I had hijacked her Trawler, then to the minefield, the vapor-filled woods—the many, many conversations we'd had. Charlie was just a young woman with a Fragment in her brain and a will to follow orders… That was what I'd seen her as. But now, lying there as she looked me in the eyes, waiting for me to answer, I saw she was so much more than that.

Charlie was how we were going to heal Earth. One of the many ways.

"It's called faith," I answered finally.

"And what is faith?"

"Complete confidence and trust in someone, or something—even if you're flying blind."

Charlie considered it for a moment. "That seems stupid."

"It's not something I can explain to you, Charlie… You won't know it until you feel it yourself."

Charlie didn't say anything after that, and after a moment of lying as still as I could, I managed to roll myself over onto my back. I dragged a hand down my face, wiping away the layer of mud.

"There's something between Hatch and Donovan," I said, thinking aloud. "Something very strange."

"Yeah, you said that already. What makes you so sure?"

"Because of how he talked about her—how he reacted. Now I've seen how he is around her…" I squinted, thinking. "Did you see his face?"

"I tried not to look at him. I knew I'd want to cuss him out if I did."

"And something Hatch said…" I ran my tongue over my lips. I tasted mud. "Something about how I looked terrified… like Donovan had. She acted like she'd known him for a while."

"Hatch isn't exactly a spring chicken. She's probably seen him around."

"No, but I think it's more than that."

"How so?"

"I'm not sure…" My answer came slowly. "I'm not sure why she's here, or what she's here for—I'm not sure about anything right now. But I recognized that look Donovan had on his face as he stood there next to Hatch. I recognized it because I used to wear it sometimes, a long time ago."

"Yeah?" she asked. "And what kind of look is that?"

"Hatred," I replied.

———————————

Hours passed. A thousand thoughts churned in my head, but my body gave out beneath their weight. I drifted and fell into an ugly sleep, collapsed in an agglomeration of muddy, swollen arms and legs. Everything paused, it seemed. I slept for the first time in what felt like forever, and the world took on the illusion of standing still.

I startled awake to the sound of an explosion, followed by a long, low, rumbling fallout; the trembling rolled through the base like a tidal wave, causing the barracks to shiver on its foundation and spidery cracks to splinter across the ceiling.

I scrambled up into a seated position, breathing hard, my eyes darting from one end of the ceiling to the next. My heart was in my mouth. There was silence as everything calmed. The scent of dust hung in the air. I listened, holding my breath. Muffled shouts filtered through the cement, followed by the shrill wail of a siren.

I jumped to my feet just as another impact shattered the temporary stillness, shaking the ground.

"Charlie!" I leaned over to clap a hand on her shoulder. "Charlie, wake up!"

"Errrmmpph…" She rolled over, swatting my hand away.

"*Charlie!*"

Finally her eyes blinked open, wide and bewildered. "What…?"

"Get up!"

She didn't have to be told twice. Another explosion rang through the air, accentuated by more sirens and the sound of engines starting aboveground.

Dust hissed down from the ceiling as it began to come apart. I pressed my back to the wall closest to the door, breathing hard, my thoughts tumbling over each other.

"Holy sh—"

A massive chunk of the ceiling crumbled away from the rest, hurtling down to flatten my cot. A cloud of dust rose, and a deafening sound rolled through the room as whatever was above us came smashing down through the hole.

"Get down!" I shouted.

Without thinking, I threw myself on top of Charlie, bringing us both to the floor as the rest of the ceiling deteriorated and came crashing down.

# CHAPTER TWENTY-FIVE

*Fin*

Hawk was sleeping. Finally able to heal the forest, I'd grown her a raspberry bush, and she'd eaten her fill before lying down in the soft green grass and falling asleep. I took advantage of the opportunity to sneak down to the nearby river.

I'd spotted it from the treetop earlier that day, a sparkling, clear vein cutting through the lifeless forest like a streak of copper in stone. Surprisingly, it was the clearest water I had ever set eyes on. I could see every pebble and rock at the bottom. I couldn't resist the temptation of dunking my feet in when I reached it. I peeled off my shirt, letting the sunlight spill over my back.

It was just like the streams my sisters and I used to play in as children after the winter sun had warmed and the rivers ran thick with melt. Chills broke out over my skin immediately. *It was freezing.*

I bent down and sifted my fingers through the rocks and pebbles until I found one that was smooth and flat. Taking a seat on the bank of the stream and holding the rock in my palm, I began sharpening my pocketknife against it, unable to remember the last time I'd shaved my face. I hadn't realized how long my hair and beard had grown.

When I was content that the well-worn blade was sharp enough, I splashed my face with the icy water and started on my beard. My jawline slowly resurfaced. My eyes followed my reflection on the water's surface as I tried desperately not to cut myself.

When I was finished, I moved on to my hair, trimming it back just as my mom always had. My head felt light by the time I was done, my wavy blond hair ending above my ears. I looked a little less like something from Greek mythology and a little more like the Fin Hawk remembered.

The river ran a little deeper than I expected in the middle. The fact remained that it was ice cold, but I decided to venture in regardless. So, pocketing my knife, I stripped off the rest of my clothes and tossed them over one of the large nearby boulders for safekeeping. I waded in up to my waist, the cold shooting up my spine to numb my brain; then I let myself plunge below the surface. For a split second my ears were filled with the whoosh of the water as it rolled past in cold torrents, blasting over my skin and through my hair. I resurfaced, gasping for the air the cold had knocked out of me, throwing my head back. Tiny droplets spattered across the water's surface to rejoin the river.

I sank back against the gentle current, kicking my legs to keep myself in place as I gazed up at the leafy canopy stretching out overhead. The water suddenly didn't seem as cold. I thought about the forest—the small patch that I'd brought back to life. I'd transformed only a small radius, not wanting to draw any undue attention to ourselves from the air again—though I doubted another incident like that would occur.

As awesome as it had been to finally feel the power flowing through my fingertips again, it was Hawk's hand in my own that I remembered even more vividly. Hawk's *human* hand. She'd looked so different, yet so much the same to me as we had run through the forest together, life seeming to explode out from beneath us, transforming the dead Earth into a paradise.

When I breathed now, I caught the scent of fresh soil and dew and blossoms. When I looked up, I saw leaves and vines and flecks of pollen floating like snowflakes in the large shafts of sunlight, and when I closed my eyes, I saw Hawk's dark brown eyes staring into mine.

I bit down on a smile and dunked my head back under the water. It was so hard to think straight; so much had happened in the last few days. The last gathering I'd attended felt so far off… yet remained as vivid as if it were happening continuously around me. Gaia and her students' revelation of the database's location, Mitsue's enraged response…

I knew Mitsue too well to assume that he would raise the white flag and let someone else steer the ship. But the council was running out of options. Their sole focus had gone up in flames. I couldn't help but wonder what initiative would replace it, and from the way Mitsue had reacted that night, I had a sinking feeling that it could be nothing good.

My mind went back to my conversation with Areos, and my conviction that Earth needed healing rather than fixing. As I saw it, it was to be expected that the database should be beyond our reach. Destruction never brought about lasting change; there had to be something else—something we were overlooking. Something that was right in front of our faces.

As I lay there, floating in the river with my face tipped towards the sky, I couldn't help but wonder if the forest was a clue, an arrow pointing to something even greater than itself. I hadn't been able to heal the trees until Hawk had come back to life in human form. I knew why, though I didn't want to admit it out loud. No longer burdened with grief, my heart felt weightless each time I looked at her.

I had been unable to contain my love for her in that moment; as I looked into her human eyes again, it had involuntarily spilled over to create something far greater than I could ever have imagined.

I lost myself in thought. Then my name cut through the stillness, pulling me back.

"Fin?" A familiar voice, soft like the wind. "Fin, where are you?"

My eyes widened and I froze, sinking down into the water up to my shoulders.

"Hawk? I'll—I'll be there in just a—"

It was too late. She stepped out from among the trees, her long white braid swaying over her shoulder as she took a few steps. "Fin, are you out he—?"

She came to an abrupt halt, her eyes widening a little before she quickly turned around. "Oh—sorry!"

"No, no, no, it's okay," I assured her, though my ears were on fire. "Just, uh…" I coughed, wading cautiously over to where I had left my clothes. "Just give me a second."

I splashed into the shallow water and stepped up onto the bank. Feverishly, I started pulling my jeans back on.

"Can I turn around now?"

"No!" I grunted, then laughed. "You can't."

Hawk waited impatiently, folding her arms over her chest. Her braid was tucked to the side; the sunlight spilled down the back of her neck and her upper back, which was visible above the low scoop of the silky white fabric. I zipped up my jeans and reached for my shirt, but she turned around before I had time to pull it back over my head.

"So you ran off and left me to go swimming?" she teased, but her expression changed before I could answer. "Whoa, Fin, you look…"

She stepped closer, her gaze sweeping over my face. My heart started racing.

"You cut your hair," she observed aloud. "And you *shaved*." Reaching up, she ran a hand over my cheek, a grin playing on her lips. "I knew you were under that beard somewhere."

I probably would have been embarrassed had my brain actually processed that comment, but my thoughts were lost in her eyes and her face. It started to register just how close she was.

"I didn't want to wake you up," I said, my voice coming out soft. "I knew you were exhausted…"

"I was…" she replied quietly, her eyes scanning my face. "But now I'm awake."

I couldn't think; I couldn't breathe. Hawk stepped back, clearing her throat.

"The raspberries." She gave me a beaming smile as she changed the subject, a few feet suddenly between us again. "I'd forgotten how delicious food tastes. I'd forgotten what it was like to be hungry."

I smiled a little, looking down. My shirt was still balled in my hand, and water was dripping down my chest. "I'm glad you enjoyed them."

Hawk made her way to the edge of the stream. She dipped one toe into the water. "What happened while I slept?"

I leaned back against the rock, watching her.

"Nothing," I replied. "The sun moved slightly; the trees swayed in the wind a bit. I went for a swim without you. I thought about a thousand things, but mostly you."

Hawk turned and looked at me over her shoulder. "What kinds of things?"

I sucked in a breath, trying desperately to clear my head.

"Nothing I haven't already told you," I replied at length. "The gathering and everything that happened there. The forest." I smiled. "The way things are—Earth, and all its messiness, and how we're going to change things."

Hawk closed her eyes and tipped her face back to absorb the warmth of the sun. "It's good to hear you talk about it, Fin, to hear your voice so full of faith…" She opened her eyes again and glanced at me. "No wonder the forest cannot help but resurrect itself beneath your every step."

"I cannot take credit." I bowed my head to look at the ground. "I just… believe what he's told us all, so many times."

Hawk's smile faltered slightly. She pulled in a firm breath as she turned to look down into the stream. "I miss him so much."

A strange feeling twisted my heart. "Who?"

"Sensei."

I breathed a sigh of relief, then immediately felt a prickle of guilt. I shoved these thoughts away.

"Sensei is always with you," I assured her. "He's the one who helped you transport back here… isn't he?"

"Yes," Hawk replied. "Yes, he came to the worlds beneath the ravine. He… took care of me. He transported to Earth too."

"Sensei's on Earth?"

"Mm-hmm."

"Why would he have transported to Earth?"

She laughed. "Fin, do you think I asked?" She shook her head. "No, these days I just trust. I've learned that much from my world and all I had to overcome there."

"Sounds like training for this world."

She smiled, but I could tell the reality of the fact was heavy on her mind.

"Hawk, have you given any thought to making an appearance at the next gathering?"

She opened her mouth to reply, then seemed to change her mind. She turned around and walked back over to me.

"Why should I?" she said, her voice quiet but level. "Why should I, when they would have liked nothing better than to watch my execution not so long ago?"

"I know," I said, sighing. "I… I know, Hawk."

She squinted out at the river, her brow creased.

"What about Icarus?" I asked quietly.

Hawk looked startled. "What about him?"

I wasn't sure what to say—how to say it. In my mind's eye I could still see his face: the dark circles under his eyes, the way he had wept, wounded and unable to go on.

"He asks about you every time he sees me," I told her. "He… he seems lost without you."

I couldn't read Hawk's expression as she stood there looking at me, the soft breeze tugging at her braid.

"Is he all right?" she asked, finally.

"I don't know. Areos hasn't returned yet."

Hawk nodded briskly, then looked away again.

"But when he does return—" I began.

"I'll think about that when it happens," she interrupted quietly, closing her eyes. We both stood in silence for a moment, listening to the bubbling rhythm of the stream as it rushed past us.

"I know what it's like," she said after a long moment. "To feel lost without someone…"

When Hawk's eyes opened, they locked with my own. My heart faltered in my chest. Finally, she looked away, then turned and walked back into the forest. I stood there at the edge of the stream, finally able to let out the breath I hadn't realized I'd been holding.

239

# CHAPTER TWENTY-SIX

## *Hawk*

I had behaved as though I were caught off guard when I'd emerged from the forest and found Fin bathing in the stream. I'd turned around while he dressed and joked about the whole thing—teasing him. But I'd actually noticed him from far off, concealed in the now leafy green birches and pines—the droplets of water glistening on his muscular shoulders, the sunlight tangled in his blond hair.

I'd watched him as he floated there, submerging and reemerging to gasp for air, tossing back his wet mane and staring up into the branches stretched out above, admiring his own handiwork.

I'd stood there, wondering why my heart seemed suddenly to pound harder within my chest. The conversation that followed only intensified this strange feeling within me.

Why was I not thinking of my duty? I was a human now. I was free to go and do as I wished. Fin said Areos had gone to look for Icarus, but that he hadn't had any word from him yet. *Why wasn't I out there looking for him myself?* Or perhaps the real question was, why didn't I *want* to—why didn't I feel that burning desire to find him, to be with him and fulfill my mission beside him?

Instead, I'd said nothing. I didn't know how to answer Fin's questions; I didn't know what to do—or what I *should* do. I would need to face the council sooner or later. I had to. I was the Sunrise, after all. I had a responsibility and an obligation to my people. I couldn't let them down.

Yet, there, alone in that patch of living woods, with only Fin for company, I found myself yearning for more time. Time to regain the strength I had lost—that was what I told him. But perhaps that wasn't the real reason. Perhaps I wouldn't even admit the real reason to myself.

The day faded away and night came. Fin built a fire and grew an apple tree, with rich golden fruit for me to devour. I sat in the soft green grass and watched him, and laughed at every joke he made, and found myself smiling as the Earth seemed to reach up to grasp his hand, yielding fresh green life to his every touch.

We talked about nothing, and everything, until we were both too tired to do much beyond lying outstretched in the grass, searching for stars we could no longer see; the sparks drifting up from the flames became their replacement.

"I remember a time like this," I told him quietly. "That day I transported to Dublin with you; tea beside the fire in your parents' house, your sisters all tangled around us."

"Mm." He smiled. "I'll never forget that day."

As quickly as it had come, his smile faded. I knew what he was thinking about. I said nothing for a moment, studying his face, a weight sinking in my chest.

"Do you ever regret it?" My question came out quiet. "Leaving them behind…"

Fin's eyes remained fixed on the sky. "Sometimes."

A cracked whisper. Yet it was enough to split my chest. He must have known the effect it had on me, though, because he turned his face to meet my gaze now.

"But when I look at you, I feel like I never left home," he went on softly. "When I look at you… I am home."

I didn't take my eyes from his for a long moment. In their dark parts I could see the sparks from the fire drifting up. And beyond the sparks, beyond the flames, there seemed to be something else. Something I was seeing for the very first time.

I looked back up to the sky and so did he. For a moment we just breathed.

Then, in the soft grass, I moved my hand just slightly towards him; the movement was barely there. I almost didn't notice it myself. But then I felt my little finger brush against his. Neither of us moved our gaze from the opaque sky. Then, slowly, his hand drifted, his fingertips brushing across mine. Chills raced over my skin. For a moment our hands just stayed like that, still and barely touching, like petals resting on the surface of water. Then my hand rolled slowly beneath his, and my fingers wove into the spaces between his own.

I felt as though I were holding back an ocean; I could feel its turbulent waves rising and crashing against the inside of my chest. I knew that if I said one word, all the sea would come rushing out with it. I wouldn't be able to hold it back anymore.

Maybe Fin knew. Maybe Fin held back an ocean too, because he asked nothing—said nothing.

Everything became more and more blurry each time I closed my eyes; the flames turned into stars. Finally, my heavy lids closed.

---

I bolted upright in the darkness to the loudest noise I'd ever heard. Breathing hard, I glanced around frantically.

*Where am I? What is happening?*

The sky was pitch black and so was everything around me—except for the warmth of a hand in my own. Suddenly everything came into clear focus. I heard his voice before I even comprehended that he was awake and seated beside me.

"Hawk—Hawk, wake up!"

"What's happening?"

"I'm not... I'm not certain..."

He jumped to his feet. I could make out his frame now as he took a few steps, my eyes having adjusted to the darkness. A low rumble penetrated the silence around us, and for an instant the ground shivered. I gripped it, then scrambled to my feet.

Then came the sound that had roused me: a sound like a crack of thunder, but a thousand times louder. The sky flashed overhead—bright white. Then there was darkness and silence, followed by a dull orange glow.

"Hawk." Fin came up alongside me. "Stay close."

"Where's it coming from?"

We darted through the trees, feeling our way through the brush and new growth until we came to a ridge where the trees fell away, opening up to the view below. In the far distance, a fire raged; the sky was red with feathers of flame. My eyes widened as I stood beside Fin.

There was a pause. Then another explosion loud enough to make me jump a little. A large broiling mushroom of the same colors roared up on the horizon.

"Oh, Lord, it can't be…" Fin breathed beside me, a tone of disbelief in his voice.

"What?"

He shook his head slowly, not giving an answer. Then he seized me by the wrist. "We have to get down there."

My eyes darted to his. "But how will we get there in time? It must be miles away—"

"We're not going to walk."

He led me by the hand back into the forest. Though I couldn't see his face, I could tell he knew something I didn't.

He stopped in front of me. "Ready?"

I gave a quick nod and his hands slipped back into my own almost just as quickly. I closed my eyes and let him lead—because I had to. I wasn't a slider anymore; I was merely a human. I didn't have the ability to conduct a transport. For the first time, I felt how Icarus must have that night I'd dragged him into the broom closet.

Everything had felt so different back then, so simple.

I pushed the thoughts to the back of my mind, letting my brain go numb so that Fin could execute the transport. An instant later, I felt my surroundings change. But this time it was not to the small enclosure of the cavern; the air did not grow cool and damp. On the contrary, wavering heat radiated against my skin.

I sucked in a breath and my eyes flew open. We stood planted in the middle of a wide-open field. The sky seemed to be on fire, and the air roared around us, rippling in angry waves. I was barely able to move. I turned and looked in the direction from where it all sprang—the coastline.

Ahead, aircraft swarmed in the rusty sky, ejecting soldiers toward the blistering inferno. Vehicles raced over the singed ground below—only to be tossed like rag dolls when another massive explosion erupted. I caught snatches of choked screams and sirens amid the utter chaos.

Before I could get one word out, Fin surged forward, running towards the firestorm ahead.

My heart stuttered over its next beat. "Fin!"

I didn't think—I ran after him, each pounding footstep heavier than the one before it. The ocean lay beyond the fire, its crashing swells illuminated like shards of broken glass as it threw itself against the cliffside.

What was our plan? We couldn't get much closer without being roasted. Fin finally slammed to a halt, then turned left and began to run again. Shielding my eyes from the blaze as I followed him, I noticed what had caught his attention: a body in the grass.

I picked up speed, coming up just behind Fin as he dropped to his knees beside the dark mangled shape lying facedown. He rolled the body over onto its side. The glow from the blaze illuminated the face of a young woman. She had deep brown skin, and her hair was shaved almost to her scalp, her cheeks were singed, and blood dripped from her forehead.

Fin sucked in a breath and leaned over her body, listening for a heartbeat. I glanced behind us, checking the progression of the fire. It was feeding its way rapidly across the grass, destroying houses and farmlands; I could hear distant screams and the wail of sirens.

"She's breathing," Fin announced, straightening up again. "I can heal her."

"Then hurry!" I panted, squinting at him through the blinding glow. "We don't have much time!"

Fin didn't need to be told twice. He gently pressed his hands to her face, concealing it from my view.

My eyes scanned the nearly lifeless body beneath his healing touch. I looked back over my shoulder as another blast roared up from the cliffside; a giant plume of flames rolled up into the sky.

"Fin, hurry!"

He didn't reply. But when I looked back, he'd pulled his hands away from the girl's face. She was staring up at Fin, blinking, as he helped her to sit up.

Her eyes were large and round, terrified, and reflecting the dancing tongues of flame.

"Lara…?" Her question was mumbled and listless; then it quickly became frantic. "Lara! Where is she? Where's Lara?"

She stumbled to her feet and immediately fell.

"Hawk, help me!" Fin shouted, stooping down to loop an arm around her torso. "We have to get her to someplace safe!"

"How? Where?" I shouted over the escalating rush of everything around us. "We can't transport with her. It will be impossible!"

The girl was in hysterics at this point, screaming the same name and struggling to escape Fin's grasp.

"We can't just leave her here!" he yelled back. "She'll die!"

"We'll all die if we stay here any longer!" I shouted hoarsely.

I grabbed the young woman by the shoulders and looked her in the eyes. "Listen to me! Your friend is gone—you cannot go back there. You will die!"

She stared at me, her expression numb and shocked.

"We have to run, now!" I shouted, pulling her forward. "We can't get any closer—we have to get out of here! The fire is spreading!"

Fin took her by the arm, and this time she didn't resist. I took up the lead, and we ran as fast as we possibly could. We reached the banks of what looked like a channel. Without hesitation, we waded in past our thighs.

"What were you doing there?" I panted, splashing forward through the cold water as we continued our way along the shoreline. "Are you a civilian?"

"Soldier."

"What's your name?" I asked.

She stared straight ahead for a long moment, sloshing forward as she continued gasping for air. "Kess."

"What happened back there?" Fin asked, his voice grave. "Who set off the explosions?"

"Lice-bag recusants," she returned bluntly.

"Recusants?" I questioned.

Kess nodded her head. "Defective hosts."

My brow creased.

"Monsters," she clarified, staring over her shoulder at me. "They just bombed our outpost! They just killed my friend!"

I didn't know what to say, so I said nothing.

Fin waded over beside me. "Lara?" he asked her, a heaviness in his voice. "Was that your friend's name?"

Kess did nothing for a moment, but then she nodded and choked back a sob.

"I'm sorry," Fin told her quietly.

"When I awoke and looked into your eyes, I thought it was…" Her voice faded. "I thought for a moment it was her… but now I've lost her too. Just like my parents."

I looked over at Fin, a heavy feeling in my chest as I saw that familiar expression cross his face.

"I know how that feels," he said, so quietly I wasn't sure that Kess even heard him.

Then he fell back slightly, leaning over to whisper into my ear, "Hawk, we have to do something about this."

"I know. I… I know."

"We have to report it to the council—we have to make them see what they refuse to open their eyes to!" He shook his head, looking back in the direction of the inferno. "This isn't just turmoil—this is butchery."

"The council, from what you've told me, has banned the use of powers beyond the walls of the Dimension," I replied quietly. "If that's the case, I don't see what they can do."

"Nothing, at least under Mitsue's leadership," Fin said tersely. "But I think the time has come for a new order to rise—wouldn't you say so?" He was looking me square in the eyes. It took a moment for it all to sink in.

"Me?" I blurted, my voice rising. "I—Fin, no, I can't. Not—not yet—"

"Hawk, you were *made* for this." His voice was filled with intensity. "What on earth are you waiting for? Of all people to hesitate at the ledge—"

"I am not hesitating!"

"What do you call it, then?"

My voice froze in my throat. I turned away from him and splashed forward.

When we reached a spot where it was safe to return to land, we plodded up onto the sandy ground and began running again until we were far from even the glow of the raging fires.

"Kess," I panted as we finally slowed to a stop, "do you… do you think you can make it back to New Dublin from here?"

She stared back at the fire, a distant look in her large brown eyes. "Yes."

We began to walk past her; she didn't move. A moment later she snapped out of it and yelled to us. "I would have died without you," she called weakly. "I don't know who on earth you are… but thank you."

Fin bowed his head in a respectful nod as we left Kess standing on the shore.

We walked in silence, Fin's words reverberating in my thoughts. The more I thought about what he had said, the angrier I became.

*You were made for this. What on earth are you waiting for?*

It was easy for him to say. Fin, who had spent the past year in peaceful, woodland seclusion in a human body—not trapped in the form of a hawk, unable to speak, unable to shift, unable to do anything to change the circumstances around him. How could he understand? How could he dare to pretend that he did?

By the time we had transported back to our camp in the mountains, my anger had begun to boil. I could tell that Fin sensed it, though he asked nothing. This only infuriated me more.

"Fine," I said at last. "Let's transport into the Dimension and speak to the council."

The light of dawn filtered through the trees now. Fin stood beside the pile of ash that had been a campfire only hours before. His eyebrows rose over his tired green eyes. "Are you certain—?"

"Of course." I cut him off coolly, stepping closer. "Didn't you say it was high time I made an appearance? Didn't you say it was time I showed myself?"

"Yes, I did," he replied. "But I didn't mean—"

"Let's not waste any more time," I interrupted again, coming to a stop in front of him. "Please assist me in the transport."

He looked down into my face, a look of concern in his eyes. "Hawk… don't go into this angry."

I gritted my teeth, speaking clearly and sharply. "I am *not* angry. Now, will you or will you not help me transport so that I may speak to the council?"

Fin's jaw tightened. He looked at me for a long moment before bowing his head in a begrudging nod.

"I will," he said finally, that same, irritating gentleness still holding its ground. "If that's what you really want."

Against my will, something inside me hesitated. Something inside me raised a warning flag—a quiet voice urged me to stop, to breathe, to loosen my grasp, to listen. I knew the voice; I recognized it.

But instead of heeding its whispered words, I brushed it away. I nodded resolutely.

"Yes," I replied. "It is what I really want."

# CHAPTER TWENTY-SEVEN

*Lara*

The hours before the first explosion were filled with dwindling candlelight and conversation unlike any I'd had in my life. In that short time, Areos had transformed from the cold, aloof stranger I had sized him up to be, into someone who made me feel as though I wasn't alone in the world. Someone who understood me.

"You are like Icarus," had been my whispered response to his story. "You're a…"

"A slider, yes," Areos had confirmed, thunderstruck. "Which is what you are…" He had gazed up at the wisteria hanging above us, then turned and glanced around at the vines covering the walls in a thick blanket of foliage. "Whether you realized it or not." He gave a little laugh, and for the first time a smile formed on his lips. "How on earth did you survive here? How did no one ever find you?"

"Since the day I met the strange man in the woods, I've moved around—constantly. Changed my identity a few times, and lived mostly in seclusion. That is, until the RGM found me."

"When did they induct you?"

"Five years ago," I replied, frowning. "And now I'm stuck. There's no way out of here without them figuring out what I am—that I don't age, that I…" I tipped my head back, searching for the right words. "That I'm a slider, as you call it. They'll exploit my abilities, no doubt; lock me up in the lab and never let me see the light of day again."

"I won't let that happen."

My gaze shifted back to his, surprised.

"You won't?" I repeated, stunned. "Who exactly do you think you are, Lieutenant?"

Areos's face flushed, but he didn't glance away. "You said that you felt like you found Icarus for a reason, didn't you?"

I nodded.

"Well, maybe I found *you* for a reason," he said softly.

A smile crept across my lips as 0159 rolled slowly into 0200 hours. And a deafening bang ripped the quiet in half, shaking the floor beneath us and rattling every piece of furniture in the tiny room.

Areos and I both started; his alert hazel eyes darted to the door.

"A bomb," he announced, his tone flat but urgent. "Somewhere close."

I jumped to my feet and sprinted to the window to peer through the cloudy glass. Above the trees, the sky glowed orange.

"Holy sh…"

I was already starting for the door by the time Areos got to the window.

"Wait, where are you going?" he asked, stunned. "You can't just go running towards a frickin' bomb, Lara!"

"I have to get back to base—I have to find out what's going on!"

He glanced from the window back to me as I zipped my jacket up to my chin.

"At least let me come with you."

I shook my head. "No, you'll be caught. You need to stay here."

"But, Lara—"

"*Promise me* you'll stay here."

Areos looked irritated, but he didn't protest, and that was good enough for me. I flung the door open and descended the few steps the same way I'd ascended them: all at once.

Rifle slung over my shoulder, I ran as fast as my legs would allow.

When I finally arrived back at base, I was greeted by nothing short of chaos.

All the Trawlers had already been dispatched. Byrds were taking off in quick succession from the middle of the courtyard. Donovan stood in the middle of it all, overseeing the soldiers as they were loaded into each one like cargo. Before he could notice me, I ducked into the entrance of the barracks, pushing against the current, as everyone seemed to be racing in the opposite direction—trying to get out.

A pair of strong hands snatched me and yanked me backwards just as a massive portion of the ceiling came crashing down. The entryway I'd been standing in collapsed.

I scrambled to regain my bearings, unable to see who my savior was until they had dragged me back outside.

"Get with it, Moron!" Kess shouted, giving me a firm shove as she shouldered her weapon. "We're under attack!"

I was coughing up dust, trying to breathe. "No! No, I have to get back down there!" I shouted, "Icarus is in there—down in the holding cells!"

"I don't care *who's* in there." She dragged me by the shoulder. "You're going to get yourself *killed!*"

"You don't understand—" I attempted to tear away from her, but my efforts were fruitless. Security already swarmed the entrance of the barracks as yet another explosion rumbled in the distance.

"Shit," Kess hissed, bracing herself as the ground trembled beneath us.

I clutched the strap of my rifle and stared at my friend. "What's happening?" I choked.

"Where you been?"

"Night patrol—I just—I just got back."

"The attack is in Howth. The lice-bags just bombed one of the outposts—the fire's spreading towards the village. We have to get to the remaining structure to rescue any potential survivors."

"Howth?" My heart sank. "Are you certain?"

"Yes, I'm certain—now shut up and move!"

She ran and joined the ranks of other young, armed soldiers lining up in front of Donovan.

My eyes locked on Donovan, my throat tightening as he turned and looked back at me.

*Howth.* That one word, scratched out in messy penmanship among the Gaelic in his notes.

*He knew. He knew about the attack.*

I swallowed hard and ran up to stand beside Kess.

"Two per Byrd," barked a shorter woman standing beside Donovan. Her hair was red, and there was a jagged scar slashed across her eyebrow. Her eyes darted back and forth anxiously, and she was screaming orders as she shoved the soldiers into the Byrds. "Move yourselves!"

Another Byrd lifted quickly from the ground and then another. This repetition continued until we were up next.

Kess locked arms with me, but as we stepped up, Donovan shook his head.

"Not you," he said, jerking a thumb for me to step out. "I need you here."

Kess didn't let go of my arm, but before she could protest, the woman beside Donovan shoved us through the open doors.

"No exceptions," she growled at Donovan. "I've had it up to here with what you've turned this organization into in my absence!"

Donovan's expression was murderous, though I never heard his response. The doors zipped shut and we rose into the air at a rapid pace. I felt my stomach turn.

That one word echoed in my mind, louder and louder: *Howth.*

*Howth, Howth, Howth.*

Donovan had *known* about the attack. And now we were heading into a death trap.

"Kess, we can't do this," I whispered, feeling as though I was going to be sick. "We can't—we can't! We have to turn this around! We can't go to Howth!"

"Lara, what the fu—"

"I don't have enough time to explain." My words came out in a fevered rush. "You just have to believe me! You have to believe me, Kess—we're all going to die!"

"Lara, get a grip!" She pulled on her helmet. "Why do I always have to be the one to get you back in line? Why do I always have to be the one to save your ass? Get your gear on and shut the hell up."

"Kess, please just believe me for once! You don't understand!"

She pulled down her visor. "No, Lara, I don't!" she shouted back. "But I do understand that RGM members who abandon their missions get executed, so I'd be grateful if you'd shut the hell up and let me do my job!"

I stood there for a moment, staring at my own reflection in her shield, breathing fiercely.

"What's gotten into you, Lara?" Her voice was muffled.

Swallowing back the bile burning in my throat, I strapped on my landing pack and slid on my helmet.

"You used to be braver than all of us…" Kess shook her head.

"Corporal Moron, Corporal Namono," ANI chimed in before Kess could get any further. "We are descending. Prepare for drop-off in two minutes."

Kess heaved an irritable sigh. "Lara, just swallow your nerves, stay by me, and you'll make it out alive. All right?"

I didn't argue. I nodded and said nothing.

Suddenly the floor bottomed out, and I was falling through the air. Below was a spinning inferno.

We landed safely on the ground, among a churning sea of other RGM members. Trawlers came as close as they could, leaving long compressed lines of tire tracks in their wakes. Our large fire fleet was dwarfed by the size of the blaze. I could feel in my gut that something was about to go horribly wrong.

"Come on, this way!"

I could barely hear Kess over my headset as we sprinted through the tall grass and shrapnel from the explosions. The Trawlers and the soldiers who had dropped from Byrds, just as we had, were all headed for the same thing: the remaining outpost building that lay about a quarter of a mile adjacent to the destroyed, burning remains of its counterpart near the cliff's edge.

The outpost. Where any survivors would be hiding. But I knew full well there wouldn't be any survivors.

"It's too late!" I yelled to Kess through my headset. "The fire's too big— we have to back off and fight it from farther back!"

A crackle, a pause. Then I could hear her panting. She was still running full speed ahead, dodging Trawlers and lunging over mangled chunks of debris. I ran only a little farther before stopping in my tracks, everything slowly fading to mute as I scanned the chaos around me. Smoke rolled violently overhead, and the ash rained down on the hundreds of soldiers around me, all dressed in black, all wearing masks, all running towards death.

Kids with guns. Going to find survivors who weren't even there.

Everything seemed to fade but the sound of my heart pounding.

Every bone in my body jolted as the earth came apart beneath me, tossing me into the air; I slammed back into the ground and started rolling. I caught a glimpse of the sky—glittering, hot orange fallout, and a Trawler sailing past overhead. I heard a crackle in my headset as Kess's signal went dead.

I clawed my way up to my feet again and ran. Not away from the inferno, but nearer to it. Nearer, where, by some miracle, I spotted her among the smoke, pinned beneath a Trawler. The driver was already dead.

"Kess!" I screamed her name, clawing back my visor. "Kess, can you hear me?"

I didn't wait for a response. I grabbed hold of the smashed vehicle with both hands and pulled up. Harder, and harder, and harder—screaming. Tears clouded my eyes.

*You're going to die—you're both going to die.*

"No, we are not!"

I yelled those words out loud. I screamed them like a battle cry, hoping Donovan was back at base listening to every last word as the impossibly heavy vehicle slowly cooperated with my fierce efforts, lifting slightly—just enough for Kess to scramble out from underneath it. I couldn't hear her through my headset, but I could see her eyes through the crack in her shield for a split second as she stared at me. I dropped the Trawler and it smashed back against the ground again.

"Run!" I screamed at her, though I could barely hear over the ringing in my ears. "Run *now!*"

For the first time, Kess did as I asked, managing to sprint despite her injuries.

The sky and earth seemed to simultaneously explode into fire in the loudest blast I'd ever heard. The outpost building ahead flashed and flew apart, concrete and timber turning to mere confetti in the arms of a swelling plume that reached up to drag its claws across the dark sky. The force threw me as if I were weightless; my clothes caught on fire. I landed hard on the ground near the cliff's edge, and I tried as best I could to roll, but the only way ahead was farther into the fire.

A scream roared out of my throat while every nerve in my body went haywire.

*There's no way out, there's no way out, there's no way out...*

Silence. Ringing in my ears.

No way out except *down.*

I took the only option I had left.

Ignoring the splintering pain, I jumped to my feet and ran the remaining stretch left between me and the cliff's edge, where the angry ocean roared below. An instant later the ground fell away beneath me and I plummeted through the air.

Down,

Down,

Down.

# CHAPTER TWENTY-EIGHT

## *Fin*

The Dimension was abandoned. I knew this as soon as I transported us in. I followed Hawk just the same as she searched the platforms and safe rooms.

"Where are they?" she seethed, storming the length of the hallway, back in the direction of the cavern. "Where did they transport to?"

"Probably Japan," I told her reluctantly. "They've been meeting there to discuss finding the database and what to do next."

"Take me there."

Her tone was sharp as nails, and her eyes glinted like ice as she yanked open the door and strode into the cavern.

"Hawk, I think we should transport back to Wicklow," I told her gently, shutting us into the small dark space. "I think you need a little time to cool down."

She cut me off with a disgusted grunt. "I don't need time, Fin—would you just stop it?"

"Stop *what*, exactly?" I asked, my face beginning to flush with anger. "Helping you? Being there for you? What, Hawk?"

"Treating me just like everyone else does!" Hawk snapped. "Stop being like the rest of them! I know what I'm doing—I don't need your help!"

The words had a piercing impact. I swallowed, something inside me receding.

For a moment I made no response. I listened to her breathing in the dark silence.

"Fine." My voice came out hoarse, barely above a whisper. "I'll transport us to Japan."

I closed my eyes, focusing in, though it was hard. Hard when all I could hear was the pounding of my own heart and the rhythm of her breathing. Slowly, though, the room transformed around us, fading from the damp, echoing atmosphere of the cavern to the warm, tungsten glow of the elevator.

When I opened my eyes, there were Hawk's, staring at me. Her hair was bathed in golden light, and her arms were crossed tightly over her white tunic. In that moment, I finally began to see how different she actually was. Not just how she looked, but how she acted, how she behaved. She felt like a stranger, but at the same time more familiar to me than myself. That was why it made me so angry—because she was better than what she was feeling, yet she was allowing her feelings to control her.

She jabbed the "open" button with her index finger. The doors rolled apart and she took a measured breath before stepping out onto the glass floor.

The room, as I'd expected, was buzzing with heated conversation; the council was seated around the long metal table. Everyone fell silent in succession. Hawk turned every head in the room, just as she always had. In one way or another.

Mitsue was the first to jump up from his chair, sending it clattering to the floor as recognition flashed in his dark eyes. Delta, at the opposite end of the table, was the first to speak.

"*Hawk?*"

I stood behind her, saying nothing. I watched as she crossed her arms and stepped right up to Mitsue, ignoring Delta altogether. "Back from the grave," she answered.

Mitsue's eyes were wide as he stared at her, his Adam's apple drifting up and down his throat as he swallowed, hard.

Hawk cracked a mirthless grin. "Did you miss me?"

"It can't be..." Delta was slowly shaking her head, still staring. "You—

you—"

"I committed suicide?" Hawk interrupted. "Sorry to disappoint you."

My jaw tightened. "Hawk."

"But you did jump." Delta rose from the table, shoving back her chair. "I know you did—Fin saw you! Fin *told* me."

Delta's eyes shifted to mine momentarily. I looked away just as Hawk slowly turned to look at me, something new mingling in her eyes with the rage.

"Yes, Delta," she replied sharply, though I could feel that her eyes were still drilling me. "I did jump, but only to save all of you from something you didn't understand. Something you still don't understand even now."

Mitsue finally spoke. Stepping forward, he jabbed a finger in Hawk's face. "You are an impostor," he growled through gritted teeth. "A fabrication. Did you actually think I would fall for this, Fin?" He looked past Hawk to me now, his eyes wild and dark. "Did you actually think you could usurp me with some stupid little prank like this?"

No one at the table said a word.

Mitsue let out a mocking laugh and grabbed Hawk's face in one hand. "Think again," he hissed.

That, for me, was the final straw. I didn't even care that Hawk resented me at the moment—no one touched her like that in my presence. I didn't care that this was an official council meeting and that Mitsue was the appointed leader. In one furious, fluid motion, I grabbed Mitsue by the throat and slammed him down on the table.

Shoving my face down into his, I stared into his startled eyes, my fingers shaking as I gripped his throat.

"If you ever touch her again," I hissed, flecks of split flying out of my mouth, "you will not live to see another day—do you understand?"

Mitsue said nothing. The room was so quiet you could have heard a pin drop.

"All hail the powerful Sunrise," he uttered, his voice strained by my grasp as he cracked a smile. "Who cannot even defend her own argument without someone else swooping in to save her."

Whispers rose around us like black water. My face burned and my fingers trembled, locked around Mitsue's throat.

"Fin, let go of him!" Delta's voice snapped me out of it.

My lips pressed into a thin line, and finally I released him with a violent jolt. I straightened back up, breathing hard. Mitsue slowly pushed himself up from the table, bringing one hand up to rub his throat. He said nothing for a moment, his face expressionless; then, without warning, he launched his fist into my face—nailing me right in the eye and sending me sprawling backwards onto the floor.

"Take your… thing," he pronounced calmly, gesturing towards Hawk. "And get out."

"But, Mitsue," Gaia piped up, her voice almost a whisper, "that… She really is—"

"I have decided the course of action we will take against the RGM and the UNC." Mitsue's voice rose to interrupt her. "I am tired of the weakness of this council! I am tired of the lack of passion, the lack of prioritizing, the lack of willingness to serve! Together, Delta and I"—he gestured towards where she was still standing, her thin lips pressed together—"have decided what must be done."

Hawk extended a hand to help me up, but I refused it, getting up myself. Not making eye contact with her.

With one last look at me, Mitsue turned slowly to face the table. "If they want to fight us with fire"—his fists clenched around the edge of the table—"we will fight them with fire in return. They kill us with their forces—we kill them with our powers. And anyone who disagrees—" he gritted his teeth, turning to look at Gaia "—will suffer the same fate that the RGM leaders soon will."

No one spoke. Mitsue turned and looked at me, his lips trembling and his face now as red as the marks around his neck.

"This gathering is adjourned."

---

The forest looked the opposite of how I felt when we transported back. The breeze was gentle and warm, and the sun glittered down through the leaves to bathe the forest floor below, like a picturesque watercolor of how everything ought to be. It was Eden and I was hell.

Hawk threw herself down to sit in the soft grass beside what had been the fire—the fire we'd lain beside the night before, holding hands, her fingers intertwining with mine, sending shivers down my spine. And now she sat there, shaking her head in disbelief. Pitying herself.

She expected me to sit down beside her—to tell her it was all going to be fine, just as I always did. But instead, I left her there. I walked past the elm we had climbed what felt like so long ago and down to the stream to wash my face; my left eye was throbbing in my skull. I heard her call my name behind me, but I didn't stop.

I walked to the edge of the water and knelt down to plunge my head below the surface. That same whoosh filled my ears for a moment, but this time the feeling was completely different. I flung my head back again, sending up a spray. I took a deep breath.

For a moment there was just the wind to match my breaths, the babbling of the water making its way downstream, and the deep quiet of the woods around me. The woods I'd brought back to life again.

My jaw tightened as I looked down into my own swirling reflection.

"Fin…" Hawk's voice came up behind me. "Fin, I…"

"You what?" I asked flatly when she didn't finish. "You wanted me to shut up and let you handle it? Sorry I ruined it for you."

I felt Hawk tense behind me. "How dare you say such a thing…"

A tired, mirthless laugh found its way past my lips. "How dare I?"

"Fin, just stop—"

"*How dare I?*" This time I shouted it, getting to my feet, stepping closer, getting right in her face. "*How dare I*, Hawk? How dare I *what*? Stand up for you because *I love you*? How dare I try to stop you from unintentionally destroying everything that comes in contact with the consuming fire that is *you*?" I shook my head slowly, looking her right in the eyes. "How dare *you* assume your actions come with no cost!"

Hawk's eyes were wide, stunned.

"How dare you think this is just about *you*, when all of the Dimension, when all of the work Sensei has ever done, when all of broken, aching, groaning Earth is depending on you! How dare you act as if this only affects *you*, Hawk—it affects *everyone*! It affects *everything*!" I yelled, tears burning in my eyes. "I spent over a year, Hawk—a year searching for you! Not for myself, as much as I would give anything—" a sob tightened in my throat as I gasped for breath, still looking at her "—*anything*, just to be with you. That's not why I stayed out here day after day after endless day, searching for you. I stayed because I believed in you—in us! In what he says of us! I *believed*, Hawk…"

Hawk's eyes glistened with tears. They were like rivers, trembling and angry. "Are you saying that *I don't* believe, Fin?" Her voice was a hot whisper. "Is that it? Is that really what you think of me?"

I shook my head slowly, my eyes still connected with hers. "Yet again, you turn it around to make it about you. Hawk, can you think of one person beyond yourself for even a moment?"

"You believe I think only of myself?" She lowered her trembling voice, stepping closer. "You are not inside my mind, Fin! You do not see my every thought! You do not understand my every emotion! You have no idea of the pain and suffering I have endured—you have no idea how heavy everything is weighing on my mind, h-h-how much everything hurts!" A tear rolled down her cheek, her eyes cutting into mine. "I *have* thought of others, Fin—of the Dimension, of Sensei, of Icarus, of Earth and what I am *supposed* to be doing, but most especially…" Hawk paused, gasping for breath. Her lips trembled, her voice faded in her throat. "But most especially of *you*…" Her voice cracked. "Because I *love you*, Fin."

As I stood there, staring at her, it seemed suddenly that there was no world. No forest, no trees, no Earth beneath us. It was as if everything fell away, and nothing remained but Hawk. Her eyes stared up into mine as she repeated the same words I'd spoken to her a thousand times over in my heart.

"I love you…" she whispered. "I need you… I've always needed you."

Hawk's eyes slowly disconnected from mine, tracing every feature of my face. Her hand came up against my cheek, and suddenly my skin was ablaze. For a moment, she just stood there, her fingers softly brushing against my face. Everything seemed suddenly frozen, though fire coursed through my veins. Hawk's gaze softened, and lifting onto her toes, she leaned closer. For a split second I felt the warmth of her breath against my lips, then even that small separation disappeared. She kissed me. My eyelids lulled shut and my insides went weightless as her lips moved over mine. Her fingers tangled in my hair to draw me closer, as if I were air and she desperately needed to breathe. At first, I was numb, high, unable to process thought. Then, slowly, a shaky sigh murmuring past my lips and into her mouth, I melted into her arms. My lips moved around the shape of hers, setting my brain on fire.

Finally, a space slipped between us again. I heard her take an unsteady breath, her forehead gently touching mine.

For a long moment neither of us said a word. The only sound in the quiet forest was our own breathless inhalations.

"Hawk," I finally managed her name, my voice barely sounding like my own, "all my life I have…" I stopped, drawing back just enough to look down into her eyes. "All my life I have dreamed of this moment…" My voice faded. "But we can't do this. I'm not…"

She drew a shallow breath, and I felt her hand slipping to my chest. "I know you're not, Fin, but…" Her voice faltered as she gazed up into my eyes, something depthless in her own. "But that makes no difference to me."

As I stood there, lost in her eyes, I wanted to tell her that, yes, it didn't matter to her now, but one day—one day soon—it would matter very much. I wanted to tell her to save her heart, to keep it safe. I wanted to tell her not to give it to me, no matter how much I would cherish it from now to eternity. I wanted to tell her a thousand things in that moment, but I couldn't seem to find the words.

Instead I found myself leaning closer, my trembling hands wrapping around her waist to gently pull her closer. Instead my heart pounded as my lips softly caressed hers once more.

Instead I kissed her,

and kissed her,

and kissed her.

# CHAPTER TWENTY-NINE

*Icarus*

"Icarus…"

That voice.

"Icarus…"

I opened my eyes and found the Dimension before me. I was at the edge of the training platform overlooking the ravine. Everything was hazy, and the rail was slick with dew.

I turned and found Hawk beside me. Her hair was white as snow, like her feathers had been, and her eyes spoke a language I couldn't understand.

"Icarus." She repeated my name for the third time. "Things cannot be as they were, Icarus."

A sinking feeling settled inside me. "Why not?"

Hawk only shook her head.

"Hawk, why?"

I reached out for her, but my fingers swept through her as if she were merely a ghost. My throat tightened as I tried desperately to hold on to her, but I couldn't. She stood before me, staring up into my eyes, yet she was unreachable. Untouchable.

"I'm sorry, Icarus." Her whispered words sounded pained but resolute.

I crumpled, the floor seeming to fall away beneath me, swallowing me up, sending the Dimension spinning overhead, spiraling out of control before vanishing altogether. Cold darkness replaced the light and warmth of the perpetually rising and setting sun.

"I want to go back," I whispered, though I could not tell if I had spoken it aloud or within myself. "I want to go back home…"

For a moment, everything felt cold and dark and lost like I was, spinning and falling. I felt like I was withering from within, but then, from that very same shrinking place, a strong, clear voice bellowed: "Remember who you are, Icarus…"

*Who I am…*

I became aware of the black bands wrapping my arms, the band around my finger, as if I were a married man. I swallowed back the tears that were beginning to sting my eyes.

"Trust in her, Icarus." The bellow ebbed to a whisper, so close I could feel it on my face. "And trust in yourself, in who you are."

*In who I am… the Sunset—with a Sunrise hidden within.*

Slowly, I opened my eyes. Everything was a blur.

I blinked away the dust, coughing as I tried to move, but I couldn't— there was something on top of me, something hard and heavy, something blocking the daylight. I felt something softer beneath me, and for a moment, I was dazed.

I felt around in the darkness, and my fingertips brushed against something. I grasped an arm, and it all came rushing back.

"Charlie," I whispered, maneuvering as much as I could within the tight space to make sure I wasn't crushing her. "Charlie, can you hear me?"

There was a long silence followed by a strained breath, then a cough from beneath me.

"Mmm."

I was already assessing the situation: rubble was heaped around and on top of us; light filtered down through the cracks. A large slab leaning up against the wall was the only thing stopping us from being completely crushed.

*You're buried alive, Ion—there's no one up there to help you.*

I closed my eyes, anger welling inside me. "Shut up…"

*No one will even be able to hear you calling for help. No one even cares.*

"Not true… I won't listen."

*This stuff weighs thousands of pounds—there's no way you can dig your way out. You're insane.*

Logic was coming through loud and clear: we were buried alive, helpless. But I had a weapon far greater than logic. I had the power that radiated inside me. I was the only one who could decide which would win or lose.

It was do or die.

"I guess you don't know who I am, then," I whispered into the war zone in my mind, grunting and pushing up against the massive cement slab with all my might. "I'm an anomaly and I'm the *Sunset*."

Ignoring the nagging voice, I pushed harder and harder and repeated in my mind, *I'm the Sunset, I'm the Sunset, I'm the Sunset.* And then aloud.

"I am the Sunset…" I growled, listening as the rocks began to grind and then to slowly move. "I am the… I am the Sunset…"

Slowly but surely, a familiar warmth began to glow inside me, flowing down my arms and causing my fingertips to tremble.

Gradually, with a guttural scraping sound, the slab tipped and fell— sending with it an almost visible bolt of energy that blasted through the rubble around us as if it were nothing more than autumn leaves to be blown by the wind. Dust swirled as I stood there, my chest rising and falling. My fingers trembled.

Charlie coughed, still crumpled on the floor, blanketed with dust.

"What happened?" Her voice was raspy.

"The floor above us collapsed," I said, panting. "But I've cleared away the debris. If we're careful, we should be able to climb up and out."

I reached out a hand to help her to her feet. I could see straight up to the sagging ceiling of the first floor. I scoped the sloping piles of rubble around us, searching for the best way out.

"This way," I said finally, gesturing. "Careful—there's a ton of broken glass and razor-sharp metal."

We picked our way carefully up the tall embankment of what had only hours ago been the barracks, climbing side by side.

"What even happened last night?" Charlie asked, still sounding out of it. "I can hardly remember…"

"There was an explosion—several."

"Coming from where?"

"No idea." I searched for a foothold before taking another step. "Close enough to do this much damage."

"Sounds like the work of lice-bags."

I shot her a look. "In case you're forgetting, I'm a lot like those lice-bags, Charlie."

She grunted, climbing past me. "You keep saying that, but I don't understand."

"Only because you keep telling yourself that you don't," I called after her. "Charlie, I have seen what you are capable of, and Frag or no Frag, you have the capacity to understand anything you want to."

"Like what?" she grunted dubiously, stopping to glance down at me. "Love? Faith? All these weird ideas you keep talking about?"

"Yes, those." I reached up to take hold of another jagged chunk of cement. "You just have to believe."

"In what, exactly?"

"In *you*," I replied. "That's the only way anything is going to change. That's the only way Earth will ever be any different—if we decide that we are more than what they say we are."

Charlie kept climbing. She said nothing else, but I could tell she was considering it. She got to the top before I did and extended a hand to help me up.

"See?" I grinned through the dust. "Concern—love."

I took her hand and she yanked me up onto solid ground; the exit lay just ahead of us.

"Survival," she corrected me, rolling her eyes. "Now let's get out of here."

Amazingly enough, the door frame was still intact, providing us with a relatively easy way out into the courtyard, where we were greeted immediately by the barrel of a long black rifle. A guard, a young guy with dark brown skin, stood behind it, wide-eyed and looking shocked.

I heard Charlie curse beside me.

"What?" I asked, glancing from him then down at myself. "You'd be a little messy too if a room collapsed on you, dude."

My joke was badly timed and clearly unappreciated; he grabbed me by the arm and dragged me forward. A female guard grabbed Charlie, dragging her in the opposite direction.

"Wait—no!" she protested, writhing in the woman's grip. "Where are you taking him?"

The only response she received was a punch in the mouth, preventing her from making any further inquiries. My jaw tightened, anger swelling inside me as I was led forward through the mass of soldiers filling the courtyard. I could feel the burn of a hundred sets of eyes staring me down as the crowd divided to make way for us.

We came to a halt in front of a pair of boots—that was all I could identify with my head shoved down. The guard slammed me in the back with the butt of his rifle, and I fell on my face, sucking back a cry of pain.

I lifted my head and looked up. Donovan stood over me, his face as white as stone. His eyes were expressionless as they stared down into mine. Taking an unsteady breath, I pushed myself to my feet, bringing myself up to his eye level.

"Lieutenant," he said crisply, "I trust you slept well."

I stared at him, trying to decipher the cold, dead look on his face. "Of course, sir," I replied, not blinking.

Donovan stared at me a moment longer; then his gaze shifted to the guard who was still standing behind me, aiming the gun at my head. "Take him to my office."

I was slammed in the back once again and led across the base at gunpoint. The morning air was thick and smoky. I noticed almost all of the Trawlers were out.

"Wait here," the guard instructed as we entered the small cement building, pointing to a chair positioned on one side of Donovan's desk.

I took a seat as instructed. The guard waited with me, gun in ready position, until footsteps finally thudded up the steps and the door swung open.

"Thank you, Stevens. That will be all," Donovan muttered, dismissing the guard.

As soon as he had left, Donovan took a seat behind his desk. For several minutes he straightened his workspace in strained silence. Finally, he folded his hands on the desk and leaned forward.

"How did you get out of the rubble? You and Charlie were buried alive down there."

I looked at him for a long moment.

"I dug us out," I replied flatly, "sir."

Donovan said nothing, then, after a moment, his lips formed a thin smile. "Icarus, I know you are different from the rest," he said quietly, keeping his eyes connected with mine. "Very few could have done what you just did."

I made no reply.

He leaned closer. "Why did you save the girl?"

"Because I had to," I replied. "I wasn't leaving without her."

"Moral obligation?"

I shook my head. "Love."

Donovan's eyebrow twitched slightly. "Icarus, why do you think you are here?"

"I'm assuming there was some sort of agreement between you and Hatch," I answered. "Hatch sent me here because I deliberately disobeyed her orders. I left the base at Section C when I was ordered not to."

"Yes," Donovan agreed, his voice hardening to almost a growl. "Hatch does like her orders to be followed… Did you happen to notice the impressive scar across her eyebrow, Icarus?"

"Yes, sir."

"I did that." His expression twitched slightly. "I made that scar—I cut her face."

"Why, sir?"

He swallowed. "Because she killed my parents. Because she shot them both right in front of me." His voice was tense, strained.

My stomach twisted as he leaned a little closer.

"I had a pocketknife, one my father had given me. I lunged at her with a burning desire to kill her…" He shuddered slightly and closed his eyes as though blocking out the memory. "That… *animal.* But I was just a stupid little boy. I sliced her face and left a permanent scar. As punishment, I spent my life, up until I was your age, being raised and trained by that monster who inducted me into this militia. The monster who slaughtered my family."

I stiffened in my seat and waited for him to go on. My mind reeled back to the picture of the young boy I'd seen hanging on Hatch's wall.

"Hatch could have killed me that day, but she didn't. She didn't, because my violent behavior had shown me up—had revealed something about me to her that she decided she could use." The color drained from his face. "Can you guess what that was?"

I could, but I was too shocked to reply.

"A recusant," he answered for me, "Hatch had found a recusant—a young, innocent boy on whom she could experiment. Yes, *experiment*, Icarus. Just as she is going to do with you."

"But I thought—"

"That I was behind it?" he interrupted. "No. Why do you think Hatch is here?" He leaned forward to look at me. "Hatch *had* initially been sending you here as punishment for your unruly conduct… but you gave yourself away when you broke out of the Bullet, Icarus. No normal Fragmented person could do such a thing."

"But how did *you* find us in the mountains?" I blurted, unable to resist. "It was Charlie, wasn't it?"

"Very observant," he granted. "Unfortunate about your inclination towards love—you could have escaped quite cleanly if you had disposed of her."

"Perhaps," I replied. "But as you say, my inclination is towards love. I would rather bear whatever consequences may come than betray myself."

Donovan nodded slowly. "You make me nostalgic, Icarus. I once thought and spoke similarly—I used to love. To speak of it boldly and act only upon my principles…" His eyes took on a faraway look. "But life… circumstances… have a way of beating that out of you. Life has a way of helping you to develop the callousness you need to survive. It may seem like a bad thing at first, but as time goes on, you begin to realize that love doesn't always win, Icarus. Justice and peace do not always prevail—morals and principles do not always serve the greater good…"

"How do you mean?"

"I mean that Hatch knows full well we cannot continue offing the population of Earth at this rate—it won't work. We'll lose the battle."

"And so?"

"And so we eliminate the recusants without killing them."

My brow creased. "I'm not sure that I follow."

"Hatch has developed a theory that recusants can be reprogrammed." He lowered his voice.

"But I thought if a Fragment is removed, the host is terminated."

"Hatch believes there may be a way to install a new Frag—one that would override the defective counterpart without it having to be removed," he stated.

"And… you were the experiment in all this?" I asked cautiously.

"I have seven Fragments in my cerebellum, Icarus, none of which were successful—they did nothing but plague me with extreme headaches. But Hatch believes she has hit on the correct formula." He gave me a knowing glance. "And she finds herself in need of fresh meat."

For a second, I was confused. Then it hit me like a slap in the face.

"Me?" I almost choked on the word. "They're—they're going to Frag-ment… me?"

"You're Hatch's new guinea pig, yes."

My mouth ran instantly dry.

*Stay calm, stay calm, stay calm…*

"If you're in on it yourself, why are you telling me all this?" My voice came out strained.

"Because I'm in on something else, too, Icarus," he answered. "Some-thing that destroyed nearly half of our troops last night in Howth."

I gaped at him, a sick feeling rising in my stomach. "The explosions…"

"Bombings," he corrected. "Carefully planned and executed by the very best of the recusant army."

"Recusant *army*?" I reiterated, stunned. "You're... acting as a double agent?"

He nodded, leaning back. "Hatch needs to be defeated. The time for revolution is ripe on the vine."

My muscles tightened. "At the cost of hundreds of innocent lives?"

His expression didn't alter. "It's unpleasant, I agree." He nodded slowly. "Last night I lost my most important asset, aside from you. Moran did not return." He dragged a hand over his face wearily. "I was going to use her to do great things in the next attack—right here in the heart of New Dublin... She could kill like no other."

"And she hated it!" I exploded, lunging to my feet. "She... she *hated* it, just like I do..." My throat tightened as his words sank in. "How could you do that to her? H-h-how could you send her out there to die? To be killed in an attack *you* planned!"

Donovan didn't flinch. "In times of war, Icarus, we must sometimes do things that go against our very nature," he responded calmly. "Which is exactly what I will be expecting you to do when the time comes."

"What do you mean?"

"I mean that soon you will be alone in the lab with Hatch, Icarus." Donovan spoke quietly, leaning forward. "She will be installing your Fragment herself."

"When?"

"That, I couldn't say," he replied.

I swallowed, feeling sick, as he slid open one of the drawers in his desk. "Why are you telling me all this?"

Ignoring me, he took something out of the drawer, then closed it again and straightened back up to look me in the face. "Because we're going to make her lifelong work blow up in her face," he replied quietly, grabbing my wrist. "I want you to destroy her, as she has destroyed..." He stood up, rising to meet me at eye level. "Make her suffer as she made my parents suffer. I need you, Icarus. Now that I..." He faltered slightly, but then his jaw stiffened. "Now that I've lost Moran."

He turned my hand over and placed a slender knife with a black handle in my palm. "I'm going to save you, Icarus." He looked me straight in the eyes as he closed my fingers around the knife. "But you must do exactly as I say."

"Or what?" I asked.

Donovan dampened his lips with his tongue and leaned his hands on his desk. "Or else your friend Charlie will join the rest of the dead RGM members we just buried."

# CHAPTER THIRTY

## *Lara*

I felt the ocean around me, her mighty folds rising in tempest strength, threatening to throw me against the cliffside. I felt her rolling rhythm beneath me, the swells as they formed and fell, rocking me gently downward. She filled my lungs and sang me to sleep in her bubbling darkness.

In listless unconsciousness, I dreamed. I dreamed of my brother and my sisters, my mother and father. I dreamed of the cottage in the woods, and my conversation with the hazel-eyed lieutenant. I dreamed of Ronan's note, his last words to us: *Never stop searching.* And finally I dreamed that the sea coughed me up on a rocky shore. I felt something pound my chest with a will to get in until I vomited seawater and breathed again. I dreamed of a voice that sounded familiar. I dreamed of strong arms carrying me.

Like a ghost of a memory, I could hear the train as it derailed and crashed. That sound that seemed to repeat, over and over, that I would never see my family again.

"No!" A sob roared from my throat. "I cannot be different—I cannot be different! I cannot leave them!"

"Shhh, Lara, it's okay…"

"I want to go back…" My head felt as though it were on fire. "I want to go back, please—please let me go back! Let me go back…"

I felt something warm grip my hand.

My shouts, like the waves that had carried me, rose and ebbed away to whimpers.

"Let me go back…" I wept. "Please let me…"

"It's all right, Lara," said a faraway voice. "You're safe now. I promise, you're safe…"

———————————

I awoke to the sound of rain falling softly. I didn't know where I was, so I imagined myself tucked beneath white sheets and quilts that smelled of lavender. I heard my mother creak open the door. I listened to her footsteps as she crossed the floor and slid open the window. The songbird chorus swept in on the warm breeze.

I felt her hand against my cheek.

"Lara, it's time to wake up."

The voice twisted and swirled in the darkness as the sounds of the birds and the wind faded away.

"Lara, can you hear me?" The warm fingers squeezed my hand gently.

My lips quivered; I felt a tear tracing down my cheek. "Yes, I can hear you," I whispered, squeezing back.

I felt strong arms wrap around me. I sobbed, gasping for air.

"Where am I? What's happening to me?" I whispered. "What happened?"

I rubbed away my tears, blinking furiously in attempts to open my eyes. As my vision slowly cleared, I found myself gazing up at ripples of wisteria vine; one large blossom in particular was reaching down to nuzzle my face. I reached up a hand to touch it, softly running my fingers over its petals. I breathed in and felt my aching lungs fill with the fragrance of blossoms.

"You're back in the cottage you so generously allowed me to take shelter in," a familiar voice replied. "Although, honestly, I think the term *tree house* is more fitting—seeing as there is a tree growing out of the center of the floor."

I looked up to find those hazel eyes. "Areos." I exhaled his name. "I thought for a moment I would not see you again."

He hesitated, looking down at my face, then slowly nodded. "Yes. Well, when you left last night, I thought the same thing. That's why I tried to stop you."

"I know… but I had to get to Icarus…"

"Did you?"

I shook my head slightly, a lump forming in my throat. "The barracks collapsed before I could get to him."

Areos heaved a sigh, pressing a hand to his brow. "*Shit…*"

"I tried…" I whispered, a tear burning across my cheek. "I'm sorry."

"Don't say you're sorry. It's not your fault."

I sniffed, swiping my shaky fingers across my eyes. "But you saved me, and I couldn't save your friend Areos—I should have been back sooner, I should have—"

Areos shook his head, sliding his hand back over mine. There was a heaviness in his eyes. "There was nothing you could have done. You tried your best, Lara," he told me quietly. "And I wasn't the one who saved you."

I slowly sat up to look Areos in the eyes. "Who, then?"

His eyes scanned my face gently for a moment; then he turned slowly to gesture beyond the window at the end of the room. "He's outside…"

There was something about the way he said it… something that stirred my soul. I took a deep breath and slid my legs over the side of the bed. "Will you help me up?"

I made my way across the cottage like a child who had never walked before: tiny, staggering steps with Areos's arm wrapped around me the whole time. The small cottage door creaked open slowly, allowing in my first taste of what lay beyond it: a breeze like the one I had dreamed of. And it was sweet.

Beyond the door, beyond the tiny porch, were trees and grass and wildflowers. Nothing was dead, nothing was dried up, nothing was faded—it was all green and golden and bursting with life.

I clasped one hand over my mouth as tears welled in my eyes.

Kneeling on the ground in the center of it all was a familiar old man pushing seeds into the ground with his large weathered thumb. He turned to look at me when he noticed me standing there, a smile spreading across his face as he stood and walked toward me.

I pulled gently away from Areos to descend the steps and run the rest of the way to collapse into his arms, the same arms that had snatched me from the cold waves.

"It's you," I whispered, sobbing into his chest. "It's you—you came… you came…"

He laughed, and I felt it roll through his chest like wind in the green hills. "Yes, dear one, I am here." He lifted my chin and looked down into my eyes. "Did you think I had left you forever?"

I shook my head, laughing, sobbing. "No, sir."

He smiled as I stared up into his weathered face. He shook his head. "I am not 'sir,' remember?" he whispered, brushing my tears from my cheek. "I am your teacher."

---

"Sensei…" I said his name quietly. We sat on the edge of the porch, overlooking the garden and the restored wilderness around us. He rolled a walnut from one of the trees between his palms. "I didn't get to the base in time to get Icarus out of the containment area before it collapsed. He was still down there."

A heaviness filled me like lead. I felt the warmth of his eyes.

"Icarus is capable," Sensei replied softly. "Trust him, Lara. Believe that all will be well."

"But how, Sensei?" Areos spoke up now, seated on the opposite side of our teacher. His arms were crossed and his brow was furrowed. "How can all be well? Icarus is probably lying crushed under a pile of rubble. That's actually the opposite of 'all being well.'"

Sensei cracked open the walnut. "Have faith." He tossed the meat of the nut into his mouth. "What have you learned from your time in the Dimension if not that?"

I smoothed the fabric of my soft gray dress over my thighs and pulled the quilt that Areos had brought me a little more snugly around my shoulders. It felt so good to be in dry clothes and warm again.

"Sensei, the Dimension…" I began slowly. "What's it really like?"

Sensei smiled. "Perhaps Areos can show you."

Areos grunted. "We can't just transport from anywhere—our portal is long gone." Then he gestured towards our surroundings. "It looks like this place—you've seen one forest, you've seen them all. I, for one, don't mind being back on Earth." His brow furrowed. "I love the Dimension, but as it used to be, not as it is now."

"Then why did you allow it to become so?" Sensei picked up another walnut from the pile he had gathered.

Areos turned to look at him, offended. "Me? What do you mean, me? What did I have to do with it all?"

"What didn't you?" he returned. "You lived there, did you not? You trained there, you slept there, you breathed the air and grew, and helped your friends do the same, did you not?"

"Yes, but Mitsue is in charge."

"No one is in charge," Sensei replied, cracking open the nut and placing it in my hand. "Least of all young Mitsue."

Areos heaved a frustrated sigh. "Well, you haven't been there in a while, Sensei, so I guess you wouldn't know."

"Do not wait for someone else to change the world for you, Areos," Sensei told him, a steadfastness in his voice. "Do not blame someone else for not changing something when you yourself sit idle."

"Idle?" Areos sputtered. "I-I am not!"

"Here." Sensei handed him a fistful of walnuts. "Crack some."

Areos angrily snatched the walnuts. "Sensei, this whole thing has been utter chaos—do you even realize that? Do you even get what we've all been going through?" He pried at the nut with his fingernails. "Where were you all this time? Why didn't you come to help us?"

"I did not hear you ask for my help, Areos," Sensei replied.

"Well, whatever—I needed it!" He bashed the nut fiercely against the porch until it shattered. "But you were probably too busy planting a frickin' garden somewhere, right?" Areos picked himself up off the porch and stormed off into the woods.

I sat there and nibbled my walnut, watching him go. "Areos is so…" I took a breath, searching for the right words. "He is cold, Sensei. Inside, I mean."

"He has allowed what is outside to shake that which is within, Lara."

"But I've… I've seen darkness too, Sensei," I replied quietly. "And it has not shaken me inside."

Sensei nodded, looking out over the garden. "I know, dear one."

Areos had made it to the edge of the trees, where he was now angrily kicking rocks. We both watched him in quiet contemplation.

"Perhaps, Lara," Sensei said finally, "*you* should be the one to show *Areos* the Dimension."

I felt my eyebrows pull together. "But, Sensei, I have never been there."

"Precisely."

"Areos said the portal is—"

"Areos is, himself, a portal between this dimension and the next," Sensei interrupted quietly. "We all are. Few realize it, but those who do can easily commute between realms without an external portal."

I looked at him uncertainly. "Do you think Areos will believe that?"

Sensei didn't reply. He only smiled a little and nodded in Areos's direction.

I took a deep breath and slid off the porch to the soft grass below. I walked through the garden, a renewed determination in my footsteps. I pushed past the brush and entered the forest. Light filtered down golden through the leafy green canopy above. I spotted Areos a few yards ahead, leaning back against the trunk of a large oak, frowning at the sky. He looked up as I approached.

"So it was Sensei who saved me and healed me," I began, giving him a once-over, "not you?"

He shook his head. "Not me." He hesitated. "However much I may have wished it."

"Well, there is something you can do for me now."

One light blond eyebrow quirked. "What would that be?"

I stepped closer and took him by the hands, looking straight into his eyes. "Teach me how to transport."

Areos looked down at our hands, seeming almost taken aback by my sudden touch. "I... I, uh." He swallowed. "I can't just transport from anywhere. It doesn't work that way. Besides, I don't know if I can bring you in there. We got in major trouble last time, when Icarus and I brought Charlie in—"

"Charlie? Charlie saw the Dimension?"

"Uh, well, yes, but—"

"Well, now I really must see it, then," I cut in, grinning. "Just try. Sensei believes you can."

Areos took a breath, looking like he was about to protest, but then he stopped. He glanced around as if we were being spied on, and then looked back to me. "Whatever." He sighed. "I guess we can *try*. Close your eyes."

"Close my eyes?"

"Yes." He cleared his throat. "Portals are usually in a small dark space... But since we don't have one to transport from, closing our eyes will have to do."

I gave him a suspicious look, then my eyelids fluttered shut. "Okay."

"Okay..."

I could feel his hands beginning to sweat. Or was that me? I couldn't tell.

"Imagine a ravine," he began. "Two craggy peaks rising, then falling to meet, leaving a big empty space between them. Imagine mist rising from the void like billows of smoke, but not angry and filled with ash. No... more like the mist that comes up from the ground after it rains, but ten times as thick. Imagine a smell like a rain forest, but sounds like a distant quartet warming up for a concert. That's the wind—the wind sounds like that there."

A smile found my lips.

"Imagine small woven dwellings, like baskets, strung across the ravine, hanging in midair. This is the dormitory, where the students live. Imagine ropes and narrow bridges connecting them all to the cliffside, and then imagine platforms—two of them. One is bigger than the other, and it's covered in a thatched roof. This is where the students train… where we train…" His voice quieted. "Imagine, at the end of the long platform, a hallway. Are you imagining it?"

"Yes. Yes, I'm imagining it."

"The hallway is lined with doors, all mahogany, and all lit by natural light pouring in through tall windows lining one side. There is one door in particular. You reach out and open it, and as it swings open, the light spills in to illuminate what looks like a thousand glittering jewels. A tucked-away cavern."

I imagined it all, leaning into Areos's every word, holding on to his hands a little tighter, though I barely noticed.

"You step inside and shut the door behind you," he continued, even quieter. "Everything goes dark. Everything begins to grow cold. You begin to hear echoes of my voice as I speak—you begin to hear the soft dripping of water as condensation rolls off the walls. You feel walls closing around you…"

Shivers broke out over my skin as the temperature around us changed. The next time he spoke, I *could* hear echoes on the edge of his voice.

"Then I reach out for the handle… I turn it." A shrill creaking sound split the silence as my eyes flew open, only to be blinded by a sudden blast of bright white light. "And we've arrived." Areos sounded surprised—stunned by what he'd just been able to do. He stepped to the side, gesturing for me to step out first. Finally, he gave me a little smile. "Welcome to the Dimension, Lara."

I took a careful step forward, squinting, blinking furiously as I brought up a hand to shield my eyes from the sunlight. Before me was a tall glass window stretching from floor to ceiling. Beyond that, a setting sun, a sheer cliffside carpeted in green and wildflower hues, and billows of fog rolling up from the yawning void below. Basketlike pods swayed in the sighing breeze, strung out like a spider's web, and in the distance, I heard the calls of birds and what sounded like the trilling soprano of a violin.

My breath caught in my throat as I stepped quietly forward, stopping to touch my fingertips to the cool glass. I could almost see the wind as it blew past, stirring the mist into swirling shapes that reflected the pink glow of the sky above.

I sighed, and my breath misted the glass. I sensed Areos's presence beside me.

"What do you think?" he asked.

"I think it's…" I trailed off, not taking my wide eyes off the landscape sprawling before me. "I think it's the most beautiful thing I have ever seen."

Areos made no reply.

I turned to glance at him. "See? Told you you could do it without a portal."

He cleared his throat uncomfortably, his face going slightly red. "Would you, uh, like to see the training platform?"

I nodded eagerly and followed him down the hallway.

"That's Sensei's office." He pointed to one door in particular. "That's where he used to work before he left us to return to Earth."

I couldn't help but notice the bitterness in his tone as we walked. "You sound as if you don't approve of his actions, Areos."

"He doesn't seem to care whether I approve or not. Sensei does as he likes."

"There I think you are wrong."

He shot me a glance. "What do you know about it? You weren't even here."

"No, but I can see in his eyes that he is every bit as grieved as you are."

"I just don't see what the point was in leaving—why'd he do it? What was he even doing, anyway?"

"Saving me from a train crash," I replied unabashedly. "And no doubt seeing what you would do with your freedom—what you all would do with it."

"I am glad Sensei saved you," he said finally as we emerged onto the wide-open platform. "But I also can't help but wonder, why you? Why you, of all people?"

I thought about it for a moment, looking across the great expanse to the sunset that lay beyond the rail. "I do not know why," I confessed finally. "I would be lying if I said I understood everything, Areos. I just… believe that it must be for a good reason."

My footsteps echoed in the emptiness as I walked over to the railing.

"I don't understand how that can possibly be enough of an answer for you," Areos countered. "There's a reason for everything—cause and effect. Why did Sensei save *you*? Is that the only reason he left the Dimension, or were there others he saved?"

"Maybe he saved me because I lost everything I knew…" I replied, looking out over the golden ravine. "Maybe he knew about what happened to my brother. Or maybe there was an entirely different reason. Why don't you ask him, Areos?"

He fell silent for a moment, pausing beside me at the rail. "What happened to your brother?" His tone had changed from cynical to sympathetic. "I mean, you didn't mention it before—you don't have to talk about it. I just—I—"

"It's okay," I reassured him quietly. "I don't mind." I kept my gaze fixed on the ravine as I took a steady breath. "Back when I was growing up, I spent all my time with my sisters and my brother, Ronan. I was the youngest—the baby. I looked up to him almost like a second father," I explained; a small smile crossed my lips. "He was a fortress. He taught me so many things, and he was always there for me—for us… But one day he disappeared. And we never found him—never even figured out what had happened to him."

Areos was silent for a moment. "I'm sorry…"

"Don't be… It was a long time ago."

"But it must still hurt."

I nodded, a lump forming in my throat. "Despite the theory, time doesn't heal all wounds. We just learn to live life perpetually wounded."

Areos nodded slowly.

I turned to face him. "But the note he left me gave me hope—in it he told me to 'never stop searching,' so I never did."

Areos's brow furrowed. "But that makes no sense."

"Not everything has to—not everything needs to be understood and explained."

"Not true," he returned stubbornly. "Everything can be explained."

"Really?" I asked dubiously.

"Really," he insisted.

I gazed up at him for a moment, into his hard, decided eyes. His face was like something that would hang in a museum: older looking than it was, and protected behind a layer of bulletproof glass, complete with a jaded frown. In one quick motion, I lifted onto my toes, pulled him closer, and placed a quick, soft kiss on his lips. I felt him stiffen under my hands, and when I pulled away, his face was flushed.

He stared at me, wide-eyed. "W-w-what was that?"

"Something for you to explain," I replied. "Since everything can be."

Areos's mouth dropped open; then he closed it again. He cleared his throat. "Uh, you, uh—you kissed me."

"Mm-hmm. But *why* did I kiss you?"

He swallowed, staring down into my face. "I can't—I couldn't say. I can't know what you're thinking."

"Can't you?"

He shook his head, still red-faced.

"Well, I can tell you're thinking about kissing me back," I told him. "And I'm fairly certain you wouldn't be able to explain that either."

He gaped at me. I could tell he wanted to kiss me and curse me all at once. I smiled and stepped past him now, walking across the platform.

"Come on," I said. "What's down this way?"

For a moment, I walked alone while Areos remained fixed where he was, recalibrating. Then he snapped out of it. "Oh, er, those are—those are just safe rooms."

"Safe rooms? What are those?"

His footsteps finally quickened and caught up with mine.

"They're rooms that are used for private meetings, training sessions, procedures, et cetera," he explained, falling into step beside me. "But it looks like no one's here at the moment, which has become the norm of late—"

Then he clamped a hand down on my shoulder. The gesture was so sudden I startled, but just slightly.

"What?" I gasped.

"Shhh." He lifted a hand. "Listen."

I did, tilting my head to the side. Sure enough, I detected the muffled tones of back-and-forth voices. I shot Areos a look, raising an eyebrow.

His eyes shifted back and forth, studying thin air. Then he flattened himself against the wall, pulling me with him, as one of the many white pocket doors rolled quickly open and closed again, letting someone out into the hallway with us: a young man with a muscular build and bright red hair.

Areos dropped his guard, recognition flashing in his eyes. "Runner," he called, straightening up again. "What's going on in there?"

The young man walked over to meet us. "Hey, what are you doing here? Who's this?"

Areos sighed, obviously irritated. "Runner, Lara. Lara, Runner," he hurriedly introduced us. "Now what's going on?"

Runner acknowledged me with a polite nod, then refocused. "Nothing good, unfortunately."

"What do you mean?"

"I mean that Mitsue's on the warpath," he explained, lowering his voice to a whisper. "Mala's covering for me so I can go tell Fin."

"What kind of warpath?"

Runner sucked in a breath, rubbing his forehead. "Why don't you guys just come with me? It would be easier to tell everyone at once."

I followed the two of them back to the cavern, and we transported again. This time, though, when the atmosphere shifted and the darkness melted away, we found ourselves in what looked, and smelled, like a dank basement.

I blinked as my eyes adjusted. I stood staring up at the massive hole above us, through which I could see straight up to what looked like an old bell tower. "Where are we?" I asked quietly. "A... a church?"

"Yeah. This is Fin's portal," Runner explained, sprinting away and leaping up to grab hold of the edge of the floor above. He climbed up and reached down to offer me a hand. "What's your name again?"

"Lara," I replied, allowing him to hoist me up to the floor above. "Who is this Fin person I keep hearing about?"

"I told you—he's another slider," Areos replied.

"He's a great guy," Runner said at the same time. "Although I'm not sure why his portal is in a decaying old church building in the middle of nowhere."

"It didn't used to be the middle of nowhere," Areos corrected him, scrambling up after us. "It used to be the outskirts of Dublin."

I gazed around at the decaying sanctuary, an eerie feeling of déja vu coming over me.

"Come on—this way." Runner waved us onward, marching towards the back door. He kicked it open and vanished outside.

"You coming?"

I turned slowly towards the sound of Areos's voice, my eyes still focused on the cobweb-covered chandeliers above. I nodded, following slowly. Areos gave me a brief reassuring smile before following Runner outside. We emerged into a dried-up tangle of what must have been a beautiful garden once, rolling out in the shadow of the steeple and surrounded by a weathered wrought-iron fence.

"This place," I said softly, skipping the steps to jump down to the soft soil. "It feels so… so strange."

"Strange?" Areos asked.

"Like, familiar," I clarified, shielding my eyes to gaze up. "Like a distant memory I can't clearly recall."

I stared up at the steeple for a moment before shrugging it off. I crossed the old churchyard to join Areos at the gate, where he stood waiting for me.

"My father was a gardener," I told him quietly. "He tended the gardens at a few churches nearby where we lived—one looked so much like this place. But I can scarcely remember; I was so young."

A thoughtful look crossed Areos's face. "Funny you should say that. Fin was just telling me that his—"

"Guys, come on!" Runner shouted through cupped hands; he was already fifty yards ahead. "We don't have all day!"

"Yeah, yeah, we're coming!" Areos waved me forward.

After a little while I understood why Runner had hurried us along. Apparently, this Fin person liked to hide himself away in the mountains— *deep* in the mountains.

We hiked through the woods, climbing steadily higher and higher, until the remains of the village below were dwarfed and then swallowed altogether by the trees. Runner told stories about a Death Vapor attack, and Areos butted in several times to accuse him of embellishing the tale, reminding him that he was the one who had been there.

Finally, just when I began to doubt whether or not we were ever going to find this Fin, Runner lifted one hand high in the air, waving to a set of figures far off in the distance.

"Fin! Hey!"

One of the figures waved back. Presumably Fin.

As we got closer, I realized that the forest around us had slowly come to life, fading from a lifeless brown to rich green hues, reminiscent of Sensei's, and even my own, abilities.

"Runner, Areos! What's going on? Did you find Icarus?" The voice belonged to a young man a little older than Areos. He approached us with purposeful steps. He was tall, athletically built, and his emerald-green eyes looked as determined as he did. Waves of messy golden hair spilled over his forehead. He came to a halt in front of us, his eyes darting between Runner and Areos for a moment before shifting quickly to me. He did a double take.

"I've found Icarus, yes," Areos replied, "but that's not the reason we're here."

Fin acted as though he hadn't heard. He squinted as he looked at me. "Who's this?" He stepped up to me, extending a hand for me to shake.

"Don't worry—she's safe," Areos quickly assured him. "She's on our side."

I glanced from Fin's hand to his face. The same strange feeling that had come over me in the church had returned. "Lara," I said, giving his hand a firm shake. "My name is Lara."

His grasp went limp in mine as he continued to stare intently down at me. "Lara?" He almost whispered it.

I nodded, slowly pulling my hand away.

Areos raised an eyebrow, giving Fin a strange look before sidling up a little closer to me.

"Fin," Runner interrupted, "I have some important news…" He stopped, his eyes going wide as he glanced suddenly at the young woman who stood silently behind Fin. A young woman with hair as white as snow, and eyes like cedarwood.

"Is that…?" Runner faltered.

"I can't believe you found her." A look of shock passed over Areos's face. "And she's…"

"Human." The young woman finished for him, bowing her head slightly. "Yes."

# CHAPTER THIRTY-ONE

## *Hawk*

I'd kissed Fin. I hadn't realized how much I felt for him until we were standing there, yelling into each other's faces. It was then, staring into his eyes, that I'd realized how much I needed him—how much I had *always* needed him.

"I don't know what to do," I'd told him quietly as we sat there watching the river roll past, my head resting on his shoulder. "I should have listened to you. I shouldn't have been so—so—"

"Stubborn?" he offered softly, smoothing his thumb over my hand. "I think it's in your nature."

"Well, now everything is ruined because of me."

"Not ruined. Complicated."

"I barged into the situation and tried to force my own will and authority—ugh! Fin, I hate myself sometimes."

"Stop it."

"No, seriously."

"Mitsue is somewhat to blame, you know," Fin countered. "He's the one who wants to use our powers for evil—to destroy the RGM simply because he doesn't see any other way out of this. He recognized you. I saw it in his eyes."

"And Delta," I added hesitantly.

Fin made no response.

After a moment I straightened up to look at him. "The way she spoke to you…" I began slowly. "The way she said that you told her I had jumped into the ravine… It made it sound as if… as if there was—"

"As if there was something between us?" Fin finished, turning to face me. "No, Hawk, there wasn't…" He trailed off, his voice quieting as his eyes stayed fixed on mine. "Not in the way that you imagine."

I asked nothing. I waited until he was ready to go on.

"Hawk, I have loved you since the moment I set eyes on you," he began. "I have always known you were our Sunrise, and I have also always been aware that you were meant to be with someone else, not me—"

"Fin, don't say that—"

"Please, Hawk." He put up a hand, an almost pained expression crossing his face. "Just hear me out."

I gave a slow nod of consent.

"I decided long ago that it didn't matter to me—that I couldn't be with you. I loved you then, I love you now, and I always will love you. But when you left the Dimension, when you left to redeem the other half of your soul, Hawk, my own ripped in half. I found myself fighting my human weaknesses, struggling just to breathe, but it seemed like everything only served to remind me of what I had lost… You, most of all…"

Fin looked down at our hands, still intertwined. "There were times, Hawk, when I forgot my responsibility as a slider—as an anomaly of Earth. There are times even now when I feel weak and human—times when I have fallen into the arms of someone else, looking for them to piece me back together when that's what I should have been doing myself." He paused. "Yes, Hawk, even I feel that human struggle sometimes—I've hurt others in the process, you included, by allowing your secret to be known."

I looked at him for a moment in silence, a strange feeling of release filling me. I could still remember a day, looking back, that I hadn't even been brave enough to tell Fin about my past. Now everyone knew, and somehow, I'd moved so far beyond it that I didn't care.

How far I had come. How far we both had come.

It was as if everything Sensei had ever told me had finally come into clear focus.

I pressed my lips together, taking an unsteady breath. "It's not my secret anymore, Fin…" I said quietly, still looking into his eyes. "It does not define me… not anymore."

Fin didn't reply right away, he just looked into my face, circling his thumb over the back of my hand. Slowly, he lifted my fingers to his lips and kissed the backs of them. He smoothed his hand over my palm, studying it for a moment like each line and wrinkle that ran across it was a star trail. He pressed it to his lips, closing his eyes, breathing in. For a moment I felt the features of his face imprinted against my hand, each so familiar. My fingers grazed his warm skin and the stubble on his cheeks.

I drew an unsteady breath as he let go, the air cool on my skin in the place where his lips had been. His eyes steadied on mine.

"It *never* defined you, Hawk," he answered, his voice quiet. "Not to me."

A lump began to form in my throat. Everything I'd wanted to say escaped me. So I said nothing.

Taking his face in my hands, I leaned in and kissed him.

His lips were soft and warm and made something inside me go weightless. I wanted to hold onto that moment—him. I wanted everything to just… stop. I wanted to forget that anything else existed but the two of us in this capsule of paradise.

But even then, it was as if I could feel something inside me pulling me in another direction. I could hear a voice on the edge of the wind, whispering my name.

I drew back a little, taking a deep breath and squeezing my eyes shut. I felt the warmth of his thumb against my cheek.

"Hawk…" Fin whispered, gently brushing a strand of hair away from my face. He didn't finish, but I could feel his gaze on my face as my throat grew tighter.

I didn't say anything because I knew I didn't have to. He already knew.

I wrapped my arms around him, resting my head on his shoulder so he couldn't see the tears welling in my eyes.

I couldn't help but feel like he was already slipping through my fingers.

———————————

I sat at the base of the elm we had climbed while Fin rebuilt the fire. I watched as he carefully placed each stick and stacked each twig, each action deliberate and thought out.

I held one of the plump golden apples in my hand but, in spite of my rumbling stomach, I didn't eat it. I was tired of *having* to eat. I was tired of needing to sleep every night. I was tired of not being able to shift, or form an energy orb between my two hands.

"You know, when I was down in my world beneath the ravine, I learned how to channel fire," I told Fin, still studying the apple. "I taught myself."

"I'm not surprised to hear it." He leaned in to nurture the tiny flame with his breath. "I've always told you you're capable of all that you set your mind to."

I watched as the flame grew gradually stronger.

"That was the easy part. It was defeating the wolves that was hard, slaying my thoughts—the only things that seemed to stand between Icarus and me…" I trailed off, looking down at the apple again. "Against getting him back. Not that it's done much good."

"What makes you say such a thing?"

"Earth," I replied flatly, looking up at him. "Earth in all its wretchedness. It doesn't seem like Icarus has done much good with the other half of my soul."

"Because he's not meant to heal Earth alone, Hawk." He continued fanning the flames. "He's just… holding on to your soul for safekeeping, waiting for you—he's believed that you would return just as much as I have. And while the Earth does seem wretched, as you say"—he cast me a look—"a wise man once told me that all is never really lost. No matter how much it may seem that way at times."

"Sensei?"

"He wrote to me before he left the Dimension. That's how I knew you weren't coming back. He told me."

My gaze shifted to the fire. "He appeared to me at the bottom of the ravine before I sacrificed my humanity to bring Icarus back. He comforted me."

Fin sat down cross-legged. "And does he comfort you now? Does he guide you in any particular way?"

"In truth, Fin?" I sighed. "I sometimes find myself struggling to even hear his voice."

He twirled a stick between his fingertips; leaves slowly budded from it as it turned. "Do not mistake that struggle for reality, Hawk. Sensei is always with you."

Before I could reply, a voice rang out in the distance.

"Fin! Hey!"

Recognition immediately flashed over Fin's face. He jumped to his feet before I could ask anything.

"Runner! Areos!" Fin started toward what I could now distinguish as three figures among the trees; two I recognized, one I did not. "What's going on? Did you find Icarus?"

My heartbeat accelerated at the mention of his name. I got to my feet and followed Fin.

"I've found Icarus, yes," Areos replied. "But that's not the reason we're here."

Fin didn't reply right away; he was studying the newcomer. She was fair, petite and green eyed, her blond hair chopped down to an RGM standard buzz cut.

"Who's this?"

"Don't worry; she's safe," Areos quickly assured us. "She's on our side."

Fin extended a hand after a second, and she shook it.

"Lara," she introduced herself. Her voice had an Irish lilt. "My name is Lara."

I could practically feel Fin tense as I came up beside him.

"Lara?" he repeated.

Areos tossed Fin a certain look, coming up alongside the girl.

"Fin." Runner spoke up. "I have some important news…" Then he noticed me standing there and gaped. "Is that…?"

Areos finally acknowledged my existence—his eyes widened. "I can't believe you found her. And she's—"

"Human," I cut in, my hand brushing against Fin's slightly. "Yes."

Fin put up a hand before anyone could question further. "Why don't we all sit down and discuss this?" He jerked his head toward the fire behind us. "It will be dark soon anyway. You won't be able to hike back out of the mountains tonight."

Areos was still studying Fin through narrowed eyes, but he complied with everyone else.

"I've just come from a gathering," Runner explained, warming his hands over the fire. "They're still gathered in the Dimension as we speak—the council has decided on a course of action, and they're informing the students now. They have agreed that since the database is beyond our reach, we must… strike where we can, so to speak."

"Meaning take the side of the recusants," Fin finished for him. "By using our powers to off the leadership of the RGM."

"Yes, but now it seems that Delta caught wind of plans for a recusant uprising in New Dublin," he went on urgently. "Tomorrow night."

"Tomorrow night?" Lara's face went sheet white.

"It seems Mitsue and the council have decided that the recusants are on the right side of the battle, and that we should side with them. That together we can overthrow the UNC—of course, I'm paraphrasing."

Fin blew out a sigh, running a hand over his face. "What do they think this is? A dystopian novel? We're not here to overthrow the government! This is not what we trained for—this is not what Sensei trained us for."

"And they're wrong about the recusants," Lara interrupted, her voice small. "While I am very close to being one myself—I don't have a Frag—I have seen the evil they, too, are capable of. They fight fire with fire—in many ways there is no right side to this battle. Both are steeped in wrong."

Fin nodded thoughtfully, though he was still staring at her with a strange expression on his face. "Just so," he agreed slowly. "We have not returned to

Earth to take sides in a war—but to start a quiet revolution of our own."

"And how do you propose we do that, exactly?" Areos grumbled from where he was leaning back against the tree. "Seeing as we have nothing to work with—not even Icarus, though Sensei seems to think he's alive. Lara was there. She saw the collapse."

My throat instantly tightened as my gaze shifted to Lara's. "What collapse?"

"The barracks," Lara explained hesitantly. "The containment area where he was being held lies below it—the bombing was enough to cause some of the buildings to cave in. Areos was correct in his instincts that Icarus was captured—the Death Vapor attack was meant to drive him and the rest of the escaped RGM members out into the open. I captured Icarus and Charlie myself. They've been held at Base New Dublin ever since."

I drew a shallow breath, my heart pounding. "And now?"

"He was crushed to death," Areos answered gravely, staring into the flames. "I mean, most likely."

"Areos, how can you say that?" Lara corrected him harshly. "Sensei said to trust that he—"

"Sensei?" I blurted, staring at her. "Sensei is... Sensei appeared to you?"

Lara nodded slowly. "I didn't know who he was—I'd met him before, long ago, but I didn't realize who he was. Areos was the one to explain everything—after he attempted to kidnap me."

"Okay, lies. I wasn't going to kidnap her," he blurted. "I knew I would need someone on the inside in order to find Icarus—"

"But what he didn't realize, apparently, is that I scarcely had access to Icarus myself," Lara cut in. "Donovan and Hatch had him under lock and key—they were running experiments on him. Last time I saw him, he told me he thought it was because he, like me—like all of us here, I suspect—doesn't have a Fragment."

"Experiments?" I repeated, stunned. "What are they doing to him exactly?"

"That I couldn't say," she said quietly, looking me square in the face. "But I've seen what he's capable of. And I... I find it harder and harder to believe, the more I consider it, that he could die in such an accident."

Fin sat down beside me, seeming deep in thought. "So now the student body is to join a recusant battle against the RGM." He rubbed his jaw, staring into the blaze. "They won't make it out alive—and those who do will find themselves in the same place Icarus finds himself now: a lab. Using our powers against the RGM will only blow our cover. But we have to stop this attack somehow."

Runner sat down in the grass. "I don't think it's gonna be easy this time, Fin. The council has poisoned the student body. They seem to believe that this is the only way to bring things back to how they were. It's like… they've completely lost track of who they are and who their true leader… *leaders* are."

I didn't look up from the ground, but I still felt the burn of everyone's gaze.

"They're only following Mitsue and the rest of the council because, honestly, they're scared—whether they'll admit it or not." Runner sighed. "I know I am. They're not bad. They just… need an example to follow. It wasn't long ago that they were ready and willing for Fin to be their leader. The only reason Mitsue took over is that Fin refused—"

"Because I knew it was not my place," Fin interjected.

"Exactly!" Runner's voice escalated. "But it's hers—Icarus's."

Slowly I looked up at Runner, then around at everyone else. "What are you saying?" I asked quietly.

"I'm saying that I think you're the one who needs to go find Icarus," Runner replied, his voice unusually solemn. "Not Areos or Lara, or—or anyone. You're the Sunrise, aren't you? Aren't you supposed to be the one to go find him and make this right, Hawk? Aren't you the chosen one?"

I never would have thought Runner's words would make such an impact on me, but now I found myself sitting there with nothing to say. I felt like I was a student and he the teacher.

Icarus was alive. I could *feel* it. He was down there, bearing my markings, waiting for me to return. He was doing his duty. It seemed this time that *I* was the one who was running from it.

Feeling as though I was collapsing beneath the weight of the questions, I jumped to my feet and sprinted into the woods, leaving Runner's words hanging in the air.

*Aren't you the chosen one?*

# CHAPTER THIRTY-TWO

## *Fin*

I followed her into the forest—I knew full well where she was headed. The river had become our place of refuge. But I'd barely escaped the clearing when I heard a set of quick footsteps behind me.

"Fin, wait."

A hand clamped down on my shoulder and I turned to look at Areos. His eyes were round and stern in the lowlight.

"What are you doing?" he whispered fiercely.

I brushed away his heavy hand, unsettled by his question. "I'm going to talk to Hawk."

"No, that's not what I meant," he came back firmly.

"I'm afraid I don't—"

"You and Hawk." His words came down like a gavel of condemnation. "Did you really think no one would notice, Fin?"

"Notice what?"

"The way she's acting around you," he hissed, stepping closer. "The way you're acting around her."

I opened my mouth to speak, but the words stuck in my throat.

"Oh, god, Fin…" He dragged a hand over his face. "You made her fall for you?"

"I didn't make her do anything," I shot back, my voice hard. "Hawk is her own free person, Areos. She does as she wills—if I could *'make her'* do anything, if I *actually possessed* that ability, she would be back with Icarus by now."

Areos folded his arms, arching one eyebrow. "Are you *sure* about that, Fin?"

A wave of déja vu came over me. Not so long ago Runner had asked me almost the exact same question.

*"You find Hawk, and she goes back to Icarus… Are you going to be okay with that?"*

"Of course," had been my confident answer. *Of course* I would be okay with letting her go. Of course. But now, here I was, on the threshold of needing to do exactly that, and I found myself holding on with shaking hands.

"Fin." Areos's voice softened as he studied me, concerned. "I know it's hard for you. I know you like her—"

"No. No, that's where you're wrong, Areos. I don't like Hawk, I love her. I… She…" I trailed off, lowering my head to draw a shaky breath. "She's all that I have left, Areos."

"I know, Fin," he said finally, quietly. "But… you can't lose someone who was never yours to begin with."

I nodded, blinking back the sting in my eyes. "Yes. Yes, Areos, I know." I changed the subject; I couldn't bear talking about this any longer. "That, uh, that girl, Lara—she's interesting."

He smiled a little, nodding. "She is, isn't she?"

"How'd you find her?"

"It's a bit of a long story. But you wouldn't believe what she told—" He was cut off by Runner calling his name. Areos sighed, then gave me a weak smile. "When you get a chance, you should really talk to her yourself."

I nodded and he started walking back to the fire. In truth, I barely heard what he was saying. The girl's name alone had thrown me off—reminding me of that hollow place in my chest that could never be filled. My mind was haunted by that day I had left them behind in Ireland.

And now I would do the same with Hawk. I had to.

The sunlight had faded away to lavender dusk down by the stream where Hawk stood, gazing at her reflection in the crystal-clear water as it rippled past.

I hesitated at the edge of the tree line when I saw her, watching her for a moment. Then I stepped forward again and came up behind her. I wanted more than anything to wrap my arms around her and bury my face in the curve of her neck, to kiss her, to breathe her scent. But instead I just stopped alongside her.

"What are you thinking about?" I asked quietly when she didn't look up.

Hawk stayed silent for a long moment. Then I saw a tear slip down her cheek. "You," she whispered.

"Yeah?" I asked quietly. "What about me?"

Hawk took a deep breath, beginning a reply, only for her voice to crumple. She pressed her hands to her face, and this time I wrapped my arms around her.

"Shhh," I whispered softly, pressing my lips to her hair. "It's okay... It's okay..."

"No, it's not." Hawk turned to me now and sobbed against my chest, wrapping both arms tightly around me. "It's not okay, Fin. It-it never will be..."

"Oh, I wouldn't say that, Hawk..." I forced my voice to stay steady. "I think you'll find that you're well equipped to handle anything that comes your way. I think it's all going to be fine..."

"How can it be?" She sniffed, her voice muffled. "How can it be when I won't be with you?"

"You'll always have me, Hawk."

She shook her head, pulling back to gaze up into my eyes. "Why couldn't I have just been an ordinary person? Why couldn't I have been..." She trailed off, shaking her head and looking down before the tears had a chance to fall.

"Because, Hawk," I whispered, lifting her chin, "you were made for the *extraordinary*. And it has nothing to do with Icarus or me or even Sensei. Your purpose and destiny are not found in Icarus, Hawk..." I brushed her tears away. "They're found within *you*."

Hawk stared up at me through wide eyes welling with tears. "I just don't want to lose you, Fin…"

"No." I leaned forward to kiss her gently on the forehead. "No, you will never lose me. But there are a lot of people counting on you right now, Hawk…"

"I know…"

"Earth, to be exact. So you need to be the brave, strong soul I've always known you to be, Hawk—enough of this human stuff." I gave her braid a little tug and she sobbed a tired laugh.

"I don't know what to do, Fin…" She sniffed. "I don't know how to fix the mistakes I've made—how to stop the attack."

"So what if you don't?" I shrugged a little. "You know the first step— the one thing you, and only you, can do."

Hawk sucked in an unsteady breath. "I wouldn't know what to say to him… how to act."

"Then don't say anything." I held her out at arm's length, looking her straight in the eyes. "Just be you, Hawk. Be you, and set this bloody world on *fire*. Okay?" I gave her a little smile.

She wiped away her tears with her forearm. "Okay," she whispered.

———————————

I lay awake, staring up at the thick, starless sky stretched above, my mind churning like a restless sea. I listened to Hawk's quiet breathing; I could easily distinguish it from the rest, I knew it so well.

Eventually I got up to tend the dwindling fire, reaching for another branch to throw into the hungry flames. That was when I noticed that our small group was short by one.

In the dim moonlight I could make out the indentations of footprints in the dew. With one last glance at Hawk, I quietly crept from camp and fol- lowed the prints. They wound through the blue-tinted trees and ended at the ridge overlooking the valley, the place where Hawk and I had only just stood, watching bright plumes of red burst up into the sky as fire engulfed Howth. A small figure stood out among the vast navy-blue backdrop, leaning against a tree and staring out over the expanse rolling below.

I came to a quiet stop beside her.

"I've been awake all night. I'm surprised I didn't hear you sneak off," I said.

Lara turned to look at me, a tiny smile passing across her lips. "I'm an RGM sniper, Fin. Of course you didn't hear me."

"True enough." I gave a little laugh. Then there was quiet again.

"They don't understand, do they?" she mused after a long moment. "What they're getting themselves into—the council, I mean. The recusants are… fierce. Angry. Not all of them, but the many who fight…" She trailed off. "They aim to kill. Same as us."

I studied her in the moonlight. "Didn't you say you were practically one yourself?"

"I'm both, Fin—and neither." She gave a mirthless sigh. "I have no Fragment, but as far as the RGM knows, I'm an able-bodied, overachieving warrior. Well, except for Donovan…"

"Who?"

"My commander," she replied, her voice suddenly troubled. "He discovered that I was a recusant when I tried to help Icarus and Charlie escape. I was going to run myself, but… it didn't work out." She sucked in a breath. "And I'm discovering there's quite a lot more to Donovan than meets the eye…"

I gave no reply for a moment, continuing to stare at her.

She shot me a look. "Not to be rude, Fin, but you've been staring at me since we met." She straightened up. "Why is that?"

I felt my face go red. "I-I know, I'm sorry. I just… I can't help but feel as if we've met before. You seem so familiar."

Lara frowned thoughtfully, then shook her head. "Not possible, you've been tucked away in that Dimension of yours for quite a while," She smiled a bit. "What a fantastic… beautiful…"

"It is, isn't it? Sensei created it and upholds it still. It's a projection of his own consciousness."

"Sensei is remarkable. I don't know what I would have done if he hadn't…"

I watched her expression closely. "He saved you?"

"He's the only reason I was able to survive on Earth as I did," Lara answered. "He gave me hope—made me realize that I couldn't run from who I was… what I could do."

"What can you do?"

Lara shot me a side glance. "What can *you* do?"

"Well…" I threw my arm in a wide gesture to the rejuvenated woods surrounding us. "I've always enjoyed gardening, so…"

Lara's eyes swept up to the trees, then down to me again. "You did this? You healed the forest? I assumed that was Hawk's doing—Areos told me so much about her and Icarus."

I looked down at the damp grass. "I know how hard it's been for Icarus."

"It wouldn't have been if I had at least tried to break him out with Areos when we'd had the chance." She lowered her head. "I can't stop thinking about all the things I should have, could have, would have…"

"I am acquainted with the feeling, believe me." I leaned back against one of the trees. "But from what I gather, it sounds like you saved Areos's arse."

Lara laughed. "He is pretty pigheaded, I'll give him that. He seems cynical about most everything—his own existence included."

I couldn't help but grin. "Areos likes to see before he believes."

"I've noticed," she agreed, looking back to the valley below. "I'm the exact opposite. I like to jump before I look; isn't that the thrill of life? If we knew everything—if we knew exactly *what* we were searching for—life would be rather dull. Perhaps if we knew, we would stop." She paused, a faraway look on her face. "Maybe we don't know so that… so that we'll never stop searching."

A strange feeling gripped my heart. I looked at her for a moment without saying anything.

"I agree," I said finally, quieter. "I… I agree with you."

Lara was still staring out at the sky, which was beginning to phase from navy to purple. Finally, she stepped away from the ridge. "We'd better get a move on if we're going to get down there before the recusants do," she said, her expression becoming serious. "We have to get Icarus out of there as soon as possible, if he's even still there. And it sounds like Hawk is just the person to do that."

I looked at her for a moment, then folded my arms thoughtfully. "Lara, you've been in the RGM how long, exactly?"

"About five years."

I nodded slowly. "So you must know the inner workings pretty well."

"I know a bit." Then she smirked. "A bit more than you."

"That's… that's exactly what we need."

Lara quirked an eyebrow. "I'm not sure I follow…"

I shook my head, gesturing for her to follow me back into the forest. "You're not going to be the one following—you're going to be the one leading."

# CHAPTER THIRTY-THREE

## *Icarus*

The armed guard threw me into the tiny room and slammed the door behind me. There was a click as he locked it tight. I stumbled forward, catching myself against the wall. A bare bulb hung from the ceiling. Charlie jumped to her feet, still covered in dust, her uniform in tatters.

"Icarus! What the hell happened?"

"Nothing," I panted, straightening up. "It was—it was nothing—"

"What do you mean, nothing?" Charlie looked startled. "Did they… did they take you back to the lab?"

"No. No, they didn't." I gulped back the sick feeling. "But they're going to."

"Why?"

"Charlie, listen." I took a deep breath. "Someone wants me to do something wrong, something that's going to make things even worse. But if I don't do what they say, they're going to kill you and…"

My mind was still reeling from my meeting with Donovan—the things he had told me. I could feel the handle of the knife burning a hole in my back pocket. I forced myself to focus and not think about it.

Charlie narrowed her eyes. "And what?"

It took me a moment to find the right words. My voice was tight when it finally came out. "And they're going to use me for experimentation." I ran a hand over the back of my neck. "They want to see if it's possible to re-Frag a recusant."

Charlie's face went white. She took a heavy step closer. "They're gonna Frag you?"

I gave a tentative nod, though this did nothing but intensify the look on her face.

"Oh no," she growled. "No, they're not."

"Charlie—Charlie, no—"

She was already heading for the door, but I put a hand on her shoulder before she could get there.

"Icarus, let *go* of me *now*!"

"Charlie, *no*." I lowered my voice. "You don't understand—"

"No, *you* don't understand!" She cut me off. "I've installed thousands of Frags, remember? It's what I did."

"Yes, I remember. And?"

Charlie's lower lip trembled as she looked me in the eyes. "Why do you think we insert them at birth? Why do you think we do it in hospital labs, where no one can see what's happening?" She pressed her finger and thumb to her eyelids. "There were babies I'd have to hold all night just to stop them from trying to smother themselves…"

I swallowed hard. Just the thought was enough to make my skin crawl.

"I've never Fragged an adult," she finished finally. "No one has; god only knows how bad the side effects would be."

Except Hatch. Hatch had Fragged Donovan. Seven times, though none of the insertions seemed to have worked.

"The only way to avoid it is to kill someone, Charlie—and this person I've been ordered to kill…" My voice faded as I thought it through. "Lots of people are going to die if I do it: it's going to start a war. But if I don't kill them… we're both as good as dead."

"Icarus, listen to me. You can't let them Frag you," she said hoarsely. "You've taught me things I have never even heard of before: you've shown me what love is—mercy, faith, all of it. You're not like the rest of us—you're what's going to wake this dead place up. You're what's going to break down these walls. Don't you get that? You can't die—you can't let them win!"

My eyes stung as I looked at her. A tear rolled down her cheek, but she held on to that same hard expression.

I thought back over everything that had happened since the day we'd been shipped out of Section C: every obstacle we'd overcome, every long conversation we'd had—the concepts she'd never understood. The things I'd tried to explain to her over and over and over again. All the times she'd given me that blank expression and told me that she didn't understand. She didn't understand love or mercy or faith.

*… or does she?*

When I spoke, my voice was barely a whisper. "Why not?"

"Because I don't want to lose you," she answered quietly.

"But *why?*" I cut in, stepping closer, a feeling of anticipation rising within me.

"Because…" She trailed off. "You're different."

"So?" I probed. "Who cares?"

Her eyebrows pressed together in confusion. "I do…"

I couldn't believe what I was hearing. Then a grin spread across my face and I punched the air with both fists. "Yes!" I practically shouted. "Exactly!"

Charlie stared at me like I'd just escaped a mental hospital.

I grabbed her excitedly by the shoulders. "Remember we talked about this before? Remember—after the Death Vapor?"

"Uh, I guess." She picked my hands off. "I mean… I helped you because I didn't want you to die…"

Charlie's voice faded; I could see the gears turning behind her eyes. She just stood there, gaping at me. Then suddenly her hands clapped over the back of her head; her eyes screwing shut as if she were experiencing a brain freeze. She staggered backward and for a moment my stomach lurched with fear.

*"Disconnected hosts are terminated instantly"…* the words spoken many times at the council haunted me.

I lurched forward to grab her by the shoulders for support. "Charlie? Charlie, are you okay?"

For a moment she said nothing; she remained hunched and grasping her head. Then slowly she sucked in a deep breath and straightened up. Her blue eyes widened, as if she were seeing me for the first time. The expression of pain melted away from her face like snow to spring, and she burst into a laugh, a sound that was like a first breath, tears brimming in her eyes. "Icarus!" She gasped my name, shaking her head slowly as tears streamed down her cheeks. "I... *care* about you. I... Icarus, I've never actually *cared* about anyone before—even as a medic, I didn't actually care if they lived or died; it was just about doing my job."

"Because they programmed you not to feel," I answered, my words tumbling over each other as my mind raced. "They didn't want you to have feelings—to love or care about anyone—because then they wouldn't have control over you."

"I've never felt anything for anyone before..." She was still shaking her head as she backed off just slightly, looking down at herself as if she were a new person. Then she looked back up at me, and I could tell by the look in her eyes that something had clicked. "Icarus, what just happened?"

"You tell me. What did you do differently?"

"I don't know—nothing! I was just thinking about you—how I wanted to protect you." She was holding her head in her hands, trying to process it all, tears rolling down her cheeks.

*Thinking of someone other than herself...*

I stared at her, my mind racing. What if the Fragment only had as much control as we gave it? Maybe our ability to reason hadn't been eliminated by the Fragments: maybe it only had as much control as we believed it did.

Maybe the only thing holding us back, maybe the only thing that was keeping us slaves was that, all this time, we had believed a *lie*. A lie about *ourselves*. That we were who they said we were—who they programmed us to be and no more.

But nothing could be further from the truth. We were *infinitely more* than we could possibly imagine. This was the greatest secret. This was what no one realized—no one knew it was something they could defeat, something they could override if they simply realized they were more powerful than the

Fragment! Charlie had been able to do it, completely accidentally, because I'd introduced her to an entirely new concept:

Love.

"Charlie, this could be it," I said, struggling to keep my voice level. "This could be what makes or breaks the *entire* system—it may have nothing to do with the database or removing Fragments. It may be as simple and as difficult as… as one person choosing: choosing good instead of evil, love instead of hate or revenge. As simple as reaching within yourself and finding the love, hope, faith—the things that are already inside us…"

I paused for a long moment and the room fell silent.

"All this time we've been looking for something external that would change everything—that would save us, but everything we need… the answer…" I slowly placed a hand on my chest, my voice lowering to a whisper. "It's already inside us."

Charlie, still blinking and reeling as if she'd just awoken from a deep slumber, stepped forward, seeming to refocus. "Icarus… I don't like that look," she began warily, drying her cheeks with the backs of her hands. "What are you plotting?"

I bit my lower lip, my mind still racing as everything came into clear focus. I stared at her blankly for a moment before I answered. "I have to know if it's true…" I trailed off, my voice a whisper. "If this is it—if this is what could send the whole system toppling? I need to know."

"What are you saying?"

I took a deep breath, straightening up. "I'm going to let them do it. I'm going to let them Frag me… and I'm going to defeat it from the inside out."

Charlie pulled in a deep, irritated breath, running a hand over her face. "So basically one of us is going to die—if not both of us."

"Not a chance. You need to get out of here," I told her urgently. "If anyone comes for you—"

"I what, Icarus?" She snorted. "Fight them off with the large arsenal of weapons they've conveniently hidden in this room?"

I shook my head. "You don't need weapons. You've defeated your Frag, Charlie—you have the ability to control your own mind now."

She quirked an eyebrow. "I… am not sure that I follow…"

Despite the seriousness of the matter at hand, I couldn't help but crack a little grin. "You know," I began, bringing my hands up in front of me. "I've wanted to show you how to do this for a while now…"

She lifted an eyebrow, starting to question, but I shook my head.

"Just watch," I whispered.

Spacing my hands appropriately, I began to sway them gently back and forth until I could feel the energy pulsating between my palms.

"In the Dimension, we call it channeling…" I explained carefully, glancing up at her just as the invisible energy began to turn light blue. "And I'm going to teach you how to do it."

# CHAPTER THIRTY-FOUR

*Lara*

By the time Fin and I had walked back to camp, dawn had come to rouse the rest of our group. I felt a new weight of responsibility as I looked around at them, Fin's words repeating in my mind.

I couldn't help but wonder if I was the right person for the job he described, but there was no time for doubt. If we wanted to get to the base before the recusants did, we had to move.

"Where were you two?" Areos muttered through a yawn, stretching his arms overhead. "I know Fin's an insomniac, but I didn't realize you were a similar animal."

I tossed him a glance. "Who has time for sleep when there's so much work to be done?"

Hawk was already on her feet. Her face was almost as pale as her long braided hair. She adjusted the belt and shoulder strap over her white tunic, looking anxious.

"We shouldn't transport. We should hike down into New Dublin," Fin announced. "We need to get the lay of the land, and goodness knows what we'd be transporting right into the middle of. We don't want to go into this blind."

"Well, I hate to break it to you, Fin." Areos rubbed his eyes. "But that's exactly what we will be doing if we just go traipsing into the RGM's detection area."

"I've thought of that," Fin responded, turning to look at me. "Which is why I think Lara should be the one to help us get down and into the base."

Hawk looked approving, and Runner, still sitting cross-legged on the ground, bobbed his head in a nod. But Areos crossed his arms.

"Sneaking into the base without being apprehended?" he quipped dubiously. "All five of us?"

"Is it so hard to believe that I could get us in there safely?" I crossed my arms to match his.

"It's not that. Of course I believe you're capable."

"You yourself sneaked in without detection."

"Yes, but I was just one person!" Areos gestured around at everyone. "This is too much—this isn't going to work."

"Why not?"

"Because, it's just…" He trailed off, rubbing his forehead. "I hate my life."

I gave him a level, disappointed stare before turning to Fin, Runner, and Hawk.

"I'm confident that if a bigmouth pilot can get on base without detection, then a sniper, plus a few extras, surely can do the same," I declared, stiff-jawed. "If Donovan knows about the attack, he'll doubtless be preparing for it… We can take advantage of that distraction."

"And if we start out now, we'll get there by noon—before any fighting breaks out," Fin added. "Which is exactly what we need: to get in and out before the fighting."

"What happened to stopping the attack?" Areos countered.

Fin looked sternly at him for a moment. "I, for one, still believe in the prophecy and in what Sensei foretold. When the Sunrise and Sunset are reunited, things will change."

"Things will change?" Areos said dubiously.

Fin nodded.

"Well, I'm sorry," Areos grunted. "But that sounds a little too much like a fairy tale for me. I think we need a plan B."

"Oh?" I asked, though I wasn't interested in hearing what he had to say. "And what might that be?"

"I don't know—fighting?"

"And you think you can take on the RGM and the recusants, Areos?" I stepped closer.

"That's what the council decided—that's what the Dimension is doing!"

"Well, that's not what *we're* doing!"

"Well, maybe it *should* be!" Areos shot back.

"Maybe you shouldn't even be here, then." I dropped my voice. "Maybe you should go fight with the rest of the students."

"Maybe I should."

"Why don't you just leave, then?"

"Maybe I will!"

"Fine!" I hissed, getting right in his face.

"Fine!" he returned stiffly.

"Guys!" Fin stepped in, hands up. "Come on. No one's leaving, no one's backing out—not now." He nodded towards Areos. "Just cooperate, okay? Lara knows what she's doing—more than we do."

He grunted. "I was in the RGM too, you know."

"Keyword: *was*," I grumbled, then turned to Fin. "Time is of the essence—since you can lead a transport without a portal, I think we should transport halfway, into the woods surrounding the foothills. Areos and I will meet you three there."

"Meet us?" Fin questioned.

"I have to transport back," I explained. "It won't take me long—I have to retrieve my uniform." I glanced down at the gray dress I was still wearing, then looked around at everyone else. "I have an idea for helping the rest of you blend in a bit better... but I'll explain that later."

A look of understanding passed through Fin's eyes.

Areos, on the other hand, gave an irritated sigh. "Why do I have to go with you?"

I didn't answer. I turned and gave him a look; it was enough of an answer.

I strode away from the clearing. Areos followed reluctantly. We walked wordlessly through the evergreens and came to a stop when we reached the ridge. I turned to look at him.

"What's gotten into you?" The question was an angry one.

Areos sighed. "Nothing has 'gotten into me,' Lara. It's *been there all along*. Since I was born."

I crossed my arms, my gaze locking with his. "Why."

It wasn't a question.

"Because."

"Because why?"

"Because I don't know, okay?" he blustered, throwing his arms wide. "I don't know—I don't understand. I don't get how any of this is going to work, how we're going to 'save the world' without getting ourselves killed! None of this seems possible to me, and I'm not one to step out on thin ice, Lara—I need to *know*." He stepped closer, his jaw tense. "I need to be able to understand."

I shook my head. "You don't *need* to: you *want* to. And we can't always have exactly what we want—sometimes we're meant to not know. It's the only way faith works!"

"Well, then, maybe I don't want to have faith!"

My muscles tightening with frustration, I grabbed him by the hands and closed my eyes. I started thinking about the foothills and the woods and the cottage hidden away in the trees.

"You're the one who taught me how to do this, Areos," I murmured, focusing. "If this doesn't take faith, then what does?"

Areos didn't reply. The air seemed to shift around us, and when I opened my eyes again, we were back where we had started: standing at the edge of the woods surrounding the clearing. I could see the cottage through the leaves. I looked up into Areos's hazel eyes.

"You can't explain everything, Areos," I told him quietly. "You couldn't even explain the kiss. You didn't even know why I gave it to you—you just enjoyed it."

He studied me like I was something he couldn't untangle. Then he frowned. "Yes, but the rest of life is not like that," he replied. "Life-and-death situations are not like that. We can't go into this blind, Lara."

"We're not."

"But what if…?" He trailed off, stopped.

I watched his tortured expression for a moment before reaching a conclusion. "You're scared."

"What? No—"

"That's the only reason you need so badly to know, isn't it? Because you're afraid of what might happen, of what might go wrong, of—of all the 'what ifs.'" I placed one hand gently on his arm. "Areos, you are well able to face whatever they throw at you—we all are. It's now or never."

Areos sighed and pressed his fingertips to his forehead. "I wish I had your faith, Lara. I wish… I wish I saw the things you see: hope where there is none." He gave a mirthless, halfhearted laugh. "Life where there seems to be death and nothing more."

I felt myself smile. I gave his arm a little tug, beckoning him in the direction of the cottage.

"Well, it doesn't happen overnight," I told him. "It took almost two hundred years."

For a moment Areos followed me in silence. Then he gave a little laugh. "I guess I have a lot to look forward to."

---

We found Sensei working in the garden. Areos stopped at a distance, tugging his arm free from my grasp. Sensei stood and brushed himself off as I approached. He studied me through shining green eyes, a warm smile pulling the corners of his lips.

Without a word, I reached up and wrapped my arms around his neck. His hand went gently to my back, and he pulled me in close. I could hear the beat of his heart in his chest; his clothes were filled with the scent of pines and freshly turned soil. I breathed it in deep before pulling back to look up into his face.

"There is to be an attack, Sensei," I informed him.

He arched an eyebrow. "An attack from whom?"

"The recusants," I replied.

"Mm." He gave a thoughtful nod. "In that case, do not tell me about it. Tell me instead what you will do."

"Fin and I believe that we must reunite Hawk with Icarus before the recusants, and the student body along with them, attack," I explained. "Hawk and Icarus are the only ones who can stop this."

"Are you certain of this, dear one?" Sensei raised an eyebrow. "Do you believe that you have no part to play in all of this? Nothing to contribute?"

"My contribution is to lead them in safely."

Sensei bowed his head in a nod, but I could see the question in his eyes had not yet been answered.

"I do not know what else will happen," I went on. "I do not know what I will do, or what I *can* do, really. But I do know that I must trust my heart, take what comes, and though I am afraid, I will be brave." I took a fortifying breath. "I just… I needed to see you once more, sir—" I caught myself. "Sensei."

Sensei placed his large gentle hand on my shoulder, looking me in the eyes. "I will be with you."

I bowed my head, placing my hand on top of his for a moment, wondering if he knew how much those words meant to me, wondering if he knew how much *he* meant to me.

Finally, we separated. I took the steps to the cottage as I usually did: all at once. I opened the door and stepped inside, walking over to where my uniform had been hung up to dry. I slid out of my dress and into the fitted black pants and shirt. I zipped on my jacket and pulled on my beret.

I sat down on the bed and reached for my boots. I began to slide my foot into the right one, but then I stopped. Something tickled the rough sole of my foot. I reached down and pulled out the familiar, faded slip of paper.

The door at the end of the room finally creaked open. Areos stepped in cautiously, then shut it behind him.

"Is that the note from your brother?" he asked gently, crossing the room to stop beside me.

I nodded and smoothed the yellowed page over my knees. "I carry it with me always."

Areos took the paper in his hands and read it over silently. Then he squinted. "This handwriting seems strangely familiar to me."

"It does?" I asked.

Areos's brow furrowed. I studied his expression for a long moment, watching as his jaw slackened and his eyes grew wide. My heart instantly beat a little faster.

"What is it?" I asked.

He lowered the paper and stared down at me. "I know who wrote this."

# CHAPTER THIRTY-FIVE

*Hawk*

"I wish they would hurry up…" Runner muttered under his breath, tapping his hand anxiously against his thigh. "Waiting around like this makes me nervous."

"They'll be here soon," Fin replied beside me.

Runner sighed and carefully rose to his feet to peek over the crest of the embankment we were using for shelter.

I closed my eyes and tried to steady my pulse. I kept thinking about Icarus. I kept thinking about what I would say and do and—and what I would feel.

What *would* I feel? It had been so long…

"You okay?" Fin whispered.

I swallowed, nodding. "Fine."

And for a moment that was true, in a way. So far nothing had gone awry; we were still on track, waiting for Lara, waiting to infiltrate the base tucked into the valley below and somehow find Icarus. But then I heard something.

For a moment I thought it was the wind whipping through the trees, but then I raised a finger to my lips.

Fin glanced over at me. "What is it?"

For a moment I just listened. Then, slowly, I crept to my feet and gestured for him to follow.

"What's up?" Runner questioned.

"Shhh," Fin whispered. "Stay where you are."

My footsteps were muted against the thick forest floor and I came to a stop after several hundred yards, ducking behind the trunk of an oak. Fin fell into place beside me, holding his breath. In the clearing ahead, I'd caught glimpses of figures—people. Familiar faces to match the familiar voices that echoed in the silence.

I turned and looked up at Fin. His expression was just as grave as mine.

"We wait for night to fall." The authoritative voice that spoke was Mitsue's. "We know that's when the recusants will strike—correct?"

"Yes. From the north." This was Delta. "Quite a few troops were slaughtered by the recusants at Howth, in the bombings. New Dublin's RGM stock is greatly depleted—they will be outnumbered. When the recusants make their entrance, we will follow them up. It will be dark—they will hardly be able to differentiate."

"And then?" Gaia spoke up. "We follow them into the attack, and what then? Slaughter along with the forces of darkness?"

"We are not speaking of any 'forces of darkness,' Gaia. We are not speaking of the RGM. We are speaking of the recusants—whose side we must support," Mitsue replied firmly. "If there is to be any change, if we are to take back Earth, it will be through—"

"Through *killing*?" Gaia cut him off harshly as a murmur arose from the many other sliders who had joined them in the clearing. "Through fighting it out, as if we were no better than humans? I cannot believe that this is what Sensei had in mind."

"Perhaps not. But it's what *I* have in mind."

"Since when was this about you, Mitsue?" Gaia launched back. "This is about Hawk, isn't it? Hawk's reappearance, our discovery about the database—you cannot stand to be wrong!"

There was a sharp sound: a slap. Gaia gasped, and a stunned silence followed.

"Mitsue!" Delta snapped. "Enough!"

"No—I call the shots, I say when it's enough!" Mitsue's voice echoed in the woods. "It will not be enough until every single one of those bastards who stand against us is dead and gone—and that includes any slider who chooses to question my decision!"

I glanced at Fin again; a troubled feeling had begun rising inside me. His eyes darted back and forth as he listened. Then, at length, he backed quietly away and gestured for me to follow. We raced back to Runner and dove below the embankment.

"The sliders have already assembled. No doubt the recusants are doing the same," Fin reported, panting. "They're planning on blending in with the recusants to support their cause—and take advantage of the chaos. We have to move—now."

"But what about Lara and Areos?" Runner questioned, getting to his feet. "They were meeting us here."

"They'll assume we went in."

"But how can we do that without Lara?" Runner's voice was low but urgent. "She's the one who knows her way around the base, not us! How are we supposed to get in there without getting caught and skinned?"

"Carefully." Fin sank back down to the ground and threw a glance between us. "All I know is, if we sit here and wait around, we will definitely get caught and skinned—by our own kind, Runner. Not by recusants."

"We can't just—just go marching in!"

"Don't worry," Fin replied quickly. "I've got an idea."

I didn't ask what this idea was. I could tell by Fin's expression that it was a good one.

"Let's go," I told him. "Lead the way."

Painstakingly, we left our hiding place and began carefully making our way down the hill. The closer we got, the more foreboding the large RGM base appeared. Smoke rose in listing pillars at one end, and large square buildings stood out against the overcast sky. Guards were posted at the gates and along the surrounding barbed-wire fence. The occasional tactical vehicle rolled out onto the long dirt road, kicking up dust. Thankfully, the grass and brush were tall enough to crawl through without detection.

"This way," Fin breathed, making a tiny motion with his finger.

On our bellies, we crawled along the fence until we found ourselves behind the back of a building—just as sirens began to blare.

"They've detected us," Runner said, his voice tight. "What's the plan, Fin?"

He placed a finger to his lips, flattening himself against the back of the building. He paused a moment, seeming to sniff the air, which reeked of ash, exhaust, and a tinge of something else. He waved us onward. We made our way along the back of the building until he halted abruptly below a window. He quickly gestured for me to come closer.

"Check to make sure it's clear," he told me, stooping down to make a cradle for my foot in his interlocked hands. "If it is, get that window open."

I nodded, clamping both hands around his shoulders and sliding my foot into place for him to hoist me up. Fin slowly stood, putting me at eye level with the glass, which was already slid open about a quarter of the way. Finally, I placed the scent: the laundry room was below me, filled with long high-speed machines that were washing, drying, and pressing all-black clothes. Uniforms.

I was catching Fin's drift now.

As quietly as I could, I slid the window the rest of the way open. I pushed off his hands and climbed inside, shimmying out onto a tall shelf that stood up against the wall and scanning the room below. Runner came through next. I climbed down and dropped to the floor, tucking myself behind one of the large churning machines. Runner dropped down beside me.

"Shhhh!" I pressed a finger to my lips. "Quiet."

"There's no one in here."

"You don't know that," I whispered back, turning to watch Fin climb down. He dropped lightly to his feet—just as the door at the opposite end of the room creaked open.

Fin froze. A soft click sounded.

Runner cursed. My throat tightened as a new voice sliced through the silence.

"Move a muscle, you die."

"Please, I didn't—I don't—"

I jumped up, ignoring Fin's immediate subtle gesture for me to stay down. The gun's muzzle flicked to the space between my eyes. For a moment that was all I saw: the barrel of a pistol. Then my gaze reset on the face behind the weapon. A *familiar* face: a young woman with dark brown skin, wide eyes and one finger twitching on the trigger. It had been dark when we met, but I recognized her instantly. I stepped bravely forward as if the gun weren't even there.

"Kess." I said her name, keeping steady eye contact. "That is you, isn't it?"

Her expression didn't change and her arms remained braced at full extension. "And who the hell are you?"

"You don't remember us?" I asked carefully, making a slow gesture toward Fin. "We're the ones who found you, out there in the field, in Howth, after the—after the—"

"After the bombings…" Recognition clicked in her eyes. "No shit—that was you guys?"

I nodded.

Kess glanced nervously over her shoulders, then gaped back at us as she slowly lowered the pistol. "I never thought I'd see either of you again. You saved my neck out there—I would have died. What the hell are you guys doing here?"

"We're here to find Icarus," I explained, deciding to be honest with her. "Lara will be here soon—she's helping us."

Kess froze. She dropped the gun into its holster. "*Lara?* Lara's *alive?*"

Fin nodded, stepping forward.

"Holy shit…" Kess murmured, rubbing her forehead. "You guys are friends of hers?"

"We are," Fin affirmed, dragging Runner out from behind the washing machine. "All of us."

Kess gave a quick glance around, then gestured for us to follow. "Then I guess I'd better help you guys before you get yourselves killed."

She led us across the laundry room and down a short hallway. The next room was a bit smaller. The walls were lined with shelves stacked high with black RGM uniforms. Kess turned and gave me a once-over before striding over to one of the shelves to snatch a black T-shirt and a pair of almost skin-tight black pants. She threw them at me. "Put those on. Hurry up."

Fin turned around and made Runner do the same while I quickly slid out of my clothes and into the starched uniform.

"Catch." She threw uniforms at Fin and Runner. "Give me your clothes when you're done. I'll hide them."

I pulled the shirt on over my head and turned to look at her as I stepped into the pants. "Lara told us she saw Icarus—do you know where they're keeping him? Since the containment area collapsed."

Kess frowned, quickly shaking her head. "I have no idea. I think one of the guys told me they saw him leaving Donovan's office yesterday and heading for the infirmary… but I don't think they'd be keeping him there unless he's sick or something. It was probably a misunderstanding."

*If only she knew…*

"And this *infirmary?*"

"Oh, that's off-limits. The larger part, anyway," she explained. "I don't even know what's back there. You'll get yourself shot if you try to get in there—what's your name?"

"Hawk."

She nodded an acknowledgment. "You'll be a dead hawk."

I glanced over at Fin as he latched on a belt. I could see the gears turning behind his green eyes.

"What would be the best way to get in there?" he asked.

"Are you not hearing me the first time around?" Kess snapped. "There is no good way to get in there—*no way, period.*"

I pursed my lips, racking my brain. "What if there was a distraction?"

"A distraction?" Kess reiterated.

"Just enough to get us in," I told her, stepping closer. "It's important, Kess—I have to get to Icarus before the attack."

Kess's expression shifted. She stared at me. "What the hell are you talking about?" she asked gravely. "What attack?"

I took a breath to answer her, but the words never came. A bloodcurdling scream sounded from outside, followed by a deafening boom.

The windows shattered.

"Get down!" Fin shouted.

I threw myself against the floor beside him as shards of glass sprinkled over us. The building's cement foundation quaked.

"I thought they planned to attack tonight," I panted, shielding my eyes.

Chaotic shouts poured in from outside, engines rumbled to life, and sirens blared.

Fin was the first to peel himself up off the floor; a thin strand of blood trickled down his forehead. "Looks like they changed their minds—come on!"

I scrambled to my feet; Runner and Kess followed suit.

"No, no, no—not that door," Kess shouted, waving us quickly to the back of the room. She brushed aside a plethora of coats and hanging gear, revealing a rusty emergency exit door. "This way."

The telltale chatter of automatic weapons split the air around us, accentuated by blistering shouts and screams from outside. Another blast shook the floor beneath me just as I slid outside and flattened myself against the building. The air was thick and smoky, filled with the roar of fire.

Kess slid her pistol out of its holster, keeping it ready as she shimmied to the edge of the building. She held up a fist for us to stop. I felt Fin right behind me; his fingers slid into the spaces between mine.

Kess leaned carefully forward to peer around the edge of the building, then ducked back just as quickly as a bullet tore through the concrete, spitting up clouds of dust and sending a uniformed body flying backward into our path. It dropped lifelessly.

I felt my stomach turn. An instant later, Kess waved us forward, shouting for us to stay down. We streaked across the small space between buildings, opening ourselves for an instant to the firefight. Kess reached down and snatched the pistol from the hand of the dead soldier as we ran. She offered it to me as we paused behind the next building.

"I don't want it."

"Do you want to die, Hawk?" she spat back. She thrust the weapon into my hand. I had no idea how to use it, nor would I. But there was no time to explain.

Kess looked back at us, jerking her head to the left. "See that white building?"

It was hard to see through the smoke or even focus over the deafening sounds of gunfire, but after a moment I spotted it. A few rugged cement structures were the only things standing between us and a whitewashed building with a rusty metal roof.

"Yes, I see it!" Fin shouted to her.

"That's it!" she yelled back. "Don't go through the door—there's bound to be guards. Find a window and break into an empty room!"

Kess leaned against the building, then peered quickly out, scanning our surroundings, before bracing her pistol out in front of her and stepping out into the open.

"Go!" she screamed over the noise. "Now!"

For a split second I was frozen in place, my heart hammering in my chest. Then I felt Fin's grasp tighten on my hand, pulling me forward. "Hawk, now!"

We ran through the smoke, crouching to stay as low as possible as we sprinted and wove around the buildings. Fin took up the lead now and Runner was behind me. I could hear Kess's shouts from a distance back—the rattle of gunfire as she pulled the trigger, covering us while we moved.

Suddenly I crashed into Fin's body as he slammed to a halt. The muzzle of an automatic slid around the corner of the building to face us head-on. A young man in civilian clothes stepped out, weapon poised—a recusant. And we were all wearing RGM uniforms.

Fin reached back and shoved me to the ground as he formed an orb in the palm of his hand. He hurled it forward just as the recusant pulled back on his trigger. The orb ripped forward and shattered the bullet in midair, sending the recusant flying backward.

"Go!" Fin shouted, a fresh orb lighting up in his hands as he stepped out into the street.

I darted to the next building. In the smoke, I could barely make out the shapes of the recusants and the glint of their guns in the flashes from the fire that was eating away at one of the buildings across the dirt road. I heard the ripple of orbs sailing through the air and exploding behind me, followed by bursts of long, hard gunfire. I stopped dead as soon as I realized Fin hadn't followed us, turning to stare into the smoke, blood surging through my veins.

"Fin!" I screamed raggedly.

A hand clamped over my mouth and I immediately countered with an elbow to my assailant's ribs.

"Hawk, it's me! Stop!" Runner shouted into my ear, working the gun out of my hand at the same time. It slid easily out of my sweaty grip. "You have to go!"

"But he's back there!" I screamed, fighting against his grasp. "I can't just—I can't!"

"You have to! Hawk, I'll go back and cover him, but you have to keep going!" He turned me around by the shoulders, shouting into my face just as another explosion blew. The ground seemed to jump beneath us, taking us both down. I scrambled back up to my feet, dizzy, my ears ringing.

"Hawk, go!" Runner shouted hoarsely, jumping back up. "You're almost there!"

I could barely hear his voice over the hiss tingling in my eardrums. It was like everything around me slowed down for a moment. I felt cemented to the ground as I stood there, gasping, my vision blurry and my eyes stinging. Runner turned and ran back the way we had come, vanishing into the fog of chaos.

I could hear the *tat-tat-tat* of gunshots, followed by a loud whoosh of orbs rolling through the air, impacting against targets.

I pressed back against the building, sick to my stomach and breathing hard as I scanned my surroundings. I could make out the shapes of figures— the bursts of bullets and orbs as they impacted. A shout, a body falling. A recusant.

I sprinted out from behind the building, running as fast as my legs would carry me, keeping myself as low as possible. I felt the singe of an orb as it flew over me, taking a strip of my shirt but just missing my skin. I was gasping for air as I dropped to the ground alongside the white building, angry, frantic tears in my eyes.

Sinking my fingertips into the ground, I clawed my way back up to my feet, forcing myself forward, forward, forward, though each one of my footsteps was like lead. I kept one hand pressed against the building, felt the cement scrape my fingertips. I blinked and squinted through the smoke, keeping my gaze locked on the windows above me.

*I can't reach them, I can't reach them, I can't reach them—how am I going to get in? I can't get in!*

I pressed my palms to my temples, forcing myself to stay calm, to think. I stopped below one of the windows: there was a large hole at thigh level where a chunk of cement had been blasted away. I slid my foot into the hole and jumped up, reaching for the window. It was closed and locked.

My breath caught in my throat, and before I could think any further, a hand closed around my ankle in a vise grip, yanking me down to the ground again. In a gut reaction, I swung around with a back fist, sending them stumbling backward, loosening their grip on the pistol just enough for me to swing my leg up to kick it out of their hand. Surging forward, I grabbed it before it hit the ground, confronting my attacker head-on: a young man—a recusant with fierce eyes. He lunged forward to grab me by the throat just as I swung the pistol up and brought the cold, hard metal down between his eyes. He staggered for a moment; then his body went limp.

Adrenaline coursing through me, I clawed my way back up the wall and bashed in the glass pane with the butt of the pistol. With one surge of energy, I pulled myself up and latched onto the sill. I felt the jagged glass sink into my skin, but I didn't care. I hauled myself through the window, then fell several feet and landed hard on a cement floor.

I jumped up, my arms braced at full extension and my index finger poised over the trigger of the gun. I pointed it out in front of me, breathing hard, blood dripping from my hands as I clenched the grip. The room around me was sterile, white and empty. A rigid examination chair was stationed in the middle of the room. I was alone.

I crossed the room in one swift motion, eased open the door and slipped out into the hallway. It was vacant.

I ran, scanning the rows of doors. Bright white lights hung from the ceiling to illuminate the long concrete hallway and the muddy boot prints that ran the length of it. I could hear voices distantly—one familiar.

I picked up my pace, then dove into an adjacent hallway as one of the doors ahead burst open then slammed shut again. I heard the beeping of a keypad followed by the loud click of a bolt lock. Then the quick, heavy thud of boots.

I didn't breathe.

A man in uniform walked briskly past. All I saw was the back of him: he was tall with dark hair. I waited until his footsteps faded, then melted back out into the hallway and darted to the door he had just exited. I gripped the handle and pulled, pushed, rattled, but it didn't budge. I glanced at the keypad: it was still lit up.

I backed up, trained the gun on the lock and pulled the trigger, blasting it open. I kicked the rest of the door aside as I burst forward and into the room. The first thing I saw was the body on the floor.

A woman in a black uniform, lying facedown in a pool of blood, lifeless.

A man stood over her with his back to me, a knife clenched in his hand.

He whirled to face me, and his eyes widened as he saw my gun.

My voice came out barely above a whisper, my heart sinking.

"Icarus."

# CHAPTER THIRTY-SIX

## *Lara*

I was stunned. I didn't know what to say—what to think. I could hardly breathe. Areos stood in front of me, wide-eyed and still holding the faded letter in his hand.

From the moment I'd met Fin, I hadn't been able to shake the feeling that there was something different about him. His abilities so like my own, the way he looked at the world, the way he saw the light in the darkness like I did—it was all so familiar. I could hardly believe what Areos had just told me, yet… nothing made more sense: Fin was… *my brother.*

I was about to respond when a deafening roar decimated the stillness. Explosions rumbled in the valley below. The attack had already begun.

"We have to get down there!" I shouted, swinging the cottage door open and bursting outside.

"Lara, just—" Areos pounded down the steps after me. "Just stay calm."

I whirled around to look at him. "*Calm?* You want me to stay calm?" My voice was hoarse. "Areos, Fin is down there! My *brother* is down there! He's counting on us. They're—they're all counting on us!"

"I know, I know! But freaking out isn't going to help us." He strode past me and then stopped, cupping his hands over his mouth. "Sensei!" he called loudly, then paused. No reply came.

I glanced around at the roses and the living trees covered in blooms. It was akin to the forest Fin had brought back to life with his abilities. I hadn't told him that night what my abilities were… that they were just like his. It all made so much sense now. It was as if the stars in my head had finally aligned, sliding into the places they were always meant to be, shining a bright spotlight through the shroud of fog that I'd been stumbling through all my life, flashing a message loud and clear.

*You are not alone, Lara Moran. You were never alone.*

"He's not here," I announced, a feeling of knowing swelling in my chest. "He's said all that needed to be said… He's taught us what we needed to learn." My eyes met Areos's. "It's time to use what he's given us."

I extended a hand and Areos took it, stepping closer to meet me in the clearing just as another explosion sounded in the valley below. I gulped, pinching my eyes shut. "You ready?"

He took hold of my other hand firmly. "Ready."

I took a deep breath and began to imagine the surrounding hills and the valley they sank into, the base and the barbed-wire fence that wrapped around it like a ribbon. I began to see the firefight, and the flash of explosions—hand grenades. A bloom of fiery red as one of the buildings went up in flames. I felt my throat tighten as my eyelids flickered open, revealing that exact reality. We were at the gates now, a crowd of armed civilians surging around us like a raging river. Everything exploded from silence to sound.

"Areos, come on!" I shouted. I sprinted forward, pulling him with one hand behind me. "We have to find them!"

No sooner had we crossed the gates than another boom splintered the air, sending billowing clouds of smoke, flame, and debris roaring up into the sky. Areos grabbed me by the shoulders, pulling me behind the cement guard shack. We braced ourselves as the ground rumbled beneath us. My hearing was muffled.

I felt Areos's arms around me. He shouted something in my ear, though I couldn't make out any of the words. I turned and looked to my right just as a ball of blue light ripped through the air and struck one of the RGM soldiers to the ground. Another soldier fired back, piercing the air with a few rounds of bullets. A scream followed and a body collapsed against the ground: the student who had thrown the ball of light.

Areos cursed. "That was one of ours," he shouted, scrambling to his feet. "The sliders beat us here; they've already joined the fight—this is going to be a bloodbath! We have to find Mitsue—and take him down."

"Areos—Areos, no, wait!" I chased after him, sprinting into the thick of it, dropping behind a mangled Trawler for cover as bullets sped by. "If you kill Mitsue, it makes you no better than him!"

Areos shook his head, panting, his eyes wild with rage as he stared into the chaos of the slaughter.

"I don't care, Lara. He has to be stopped!" he shouted back. "We'll all be dead before this thing is through! We have to retreat—we have to make him stop!"

Before I could say another word, he dodged out from behind the Trawler, jumping over a body and racing back out into the smoke.

"Areos!" I yelled hoarsely after him. "Areos, wait!"

I was wasting my breath and I knew it. I stole the weapon off the body sprawled on the ground and streaked across the courtyard, bashing a recusant in the face with the butt of the rifle before they had the chance to neutralize me with their own weapon.

My breathing frantic, I searched for Areos as I sprinted. A bullet nicked my shoulder, sending a surge of searing pain down my arm. I finally caught up to Areos just as he began to form a pulsating orb of energy in his hand.

"Areos—Areos, stop!" I shouted at him. "You're going to get us killed!"

Between two buildings, I caught a glimpse of a glowing red orb wielded by a figure I presumed was Mitsue—a tall young man with dark hair pulled back in a braid. Shouting above the noise, Fin stood in front of him, only a few yards away, blood trickling down one of his arms.

Suddenly, it was as if everything muted and froze. My mind reeled back—over a hundred years back. Back to those days of normal life, of my family and my sisters, and my brother—Ronan.

"Fin—get down!" Areos shouted, throwing the orb in his hand.

Fin's gaze flicked to us, and then he dove to the ground. Mitsue noticed just a second too late. He folded to the ground, roaring in pain as the orb seared into his shoulder.

"Now!" Areos waved me forward, ducking down and racing across the dirt road now littered with bodies and burning debris. I followed, staying low.

Fin had jumped back to his feet, forming an orb before Mitsue had a chance to counter. "Mitsue, you have to stop!" he yelled. "There's too many of them! The sliders of the Dimension will be no more. Is that really what you want?"

Blood dripped from Mitsue's nose. He clawed his way up to his feet and glared at us. Backing Fin up, Areos raised his arm, forming an ominous pulsing orb. We were partially hidden now between the two buildings.

"We cannot go on—we have to pull back!" Fin yelled in Mitsue's face. "You have to tell them!"

"Why?" Mitsue screamed back, bringing his hands up in front of him. "Why, Fin? Because *you* say so?"

Suddenly, a movement from across the road caught my eye. I turned, every muscle tensing. A familiar uniformed figure emerged from one of the buildings, silhouetted against the smoke.

Donovan.

He stood between the building and a Trawler, scanning the chaos he had created like a king overlooking his subjects. I could see him, but I was fairly certain he couldn't see me.

My pulse pounded in my skull, and my eyes burned from the smoke. Bullets shattered in midair as orbs collided with them, sailing onward like heat-seeking missiles to explode in the faces of the soldiers, knocking them to the ground.

"Because we will not survive this!" Fin shouted back. "Look at us! My god—we're fighting each other! We cannot do this!"

"Yes, we can!" Mitsue growled, backing away from Fin's fury. "*Yes, we can!* You're not the leader, Fin—I am!"

I flattened myself back against the wall just as Donovan took aim at one of the fighting RGM members—one of his own trainees—and pulled the trigger. He then turned the gun on Mitsue.

"Mitsue, stop!" Fin shouted. His voice was tight and urgent, and at once

I knew he too had just noticed Donovan leveling Mitsue in his sights.

"We will not stop," Mitsue yelled back, getting ready to throw his orb. "We will—"

Fin dove forward, ducking beneath Mitsue's orb as it flew out of his hands, and knocking him to the ground. Staggering, Fin caught himself before Mitsue could pull him down with him.

I felt sick to my stomach; the earth swirled. For a moment everything felt like slow motion. Mitsue fell and rolled several times through the dirt. Fin staggered forward a few steps. Areos tensed beside me. Shots were fired one building over; screams pierced the air. Donovan's face lowered to his weapon. Then everything snapped back to normal speed.

"Fin, look out!" Areos yelled frantically. But I knew his reaction wouldn't be fast enough.

But I was a soldier. An RGM sniper. My reaction was second nature— it was instinct. And I hadn't come all this way, I hadn't searched all these years, just to lose my brother a second time.

My heartbeat stumbled as I surged out from cover, sucking in a smoky breath to scream his name.

"*Ronan!*"

Fin turned, wide-eyed, to look at me, his face streaked with blood and dirt. Just as his lips began to form words, I threw myself in front of him. I heard the shot fire.

Then a bullet buried itself in my chest.

# CHAPTER THIRTY-SEVEN

## *Icarus*

Darkness came. I saw the light fade through the small bulletproof window at the far end of the room. Charlie eventually fell asleep, but I stayed awake. I was exhausted, but I felt like a tempest inside. I wore grooves in the cement as I paced back and forth that night.

*If you don't kill Hatch, if you let her Frag you, Donovan will doubtlessly kill you himself. What happens to Hawk if you die with her power inside you? You carry her soul, Ion.*

"Shut up, shut up, shut up! I'm not going to die, and—and my name isn't Ion."

*Oh. Of course not. Because you still think you're Icarus—the Sunset. The slider with superhuman abilities. If you're so powerful, why don't you just escape now?*

"People are counting on me. I'm staying. I'm staying for them."

I repeated that over and over and over again under my breath as I walked back and forth.

*I'm staying for them. I'm staying for them. I'm staying for them.*

It didn't really help. I was no less afraid, but it kept my mind focused on the fact that there was something bigger at play than the fear chanting in my head. It was one of the hardest nights of my life, and it ended when the door creaked open. But this time it wasn't an armed guard.

Donovan was like a ghost, standing there in the doorway with shadows concealing half his face. His eyes were empty.

Keeping silent so as not to wake Charlie, I let him strap on the bands and lead me out of the cell.

"What's going on?" I questioned, keeping my voice low.

"There's been a change of plans," he answered bluntly, keeping a firm grip on my upper arm. "The time is now, Icarus."

"Now?"

We stopped dead in the middle of the long hallway just before reaching another door. Donovan's gaze squared with mine; there was something steely in his eyes.

"Do as you're told, Icarus, and I'll make you one of the greatest men who has ever lived. History will remember you as a hero—a hero who did not fail them at the beginning of their revolution."

I looked at him, saying nothing in reply. I could feel the knife in my pocket.

"I had hoped one day to say the very same thing to Lara," he went on quietly. "This was the favor I would ask of her…"

I raised an eyebrow. "Favor, sir?"

Donovan shook his head. "It doesn't matter anymore."

We emerged into another hallway lined with doors on either side. We passed room after room until we finally came to a halt.

I looked over at Donovan, taking a shallow breath as he turned to look at me.

"You may hear some commotion outside." He spoke quietly, a strange knowing look in his eyes. "Not to worry."

A sick feeling sank into my stomach. I opened my mouth to say something, but Donovan spoke up first.

"Ready to enter," he stated. An instant later there was a series of beeps and the door swung open.

My eyes were dazzled for a moment by the blinding lights, but they adjusted quickly. I blinked and saw Hatch standing there, dressed in a long black tunic and a black cap. She took a sip from the small flask in her hand.

"Thank you, my dear boy." Her gaze shifted to Donovan. "We won't be long, I'm sure—you know how it goes."

Donovan said nothing. I took a few uneasy steps and then looked back over my shoulder at him just as he turned to leave.

"Come in, Icarus," Hatch greeted me, waving me inside. "Have a seat."

I stepped forward cautiously, and Donovan shut the door behind me, closing me into the sterile white room alone with her.

"I hope they've been treating you respectably here, Icarus," Hatch went on, walking over to a long table, which held a variety of instruments and vials of clear liquids. "If you hadn't been such a bad boy, I wouldn't have had to send you away, you know."

I watched her carefully, not moving.

"It's just a checkup," she assured me, noticing my blank expression. "There's no need to worry. Have a seat."

*Did she really think I was that stupid?*

My heart was pounding as I forced myself to walk across the room. I paused beside the chair.

"We can get rid of these now…" Hatch said, undoing the bands. "I trust you enough."

"You never trusted me when I was at Section C."

"That's because I was your commander, Icarus. You were my responsibility. Your disobedience reflected upon me. I couldn't have that." She loaded a needle. "Let's get you comfortable. You might feel a little tickle…"

I sucked in a breath, wincing as a long needle pierced the skin at the back of my neck. At first nothing felt different, then gradually the back of my head went numb. I swallowed back a nauseous feeling.

"What's happ… ening…?" My tongue grew heavier in my mouth.

"Morphine, Icarus." Hatch suddenly sounded far away. "It will kill the pain…"

The fluorescent lights overhead sizzled, burning my eyes, as the chair tipped back. My body felt light. I heard beeps and clicks.

"Just relax and enjoy the ride, Icarus…"

I felt one cold hand wrap around my arm. I winced and tried to pull away, but she shushed me again.

"It's okay, Icarus…"

There was something in her hand—something that looked like a gun, but different. Dimly, I remembered the knife in my pocket, but I made no move to reach for it. Her face blurred above me, wavering.

I felt myself slipping backwards, as if something were sucking my soul out of my body. My fingernails dug into the fabric arms of the chair.

The room spun and faded to a blown-out white; the blurry outlines of Hatch's face morphed and became something more familiar. The white turned to green: cliffsides and sky and billowing clouds. The drop yawned before me.

*This is where we jump, Icarus…*

"This will all be over soon, Icarus…" I felt hot breath against my face as the world fell away. "This will all be over soon…"

My eyelids were heavy. The hand was still there, but I could no longer feel the icy fingers. I felt a slight pressure against the back of my head; that was all.

A gunshot ripped through the air.

My eyes opened just as Hatch clutched her chest. I blinked a few times, sitting up straighter. I tried to speak, but my words were unintelligible. Her eyes widened and crimson oozed out between her fingers as she hunched forward, gasping, then crumpled to the floor.

I tried to get up, but the room spun with my every attempt to move. My vision blurred. What appeared to be two doors stood open at the end of the room. Two men in black uniform stood there, and each held a pistol. I heard the thud of boots. I felt a new shadow over me now as the figures came closer and closer, until they merged into one. One familiar, expressionless face.

"I thought I could trust you to carry out an order, Icarus." Donovan slid the pistol into his holster just as the floor began to shake. I heard a rumble like an explosion.

"But apparently—" his voice sounded distant as he stooped to pull something out of Hatch's hand "—I was wrong."

Donovan straightened back up and now I could finally see clearly enough what was in his hand—what Hatch had been holding. A strange-looking gun with a flat muzzle. A green light flashed on the side.

"You can't be trusted. You're too innocent—too convicted." He shoved me backwards, hard. "I was going to save you, Icarus. I was going to make you great—if you had obeyed me."

Donovan leaned over me and I felt cool metal slide up against the base of my head.

"You could have been a hero, Icarus," he told me, his voice muffled and faded. "Now you will be nothing more than a machine."

He pulled the trigger. A dull thud pounded through my head. My vision blurred again and my eyelids fell shut.

I heard the clatter of metal, then heavy boots. Steps… A door slamming. Another explosion, shaking the floor.

My arms and legs tingled and my stomach lurched. I felt something strange and soft in my mouth, but I couldn't seem to swallow it. I felt the rush of air in my lungs, but I couldn't seem to breathe. I felt my fingernails puncture the fabric of the chair as I clawed my way up to my feet—then fell again. The world shook underneath me. I could see the blur of a woman's body several feet away. The bright lights flickered incessantly overhead.

Everything was like a dream. Nothing felt real. My skin was heavy on my bones. I lay there. My hands were shaking as my fingernails bent and cracked against the floor tiles. I rolled to my side and felt something in the pocket of my pants. I slowly fumbled the object out into my hand.

I couldn't decide what it was. There was something thin and silver protruding from its side. I pulled on it and it flipped open. I stumbled to my feet, gripping the handle. I walked a few steps, then stopped. My knees shook, threatening to give out underneath me.

I squinted up at the lights and then down at the object in my hands. I knew suddenly what it was: a knife, and I was gripping the blade end. Blood oozed from the palm of my hand.

I heard the door creak open behind me.

"Icarus?"

The voice came to me like it was pounding through water. I turned to face it.

"What have you done?"

There were five open doors and five white wolves. They walked across the room and went to the body on the floor, as if to devour it. They looked up at me. I backed slowly away.

"Icarus…" They howled my name.

I stumbled into a table. Glass bottles rocked and fell, shattering with a sound like gunshots. I fell to the ground as the room was pulled out from under my feet. Suddenly the bright lights were gone; the floor faded away to soil. When I rolled over, there were trees over my head. Burning trees.

I inhaled and started choking on the smoke. I squirmed backwards, still clutching the knife in my hand, pointing it at the wolves as they crept closer, following.

"No, no, stop!" I shouted back, my voice echoing in my ears.

The sky was black and dripping down through the trees. I could hear the wolves; I could see their eyes glowing in the light from the flames. I scrambled to my feet and bolted into a run. Though I saw nothing before me but open forest, I hit a wall.

Gold flecks danced over my vision as I fell to the ground, swirls of hot red reaching up around me. I cried out, but I could barely hear my own voice. I hit the ground face-first, but the ground was now pavement. I lay there on my stomach for a moment, sucking in air, my entire body trembling.

I looked up slowly to find that the wolves were gone. The forest had been replaced by tall buildings. A single flickering streetlight shone overhead. Cars were parked around us—*us*. There was suddenly someone else. A girl.

A black hoodie, piercing eyes, short red hair.

"Ion, what is wrong with you?" she asked, the pitch of her voice bending and twisting. "You're such a freak—"

She was suddenly close; one fist held a bottle, and the other launched toward my face. With a fire welling up inside me, I struck her back. A sick feeling twisted in my stomach as she flew backward and hit the windshield of a car. Suddenly she was no longer a female, but male. The buildings seemed to morph, closing in around us.

There was broken glass everywhere. He got up slowly, breathing raggedly.

I held out the knife. "J-j-just stay away from me! Just stay away—"

"Icarus, it's okay!" he called.

I shook my head, backing up, crunching through broken glass as he came closer. "No, no, no—no, it's—it's not."

"Icarus, just listen to me." He lowered his voice. "Please listen…"

The walls seemed to melt, dripping away to clouds of white mist. I could see the blurry outline of a cliff behind him. Wooden floorboards creaked under my feet.

I clenched the knife in my shaking hand.

"Icarus, don't…"

I disobeyed, winding back my arm.

"Icarus, no!"

I threw it, slicing my own hand again in the process. The knife circled in the air, twisting, and then—he caught it.

I hit something hard; more glass shattered. I leaned back against the wall and slid to the floor, shaking. Blood trickled down my arm.

I closed my eyes and opened them again: a wolf stood before me—then suddenly, a girl. Breathing hard, my heart throbbing in my skull, I blinked fiercely.

A garden came into focus; a white picket fence. A hose and a mist of water. A figure like someone from a dream. Arms bearing black bands that glistened in the sunlight, brown hair pulled over one shoulder, dark brown eyes that looked up into mine.

I felt a hand on my face as I closed my eyes.

"Icarus, it's me…" she whispered. "It's me… it's me…"

Fingers brushed against mine, entwining with my own, locking. I felt something warm like blood in my own wound. Then it grew hotter. I wanted to speak, but I couldn't. My body felt weightless again. My blood ran cold for an instant; then it turned to fire.

When I opened my eyes, my vision had cleared once more. I peered around the sterile white room, but I was no longer on the floor; I floated in weightless suspension, with the familiar hand still locked into my own. The markings on my arms remained, but as I looked down at our hands, I began to notice a black band forming around her finger to match the one on my own. A girl with a long white braid that slowly began to warm with color—a face more familiar to me than my own.

Hawk took a long, deep breath, and then, as if a switch had been flipped, she opened her eyes and we fell to the floor. A circular burst of energy whooshed out around us as we landed hard, gasping for air. The room seemed to spin around us and then settle. Everything came into focus once again, and she was still there. Unlike in all my dreams, Hawk was still there.

For a moment we both lay there, blanketed in the sudden stillness, gasping for breath as if we'd just made it to the other side of hell. Then Hawk pressed up off the floor, rushing to my side.

I stared up at her as she knelt beside me. Dirt streaked her face, and there was a pistol at her hip; she wore a black RGM uniform.

"You came back…" I whispered, my voice cracking. "You… you came back…"

"Of course I came back, Icarus." She gave my hand a little squeeze. "You're part of me."

I pinched my eyes shut and drew a slow breath. "I'm so sorry, Hawk…" I whispered. "I…"

"Shhh." She shook her head a little as I opened my eyes. "It's okay."

I swallowed the lump that was already forming in my throat. "It was my fault… it was my fault you were…" I pressed my lips together and closed my eyes, unable to finish. "I should never have—"

Hawk placed a finger to my lips. Swallowing hard, blinking back tears, she shook her head. "I would do it all again, Icarus," she whispered, her warm fingers folding between mine a little tighter. "I would do it *all* again."

Wordlessly, choking back tears, I pushed myself up off the floor and collapsed against Hawk, wrapping my arms around her, holding on to her like she was the only thing keeping me from falling off the face of the earth. My face rested in the curve of her neck, and I heard her draw a quiet breath.

One of her arms wrapped around me; her other hand tangled in my hair.

For the first time in what felt like an eternity, something was right again.

"My god, what a nightmare…" I finally whispered. "I never thought I would find my way out."

"Out of what?" Hawk asked softly.

I reached up to carefully touch the back of my head. I could already feel a swollen scrape where the Fragment had been inserted—now I would have a real scar.

"They Fragged you?" Hawk's voice cracked, her eyes going wide. "Icarus—"

"I beat it." I placed a hand over hers. "I defeated it, Hawk, we… we defeated it." I looked her in the eyes now. "I would never have made it out alive without you."

Hawk placed a supporting hand behind my back, looking into my face. A little smile passed over her lips.

Rising slowly to my feet, my attention shifted back to Hatch's body sprawled on the floor, a heavy feeling of resolve settling in my gut as it all came rushing back.

"Hawk, he killed her."

"Who?"

"Donovan. Donovan killed Hatch—and he's out there." I looked at her—looked into her face for what felt like the first time in ages. "He's—we have to—we have to find him. We have to stop him!"

"Okay, okay. Just slow down." Hawk caught me as I stumbled forward. "We will—together."

I steadied myself for a moment, studying her. She was so different, yet the same.

"I have missed you… so much," I said softly, my voice breaking.

Hawk's eyes flickered over my face for a moment before she dropped her voice to a whisper. "I missed you too."

There was another loud blast from outside, followed by the sound of glass shattering.

"You ready?" she asked.

I looked at her. "Now that you're here?" I nodded slowly, glancing down at our hands, the two black bands around our fingers. "I'm ready for any-

thing."

# CHAPTER THIRTY-EIGHT

## *Fin*

I stayed behind. I stood between two buildings pocked by bullets and orbs, and watched Hawk disappear into the smoke with Runner as I covered them. A moment later, I heard Hawk scream my name. The sound pitched and bent, twisting through the air to hit me like a bullet. Everything inside me ached; everything inside me whispered a frantic prayer with every beat of my heart.

*Let her get there safe, let her get there safe, let her get to Icarus…*

Two recusants emerged from the street, shouting, keeping their automatic rifles trained on my head.

"I'm on your side!" I shouted at them, forming an orb in the palm of my hand, holding my arms out in front of me. "Don't shoot!"

One of them answered by pulling the trigger.

I let go of the orb, shattering the bullets in midair and knocking the recusants backward. One was thrown back against the building behind us, blood flowing from his ears as his head sank back.

I wasn't a soldier. I'd never killed anyone. My heart was pounding in my chest as I staggered backward, my eyes widening as the life went out of his. It was enough of a delay for the other recusant to fire. I didn't react fast enough; a bullet embedded itself in my arm.

An agonized cry swelled in my throat, and I sank back against the cement wall of the building opposite, struggling to breathe as hot tears stung my eyes. My teeth sank into my tongue until I tasted blood. I met the recusant's eyes through the smoke. Dark brown. Terrified.

I fired an orb at her rifle, blowing it out of her hands and bending it in half. She stumbled backward, then turned and darted out into the street—where she was immediately shot. Her body crumpled to the ground.

I clenched my upper arm as I felt the warmth of blood spill through my fingers.

Doubling over in pain and dizziness, I gagged on the smoke. Sweat trickled off my forehead; my entire body shook.

I quickly straightened, coughing and gasping for air, and heard an orb ignite behind me. "It's me—" I shouted, choking. "It's Fin—"

Mitsue's dark eyes stared into mine, searing through the smoke. He held a flickering red orb over his head; his expression of fury was marred by dirt and blood.

"Fin? I thought you didn't believe in fighting," he sneered, stepping out of the street just as more bullets sped past. "I thought this 'wasn't Sensei's intention.'"

"Does this look like how things are supposed to be?" I shouted hoarsely, spit flying from my mouth as I blinked away tears. "Does this look like what Sensei had in mind? Mitsue, you've become no better than the RGM soldiers, no better than the violent recusants!" I stepped closer. "*You* have made *us* no better!"

Mitsue shook his head, his mouth trembling with a thousand words he couldn't bring himself to say. He threw the orb, but I countered it with one of my own, taking his out and nicking his dominant hand.

"Mitsue, we will all die here—is that what you want?"

"No, Fin!" he roared back, forming another orb. "That's where you're wrong!"

He threw it at me, but I ducked.

"We will not die," he shouted between gasps, his expression wild and twisted. "We will win—without you."

He wound back his arms, about to throw.

"Fin, get down!" A familiar voice cut through the chaos.

I caught sight of two figures—two blurs on the other side of the narrow strip of dirt; one was Areos, and he wielded an orb. I followed the order, dropping to my belly just as Mitsue fired—and then tumbled to the ground as the channel of bright blue energy struck him.

I jumped to my feet, finally gaining the upper hand. "Mitsue, you have to stop!" I shouted, holding a wavering orb of energy above him. "There's too many of them! The sliders of the Dimension will be no more. Is that really what you want?"

Blood gushed out of Mitsue's nose as he climbed back up to his feet.

Areos slid to a stop in the dirt at my side, wielding his own throbbing orb. Lara was beside him.

"We cannot go on—we have to pull back!" I pleaded, stepping closer to Mitsue. "You have to tell them!"

"Why?" Mitsue screamed back, bringing his hands up in front of him. "Why, Fin? Because you say so?"

"Because we will not survive this!" I shouted. "Look at us. My god— we're fighting each other! We cannot do this!"

"Yes, we can—*yes, we can!* You're not the leader, Fin—I am!"

Something caught my eye across the street: a uniformed soldier crouched between a tactical vehicle and a building, his rifle aimed directly at the back of Mitsue's head.

"Mitsue, stop!" I shouted just as he radiated another ball of energy.

Everything muted as I dove forward. I ducked past his orb and tackled him to the ground, catching myself before he had a chance to take me down with him. I staggered forward for a moment, smoke stinging in my lungs as I gasped for air. Then I focused on the barrel of the gun—now aiming right at me. My heart stopped.

I heard Areos yell something, but I couldn't make out the words. The only sound that seemed to reach me through the sudden ringing in my ears was my own heart as it throbbed in the back of my head. Then a voice rang out like an echo from the void of my past.

"Ronan!"

I turned and locked eyes with Lara, gasping for words as she surged forward, throwing herself in front of me. Just as the shot was fired.

The impact took us both down; her body was thrown back against mine. We hit the wall, and for a moment everything blurred. I heard Areos shout her name, just as Lara had screamed mine only a second ago. When I looked down, I saw that her chest was covered in blood.

"*Lara!*" My voice was a roar, a broken, aching scream.

I rolled her gently over onto the ground, resting her head in my lap as she took ragged breaths for air. Tears welled in my eyes; my heart felt as though it would thunder out of my chest.

"Lara, can you hear me?" I cradled her head in my hand, leaning over her. "Lara!"

Mitsue scrambled to his feet, gasping, staggering closer. When he saw Lara, he tried to speak, but Areos cut him off, lunging forward and grabbing him by the throat.

"I didn't mean—" Mitsue choked.

"*Get out!*" Areos roared. "Get out before I kill you, you bastard!"

Mitsue wrenched out of Areos's grip, turned and ran.

Areos dropped down beside me. "Fin, heal her!" he shouted into my face, tears streaming down his own. "Heal her!"

My hand was already pressed to the wound—I was trying. But the storm around me and within me was raging, screaming in my ears with the sounds of her gasps. Hot tears burned in my eyes as I squeezed them shut, trying to focus, trying to stop thinking—trying to stop.

"Ronan..." My name snagged in her throat as I leaned over her. "Ronan, l-l-l-look at... look at me..."

A sob caught in my throat; my eyes blinked open and met her familiar green ones. Blood still welled from the wound beneath my hand.

"Ronan..." she whispered; then a smile flickered across her lips. "I n-n-n-never... I never stopped searching..."

She sucked in a ragged breath and let it go. The light dimmed in her eyes and her body grew heavy.

Areos shook his head beside me. "No..." he whispered. "No..."

I said nothing. I did nothing. I was numb. Areos got to his feet, staggered several steps, and fell heavily against the cement wall. He pressed his head against it and sobbed.

I heard footsteps behind me and turned to see the man who had tried to shoot me—the man who had instead shot my little sister. His face was sheet white. I saw his lips moving, but I heard no sound.

For a moment he stood there like he was frozen; then he turned and ran.

I looked down at my little sister's pale, still face. I stared into her lifeless eyes, tears welling in my own. Something like actual hell grew like a tidal wave inside me; a tsunami receding, vanishing—then, all at once, rushing back.

Throwing myself forward, leaning over her body, I dug my fingertips into the ground. A sound far louder than I thought myself capable of making roared out of my lungs and split the air. For a moment, time stood still; a raging heat flowed through my arms.

Then the ground around me exploded.

Green surged over the dead ashy ground and then parted as roots burst up through it, winding and surging up to crack the sky like a massive looming giant: an enormous oak surged up out of the ground, its roots snaking around and through the two buildings beside us, wrapping around them like a boa constrictor until they both collapsed. The roots pulled up the foundations like unwanted weeds and rocketed up to hold them in suspension.

I dragged my fingertips across the ground as I got up and stepped out into the street. Massive trees shot up from the ground, growing ten times their normal size as they reached up around me, bellowing like a mighty wind on the sea as they waded forward through the soil—their roots rising and whipping every which way, wrapping around buildings and snatching weapons out of soldiers' hands. I stood in the middle of the street and watched.

Deep green branches climbed higher to fan out against the sky, and dark clouds blossomed around them, sending rain shimmering down, hissing as it made contact with the fires. Soldiers and recusants alike screamed as their weapons were wrenched from their hands and broken in half. Those who still had weapons dropped them and began to run.

The soldier who had shot Lara sank to his knees in the middle of the courtyard and wept.

Tears trickled down my own face as I stood there, blood flowing down my shaking arm. Tiny sprouts sprang up around my feet, growing rapidly to spiral skyward around me, turning into trees. Their roots raced up through the soil and swam forward, growing up and over the buildings—flattening the base and covering it in green and vines and life. When the trees reached the infirmary building, one massive oak moaned and swayed to a stop. Lifting itself up by the roots, it rose into the air to form an archway. Flowering vines burst up from the ground to wrap the roots in ribbons of white and bright orange.

The door to the building burst open in a flash of invisible energy. Hawk stepped out, and the Earth shook beneath her. The blackening sky cracked, and for the first time in what felt like an eternity, shafts of what seemed like the light of dawn filtered down. Icarus stepped out after her, and the light turned sunset orange.

The clouds dissipated, bursting into fragments of light that came showering down to ignite the white flecks of ashes accumulating on the ground like snow. The fires sizzled and died, their smoke rising in gray pillars against the pink sky as it ripened with the colors of sunrise and sunset. Everything around us was still, and then, suddenly there was a great rumble as the long lines of trees bowed in reverence. The growth flattened the barbed-wire fence to spill across the landscape, covering the dead hills and valleys in flowers and trees and life.

Hawk's eyes met mine across the wide expanse between us, light shafting down through the clouds around her to illuminate her face and her once again dark brown hair. I bowed my head, tears spilling down my face.

Icarus was dressed all in black, and his eyes were wide as he stepped farther out into the light, gazing up like he'd never seen the sun before. Hawk took him by the hand, and the crowd of mud-spattered soldiers parted around them as they walked forward, the trees separating to create an avenue around them. With a sound like rock splitting, the buildings burst at the seams, the roofs exploding open as oaks burst up through them, bright green leaves taking flight on the breeze—then catching fire, morphing, turning… into sparrows.

Through the archway the tree had created, I no longer saw the building on the other side, but a vast and sprawling landscape, a wilderness covered in ice, but melting away before my eyes to life. Streaming out through the archway behind Hawk and Icarus came a warm summer breeze along with birds, insects and woodland animals. A pack of white wolves flanked them, like guards of some divine nature, their massive heads bowed in reverence.

A soldier stepped forward. He stopped before Hawk and knelt down on one knee. He bowed his head, taking off his cap. Then, rising, his appearance transformed. His uniform gave way to the plain, but familiar, robes of our teacher.

Hawk looked up into his face, then surged forward to throw her arms around his neck. I wanted to go to her—to them. I wanted to be beside her, but something inside me was frozen in place. I watched from a distance. I listened, with the few hundred others, in silence.

"Welcome home." Sensei pressed his hands together and bowed his head again. "Sunrise."

He turned to Icarus, motioning for him to step up. Slowly, Icarus stepped into place beside Hawk.

Sensei bowed to him. "Sunset."

For a moment Icarus spoke to Sensei, but then his eyes turned to me. In them were a thousand words and questions. I answered by bowing my head in a sign of respect. Then, to my surprise, Sensei turned around and faced me. His eyes locked with mine; I held his gaze, blinking away tears. He walked towards me, each step sending up bursts of vines that raced outward and up the trunks of the trees. From the hem of his robe, a river flowed out behind him, splitting to branch off in two different directions, each spilling into the valley.

He stopped in front of me, looking me in the eyes for a long moment, asking nothing. Understanding everything.

"Fin, you fulfilled your mission and the prophecy by protecting the Sunrise and the Sunset, the patriarchs of the Dimension, the protectors of Earth," Sensei began, still looking deep into my eyes. "They live, they are reunited, because of you, my son."

I stared at him, not saying a word. A single tear rolled down my face.

Sensei lowered to one knee, bent into a deep bow. Then he stood once more. "The patriarchs will remain on Earth," he continued. "They will continue to heal, to love, to restore. The sliders with them."

"And you, Sensei?" I asked, my voice a broken whisper.

Sensei smiled. "I am the wind, Fin. You will hear me, though you may not know where I am, or where I am going. But I will be with you—as you, too, take your rightful place." Then, rather than pressing his hands together into a prayer position, he lifted my own and then flattened his palms against mine. "Sensei."

I opened my mouth to speak, but found it impossible. My mind could process nothing beyond the sudden burst of what felt like fire as it surged through my arms and into my chest; into my heart. For a moment I thought I would faint, but when I began to fall, Sensei caught me, just as he always did.

I looked up at him.

Sensei's expression became serious now. "Fin, everything I have is yours," he said quietly. "I have taught you, trained you, and loved you as a son. Love them, as I have, Fin. Train the next sliders."

"But there are no sliders, Sensei," I whispered. "Not from this far in the future."

Sensei looked at me firmly. "Are there not, Fin?"

His focus shifted. I followed it to Charlie, who was standing at the edge of the road, watching in awe.

"Or is that simply what you have believed?" he asked.

Sensei placed a hand on my shoulder. Tears flooded my eyes as I stared at him, breathless. He pulled me into an embrace, and I wrapped my arms around him tightly, weeping.

"Wake them up, Fin," he whispered, though it felt like a roar. "Wake them all up."

I held on to that moment, pressing my eyelids shut, letting it all sink in. Finally, looking into Sensei's eyes one last time, I stepped away, fresh green life still drizzling from my fingertips. The onlookers parted as I turned and walked back to the place where Lara still lay lifeless.

Areos was hunched beside her, his face in his hands. I touched his shoulder gently as I knelt down beside him. He looked up at me, tears streaking his face, but said nothing.

My hands shaking, I lifted my little sister from the cold ground to cradle her in my arms. I leaned closer until our foreheads touched. I inhaled deeply and breathed over her face, murmuring soft words that seemed to shake the ground beneath us.

"It's time to wake up."

# CHAPTER THIRTY-NINE

## *Icarus*

I could already see beyond the shattered window into the courtyard. I could already see trees growing up out of the buildings, their roots winding out of the ground like massive arms, snatching weapons to break them in half, ripping structures up by the foundations. Smoke blackened the sky, and blood ran in the street. Soldiers stood, trembling, staring, then dropped their weapons and ran.

Fin led this army of trees; fresh green grass infected the ground with each step he took. Streams of life paved a way before him. I felt my heart hammering in my chest as I turned to look at Hawk. She was beautiful—no, she was so far beyond that. She was *everything*. Who was I to stand by her side? Who was I to be her other half, when Fin had spurred a revolution?

The same voices plagued me: *Who are you, Ion, that you should be worthy of the Sunrise? Who are you that the Earth now roars for you to awaken?*

Swirling her hands in a circular motion, Hawk carefully channeled a large trembling orb of invisible energy between them. I watched, tuning out of everything else. I couldn't help but notice the black band wrapping her finger and feel the one on my own burning, as if in response.

I looked down at my hand, the palm where blood still trickled from the cut. I studied the droplets of crimson for a moment as Hawk continued to channel, my thoughts racing back to the hallucinations I'd only just emerged from—the side effects of the Fragment insertion.

I'd defeated the Fragment Donovan had implanted in my cerebellum—I would not be controlled or commanded by any outside force. Realizing I could control my own thoughts had shown me I could be the master of my own mind, and had robbed the Fragment of its governing power. My thoughts had helped me conquer it—but, unchecked, my thoughts could also take away my *own* power. I'd watched that happen my whole life. The only difference was that now I could see that it was *my choice.*

I chose which wolf won. I chose whether I was up against a Fragment or something far more dangerous: my own destructive thoughts.

Standing there in that hallway beside Hawk, I took a steady breath, closed my eyes and placed my hand over the cut, applying some pressure.

*Your name is not Ion anymore. Your name is Icarus—the Sunset.*

Heat pulsated through me, spreading through my torso, up into my face, and rushing the length of my arms to spill out through my fingertips. My other hand felt as if I'd stuck it into a fire. The sensation was quick and dizzying. It vanished just as Hawk threw the orb and the door exploded open. I opened my eyes just as light streaked in to blind them; a massive tree lifted from the ground by the roots, with a roar like a bear's. It grew to form an archway laced with vines.

Hawk reached for my hand. "Icarus, come on."

I studied her for a moment, standing there with my heart beating in my throat. Then I looked down at my own hand, taking my fingers away from the cut. The cut that was no longer there.

I'd healed myself. For the first time, *I had healed myself.*

Something big and strange and sweet that couldn't be described or named swelled inside me. Something like the dawning of a new day, the turning of a page, a blank canvas. The feeling that came with melting snow and the promise of spring. Something indescribably new.

Suddenly, the room around us changed. The walls seemed to melt away to some new reality—a sprawling landscape of melting snow and blossoming trees, birds, and insects. Rabbits and foxes and familiar white wolves darted among the trees and wound their way over to us. I would recognize this place anywhere.

"Your world," I whispered, barely able to get the words out. "It's... it's..."

Hawk gave me a little smile. "It's about to invade this one."

I grasped Hawk's hand in my own, taking a deep breath as I stepped up beside her, and together we walked forward, flanked by white wolves, through the archway and out into the crashing waves of new life. For a moment everything spun like a hurricane, but then everything slowed and fell away as one soldier stepped forward and dropped to his knees before Hawk and me. When he rose, it was as if everything else had vanished.

The young, rugged face gave way to one that was aged and familiar, with eyes brimming with wisdom. Hawk immediately embraced him, burying her face in his chest.

"Welcome home, Sunrise," he whispered, stroking his hand over her hair.

Then in turn, his eyes fixed on me. As he slowly separated from Hawk, I instinctively made a motion to drop to my knees before him, but he stopped me. Sensei bowed his head to his chest. "Sunset."

I swallowed, my knees shaking; I hoped he couldn't tell.

"Sensei, it is I who should be bowing to you," I whispered.

Sensei placed a hand on my shoulder. "Icarus, you have fulfilled what was written."

"But, Sensei, I..." My voice cracked as I stared at him, his face suddenly the only one I saw. "I am still—even now I am still afraid. I do not think I am ready."

"It is because you believe that you are not, that you are indeed ready, Icarus; trust in who you are." Sensei smiled, speaking only loud enough for me to hear. "Trust in who she is."

I stared into Sensei's eyes, unable to answer. In his eyes I saw myself, so many years ago, when I'd sat across from him at the kitchen table. When he had asked me what I wished to learn, and I, in my ignorance and pride, had answered, "Nothing." How far he had brought me, leading me by the hand— how much I had grown! How much he had *taught* me.

Hawk, the Sunrise. The other half of my soul. I didn't need to tell Sensei anything; he already knew the depths of my heart, how much I loved her. How terrified I was of losing her again, in a different way. He knew all of this, and his answer cut past the mire of my thoughts to strike my pounding heart.

*Trust her. Trust Hawk.*

With one last look, Sensei turned and walked across the courtyard toward the place where Fin still stood. Hawk took a few steps forward, almost as if wanting to follow.

Fin's eyes met mine for a moment. He bowed his head in a nod. Somehow it was more than a gesture; it was a message. One I returned, this time without that feeling of fear. This time with gratitude, as I remembered all that he had done for me. Fin hadn't let me forget who I was, even when I wanted to. He'd pushed me like a brother would, and I loved him like one.

"Icarus!" A familiar voice pulled me out of my thoughts.

Turning and scanning the crowd, I spotted Charlie, her eyes wide and her face marred by dirt and scrapes. The crowd separated around me as I walked over to her.

"Are you all right?" I asked.

"I'm fine. I got out," she responded, glancing down at her hands. "Thanks to you."

A sparkle of white formed and hovered over the surface of her palm for a moment before she killed it, rolling her fingers into a fist. Then she looked up at me questioningly.

"Did they…?" She didn't finish.

I tapped the back of my neck in the affirmative.

"I didn't let it beat me." I sucked in a breath, dropping my hand. "I remembered who I was—even with the Frag. I remembered love." I smiled. "And faith and mercy. I followed your example."

Charlie quirked an eyebrow. "Mine?"

"Yours. Who would have thought an RGM member programmed since birth could overcome the system that controlled and employed her? But you did—not with external weapons, but with what was already inside you. You're what made me realize it was possible, Charlie."

She looked at me thoughtfully, then at her hands, then back up at me with something new in her eyes. "Icarus, if I can do that—if we can both override the Fragment..." Her eyes widened, taking in the transforming landscape around us. "Anyone could."

That same feeling I'd had when I'd healed myself for the first time came flooding back. The blank canvas, the endless possibilities.

"Anyone..." I repeated slowly. "Anyone who realizes they can... The bottle has already been uncorked."

She nodded slowly, her expression turning serious. "They're going to do everything they can to try to stop us, Icarus."

"The RGM can stop many things... but they can't stop an idea," I answered, my voice soft but resolute. "They cannot stop belief."

I turned and saw Hawk just as she turned to look at me.

"Belief is what will set this world on fire..." My voice dropped into a whisper; my eyes became lost in hers. "And the darkness will never put it out."

# CHAPTER FORTY

*Lara*

My brother was the first thing I saw when I opened my eyes. I breathed in, and my nostrils filled with the scent of roses. I stared up at him for a moment, into his green eyes that were so much like my own.

"Ronan." I managed a whisper, a smile curving over my lips.

Leaning forward, he scooped me up in his arms and wrapped me in an embrace. I could feel his heartbeat pounding against mine. My arms wound around him and I buried my face in his chest, weeping. Weeping because I had finally, finally found my brother. Weeping because the sky was pink and purple, and the sun was coming down in shafts brighter than ever. Weeping because I could hear birdsong on the breeze; because flowers grew around me.

He pulled back, taking my face in both hands; his eyes filled with tears. He placed a soft kiss on my forehead and then drew a breath.

"I can't believe we're together again," Fin whispered. "I can't believe I..." His voice broke off and a tear slipped down his cheek.

I pulled him back into my arms, shaking my head. "I knew one day I would find you," I said quietly.

I gave my brother a smile as we separated, sniffing back tears as he helped me to my feet. I turned slowly, gazing at our transformed surroundings. The buildings that had been beside us now hung in midair above our heads, suspended by the massive roots of even more enormous trees. "It would seem as though we have a similar ability," I said.

Fin smiled, drying his eyes, stepping away to reveal Areos, who stood frozen in place, his eyes wide with awe. Running to him, I fell into his arms. He caught his breath, burying his face in the curve of my neck.

"I thought I'd lost you, Lara."

I pulled him in tighter, about to answer when, past Areos's shoulder, I saw Kess walking towards me, tears welling in her eyes. Slowly pulling away from Areos, I met her halfway and put my arms around her.

"You made it out of the fire. H-h-h-how?" she stammered, swallowing back tears. "How did you make it out of there? I saw you–I saw you jump–"

"Someone was there to catch me, Kess."

She pulled away, staring at me, staring around us at everything: the light, the trees, the parted clouds, the foxes and lambs and wolves and birds. "But how?" she asked, whispered. "How?"

I smiled a little, placing a hand on her shoulder. "Not everything can be explained, Kess." I shot Areos a little glance and he smiled. "Sometimes, it has to be believed."

I turned and walked back towards my brother. "I have so much to tell you."

"And I you," Fin said. "But for now we need to get out of here—before this place is crawling with reinforcements that are probably already on their way."

I nodded in agreement. "We need to find a place to hide for the time being."

"Yes, but where?" Areos asked, coming up behind me.

I thought for a moment; then my gaze switched back to my brother. "Gather the rest—I know just the place."

---

"Are we there yet?"

"Not yet," I chided him.

"Can I look?"

"No! Now stop that." I laughed as I led Fin by the hand, pushing aside the brush surrounding us. "Just a little farther…"

We'd fled the base, which now looked more like a forest. The sound of Griffons whirred in the distance as we made our way through the trees. I held Fin's hand in mine, and our feet carried us over the now mossy green forest floor. Birds chattered in the treetops, acclimating to their new home. Butterflies and moths streamed in the air around us. When we were finally close, I made him close his eyes, though he barraged me with questions nearly every step of the way.

I reached out and brushed the curtain of flowering wisteria vine aside, leading my brother forward into the clearing. The cottage door was wide open. Icarus was seated on the edge of the porch, talking with Runner and Kess. Areos and Charlie stood a ways off in the garden, seeming locked in conversation. Icarus noticed us right away and passed me a grin as I centered Fin in front of the cottage.

"Okay," I told him quietly. "You can open your eyes now."

Fin's eyes blinked open—then widened. His jaw slackened as he stared straight ahead, at the cottage we had built together with our sisters so long ago.

"I kept this place alive," I explained after a moment of silence. "I lived here until I was inducted. But even after that, whenever I had a chance, I kept coming back. I didn't want to forget you. Or them… any of them." I paused, steadying my voice. "When I was here, I could feel you. And Brigid and Anna and Mom and Dad. When I was here, it was like everything was how it used to be…"

Fin looped an arm around my shoulders, saying nothing. For a moment we stood there in silence, listening to the birds chatter along with our friends, gazing at the cottage that was now bursting in shades of green and gold and pink, covered in blooms and foliage and life.

"We have each other now, Lara," Fin said softly, resting his chin on the top of my head. "We will not lose each other again."

I smiled, but before I could say anything, I saw his gaze shift as footsteps approached behind me. I turned to see Hawk approaching. She was still clothed in an RGM uniform, but her long hair was now a dark cocoa brown, flowing over her shoulders.

"I knew there was something familiar about those eyes," she told me with a little smile, casting a quick glance at Fin. "I can't tell you how full my heart is—that you've been reunited."

"Thank you." I smiled.

Hawk shook her head. "Thank you… Without you, we might not have had the victory we did today. You saved Icarus—and Fin. You survived as a slider independently all those years."

I smiled. "Not quite independently."

I glanced past Hawk to where Areos was standing alone at the edge of the forest. I looked back to Hawk, who was staring at Fin. I cleared my throat slightly, bowing my head in a nod. "Excuse me a moment."

I slipped away, leaving Hawk and Fin to start conversing with more than just their eyes. I crossed the garden and entered the forest after Areos. The light came down in the soft colors of the sunset. He was leaning against the same massive oak, staring up into the leaves.

I bit back a little smile, walking silently until I came to a stop in front of him. He didn't look down at first, but when he finally did, he startled.

"Holy—I didn't hear you."

I laughed. "I wasn't a sniper for nothing."

Areos was blushing, but he laughed as he straightened up. He took a deep breath and let it out again, scanning my face. "Gosh, these past few days…" He shook his head slowly. "They've been so…"

"Filled with explosions?"

Areos grinned. "Lots of those, yes, but…" He trailed off, looking down at the space between us. "The outward ones have been nothing compared to the inward ones."

"Is that so?"

"I've lived more in the past few days than I have in my entire life." His hazel eyes shifted back up to meet mine. "Because of you, Lara. Not just because of… of how much I like you… but…" He paused, steadying his breath. "But because you took a stick of dynamite and threw it into the way that I looked at the world. The way I looked at everything—I used to despair of the world, even when I was growing up on Earth. It was so easy to see the darkness, even in the light… yet you seem to find light even in the belly of darkness itself. Even if you have to create that light yourself."

Areos glanced around us for a moment. "It's a small start, really, what happened here today. There's still so much to be done." He smiled. "But because of you, I have hope now. I've learned from watching you that we don't need to know it all… We don't need an explanation for everything in order to move forward. We just need to believe."

Areos took me by the hands, looking down at them as he rubbed his thumbs over my fingers. Then he looked deep into my eyes. "You gave me hope, Lara."

My lips curved into a smile. I wove my fingers in between his as he leaned closer and pressed his lips against mine. For a moment everything went silent.

But it wasn't actually silent anymore: the birds sang around us.

# CHAPTER FORTY-ONE

## *Hawk*

Fin and I watched as Lara wandered across the garden and into the forest after Areos. The two of them disappeared among the wispy green birches and evergreens.

"She's grown up so much," I mused, thinking back to the day in Howth, to the tiny girl who had frolicked among the flowers with her sisters in a little pastel dress. "And today you saved her... Sensei."

I cast him a look and his face flushed. "I'll never get used to that title—ever."

"You'd better start. You'll be hearing a lot of it."

"And I'm already beginning to feel like I'll have to save her a second time." He rolled his eyes, shooting a glance in the direction of the forest, where Lara and Areos had slipped away.

"Oh, come on." I nudged him in the ribs. "Areos is harmless."

"No guy is harmless."

"Well, now she has you to keep an eye on her," I said, turning to make my way through the trees. "Though you'll have your hands full with all the other sliders you'll be training."

Somehow, I felt years older. Everything felt different—even Fin, though the sensation was both comforting and alarming at the same time.

When Icarus and I had emerged through the archway, my world had opened and bled through to this one. The battle had fallen away. I'd never forget the look on the child soldiers' faces as they stood and stared, their weapons suspended from the roots of the trees like ornaments. I'd never forget what it felt like to see that one soldier approach and bow, then rise again only to morph slowly into that familiar face I knew better than my own. Sensei. And it seemed almost fitting, for didn't Sensei disguise himself in all of us? In Icarus and me, and in Fin—but also in the less likely ones: Charlie, Kess, Runner… Everyone, no matter how unlikely it seemed, had some little fragment of Sensei swirling in their soul, peering out from behind their eyes, longing to escape and set the world ablaze.

I stopped beside a tree, reaching up to place a hand on its moss-covered bark. "Earth will heal now, Fin." I spoke softly. "The Dimension and Earth are no longer separate… They are one."

Fin stopped alongside me, seeming to consider what I was saying. Then he nodded. "They are, Hawk. We'll remain on Earth now."

We were quiet for a moment. Then I turned to look at him. "You'll train the next generation of sliders?"

Fin nodded, running his fingertips over the soft moss. "I'll be here—on Earth, finding them. Gathering them. Just as Sensei always has."

"What about Mitsue—the council?"

"We haven't found Mitsue yet."

I lowered my eyes. "Do you think he's alive?"

"I don't know," Fin replied quietly. After a moment he drew a breath. "But I've seen what authority and losing sight of what matters did to him, and to the rest of the council. I will not let that happen again. If I learned one thing when I was out there, searching for you, all those long days and nights, Hawk—" he exhaled, turning to look at me "—it's that we answer to a higher authority than ourselves… that voice within us."

I looked up at him, studying his face for a long moment before speaking.

"I think the next generation of anomalies is in good hands, Fin." My voice was a whisper.

His eyes scanned my face. I felt his fingers brush against my own and then intertwine in the spaces between them. He said nothing for a long moment, almost as if he couldn't. He stared down at our hands, at the black band that once again wrapped my finger. Then he drew a quiet breath and looked straight into my eyes.

"I think the future of Earth is in good hands, Hawk."

I stood there silently, gazing up into his sparkling emerald eyes. There were a thousand things I wanted to tell him, but in my heart, I knew we were beyond words, he and I. So we stood in the warm silence of the forest, listening to the birds as they sang around us. And for a moment our eyes were separate galaxies intertwining.

Finally, I pulled him into my arms. I felt the warmth of tears welling in my eyes as I buried my face in his chest. His arms folded around me and he held me tight.

"Thank you…" I managed a whisper.

"For what?"

"For believing in me…" I drew a shaky breath, listening to his heartbeat. "For never letting me forget who I am."

Fin pulled back slightly, looking down into my face, his eyes glistening with tears. "I love you far too much to let that happen," he whispered back. "I know what you were made for, Hawk—this is only the beginning."

I nodded. "I know…" I trailed off, blinking back tears. "But I… I will never forget, Fin."

A faint smile passed his lips. "Nor will I." He lifted my hand to his lips and kissed it gently, a single tear rolling down his cheek. "I will always be there for you, Hawk," he said softly. "Always."

I took in his face for one moment longer; then I bowed my head. Our hands separated and, slowly, blinking back tears, I turned and walked away.

I found Icarus in the garden, between the tall rows of sunflowers, which tipped their faces toward the setting sun. He looked thin in his black uniform. His icy blue eyes studied me inquiringly as I approached and came to a stop in front of him.

"Where will we go from here?" I pondered aloud. "The RGM will be pursuing us—we totally destroyed their base."

"I think they've already noticed."

"I guess we'll start afresh somewhere else. Which won't be a new sensation… for either of us."

He smiled a little. "Not at all."

I reached out to touch one of the bright green leaves draping from the stems of the sunflowers.

"Earth has begun to wake, thanks to you," I said quietly. "I thought I had lost you for a moment there—back in the lab when I was trying to get you to wake up, to break out of the Fragment's hold over you."

Icarus blew out a sigh. "My life rewound and replayed, Hawk. It would have swallowed me whole if you hadn't…" His voice tapered off. "If you hadn't been there."

I turned to look at him, and our gazes locked. For a long moment neither of us spoke a word.

"I can't believe it's all over," he said finally, his voice a whisper.

I glanced up at the sky, taking a deep breath. I could hear voices and laughter drifting out of the cottage, the sounds of engines in the valley below.

"We've won the battle, Icarus," I replied softly after a moment. "The first of many, doubtless."

"I didn't mean the battle."

My eyes shifted back to his blue ones.

"I meant…" He trailed off, swallowed. "I meant life without you. Lying awake each night, imagining your face…" His voice cracked a little, then dropped to a whisper. "I was so afraid, Hawk…"

I stepped closer. "That I wouldn't come back?"

Icarus shook his head, looking back up at me. "That you *would* come back. And that I would not be worthy to stand by your side."

"Icarus—"

"That I would not be enough, because I'm… well, I'm *Icarus*…" He tripped over his words, breathing back tears. "And you are the sun."

I looked at him for a long moment, my eyes tracing every detail of his face in the faint colors of the pink sky. How often I had thought of his face— longed for it, all those lonely days and nights. And now, finally, I reached out and touched it. I took it in both hands, lifting his chin so that his gaze finally met mine.

It was as if the space between us pulled us together until we were one. I kissed him and felt fire pass through my veins. The moment stretched, froze, and then pulled us back to the surface for air; the colors of the sky pushed between our faces, though our foreheads remained connected.

"The universe was born between two halves of the same soul..." I whispered. "I am your Sunrise." I slid my hand into his, our fingers intertwining, the matching bands around our fingers brushing against each other. "And you are my Sunset, Icarus."

A smile passed over his lips and a tear rolled down his cheek.

Softly, I kissed his lips again, then pulled away just enough to speak. "Are you ready?"

He said nothing for a moment, his forehead resting against mine; then he pulled away and looked down into my eyes again. "For what?"

Slowly my gaze separated from his as I turned to look out over the rolling forest ahead, the sprawling hills and the mountains: Earth, waiting for us.

A fire rose inside me as our eyes locked.

"To take back what's ours."

# THIS IS NOT THE END...

Unlock a world of bonus content including...

- What Is Your Anomaly Ability quiz
- Exclusive Q&As with the author
- The Blood Race merch
- The series' official playlists
- The Blood Race vision boards
- Giveaways

www.thebloodraceseries.com

(A whole website of bonus goodness!)

Did you enjoy Resurgence? If so, I would be so grateful if you could drop me a short & sweet review on my Amazon/Goodreads pages. Reviews are critical for indie authors such as myself. We aren't backed by large corporations, publishers, or marketing companies. You are the one powering this book! Review's really do make a huge difference. I love and appreciate every reader who takes the time to review my books.

Don't want to miss when I release new books? Join my email circle and receive personal updates from yours truly – sign up at: www.kaemmons.com

Also follow me on:

- youtube.com/kaemmons
- facebook.com/kaemmonsauthor
- instagram.com/lonehawkwriter
- twitter.com/lonehawkwriter

# ABOUT THE AUTHOR

When she's not hermiting away in her colorfully-painted home office writing her next science fiction, passionate story-teller and adventurer Kate Emmons is probably on the road for a surf or hiking trip, listening to vinyls, or going for a power run. Emmons lives in the often-snowy hills of rugged Vermont with her husband and dog named Rocket.